PHILIP NOLAN

PHILIP NOLAN

THE MAN WITHOUT A COUNTRY

CHUCK PFARRER

Naval Institute Press
Annapolis, Maryland

This book has been brought to publication with the generous assistance of Marguerite and Gerry Lenfest.

Naval Institute Press
291 Wood Road
Annapolis, MD 21402

Library of Congress Cataloging-in-Publication Data
Names: Pfarrer, Chuck, author. | Hale, Edward Everett, 1822–1909. Man without a country.
Title: Philip Nolan : the man without a country / Chuck Pfarrer.
Other titles: Man without a country
Description: Annapolis, Maryland : Naval Institute Press, [2016]
Identifiers: LCCN 2015043881 (print) | LCCN 2015048278 (ebook) | ISBN 9781591145646 (hardcover) | ISBN 9781591146650 (ebook) | ISBN 9781591146650 (ePDF) | ISBN 9781591146650 (epub) | ISBN 9781591146650 (mobi)
Subjects: LCSH: Burr Conspiracy, 1805–1807—Fiction. | Stateless persons—Fiction. | Soldiers—Fiction. | Exiles—Fiction. | BISAC: FICTION / Historical. | FICTION / War & Military. | GSAFD: Historical fiction. | War stories. | Adventure fiction.
Classification: LCC PS3616.F37 P48 2016 (print) | LCC PS3616.F37 (ebook) | DDC 813/.6—dc23
LC record available at http://lccn.loc.gov/2015043881

Title page image: Oil on canvas by Michel Felice Corne (1752–1845), courtesy of Naval History and Heritage Command.
All other images are from the author's collection.

24 23 22 21 20 19 18 17 16   9 8 7 6 5 4 3 2 1
First printing

OTHER TITLES BY CHUCK PFARRER

Nonfiction

Warrior Soul: The Memoir of a Navy SEAL

SEAL Target Geronimo:
Inside the Mission That Killed Osama Bin Laden

Fiction

Killing Che

Minsky, Pinsky, and Paddy

Land, Sea, and Stars

Contents

FOR THE HERO OF THIS NOVEL I GIVE CREDIT TO A SUPERIOR MIND AND MORE graciously fluent pen. Philip Nolan was the protagonist of a short story entitled "The Man Without a Country," first published in *The Atlantic Monthly* in 1863. Its author, Edward Everett Hale, set his story during the presidency of Thomas Jefferson and cast as his arch-villain a real-life Revolutionary War hero turned renegade—Aaron Burr. In Hale's story, Philip Nolan, a young Army officer, becomes embroiled in Burr's plot to invade the lands of the Louisiana Purchase.

"The Man Without a Country" was a magazine piece, barely seven thousand words. To make the story into a novel it was necessary to expand the plot, add characters, and shamelessly indulge a lesser author's whim. Though charting a course as close to history as possible, I have retained a novelist's prerogative, creating a sister ship to USS *Constitution* and naming her what I pleased. Naval historians will also see that a very real act of valor, the cutting out of USS *Philadelphia*, has been both dislodged in time and attributed to fictional heroes.

Edward Everett Hale created in Philip Nolan the first antihero in American literature. Though treated harshly by the court that judged him, the peculiar severity of Nolan's sentence makes him worthy of our sympathy. Two hundred years before "extraordinary rendition," Philip Nolan was made into a sort of stateless prisoner, a fate and judicial status still chillingly relevant at the beginning of the twenty-first century.

In Hale's account, Nolan becomes a sort of Flying Dutchman, never touching land, forgotten by his country, a broken man who would die repentant after decades at sea. In *Philip Nolan*, the reader will discover a different fate for America's first secret prisoner.

Oh let death deliver me
bring my days to their fatal end
For there's no affliction worse
than losing one's own country

—EURIPIDES

A NOTORIOUS PERSON

H E HAS BEEN ERASED FROM HISTORY. WERE IT NOT FOR A LETTER PUBLISHED in a gentleman's magazine and a small scrap of newspaper, the world would not know of Philip Nolan at all. Charged with treason, Nolan's prosecution was irregular, his trial peremptory, and his punishment vindictive. After his court-martial at Richmond in 1807, the records of his birth, his education, his military service, the transcripts pertaining to his indictment and sentence— all were made to disappear. Nolan was then exiled, and it fell to the United States Navy to incarcerate him.

From the first day of Nolan's confinement until the day of his death, the government made no public mention of him, published nothing relating to his trial or conviction, and allowed no citizen of the United States to inquire about him. The officers and men who held him aboard their ships were honor bound to keep the secret of Nolan's verdict and the stern conditions of his punishment. They carried out their instructions to the letter.

More than four decades after Nolan's death, the government that made him vanish allowed an obituary to be published in an obscure portion of the *New York Herald*:

> NOLAN. Died on board the United States corvette *Levant*,
> latitude 2° 11' S, longitude 131° 0' W. On the 11th of May.
> PHILIP CLINTON NOLAN.

Nolan was dead, but every other word was a lie. He had been buried at sea decades before USS *Levant* ever swam, and the latitude and longitude in the notice of his death are halfway across the globe from the place he'd laid down his life. By the time the *Herald*'s obituary was printed not one of his family survived to mourn him and almost none of the men who knew him, served with him, or administered his sentence remained alive. Even as they acknowledged his death, the powers that abolished Philip Nolan pushed him deeper into shadow.

There can be no possible harm in telling poor Nolan's story now. Those of his persecutors who would be disgraced by their treatment of him are, like Nolan himself, long beyond care. It is worthwhile to tell a little bit of Nolan's life and of his captivity by way of showing what it is to be a man without a country. His story is an obscure bit of history but real enough; presently the reader may judge the facts. And though the tale is grim, it might as well begin on a pleasant spring day.

———————

AN HOUR BEFORE DAWN ON A PALE MORNING—WEDNESDAY, THE 10TH OF JUNE, 1807. In the dark places of the forest locusts chattered, and the air was thick with the cloying scent of honeysuckle. Below the Chimborazo Hill, split rails followed a gravel road to the place where the James River narrowed and turned south. There, the sandy towpath branched past a sawmill and a squat, yellow tavern that was the southernmost habitation of the city of Richmond, Virginia.

Up the dim road, jingling and rattling, came a dray wagon pulled by a pair of sullen mules. Behind the team, a farmer slumped with the reins in one hand; a little boy in a straw hat lounged next to him on the box. Shifting his tobacco, the farmer saw a rider descending the long grade past the tavern. The horse was creditable, a dappled mare of nearly sixteen hands, and seemed to be handled by a gentleman. It was the farmer's experience that swells abroad at dawn were frequently drunk, and often not riding their mounts as much as being carried by them. The farmer was not inclined to wish the man good morning, for as mount and passenger came on he could see that neither was paying much attention to the road.

As the rider approached, the boy noticed a silk cockade on the side of the man's round hat, and then, paying attention, he picked out the details of a uniform. A tall, solid frame overflowed the saddle, and long legs in high Hessian boots kept easily in the stirrups. The man was wearing a blue cutaway with red collars, lapels, and cuffs, though in the early dawn the colors were much the same. The soldier's sword was undone, and its curved scabbard hung from the pommel and coursed indifferently back and forth. For a long moment it was the glory of the uniform that the boy fixed upon—only when the horse drew abreast did he lift his eyes to the rider's face. Under the round hat was a pair of deeply set gray-blue eyes ruled by fair, even brows; the face was angular, the nose narrow and aquiline, and the man's jaw was set firmly above a crisp linen collar and neatly tied black stock. Despite an expression of firm purpose the rider seemed distracted, perhaps even fretful.

The boy cleared his throat and piped a bit too loudly, "Good morning, Your Excellency."

At this, Philip Nolan's face changed from a blank expression to a look of baffled curiosity. Nolan had hardly registered the oncoming wagon, and were it not for the good sense of his mount he might have ridden them both squarely between the mules. Collecting his reins, Nolan's eyes searched the boy's face; in an instant he determined that the officious greeting was not a jab. Nolan smiled, lifted his hat to father and son, and said pleasantly, "Good morning to you, gentlemen."

They passed on the road, the wagon headed north to market and the waking town, horse and rider heading south to the plank bridge at Bloody Run. The mules capered a bit, and the farmer clucked at them. A mile back, where the river turned, a dozen other gentlemen had come together: men on horses, and men in a fine gilt coach. They had about them an expectant, furtive air, and had it not been for their elegant clothes and fine saddles they might have been mistaken for a gang of highwaymen. As the mules clopped past the yellow tavern, the boy could not help but look back; it was certain the officer was keeping a rendezvous. Father and son knew the infamy of the place where the men were gathered, a barren field marked by a lightning-stripped oak. The clearing was well known, even to local children, as the Bleedin' Bones. That scrap of bleak, unhappy pasture was the place where Richmond's gentlemen settled affairs of honor.

IN THE DAYS WHEN OUR REPUBLIC WAS YOUNG, AN OFFICER'S REPUTATION WAS a precious and fragile thing. A careless word, a deliberate bit of incivility, or even one's choice of associates might give mortal offense. Immutable integrity, an urbanity of manners, and the practice of every commendable virtue were recommended in the finishing of an officer.

Personal honor was the foundation upon which two other great virtues were built: loyalty and duty to country. Philip Nolan's upbringing, the station of his parents, his pleasant, forthright nature, and native honesty marked him as a person in whom trust and responsibility could safely be placed. His father was a military officer, a respected man; his mother a woman of grace and exquisite manners. Both cared for him and saw that he was given the advantages of an education, the comportment of a gentleman, and a modicum of plain good sense.

After graduation from West Point and a stint as an aide to General Henry Dearborn in Washington City, Philip Nolan was commissioned a second lieutenant of artillery and assigned to duty on the western frontier. Those who knew Nolan as a boy on the frontier, at university, as a cadet, and as an officer esteemed him as a person of determination and great promise. They might also have said that Philip Nolan was as proud as Beelzebub and as stubborn as a tenpenny nail. But these are minor defects in a lieutenant commanding a battery of horse artillery; and for a young officer in that station, pride and fortitude might even be pronounced virtues.

Philip Nolan first met Aaron Burr at Fort Massac on the Ohio River. That log-and-wattle fortress was then the United States' outermost frontier station and the headquarters of what was styled the "Legion of the West." The former vice president had arrived at the fort ostensibly on a tour of the Ohio country. He was, in fact, reconnoitering the men who garrisoned America's western border. The staggering sum of eighteen million francs had recently purchased the Mississippi watershed from Emperor Napoleon Bonaparte. The transaction had nearly doubled the landmass of the United States, but left the young American republic and the Empire of Spain to carp over the boundaries of an almost infinite wilderness.

After a staunchly patriotic banquet given in his honor, Aaron Burr sought a private word with Nolan. Burr made a point of learning about the persons who could be of use to him, and he'd made a careful study of Nolan. The young officer's aptitude for languages, his ability with maps, and above all his family connexions made him an asset to be cultivated. Recently graduated from West Point, Nolan was the only trained artillerist and cartographer at the fort. Burr flattered him by saying he had seen several of Nolan's maps at Washington City; why, in fact, he had one just at hand. Nolan bowed, and the small, keen, dapper little man rolled out a map of the Orleans Territory.

"I dare say you know this country, Mister Nolan, and the land west of the Sabine?"

"Well enough, sir." Nolan answered, "My mother had a *porcione*." He put four fingers on the map. "Here, near to Puebla Magda. I spent most of my boyhood there."

"Texas," Burr said, "should be a republic."

"The King of Spain would disagree with you, sir."

"Damn the King of Spain, Mister Nolan. I mean to take Texas from the Spanish."

Nolan was astounded. He had his own reasons to want to burn powder against the Spanish; Philip's brother, Stephen, had been shot by a troop of Mexican cavalry after leading a party of settlers across the Brazos. The death of Nolan's older brother had driven his mother to drink and shattered their family. It was these heart wounds that had turned Nolan from a rambunctious little boy into a soldier. Burr knew this as well.

"The purchase of the Louisiana territories has expanded the nation," Burr continued. "But Mister Jefferson has made a bargain with the devil. The wars that convulse Europe show that Napoleon can never keep his word. His treaties are worthless, and if Jefferson were to send him all the dollars in the world, it would do nothing to secure the lands the French tyrant has pretended to sell to us."

Burr looked directly into Nolan's eyes. "The Spanish are now the allies of the French. Should Napoleon decide to snatch back what he has sold to Mister Jefferson, it is the *dons* who will do the taking. The Spanish are already moving troops from Monterrey and Mexico City."

"Then they should be kept away," said Nolan. "Driven across the Rio Grande if necessary."

The little man smiled. "You have grasped the matter perfectly."

Burr told Nolan that two nations could not share the destiny of a single continent, and that Texas and the lands all the way to the Pacific were the legacy of the United States alone. No one spoke the word "treason." The old politician was too crafty, and Nolan's simple patriotism was too well rooted. Burr's scheme was to start a war with Spain and then seize the territory west of the Mississippi. The plot was no idle daydream. Burr had raised tens of thousands of dollars, purchased rifles, cannon, and powder, and commissioned a flotilla of riverboats. Burr had private discussions with the military and political leaders of America's frontier, obtaining their acquiescence, if not their publicly declared support. Andrew Jackson, the future president, and Major General James Wilkinson, commander of the United States Army, were among Burr's intimates. The ex–vice president had a genius for manipulation, and he knew exactly where to press the young lieutenant. Burr had ready cash—he could pay for a thousand soldiers—but he needed officers, men of honor, to lead them. Burr asked Nolan to join his venture; glory awaited, the deceiver whispered. All it required was men with pluck.

Nolan's consideration of this fatal offer was all too brief. He reflected on the object of Burr's scheme rather than the means by which it should be accomplished. Nolan did not appreciate that others, besides Spain, might object to what was, in fact, an unlawful and unjustifiable use of force—a *filibuster*. What Burr proposed was a military adventure, and Nolan saw in it not only a place for himself, but vindication for a brother he had loved.

Burr dictated a pair of letters, which Nolan dutifully copied down. These were then transcribed into a hieroglyphic-like cipher that Burr produced from a slim iron box. The letters dealt chiefly with the movements of men and materiel. There was some political language as well, but truth be told, the encryption process proved so laborious that eventually Nolan merely assembled words and did not pay strict attention to what they entailed.

Working through a long night, Nolan made fair copies and in the morning submitted them to Burr for review. They were pronounced accurate, and Nolan was delighted to be charged with delivering them to General James Wilkinson, the military governor of the Orleans Territory. The grand design, it seemed, was coming to life. Burr arranged a leave with Nolan's commanding officer and made sure he was well provisioned. Carrying Burr's dispatches, Nolan rode south from Fort Massac to the Orleans Territory, and into the noose of doom.

On the day of Nolan's arrival, the wily general received him kindly and accepted the letters. In a show of military courtesy, Nolan put himself at the general's service and was shown to a tent within the confines of Wilkinson's headquarters. That night, exhausted from his seven-hundred-mile journey, Nolan fell asleep, convinced that his future was about to blossom.

Though he had been an early and enthusiastic supporter of Burr's plot, General Wilkinson was a calculating man. Unknown to his superiors in Washington and unsuspected by Burr or his brother officers, Wilkinson was in secret correspondence with the viceroy of Mexico. In this mercenary, treacherous arrangement, Wilkinson was known to the Spanish as Agent 13. Burr had no inkling, and Nolan had no idea at all, that they were dealing with a dyed-in-the-wool traitor.

Perhaps the old general had heard the rumors that revealed him as Burr's principal co-conspirator; perhaps he had been ordered by his Spanish paymasters to thwart Burr's plot. Whatever the reasons, General Wilkinson found it in his interest to suddenly denounce Aaron Burr, repudiate their previous agreements, and renege on his promise to add the battalions in his command to an attack on Mexico.

Wilkinson had changed sides. He now had to cover his tracks.

At dawn Nolan was arrested in his tent by Wilkinson's adjutant. He was taken again to headquarters, and there found the general a changed man. Sitting behind a field desk, Wilkinson's broad bottom was propped on a saddle put down upon a milking stool. The general pointedly asked if Nolan had been granted permission to leave his post at Fort Massac.

"Verbal permission, sir."

"Then you can show me no orders?"

In a corner, Nolan caught sight of a clerk dipping his pen and rapidly scribbling. "Respectfully, sir, if I have deserted, I have done so in uniform, and fled to the headquarters of my commanding general."

The great bulk was unmoved. "I understand you have been in contact with His Excellency Colonel Burr?" Wilkinson huffed.

"I have, sir. He asked me to carry to you the letter you have at hand."

In the corner, the scratching stopped and the clerk looked up. Wilkinson's eyes narrowed. "What else did Colonel Burr say to you, Lieutenant Nolan?"

"I was offered a place in his expedition, sir. I heartily accepted it."

Wilkinson smirked like a mandarin. "You are dismissed," he wheezed.

The adjutant said sternly, "Consider yourself confined to post."

It seemed at first to be some sort of prank. The next day a dragoon guard escorted Nolan south to Fort St. John and confined him in a casemate. Nolan was certain that when Burr arrived in New Orleans the matter would be resolved. It only added to his bewilderment when a guard told him that Aaron Burr was now a fugitive with a federal price on his head. A scrap of newspaper shoved though the bars of his cell confirmed it.

A week passed. Then, with great fanfare, General Wilkinson announced that he had "intercepted" a coded letter revealing a diabolical plot to dismember the Union. Nolan's heart sank. There could be only one such letter—and Philip Nolan had placed it into General Wilkinson's fat, moist hand.

Wilkinson declared martial law in the city of New Orleans and his provost marshals rounded up dozens of potential conspirators, including members of the local militia, political rivals, and several of the general's creditors. In the renaissance of his patriotism General Wilkinson found traitors everywhere, except in the mirror. By the end of November, Nolan found himself under close arrest and marching north to Washington City with a dozen other officers and civilian officials. After more than a month on the road, prisoners and escort were met by a United States marshal, transferred from military into federal custody, and diverted to Richmond.

In an icy rain the escort drove the prisoners on past Staunton, through Rockfish Gap, and down the long Three Notch'd Road past Charlottesville and under the frowning brow of Monticello itself.

Arriving at last in Richmond, Nolan was placed in the city gaol with a colonel and a major, both formerly members of General Wilkinson's staff. During the long march from New Orleans neither officer had shown Nolan much courtesy. Soon after they were lodged in the Richmond gaol, these officers were paroled almost at once. For reasons not explained, Nolan was turned out with them. On a blustery morning, the officers left Nolan standing in front of the hoosegow with his baggage and saddle piled at his feet. As it began to rain, Nolan's cellmates climbed aboard a carriage provided by the Richmond Federalist Club. They did not say so much as adieu.

Nolan felt anger rising, the mailed fist of self-pity, and for the first time since his troubles began he considered tossing off his uniform, saddling a horse, and riding away. That he did not abscond said more about Nolan's doggedness than his sense of duty.

With his last few dollars he took a room at the St. Charles Hotel. Nolan found it a pleasant if somewhat noisy place, and not many of the lodgers seemed to care that he was still, technically, a federal prisoner. From the St. Charles, Nolan wrote confident letters to friends and a less hopeful one to his mother, gone long ago to Vera Cruz. In each, he told the story of how he had come to be arrested. Nolan could state honestly that he did not fully know the contents of Burr's letter, but he understood that it dealt with some sort of military combination against the Spanish. Nolan thought sincerely that any such grand machination must have been approved by President Jefferson. In this he was flatly and fatally mistaken.

Two weeks after his arrival in Richmond, Nolan was joined by Wendell Fitzgerald, a friend from university and West Point. Fitzgerald had bravely acceded to Nolan's request to serve as his attorney, and he sweetened their reunion by escorting his wife, Alden, and her cousin Lorina Rutledge to Richmond. As spring came to the Tidewater, Fitzgerald went back and forth to the House of Delegates, collecting the particulars of Nolan's alleged crimes, copying depositions, and conferring with the prosecutors.

Nolan had ample time to escort Mrs. Fitzgerald and Miss Rutledge about Richmond. The three were often seen about town, and more was known and said about the young officer than he could have imagined. The talk led to an unfortunate incident on Grace Street. As Nolan was passing by with Miss Rutledge, a local nabob, Randolph Creel Bell, an inbred, ill-mannered minor scion of several of the First Families, sniffed, "There goes dessert, arm and arm with disgrace."

Nolan was inclined to let the remark pass, and had he been alone he would have, but as he was escorting Miss Rutledge he was bound to ask the man for an explanation.

There was a short, escalating exchange, and Colonel Bell, as he styled himself (he held militia rank), refused either to withdraw his comment or to clarify it. As Alden and Lorina looked on, Nolan slapped the beaver hat off the colonel's lump-shaped head. It tumbled into the mud and Nolan crushed its crown under the heel of his boot. "My name is Philip Nolan, sir. And should you choose to resent this, I may be found any morning at the St. Charles Hotel."

The colonel had no choice but to resent it, for there was no affront more serious than a blow. Notes were exchanged and satisfaction was demanded.

Wendell Fitzgerald first declined to serve as a second, and did so only after Nolan pointed out that should he allow the affront to pass, Bell would post him as a coward, rascal, and poltroon. Such dishonor would unquestionably prejudice his case.

Fitzgerald understood that Nolan would be tried not by expedient men, citizens, or politicians, but by fellow officers. For them all, the notion of personal honor was placed on the same pedestal as duty and love of country. Nolan had no choice but to meet Bell on the field.

On the morning of his interview with Colonel Bell, Nolan rose early, breakfasted alone, and wrote a note to Lorina Rutledge. His were plain soldier's words, and the possibility that they might be his last gave a certain grace to his composition. He told Lorina that he regretted that she had been exposed to unpleasantness on his account, but he found it both a pleasure and an honor to discharge his duties as a gentleman. Nolan slipped the letter under the door of the house she shared with the Fitzgeralds and rode south under a humpbacked moon.

The stars were fading by the time Nolan crossed the plank bridge at Bloody Run. As he turned his mare into the clearing, the wheel marks of Colonel Bell's carriage were still plain in the dew. Nolan might have been excused a flush of excitement or even fear, but he had previously been a party to several affairs of honor, as both a principal and a second. This morning, to his own surprise, he felt nothing beyond a dull sort of annoyance.

Bell's carriage was parked beneath a dogwood tree, and several horses were tied to its rear wheels. With the most exacting courtesy, Nolan touched his hat as he rode past. The colonel chose rather dramatically to look away, and his several friends stopped their murmuring and followed Nolan with hard eyes. Bell kept his gaze scrupulously elsewhere, but Nolan, who had no impression to make, studied the colonel for several seconds.

Randolph Creel Bell was Nolan's senior by at least twenty years. He was dressed in a silk waistcoat and breeches, and the thought occurred that the colonel did not wear his uniform because it could no longer be pulled across his preposterous belly. Nolan and his adversary presented two perfect opposites. Bell was visibly distracted, and Nolan calmly indifferent—but, in truth, neither man had wished the incident to go this far.

Bell had considered Nolan's situation and projected on it his own arithmetic. He figured that Nolan could gain nothing by fighting a duel while facing a court-martial; win or lose, a duel would adversely affect his case, especially by taking the field against a nominally superior officer. Bell had expected Nolan to do the most expedient thing: endure the affront, decline the meeting, and preserve his life. Bell's original insult had been thus calculated, and he had truly thought he could make a joke at Nolan's expense—and make it stick.

For his part, Nolan still expected Bell to render an apology; perhaps one would come. Nolan had made inquiries, and his opponent's reputation was not that of a fighting man. The present Colonel Bell, long ago a captain, had been attached to the staff of Revolutionary General Horatio Gates. Bell, along with his notorious principal, was at the Revolutionary War Battle of Camden, the most ignominious defeat of American arms in history. In the midst of that fight Bell had been assigned to carry a dispatch to General Baron De Kalb, then commanding the American right. Quailing behind a stone wall, Bell watched as De Kalb was shot down when the British flanked and then overwhelmed that position. In the face of a British bayonet charge, young Captain Bell consulted his own safety and was one of the first officers to bolt down the Camden Pike. As the American line collapsed, Bell rode north. Fleeing the disaster, commandeering post horses at gunpoint, Bell had outflown even the craven General Gates himself, arriving in Charlotte, sixty miles away, before dusk.

Bell's account of his conduct at Camden improved the farther he was from the field. And though he did his best to recast himself as a hero, he was considered by his betters to be nothing more than a skedaddler and blowhard. Bell never again saw combat, and his appointment to Thomas Jefferson's staff and a vacant colonelcy in the Virginia militia was due to a finely honed talent for self-preservation and the obsequious cultivation of an uncle in the Continental Congress.

Confident that Bell would apologize rather than face him in a duel of arms, Nolan rode to the far end of the clearing and dismounted, hanging his hat on the pommel of his saddle. Wendell Fitzgerald stepped forward to take the bridle. A head taller than his friend, Fitzgerald was a bear of man, nearly as broad as Bell but immeasurably stouter of heart. Nolan glanced around; on his side of the clearing there was only Fitzgerald. He had no other seconds or partisans.

"You seem to have sauntered down," Fitzgerald said.

Nolan glanced at a blanket draped over a tree stump—on it were a set of pistols in a box. "Pistols for two and coffee for one."

Fitzgerald said nothing. He was not a glib man and did not care much for dueling.

"Bell seems disappointed I have kept my appointment."

"You both may be disappointed." Fitzgerald picketed Nolan's mare next to his own. He said quietly, "Where is our friend Doctor Kosinski?"

"He sends his best compliments but does not wish to come," Nolan said. "He told me that dueling is for imbeciles and advised me to skip breakfast in the event I am shot in the belly."

"That was sound advice." Fitzgerald glanced at Bell's crowd of seconds, one of whom was an old-fashioned gentleman in a grizzled physician's wig.

"Perhaps we'll not have need of a surgeon," Nolan said. "I don't think this man will fight."

"You are ever hopeful, friend." As Fitzgerald walked toward the carriage, Bell's chief second, a judge named Macon, came purposely forward.

"Good morning, sir."

Macon did not answer.

"On behalf of my principal, I ask again if bloodshed might be avoided and a misunderstanding put to rest."

"If there is a misunderstanding, Mister Fitzgerald, your friend is responsible for it," Macon wheezed. "Colonel Bell stands ready to accept a full and complete explanation."

Nolan removed his jacket and placed it over the picket line. Rolling up his sleeves, he walked into the meadow next to Fitzgerald. "I would be pleased to offer my compliments to Colonel Bell," Nolan said, "but I am afraid he has underestimated my regard for the lady in question."

"No offense was intended to your female acquaintance," Macon answered.

"She is more than an acquaintance, sir. On that afternoon she was under my protection. And as much as it pains me to discomfort the colonel, I expect an apology."

Bell snorted and for the first time walked forward. "I am obligated to explain myself only to a gentleman."

Fitzgerald said patiently, "A misunderstanding is—"

Bell was agitated and interrupted: "There is no misunderstanding. Philip Nolan is an accomplice of Aaron Burr, and a damnable traitor."

"Of the first accusation, sir, I readily admit to being acquainted with Colonel Burr. But I am no traitor."

"You are a damned liar, sir. And a bastard."

Fitzgerald saw the plain, inimical expression on Judge Macon's face and the pinched, disgusted attitudes of the men standing by the carriage. There had indeed been more said about Philip Nolan behind his back than to his face. Some of the gossip was merely that, tattletale and innuendo, but some of it was fact.

Bell now mentioned some of the embarrassing circumstances surrounding Nolan's birth, and spoke with frank disgust about an infamous liaison between Philip's mother and the British general Sir Henry Clinton during the occupation of Newport in the Revolutionary War. Rising in his own indignation, Bell affirmed Nolan to be not only the miserable by-blow of a skulking British lord, but a traitor sprung from a long line of unchaste, vexatious, and loud-mouthed slatterns. In the face of this harangue Nolan stood rigidly, humiliated and speechless.

It was only Fitzgerald's parade-ground voice that overcame Bell's yammering. He barked, "Enough, sir. That is enough." It was, in fact, more than enough. Shaking with rage, Nolan turned toward the stump and snatched up one of the pistols. The move was so deft and furious that Fitzgerald saw fit to place himself between Nolan and Bell. "Steady, Philip," Fitzgerald said. "Steady."

When Nolan had taken possession of the weapon, there had been a flurry among Bell's partisans. There were half a dozen, and all were armed, except the physician. Should it come to a general engagement (and such things happened in the South), Fitzgerald and Nolan would be at a singular disadvantage.

Fitzgerald was embarrassed for his friend, but he kept rigidly to the protocol of the matter at hand. Fitzgerald turned to Macon. "I assume that we are at an impasse?"

There was a moment of silence. Every man present knew this business must now come to blood. There was no way for Bell to climb down, and as Macon seemed unable to find his tongue, the colonel tried for something poetical. Bell rumbled, "I care more for my honor, and the glory of my country, than I do for my life."

Nolan stifled a guffaw. "You pompous jackass. You can polish a saddle—now let's see how you shoot."

A second pistol box was opened, and Bell took up a weapon. He made a brief show of examining the lock and mechanism and walked about the field aiming it here and there and checking the light. He eventually had a flunky go to the carriage and retrieve his spectacles. He put them on and walked to the spot where Nolan and Fitzgerald waited. The two principals faced each other and the seconds withdrew. Fitzgerald pulled a handkerchief from his waistcoat, and Bell and Nolan turned their backs.

Fitzgerald said, "You may ready your pieces."

The locks snicked back, and Fitzgerald noticed that although Nolan's expression was firm, even malicious, his hand trembled as the pistol cocked.

"Gentlemen, the distance is ten paces. Upon my signals, you may turn and then fire."

A horse stamped and blew.

"Colonel Bell, are you ready?"

"Ready."

"Lieutenant Nolan, are you ready?"

"I am, sir."

"*Vous pouvez commencer le marche,*" Fitzgerald said. The men stepped out in long soldier's strides. Fitzgerald lifted the handkerchief to his shoulder. Eight steps. Nine steps. Ten steps.

"*Présent!*"

Bell lumbered about to find Nolan already facing him, weapon leveled. They stood opposite each other for several seconds while Fitzgerald held the kerchief aloft. Finally Fitzgerald said, "*Allez,*" and the handkerchief floated to the grass.

Almost at once there was a snap and flash in the pan of Nolan's weapon. The noise was not loud, only a crack and hiss; it was immediately apparent that Nolan's pistol had been half cocked and had not discharged. All agreed that this much happened.

The accounts from this point diverged greatly. Nine men were present in the meadow, including the duelists themselves. Five of the witnesses were sworn partisans of Colonel Bell, and only Fitzgerald would ever repeat a version of events that favored Philip Nolan. Bell's surgeon, Doctor Van Sutter, forever after claimed neutrality, insisting he was not in a position to witness the action or to even to comment as he was not familiar with the code duello.

When the final command was given, Fitzgerald saw plainly that the muzzle of Nolan's pistol was pointed down and away from Colonel Bell. Though his weapon had misfired, Fitzgerald firmly believed that Nolan had intended to throw away his shot. Even Macon saw that Nolan's hand was no higher than his waist and his wrist was turned out and away from Bell. Nolan had been first to pull a trigger, but even if the weapon had functioned, the ball would have thumped harmlessly into the ground.

Bell's supporters claimed that the two men fired "almost instantaneously." In reality, several seconds passed between the moment Nolan threw away his shot and Colonel Bell aimed and fired. On the field that morning, those several seconds unfolded like a parade of seasons; it was enough time for minds to shape thoughts, for heads to turn, and for words to form. And it was time enough for Colonel Bell to aim deliberately, squeeze the trigger, and hit Nolan squarely.

The ball struck Nolan six inches under the left clavicle, tearing open his shirt and knocking him onto his back. The wound was thought to have killed him instantly. On the ground, Nolan remained motionless for the several seconds it took Fitzgerald to reach him. From the other part of the clearing, Bell yelped with pleasure and there were shouts and halloos from his supporters.

Nolan did not utter a sound, but eventually pulled up his legs and rolled onto his side. The meadow was completely silent; even the locusts and birds were still as Nolan came first to his hands and knees and then, reeling, to his feet. Frothy pink fluid pumped from the wound as he shook off Fitzgerald's help.

"I can stand," Nolan choked. His eyes were like an animal's.

Bell was huddled with his seconds. Nolan said hoarsely, "I shall have a second pistol, Mister Fitzgerald." Nolan swayed on his feet, and it looked like he would fall any second.

Bell said, "The affair is ended."

"It is not, sir." Nolan's face was ashen. "Two passes must be made before a resolution."

"Both parties have fired," Macon said to Fitzgerald. It was not mere hairsplitting. Nolan had pulled the trigger, and neither the accident of his misfire nor his intent to throw away his shot disqualified his actions.

"I am accorded two passes by custom," Nolan panted.

"He is in no condition to continue," Macon sniffed. "Look at him."

Nolan bellowed, "Damn you for a coward, sir. Arm that quim friend of yours or I shall fight you next."

Fitzgerald handed Nolan his second pistol. The code did undeniably call for two passes should either principal demand it.

"Colonel Bell, prepare to receive Lieutenant Nolan's second volley."

Bell considered the situation. Though Nolan looked like he might use his pistol instantly, the colonel did not consider Fitzgerald and a raving, wounded maniac a match for six of his friends. Bell's expression changed when he surveyed the men standing by his carriage. They were solemn and unanimous in their opinion that the affair was not finished.

"Colonel Bell," Fitzgerald barked, "arm yourself."

"You are not serious," Bell sputtered. "This matter is concluded. I am satisfied."

"I am not," wheezed Nolan. Blood dripped from his shirt and blotted his trousers.

"Judge Macon, do something."

"Two passes are stipulated, Colonel," Macon said firmly. "It is what honor requires."

Fitzgerald said, "We are in earnest, sir. Return to the field."

Bell took a step backward, and Fitzgerald lifted his saber. "Stand your ground, sir, or by God I will strike you down."

"Fitzgerald, for Christ's sake, stop this farce," Bell stammered. "Goddamn it, Nolan. Our affair is settled."

"It is not, you sack of shit," Nolan rasped. Using both hands, he managed to pull back the hammer of his pistol.

Macon came slowly forward and pressed a second pistol into Bell's hand.

"Ready your weapon, Colonel Bell," Fitzgerald intoned. He used his sword point to lift the handkerchief from the grass, and Bell hurriedly snapped back the hammer of his weapon.

"This is insane," Bell spit. "It is simple murder."

"Gentlemen, to your places," said Fitzgerald.

At the other end of the field Macon whispered something to Bell, then walked slowly back toward the carriage, obviously taking his time. Bell narrowed his eyes at his adversary; Nolan presented an unsteady, perhaps even defenseless target—he had yet to raise his pistol. Bell turned smoothly sideways, placed his feet with deliberation, lifted his weapon, and aimed exactly at the livid stain on Nolan's shirt.

Panting, unsteady on his feet, Nolan's world had become a constricting circle of agony. He could see Bell only through a wavering blur of pain.

"Colonel Bell, are you ready?"

"I am."

There was a banshee's howl in Nolan's ears.

"Lieutenant Nolan, are you ready?"

Struggling to lift his pistol, Nolan did not answer.

"Mister Nolan?" Fitzgerald repeated.

"Yes, goddamn it," he grunted. "Finish it."

Fitzgerald lifted the kerchief. *"Présent."*

Nolan saw Fitzgerald's lips move, and in a strange elongation of time he watched the handkerchief flutter toward the ground. He never heard the command to fire. There were simultaneous flashes of orange light, and gun smoke roiled across the meadow. Bell's shot trilled past Nolan's ear and went away through the trees, cracking at twigs and bark. Nolan's ball traveled flat and straight, struck Bell above his right eye, and blew off the top of his head.

Nolan staggered backward, and the pistol dropped from his hand. Folded by heaving agony, he toppled onto the seat of his pants. As pain closed its fists around him, blood pooled under Nolan's tongue in thick, salty mouthfuls. Arms crossed and legs drawn up, Nolan rolled onto his side and a low groan rumbled in his throat.

Fitzgerald knelt and bundled him into his arms. Light was coming over the trees now, and it seemed suddenly and unbearably bright. Across the meadow, one of Bell's men placed a cape over the colonel's shattered, lopsided face. Oddly, his spectacles were still perched on the end of his nose.

Nolan coughed and felt his body going strangely numb. Fitzgerald held his friend, horrified to see blood pooling in the dirt beneath them.

Nolan whispered, "Hold me, Fitz. Hold me. Now I am surely killed."

Colonel Bell's corpse was hurried back to Richmond in his fine coach and four, though the reason for such dispatch was not obvious. News of the duel reached Doctor Rikard Kosinski in the breakfast room of the Union Hotel, and he mounted and rode south. He met Wendell Fitzgerald leading Nolan's horse and a hay wagon near the Chimborazo Hill. Kosinski found Nolan sprawled on a carpet of filthy straw and at first judged him mortally wounded. Fitzgerald asked a tavern owner if Nolan might be taken to a bed. For various reasons the proprietor found this not convenient, and Nolan was trundled another several miles through cobbled streets to his room at the St. Charles. That Nolan survived this journey, and eventually his wound, was to be the last bit of luck that would ever attend him.

After some difficulty Doctor Kosinski managed to draw the ball from Nolan's chest; in a long career as a surgeon, he had never known a man to survive such a wound, but kept this prognosis to himself. Weeping, Lorina was allowed to sit at Nolan's bedside, but he did not open his eyes. While Nolan hovered near death, Fitzgerald and Judge Macon composed a joint statement for the newspapers, as was part of their duties. It was not surprising that they did not see eye to eye on the particulars.

When their letter appeared the next day in the *Richmond Intelligencer*, an attached, anonymous commentary skewed the events in Bell's favor. The colonel's lapsed marksmanship gave rise to a myth that he had attempted to spare Nolan's life—though every man on the field that morning saw Bell aim and fire precisely. A separate obituary mentioned Bell's "arduous and dangerous" service during the Revolutionary War. Forgotten utterly was Bell's shared disgrace with the coward General Gates and his loitering attachment for the rest of the war to Thomas Jefferson's staff in Charlottesville.

Bell's funeral took place on a Friday, and many of the businesses in the city were obliged to close their doors. There were muffled drums, and a pair of house slaves dressed in white turbans and green pantaloons sat atop the hearse. A groom in a powdered wig led his master's horse with boots reversed in the stirrups. Some found it particularly affecting that a young mulatto girl carried the colonel's spectacles on a satin pillow. The cortege included many of Richmond's persons of quality, but the route to Trinity Church was not thronged with onlookers. Colonel

Bell's firmness as a businessman and punctuality as a landlord were well established among the working class. Some of Richmond's citizens could not appreciate Colonel Bell's qualities with the same esteem as the moneylenders and plantation owners who were his relations and friends.

Nolan lay two days in a coma, tended around the clock by Doctor Kosinski, Alden Fitzgerald, and Lorina Rutledge. He woke in the middle part of the third morning, almost cheerful but in great pain. The windows were thrown open and the room was made airy, a particular tenet of Kosinski's unique ideas of the practice of physic. Nolan was prevailed upon to take some barley water and a salted egg. After taking them he showed every sign of improvement, and during the day Lorina read aloud and Alden spoke quietly to him. Nolan lay listening, and sometimes he would smile and look at Lorina with his eyes half closed. Occasionally he answered with a word or two and sometimes a sigh. On the fourth night, the pain overwhelmed him; Nolan slipped again into unconsciousness, and his fever reached a new and dangerous peak.

In delirium Nolan poured out the secrets of his soul. Some of what he said was meaningless fever talk, but some of it was the stuff of his darkest fears. Nolan had imbibed French during a childhood spent in New Orleans, and Spanish on the Texas frontier. Much of his delirious raving was in these languages, and although Lorina spoke only a smattering of French, what she heard was heartbreaking. In a sweat-blotted frenzy Nolan twitched and moaned and spoke of all the errors and weaknesses and aching wants of his life. Doctor Kosinski did what he could to ease Nolan's pain, and Alden and Lorina sat sometimes sponging Nolan's brow, taking away bowls of bloody bandages, and listening unwillingly to the patient's shouts and sobs. Alden had known him longest and admired Philip above every man she knew except her husband; for her, his rants were sometimes wounding. Once she placed a finger against lips to quiet him, but still he spoke of naked anguish and shame.

Lorina had seen only the proud face Nolan showed to the world. In their time together he had seemed to her carefree and blithely above the scorn and calumny that had been poured on him. From his nightmares Lorina discovered how deeply Nolan suffered the accusations made against him—steeped in months of frustration and disgrace, his ravings were heartbreaking to hear.

Dawn came, and then daylight. Nolan became quiet and the muscles around his jaw relaxed. He slept, woke, and slept again. Nolan's iron constitution triumphed, and on the following day the fever abated. Nolan's senses returned to him at last and, trembling, he took a sip of water.

The doctor felt Nolan's pulse and smiled. "I am glad you are with us again, Mister Nolan."

Nolan saw in the small circle of his room the faces of Wendell and then Alden and Lorina. They had passed the long ordeal at his side, and they too looked drawn and haggard. Nolan lifted his hand and Wendell took it in his own.

"Friend," Nolan whispered hoarsely. Then, looking at them all, he said, "My friends."

———————

IT IS A HEADY THING FOR A YOUNG WOMAN TO REALIZE THAT SHE HAS BEEN THE reason for gunfire. For Lorina Rutledge, Nolan's wounding had been the gravest calamity of her life, and his recovery one of her greatest joys.

It could be said that until the duel Lorina had not felt any particular attachment to Nolan, nothing much beyond an appreciation for his fine, attentive manners and his continuing good cheer. The nights she spent at his bedside had been like a passage through a storm. She had insisted to be allowed to help Doctor Kosinski; her father had been a surgeon, and she was not what anyone would call fainting. Through the long period of danger she impressed Kosinski and Alden alike with her determined composure. The experience kindled in her a tenderness that found delight in the small, daily triumphs of Nolan's recovery. They were attached now, mutually, by feelings of obligation and growing affection.

Nolan's steady improvement was seen as something of a marvel and wonderfully confirmed Kosinski's reputation as a physician and surgeon. In ten days, Nolan was taking halting steps across the room, and the next week he was taking the air on the lawn behind the St. Charles. In the mornings, after the dew lifted, a pair of porters would bring him down the stairs and sit him in the shade of the spreading elms. There he was attended sometimes by Alden and more often by Lorina, who plied him with spoonfuls of Turlington's Balsam and snippets from curious pamphlets by William Blake.

Lorina was touched by Nolan's sincere gratitude—his thanks were heartfelt—and as his strength returned she found his boyish enthusiasm charming. In their conversations everything seemed mutually interesting; they pleased each other with trifles and were fascinated by the small things they had in common. After the colonel's funeral, tattle painted Nolan as something of an infamous person. Lorina knew that Alden adored him, and she did not imagine half of the things she'd heard said about Nolan could be true. It could not rightly be said that Lorina had courted scandal herself, but they had occasionally danced. Her doting father guarded his daughter's reputation with all the trappings of virtue. He had reason to strengthen her defenses. Lorina's suitors were many, and only a few of them were judged suitable. At her father's insistence, Lorina taught Sunday school at Trinity Episcopal and often read her catechism. Even if she had not strictly upheld every verse, she did know and follow the Ten Commandments, and at least three of its mortal sins were beyond any evil she could even imagine.

Pleasant to look at, clever, and rich, Lorina might have been guilty of thinking a bit too well of herself, and of generally having things too much her own way. Though others frequently made accommodation for her, she was always unabashedly herself. Lorina had her own secrets. She had concealed from Nolan the fact that her family was wealthy. A dowry changed things, she knew. Money turned men into puppies or reptiles, and she did not want Nolan to reveal himself as a whelp or a fortune hunter. For his part, Nolan did not mention the name of his father, or say much at all about his upbringing except to confirm that he had been born in Rhode Island and moved at a young age to New Orleans and then to the country of Texas.

Nolan had very few friends in Richmond before the arrival of the Fitzgeralds, and after the duel he found he had none. Wendell and Alden he had known for years, and they were unfalteringly attached. Alden Fitzgerald had once been Alden Schuyler (of the New York Schuylers), and her family was too prominent to be trifled with; there was not a chance she would be insulted in the street. She had known Philip and Wendell since they were cadets, a very happy and long time before. No gossip reached Alden's ears, and she was not interested in the things said about a friend behind his back. Oddly, the insults Lorina heard about Nolan, especially the more outrageous ones, served only to make her more stubborn in her affection.

Nolan was not invited to the governor's dinner, but Wendell, Alden, and Lorina were. Lorina was connected enough to make certain they were seated together at a table where they could see, but not necessarily hear, the speechification from the dais.

Between amuse and intermezzo, Lorina asked, "Please tell me, Wendell, what is misprision of treason? I have heard it said about Philip."

"It is having knowledge of a treasonable act."

"It is a crime to simply know of treason?" she asked.

"You might say that." Wendell poured the wine, a dusty claret that had not traveled well. "It is a stipulation of English Common Law that treason is considered the very apex of felony—equal to regicide itself. All persons are obligated instantly to put it down. Failing to report even a suspicion of it is a crime."

"Philip is not a traitor," said Alden.

"Misprision of treason is unique in that guilt is determined not for acting unlawfully but for *failing* to act," Wendell said. "The accusation is that Nolan knew of Burr's treason and did not report it."

"How I detest an informer," Alden frowned.

"Do you think he is innocent?" asked Lorina.

"Innocence is a measure of virtue," Wendell answered. "And I would not say that our friend is superior to other men. He's no goody-two-shoes. If you are asking me if the charges against Philip are true, I would say that no act of treason has yet been proven—by Burr's accusers or anyone else. Not yet."

Wendell helped himself to a slice of venison pie and said, "At West Point, Nolan swore the same oath as I, to uphold the Constitution. All the officers of our service take an oath—not to the government, or to the president, but to the document itself, to the law of the land.

"While we were cadets, Philip came to blows with a classmate, Joseph Swift. Their disagreement was whether or not the president or the Constitution was the supreme deity. Swift had it that the commander in chief was Jehovah—I should say Moses, rather, we were after all just cadets—but Nolan held that we were all serving the law. We served *it*, you see. Our one loyalty was to the Constitution and not the officers appointed above us. Nolan thought that people were fallible, but the law served us all. It was a bit optimistic, but Nolan thought the ideals enshrined in the charter were more important than any elected leader. Philip insisted even the commander in chief must serve the Constitution. The spirit of the law was for Philip the burning bush. Well, Joe Swift called Nolan an insubordinate puppy. And Philip broke Swift's nose."

Lorina held out her glass to be filled. "He seems a confirmed patriot."

"He is that. And was nearly expelled from the Academy."

"I must ask you directly, Wendell, how much of it is true? How much of what is said in the streets about Nolan? I cannot think that he is truly wicked."

Fitzgerald looked at Lorina. "He is not. Pray, what have you heard?"

Lorina said, "Nolan is held out as one of the most ardent and desperate of Burr's conspirators. It is put about that he shot dead the first marshal sent to arrest him, and that he is the son of a British lord."

Wendell examined his wineglass carefully as Lorina spoke and quietly cleared his throat. "Philip has yet to be proven guilty of any crime, and I know of no harm he has ever done to an officer of the court. He is not, and has never been, gratuitously violent. That he is a desperate conspirator is all havers and nonsense, I assure you. There is much taking of sides, sure. And Colonel Bell, though not much esteemed when he was alive, has been transformed into a hero, while Nolan is called both Judas and a mercenary."

Alden said to her cousin, "Those who know Philip know better than to judge him by gossip."

"But he carried a ciphered letter to Colonel Burr, did he not?" Lorina asked this with a blush of shame. "I read it in the newspaper. Is it not incriminating that the letter was in code?"

"It is not," Wendell answered. "Officers frequently carry coded messages."

"Is it really true that he could have carried Burr's dispatches and not have known what was in them?" Lorina asked.

"It would be the rule rather than the exception," Wendell said patiently. "As it bears on the case, it is less germane that the letter was encoded than what exactly Burr requested Nolan to do."

"Burr is a vile, grasping creature." Alden shuddered. "I remember him from Manhattan. He is perfectly odious."

"Nolan was unfortunate to trust the man. But that is not a crime."

Alden's face took on genuine displeasure when she said, "What is it that Mister Jefferson called Burr? A Cataline. That was it, a new Cataline."

Lorina felt a strange flutter.

"The government must prove its case, first against Burr and only then against Nolan," Wendell said. "Philip can hardly be party to an imaginary act."

———————

SOON AFTER LORINA WROTE A LETTER TO HER PARENTS THAT ALARMED THEM greatly. Before her father had agreed that she might go with the Fitzgeralds to Richmond, Doctor Rutledge extracted from his daughter a promise that she would consider—at least consider—the marriage proposal of Richard Graff, the wealthy and moonstruck son of the chancellor of the University of Pennsylvania. Graff had a thriving medical practice and had recently published a well-regarded book on phrenology. Her father thought Doctor Graff a perfect match—Graff's future was as bright as Nolan's was bleak—and although the young surgeon was thought highly suitable, everything that recommended him had begun to make him wearisome to Lorina.

As Nolan returned to health before her eyes, the far-away Doctor Graff was made into a sexless, bloodless shadow. Lorina wrote that she no longer wished to entertain Graff's proposal. The news was most disappointing to her parents and fell like a thunderbolt on Graff, who had believed that an understanding was imminent. When he received the intelligence of Lorina's dismissal, Doctor Graff published a melancholy sonnet in the *Philadelphia Gazette*. Then, after sending several alarming notes to his friends, he retired to his rooms and took a very mild overdose of calomel and laudanum. Both poem and potion fell somewhat short of the mark. Graff's stomach was pumped, and he did his best to pine away in conspicuous and brooding melancholy.

Lorina's parents considered having Alden return their daughter but relented, thinking that her cousin (who was after all a respectable married woman) would speak plain sense to Lorina. Doctor Rutledge went so far as to write Alden, urging her to tell Lorina that a prompt marriage to Doctor Graff was preferable to spinsterhood or gossip. Of course, Lorina's parents knew nothing of Nolan, as his infamy was yet confined to Richmond and the federal charges against him were not yet public. Had they any inkling of their daughter's attachment to the young officer, they would have coached down by express and returned Lorina bodily home to Philadelphia.

Nolan knew nothing of this. Miss Rutledge had said nothing about it to him, and she wished harm to no one—not even the swooning doctor. Nolan's own feelings were anything but clear to him. He had never before in his life felt such reciprocal affection, and his own innocence gave him no measure by which to understand the things he felt. Those around him saw it more plainly than he could; Alden certainly did, and Wendell too. Both hoped brightly for the couple.

Although his cheerfulness returned, Nolan had a hundred reasons to doubt himself. His future was clouded and he had a secret in his past, one he felt that put him aside from respectable people. Nolan knew that his illegitimacy and his mother's mottled reputation posed an impediment to his social connexions. The Fitzgeralds loved him, but they had known him for most of a decade. It pained them very much to think that Nolan might be found out to be unworthy of Lorina's attentions.

THEN, ON A BRIGHT APRIL MORNING A SQUADRON OF CAVALRY RATTLED ACROSS Mayo's Bridge. Word spread quickly that Aaron Burr had at last been brought to heel. After a months-long manhunt, he had been captured in the Alabama territory under circumstances as ambiguous as his plot. Townsmen surged down Cary Street to see the most nefarious person in the Republic handed down from a wagon by a file of grim-faced Marines. The short, spare fugitive was wearing an outrageous sombrero and canvas chaps—the same outfit he'd been arrested in six weeks earlier near the Tombigbee River.

Burr was lodged in the state penitentiary, where he was given the entire top floor. Carpets, drapery, and furniture were sent up, and he received visitors like an emperor. Burr's supporters may have chosen to remain anonymous, but they were generous. When bail was set in the staggering amount of ten thousand dollars, it was put forward in gold. A second subscription raised more than a thousand dollars to buy the former vice president clothing for court. Dressed in silk, Burr went to levees and banquets. Most of the derision formerly directed at Nolan was now aimed at Burr. Beyond a cordon of supporters and sycophants, the crowd howled for Burr's head. The little man seemed to revel in the frustration of the mob.

Burr made no attempt to speak to or correspond with his former courier. He had used Nolan as he had used everyone else. The federal prosecutors, predictably, had less time to devote to the secondary cases, and Fitzgerald hoped that the gathering storm would pass over his client.

As Nolan continued his recovery, Aaron Burr's trial went forward. Burr was defended by some of the ablest lawyers in the nation: Luther Martin, Edmund Randolph, and John Wickham. The proceedings were closely monitored in Washington, and the federal prosecutor, Mister Hay, dispatched daily summaries to President Jefferson. On most mornings, Wendell Fitzgerald was in the gallery and paid close attention to a contradictory flood of testimony. The prosecution's chief witness, General Wilkinson, was so ludicrous as to make Fitzgerald suspect that the charges against Nolan would be quashed.

Questioned by Luther Martin, the sweating general admitted that he had received the coded letter from Aaron Burr. Nolan was identified as the courier. Cross-examination revealed that after deciphering the letter, Wilkinson had rewritten the contents before sending them along to Washington. Under a with-ering barrage of questions Wilkinson confessed that his editing had removed several sentences regarding his own foreknowledge of Burr's plot. Each word out of the general's mouth seemed to implicate him further, and many in the gallery believed that Wilkinson himself would be charged with treason and perjury. The government's case against Burr was falling apart, but Fitzgerald was slow to admit optimism.

Despite Wilkinson's buffoonery, the prosecution was relentless and eloquent. Mister Hay, the chief prosecutor, distinguished himself in the government's closing arguments, calling Burr an arch deceiver and a threat to American posterity. From Washington City came news that President Jefferson had told Congress that Burr was "without question" guilty of treason. These were unprecedented words from a sitting executive, but reflected the mood of the nation. At the end of August, Chief Justice John Marshall rendered an opinion that Burr's indictment was flawed, but nevertheless turned the matter over to the jury.

The nation held its breath and Fitzgerald waited in the packed courtroom until the verdict was announced. On hearing it, Wendell made his way through the stunned and angry crowds. He walked first to the offices of the military provost and then at once to the St. Charles. Wendell went upstairs and into the bright front room where Philip had been moved.

Nolan was propped up in bed, and Lorina sat by the window reading aloud from *The Age of Reason* by Thomas Paine.

"Ah," Nolan said. "The second most hated man in Richmond."

"Perhaps the third. How is your patient, Lorina?"

"Not as well or as charming as he thinks."

Nolan studied his friend. "What news, Wendell?"

Fitzgerald sat down and tapped his fingers on the table. "Aaron Burr has been acquitted."

Nolan made no attempt to hide his delight. Lorina put down the book and went to his side.

"He is free?" Alden asked.

Wendell nodded. "He walked out of the courtroom. They may charge him on misdemeanors relating to filibuster—I think they will—but he has escaped the noose."

Nolan squeezed Lorina's hand. "And when I can walk, we will dance out of Richmond."

Fitzgerald alone was not smiling.

"What is the matter?" Alden asked.

"It has been decided the military trials will continue." Fitzgerald walked to the window. "Feeling runs particularly high against you, Philip, following the death of Colonel Bell."

"I would dig him up and shoot him again."

"He would still be a nephew of Patrick Henry. And that has not helped your case."

Lorina paced the room. "How is it that Burr is found not guilty when he intended to set himself up as dictator?"

"No one is sure anymore what Burr set out to do. His followers are at each other's throats. Wilkinson made a fool of himself trying to keep his own skirts clean. That the general gave false testimony is obvious. His credibility is blown, and he may face his own trial."

"Then his charges against me are valueless," Nolan said firmly.

"Normally, they would be. But Wilkinson's duplicity has cast doubt on the loyalty of the entire Army. President Jefferson has spent several hundred thousand on this trial. He intends to make an example. He must. The case against Burr has miscarried so badly that the prosecution will now proceed with great caution. Perhaps even incrementally." Wendell looked at Nolan. "They are very likely to start with you, Philip."

Lorina frowned. "Why?"

"A case against a junior officer would involve a more straightforward application of the law. Military law."

"Because of Wilkinson? Philip is one man—not the Army," Alden said.

"He is a serving officer."

Nolan's face darkened. "So I am a symbol."

Below the window, a cart passed and a vendor shouted. Fitzgerald turned, the sun on his broad shoulders. "The provost informs me that if you plead guilty to a charge of manslaughter regarding Colonel Bell, the military court will drop the specifications of desertion and sedition against you."

"Manslaughter?" cried Nolan. "It was an affair of honor."

"Honor, my friend, is going out of fashion."

"So this is their bargain? I am to plead guilty for being a gentleman? Half the men of the court have fought duels before me. They are a mumping great set of hypocrites."

"The law does not blush at hypocrisy, friend. They mean to have something, someone, after this. Burr's acquittal has brought them to a perfect boil."

"Let them stew, damn them."

Lorina shook her head. "This has been a wicked farce. Is Philip to make himself a sacrifice for Mister Jefferson's grudge? What could be more low?"

"Philip, I know you to be brave, even fearless," Wendell said. "But choose your course carefully. Burr is acquitted, but the government believes that he intended not only to start a war, but also to separate the western territory from the union."

"They proved none of that."

"But it is widely believed."

"I do not believe it." Nolan's face twisted and he winced as he drew breath. "I volunteered to lead a battery against the Spanish, not make Burr a dictator."

"I am sure of that," Fitzgerald said. "But all of the evidence gathered against Burr will now be brought to bear against you. As your attorney—" Nolan started to say something that was likely to be indelicate, and Wendell cut him off. "—as your *advocate*, I urge you to consider the offer. There are some members of the court, particularly Colonel Morgan, who have told me in confidence that they find you a brave and likeable officer."

"But consider me guilty."

"They will likely take your commission, Philip. Be careful lest they take your life."

IN THE EVENING THE PORTER ANNOUNCED THAT NOLAN HAD A CALLER IN THE public rooms. A pair of footmen helped Nolan negotiate the stairs and brought him into the alcove at the back of the main floor. Lorina was there. In the moonlight outside the bowed windows Nolan could see a hired carriage—a four-in-hand with its lamps lighted.

Lorina helped him into a chair and called for two pints of sherry.

"You are risking tattle, madam," Nolan smiled.

"So I am," she said. The wine was put before them. "I hope you will allow me to speak as your friend."

"Of course."

"You may not take to what I have to say, but I want you to deliberate upon it. I want very much to persuade you, but I do not want to be considered a scold."

"Never in life," Nolan said.

"The newspapers came today from Washington filled with lurid ravings. The administration is incensed at Burr's release, and Mister Jefferson's partisans are in full bay—"

Nolan's ribs creaked as he drew a laborious breath. "Damn them. I am not to be convicted by the president's editors."

"You are not. But there was much grumbling today in the market and on the streets. Burr's acquittal has enraged the larger portion of the town, both above and below Broad Street." Nolan started to say something, but Lorina touched his hand. "Please, hear me. I know that you do not care a fig about politics and consider the practitioners as less than, well, as diminished beings, but I must mention to you that today I heard four different speakers, members of the House of Delegates, agitating about the failure to punish Burr."

"No one knows what Burr intended—least of all the government, for they have failed in all their proceedings."

"And Burr is hated all the more for it. He has had the good sense to leave town."

Nolan leaned back in his chair and frowned.

"Colonel Bell's partisans are putting it about that Burr's true purposes were to raise troops to attack Washington City and arrest the Congress."

"That is absurd," Nolan scoffed.

"Some people believe it, Philip. Bell's cousin paid for a public house to distribute beer and liquor gratis while a series of noxious speakers harangued against Burr and you personally. The crowds they have incited are planning to gather at the armory tomorrow for your court-martial." She paused. "There may be a riot."

Nolan looked at her with a detached expression. "Let them burn their own hovels."

"Philip, whether you think it or not, a public clamor is very likely to affect the government's determination to punish."

Nolan collected himself with a sip and said evenly, "I thank you for the things you have said. For your concern I am deeply beholden. I know very little of law or lawyers and, as you say, even less of politicians, but I will be judged by a military court, composed of fellow officers. They are men very far removed from politics. Since Burr has been found innocent, I see no way that they can convict me."

"You *did* leave your post. Is that not a mortal offense? And how can you know that the military judges do not want command of a regiment or the governorship of a territory? Would not President Jefferson have it in his power to reward them for your conviction?"

Nolan was silent. Across the dining room he watched as an infantry officer poured wine for his wife. They were laughing.

"I care for you, Philip, but you are nothing to the prosecutors. You are a statistic, a jot on a clerk's ledger. You said you will not allow yourself to be made a scapegoat."

"I will not."

She leaned forward. "Then you must leave the city. You must."

"Don't be ridiculous. I have given my parole."

"Words."

"I nearly lost my life over a few words, madam."

"Do you not understand that they *must* have a conviction? This is no longer a storm that is passing overhead, Philip. You cannot be so proud as to attract lightning. What I have is yours. I have enough, more than enough, to get you away and keep you in a safe place."

"Keep me?"

"To keep you safe."

"I do not wish to be kept."

"Kept from the noose, then, Philip. The coach is there in the livery yard. You can be on the packet in Newport News before dawn tomorrow and can take ship to Charleston or even Savannah. I will go to meet you as soon as I can."

"And then what? Would I pretend to be someone else?"

Lorina blinked at Nolan as though he were an obstinate child. "Would you stay here and be lampooned by a crooked court?"

"If I lied to you, would you still care for me?"

"I would not. I would be mortally offended if you lied to me."

"So I am to lie to everyone but you?"

"Have you not been lied to by Burr? And that greasy oaf Wilkinson—he couldn't tell the truth except by accident. Don't be a fool Philip, and don't be too virtuous to walk through a door that has been opened for you."

"Don't tell me what is right or wrong."

Lorina felt indignation warm her face. "You are ungrateful."

"Is this how you would have me show gratitude to Wendell and Alden? By bolting?"

"Is your pride so cast iron that you will not step out of a fire?"

"To go where? Into some cloud of perfume? To hide under your petticoats?"

"I am offering you a way out."

"If I did sneak aboard a ship, would you come for me? Even if you did start, you would soon think better of it. You would turn around halfway when you realized that a man willing to turn his back on his friends must inevitably betray you as well."

Lorina's eyes flashed. "Then damn you for a fool, Philip Nolan."

"I have been fool enough—for you."

The trembling silence between them went through the close room like a ripple across a pond, working itself between the laughter from other tables. The tavern keeper turned and peered into their circle of candlelight. He watched Nolan say something. He could not hear it but he saw Lorina stand and place her napkin on the table. It was a gesture of poignant finality.

The keeper came over and bowed. "May I be of assistance?"

"Mister Nolan is tired," Lorina said coolly. "I am afraid I have kept him up too late."

"I'll have the porters bring you to your room, sir." The tavern keeper went away to fetch the footmen, and almost a full minute passed in silence.

Lorina said quietly, "Shall I see you in the morning?"

"You may do what you wish."

Lorina turned and walked out of the salon, and Nolan heard the inn door open and then close behind her. Until this moment he had not known that anything other than the swirl of battle could confuse and stab him so.

BEFORE A MILITARY COURT

NOLAN COULD NOT SLEEP, AND SHORTLY AFTER MIDNIGHT THE WOUND in his chest burst open. Kosinski was summoned and administered a blue pill and a vile-tasting draught. When that failed to calm the patient, a healthy bleed and a strong dose of laudanum appeared to address the pain. But these remedies made the other, less physical, complaints very much worse. Through the night Nolan remained agitated and restless. Near dawn Nolan succumbed to a short scrap of sleep, but woke, instantly lucid, as the sun came up.

"You are not a theatrical man," Kosinski said. "And I, too, try to avoid melodrama. You are not well enough, my friend, to endure any further emotional shocks. If you do not rest, you will come upon a dangerous, perhaps even lethal, pneumonia. I recommend to you a stout breakfast—perhaps burgoo, bacon, toast, and even a moderate dram of coffee—to stimulate the humors and give you energy for what may prove a trying day."

"I have had a bellyful of nonsense." Nolan winced. "I need this to be over." He sat up in bed and was bound tightly in clean bandage. Kosinski carefully placed Nolan's left arm into a sling and he was carried like a parcel from the hotel to the armory. The short trip was made in the early morning, for reasons of safety and public order. As word of Burr's acquittal filtered through the city, it had produced a spectrum of opinion. The prosecution had been singularly important to the party of President Jefferson, and the verdict of "not proven" had dismayed the Washington City establishment greatly. Unexpectedly, some of Richmond's bluebloods took a discreet pleasure in Thomas Jefferson's setback. Although the president was one of their own, Jefferson was not held in universally positive regard. Landowners found the president a reliable supporter of their "peculiar institution" of slavery (Monticello was, for all its glamor, a working *plantation*), but Richmond's elite considered Jefferson's enthusiasm for democracy a bit overdone. Not that planters or money men would have done Nolan any violence; it was President Jefferson's partisans on the more incandescent end of the spectrum—the laborers, mechanics, and shopkeepers—who were appalled that Burr had slipped the noose. To these citizens, Burr's plan to split off the western territory was an unforgivable sin; they saw the lands beyond the Mississippi as their patrimony and the legacy of the Republic. Their fury was aggravated by testimony that Burr had conducted a secret correspondence with Lord Merry, the British ambassador at Washington, begging for the Royal Navy to help him subdue New Orleans. This scrap of evidence burned like a spark; repeated in public houses, amplified by alarm and indignation, by the morning of the court-martial a rumor circulated that even now Burr was planning to lead a British squadron into the Chesapeake to bombard Norfolk.

By the time Nolan was carried into the armory, two or three hundred persons had gathered around the building, and a company of dragoons stood guard. The crowd outside hovered and grumbled, but inside the armory the deliberate course of the proceedings anesthetized all but the most passionate.

The three chairs of the court were arrayed behind a heavy, book-covered table. Behind them, draped in bunting, was a portrait of General Washington. In front of the judges' bench were two desks and chairs for the defense and prosecution, right and left; immediately behind them were a pair of sawhorses, also draped in flags. These patriotic barriers separated the gallery from the court proper. Some fifty citizens and officers had been admitted as spectators; they had divided themselves as does a crowd at a wedding, sorted on this occasion not by relation but by sympathy for prosecution or defense. There were noticeably fewer civilians on the left side of the room, and there was not a single officer seated behind the desk at which Nolan and Fitzgerald waited. All of the long morning was spent in preamble, and the early afternoon in grinding formality. Nolan slumped in his chair, alternately bored, harried, and agitated.

His hopes had risen when old Colonel Morgan, who presided, said that the charges of misappropriation and mutinous utterance had been dropped. Nolan's heart sank just as quickly when Morgan pronounced that the court would consider the circumstances surrounding the death of Colonel Bell and render judgment on a charge of willful desertion.

A few minutes after one, Alden and Lorina entered through a door in the left-hand wall near the barrier. They found chairs two rows behind the defense table, and as they sat Lorina looked at Nolan. He was in physical pain, and a scowl lined his mouth; she had never seen him so dejected and resentful. For the rest of the morning Nolan sat with his back turned, frowning at the judges.

The prosecution put forward its arguments, and as Fitzgerald had predicted, they did their best to portray Nolan as a conspirator as vile as Burr himself. Some of it was bombastic stuff. The prosecutor, Major Teague, eventually realized that he was spinning a grand tale around a central character who was, after all, only a lieutenant of artillery. He quickly reverted to fact and summed his case: Nolan was assigned to Fort Massac and had been arrested seven hundred miles away on the Sabine River. Nolan had neither permission to travel nor lawful military business there: *eo ipso*, he was a deserter.

Fitzgerald had intended to call Major Giloughly, Nolan's commander at Fort Massac, to testify that Nolan had verbal permission to leave his post. These hopes collapsed when it was announced from the bench that Giloughly himself had pled guilty to conspiracy at Nacogdoches in the Mississippi Territory.

Nolan was furious; in a choked, bitter voice he blurted out: "Then I shall be happy to wait upon the major's arrival. I was given leave, and he can confirm it!"

The gavel banged and Colonel Morgan glowered. "Mister Fitzgerald, does the defendant wish to take the stand?"

Wendell stood, pressing his hand down on Nolan's shoulder. "No, sir, he does not." As he returned to his seat, Fitzgerald hissed to Nolan, "Hold your tongue, Philip."

Had Nolan taken an oath to testify he would have opened himself to Major Teague's cross-examination. It would not take much dexterity to lead Nolan to admit the damning fact that he had volunteered to carry a ciphered letter for Burr. Close questioning would also confirm that Nolan had publicly stated that he was proud to have joined the expedition. None of these facts would accrue to his favor; nor could Fitzgerald trust his friend to remain even-tempered under questioning. It was certain that nothing further in the way of outbursts would be tolerated.

Fitzgerald arranged some papers on his desk and stood. "If it pleases the court, a written deposition has been prepared regarding the circumstances of Lieutenant Nolan's interview with Colonel Bell." Fitzgerald walked forward and placed the document in front of Colonel Morgan. "With your permission, the affidavit is submitted in lieu of testimony."

"Any objections, Major Teague?"

The major glanced at Fitzgerald and shook his head. Teague, long ago as a corporal, had served as a color bearer at Camden and survived honorably. He was no admirer of Colonel Bell. "We have no objections, sir," he said.

The gavel banged again, the provost marshal intoned, "All rise," and the court adjourned to consider the evidence.

As they sat at the table Fitzgerald drummed his fingers. "You are not doing yourself any favors, Philip."

"I expect none."

"It doesn't help to be petulant. You are not a child."

No man is quick to think himself a pawn or an expendable thing; it is even harder for a common person to understand the schemes of men who intend to make history. Nolan had no appreciation of politics, and understood even less the manners of great men. His own relations had been governed by scrupulous, even credulous, honesty, but he understood now that he had been used, and that he stood on the brink of being made a scapegoat for it. Burr's acquittal and Wilkinson's perjury had made Nolan sure that his own charges would be dismissed. Even as the case against Burr collapsed, the prosecution remained dogged; failing to convict the prime movers, Jefferson's adherents were determined to make an example of whomever they could. At first, Nolan could not comprehend that futures were to be made by bringing the president as many convictions as possible. Could that be true?

Until this moment, patriotism had brought into Nolan's life a sense of belonging and confidence. Now, as that devotion crumbled, he saw how precariously he had trusted and how unrequited was his loyalty. Had Nolan possessed some other anchor besides love of country, some other faith or belief in a greater purpose, he might not have been so resentful. But he did not believe in anything greater than his duty, and since his days as a cadet he had believed that the obligation he felt for his nation had somehow been reciprocated. Nolan adored his country as Burr never had; Nolan's love had been unquestioning, and now it was turning into an equally irrational and unreasoning disgust. Believing he had been wronged, Nolan recoiled with heartbroken anguish.

Nolan stared at the flags gathered behind the bench; the colors had once been living things to him, totems of duty and even glory. Now it was as though the meaning had been wrung from them—water from a dishrag. It was excruciating and humiliating for him to sit before the emblems of his country and be made to feel that he was alien to them and somehow unworthy of their mercy. The tremendous consequence of this emotion blossomed in him like a poisonous flower.

The wound in his chest was suddenly an agony and with every breath Nolan could feel the bandage growing wet under his shirt. His fists clenched, his heart throbbed, and the room swam before his eyes. Exhausted and in great pain, Nolan's thoughts became the empty shadows of his feelings, roiling and black. No outward sign did he show; he did not shed tears or curse, but it was there, in an armory made into a place of judgment, that Philip Nolan failed as a man. Pouting at the defendant's table, awaiting verdict, Nolan's virtues were eclipsed by bitterness and self-pity.

A lieutenant of dragoons entered the court and bid all to rise. Fitzgerald helped Nolan to his feet and the judges entered. As they took their places, news that the verdict was at hand passed through the town. Shadows loomed into the courtroom as people took places to gawk through the long windows.

Fitzgerald whispered, "Please friend, if you are asked to speak, contain yourself."

Nolan's tongue rattled in his dry mouth. "I'll do what I can."

"Do the best you can, Philip."

Fitzgerald noticed that Nolan was trembling rigidly as he stood. At the bench Colonel Morgan arranged papers in front of him. Nolan could hear voices from the street outside; in one of the close windows, a man held a little boy on his shoulders so he could see.

Colonel Morgan said, "The court has reached an opinion regarding the death of Colonel Randolph Creel Bell of the First Virginia Regiment of Light Infantry."

Nolan's face twitched.

"Regarding the death of Colonel Bell, the court finds the defendant *no es factum*."

There was a murmur among the gallery. As it subsided, Fitzgerald said quietly, "It's less than an acquittal—but they hold you not responsible."

From beyond the windows there were whistles and jeers. Colonel Morgan pretended not to hear, but the catcalls made Nolan clench his jaw.

"Philip Clinton Nolan, this court has considered the evidence and the circumstances surrounding your absence from Fort Massac. The court finds you guilty of the crime of willful desertion from your appointed place of duty."

Fitzgerald turned at once toward Nolan but could not will him into silence.

"If I am a deserter, then why did I go to the Sabine?" Nolan barked. "Why did I travel in this uniform, and why did I report to the general officer commanding the Louisiana Territory?"

Someone hissed, "Treason!" Another bawled, "Hang him!"

Nolan shouted over them, "Did I skulk like His Excellency Colonel Burr?" Nolan's fist plucked at the lapel of his uniform. "Or was my crime to remain in a clown's costume while I rode?"

The crowd began to howl. In the gallery, Alden took Lorina's hand. Colonel Morgan thundered the gavel onto the bench. "Order! Or I shall clear the courtroom!"

"Will you have no witnesses?" Nolan growled. "Caesar has walked free! And I am left to pay his reckoning!"

"Silence! Mister Fitzgerald, still that man or I will have him gagged!"

Nolan collapsed into his chair, sallow and panting. Trembling with fury, he went numb without and hollow within.

Colonel Morgan's voice came sternly from the bench. "Lieutenant Nolan, you are convicted under the laws of your country and the service which you have had the honor to serve. Is there anything you wish to say in to this court to show that you have been faithful to the United States of America?"

Nolan choked out the most fateful words of his life: "The United States? Goddamn the United States, sir! I wish that I might never hear the name of the United States again as long as I live!"

The walls echoed his words, and not a soul drew breath.

Lorina sat in stunned, rigid anguish. From the bench, Colonel Morgan fixed Nolan with a baleful glare. Fitzgerald put his hand on Nolan's shoulder and squeezed. The gesture was intended both to quiet his friend and to conduct away the thunderbolt he was certain would be hurled down from on high.

Morgan at last said quietly: "The prisoner will remain in the courtroom while this court determines sentence." The judges retreated behind the flags, and everyone stood—all except Nolan.

When the judges closed the door to their chambers, Fitzgerald collapsed into his chair. "You are done now, friend," he said quietly.

Nolan muttered, "I was done before I ever came here." He pretended not to notice the crowd outside, but their words were ugly and threatening. "They could not have Burr, so they will catch whomever they can. Damn them for a pack of vexatious political bitches."

Fitzgerald sat with his hands folded and Nolan took up a pen from the desk. He dipped it and wrote five words on a sheet of paper, folded it, and struggled to his feet. Thinking Nolan might bolt, one of the dragoons stepped forward, a wall of crimson and white. Nolan leaned past him and thrust the paper into Lorina's hand. She looked at him, her eyes brimming. Her expression would be fixed in Nolan's memory forever; a mask of shock, pity, and anguish. She took the paper but did not unfold it, and Nolan sat and turned his back to her.

Fifteen minutes passed, each second dragging on like an eternity, until from the front of the room the provost again said, "All rise."

Nolan remained sprawled in his chair.

"Get up." Fitzgerald said. "I will not help you tie your own noose."

Nolan swayed to his feet. The judges had seemed all day to be ancient, somber, and grave; now they appeared to be made of iron. All had served in the Revolutionary War, and each had risked his fortune, as well as his neck, for the very thing Nolan had so wildly damned. The three old colonels projected attachment and shared outrage, sentiments so powerful they pulsed into the room.

Colonel Morgan's voice could be heard by all. "Prisoner. Hear the sentence of this court. Subject to the approval of the commander in chief, you shall never hear of the United States again."

Nolan laughed, but no one else did. Lorina lifted her hand to her mouth and stifled a sob.

"Provost Marshal. You will see that the prisoner is taken by armed boat to Norfolk and remanded to the naval commander there. See that no one speaks of the United States while he is in your custody. You will receive written orders before you depart."

Colonel Morgan's stern eyes fixed Nolan. "Mister Nolan, may God have mercy on your soul." He banged the gavel, and the crowd outside exploded in a roar of curses and threats.

The judges retired slowly from the bench, and the haranguing of the crowd became louder. Outrage had accumulated and condensed since the acquittal of Aaron Burr—and now it found vent. Weeks of frustration and apprehension rolled forward as though a sluice had been opened. The mob had been denied Burr, but now they had a convicted accomplice.

Stones sailed through the windows, raining glass and wood shards onto the tables. First one man and then another came across the broken windowsills into the courtroom; a dozen more quickly tumbled after, and the doors in the rear of the chamber burst open. The crowd heaved through the barriers on the prosecutor's side. There was a shout; the table was turned over and papers were flung into the air. A pair of guards snatched Nolan up and carried him bodily toward the door. There were cries again of "traitor," and a brick smashed through a transom window.

Nolan saw Fitzgerald push toward Alden and Lorina; his big arms swept them together, his wife in tears and Lorina's face wrenched with misery. Struggling free of the guard, Nolan reached out. Her fingers closed around his hand, but her expression was a mask of desolation. Her eyes did not meet his; she seemed to be looking past him.

A corporal shoved Nolan back, but when he did not let go of Lorina's hand a rifle butt flashed up—a glimmer of wood and brass. A peal of darkness crackled between his ears, and Nolan found himself on the floor next to a broken chair. He struggled to his hands and knees, and the rioters surged over him. Shards of glass on the floor laid open his hands, and he was kicked a dozen times before the soldiers lowered their bayonets and the mob tumbled back, scrambling away from the jutting steel.

The blow to his head made him almost deaf. Time slowed and yawned open. Nolan could hear nothing but the grunts of the troopers who lifted him and the crack of broken glass under their boots. The room was filled with slanting shafts of darkness. Nolan caught a last glimpse of Lorina holding tight to Wendell as he hurried her away. He called to her, but she did not turn. Nolan had become a ghost.

The soldiers formed a ring around him, and beyond them was a jostling murk of hateful faces. The officer commanding the guards used the flat of his sword to hack a path to the door. Nolan was dragged toward it; his head lolled, and blood spattered the floor in thick, black drops. Darkness poured into his ears and eyes. He could not draw breath, and neither his arms nor his legs would do their duty. Nolan felt himself falling into a stupefying void, a whirlpool of grief so vast and wild that it drowned the world.

NOLAN WAS KEPT OVERNIGHT IN A CELLAR UNDER THE STATE PENITENTIARY. A gruff barber-surgeon pricked a dozen stitches into his scalp, bound the wounds on his hands, but declined to change the bandages stuck to his chest. The dragoons gathered Nolan's things from the St. Charles. His saddle, sword, and scabbard were returned to the court, and he was ordered to take the epaulets and buttons from his uniform. His remaining possessions were picked through by the guards. His fob, dividers, and drafting tools went to the quickest; the other troopers cut cards for his leather belts, spoons, shoe buckles, and compass. The few things not taken were tied into a strip of woolen blanket.

At dawn, fife and drum played the Rogue's March; Nolan was taken up from the cellar and made to walk at the cart's end toward the river. Manacled hand and foot, carrying his possessions in the scrap of blanket, Nolan could barely stagger. The pain in his chest made it impossible to catch his breath, and blood dripped though his shirt and ran in rivulets down his wrists and hands.

He fell three times on the twelve-block journey to the river. Twice he was prodded to his feet by a soldier's bayonet. The third time, a black man came out of the whistling, shouting mob and helped him to his feet. The slave carried Nolan's blanket over his shoulder and led him the last desperate steps to the quay. Nolan kept his head high but dared not look into the crowd; he dreaded seeing Wendell and feared that his heart would break if he caught sight of Lorina or Alden.

Jeered at from shore, Nolan went aboard an armed galley and was rowed down the James River toward Norfolk. Below Richmond, the river became still and the clouds grew increasingly dark. Thunder rumbled in a lowering sky, and during the long, black night Nolan was kept on deck. By the time the sun rose livid above the Elizabeth River, Nolan had been soaked to the skin. As the galley came into Hampton Roads, all of the officers stood watch and Nolan saw the reason for their keen attention to duty.

Norfolk spread to the south, a low, commercial place pricked here and there by steeples. There were dozens of merchant ships in the confluence of the James and Elizabeth Rivers, all of them looking shabby. Conspicuous among them were a whale ship hard aground near Willoughby Spit and a China ship careened by Ragged Island, both forlorn and empty, victims of a British blockade. The officers aboard the galley pointed their telescopes, and as Batten Bay passed to starboard, Nolan could see the three tall masts of the frigate USS *Chesapeake*. That once proud ship listed to port, her yards gone by the slings and several of her port lids beaten in. Tops and yards strangely out of plumb, the frigate looked like a toy cast aside in some gigantic tantrum. That impression was made sinister by the ochre tailings of blood—human blood that even now daubed her sides.

Just weeks ago, *Chesapeake* had been preparing to escort a convoy of merchants to the Mediterranean. Not yet out of soundings, just off Cape Henry, *Chesapeake* was set upon by HMS *Leopard*. The British frigate ranged alongside, demanding that *Chesapeake* heave to and submit to a search. The American ship refused; words were shouted back and forth, and the British fired first. In the initial broadside, three of *Chesapeake*'s crewmen were blown to bits and a score wounded; and most appallingly, Captain Barron had struck his colors. He then allowed the British to board his ship and take into custody four of his sailors who the victors claimed were the king's subjects.

USS *Chesapeake* limped back into Hampton Roads, little more than a floating wreck. The incident came very near to sparking a war; it succeeded in blackening the prestige of the American Navy. Emboldened by the timidity of *Chesapeake*, the British advanced a squadron into the mouth of the bay, moving up from Lynnhaven Inlet and anchoring finally just off the Hampton roadstead. A pathetic line of American gunboats was all that lay between three British ships of the line and the city of Norfolk. Day after day the British stopped and searched arriving ships, removing men they claimed were British citizens. No American vessel dared put to sea. Norfolk was, for all intents and purposes, under blockade. Valuable cargos piled up in warehouses, fortunes were extinguished, and merchantmen swung in endless circles, tide after tide.

Nolan was put aboard a United States schooner fitting out to run the British blockade. The captain received him with cold civility, and while the ship took aboard powder and stores, Nolan was largely ignored. After his long night in the rain, Nolan came down with fever, and as Kosinski had predicted, he eventually was taken by a dangerous pneumonia. Without much sympathy, the surgeon's mate bled him and made Nolan swallow a strong, stinking brew of sulfur and fenugreek.

Each time a boat came alongside with supplies or men, Nolan expected letters. None came, nor would they ever come. Confined to his hammock, unable to lift his head, he stared through the gun ports at the beaches and wharves, looking for the familiar shape of Fitzgerald on horseback or Lorina or Alden in a carriage. He would never see them.

Working double tides, the schooner completed her stores and then took on powder and shot. As all was made ready for sea, a last boat pulled off from Norfolk, bringing the diplomatic pouch and a set of papers confirming Nolan's incarceration.

The original copies have long been lost, and the cover letter, too—perhaps the souvenir of some captain's clerk. But copies there were, one for the ship's log and another for the captain's confidential file. Written out in fair copperplate, a duplicate in a leather envelope would accompany Nolan from ship to ship for the rest of his life. Oddly, Philip Nolan would never actually read the instructions handed down about him, though he would figure them out soon enough. They read, in their entirety:

> The Office of the Secretary of the Navy
> at the City of Washington
>
> To the Master Commandant
> of the United States Armed Schooner *Revenge*
>
> Sir—
> You will receive the person of one Philip Clinton Nolan,
> late a lieutenant in the United States Army. You will take the
> prisoner aboard your ship and prevent his escape. During his
> confinement he is to be exposed to no violence of any kind, but
> under no circumstances is he ever to hear of his country or see
> any information regarding it.
> Your instructions are to remain a confidential matter, and
> the officers and men on board your vessel will take any arrange-
> ments acceptable to themselves regarding his society.
> Under no circumstances is he ever to hear of his country or
> to see any information regarding it; and you will especially cau-
> tion all the officers under your command to take care that in the
> various indulgences which may be granted, this rule, in which
> his punishment is involved, shall not be broken.

Before the end of your cruise you will receive orders, which will turn said prisoner into another outbound ship. It is the intention of the government that said prisoner shall never again hear of, or return to, the country that he disowned.

Respectfully,
R. Southard
for the Sec'y of the Navy

Under the signature was a notation in purple ink. It read: "Approved, dispatched, Tho. Jefferson."

From that moment on, no member of the crew said a word to Nolan, and a silent Marine stood guard over him, watch upon watch. On a moonless night, USS *Revenge* weighed anchor and made her way past the ships in the outer roads. Nolan crawled up the companion ladder and found a place to sit in the forepeak. *Revenge* showed no lights and ghosted first past Old Point Comfort and Thimble Shoals, then south by east into the mouth of the bay.

With muttered commands, *Revenge* cleared for action, and the smell of slow match wafted fore and aft. Nolan pulled himself to his feet and gripped the larboard rail next to one of the short, deadly carronades. The crew was tense, determined, all of them infuriated that an American ship should have to skulk out of her own home port like a smuggler. But there was little choice; from Lynnhaven Inlet a British squadron was anchored in a wide crescent: a trio of 74-gun ships of the line—*Bellona*, *Triumph*, and *Bellisle*—and between them the frigate *Melamphus* and the store ship *Cichester*, all of them spoiling for a fight.

As *Revenge* turned by Desert Cove, her gunners kept a grim vigil. Patrolling among the British ships were guard boats with dark lanterns and muffled oars. Every man aboard *Revenge* knew what would happen should the schooner be seen—the glare of signal rockets and then a merciless series of broadsides delivered point-blank.

But a rainsquall did them a kindness. The schooner slipped though the outer anchorage and close through the Cape Henry Shoals. A thin sliver of moon rose above the trees near Little Creek and was quickly swallowed by cloud. *Revenge* glided through the shoal waters, dark and silent. In the bow, Nolan listened to the leadsman whisper, "By the mark, three, and a half three," like an incantation.

The rain fell steadily as they coasted near the mouth of Lynnhaven Inlet, and then past HMS *Leopard* herself. The frigate towered in the darkness, masts and rigging obscured by blowing cloud, and her bright gun ports open, throwing rectangles of light into the drizzle. From somewhere within, a fiddle tittered away and men could be heard laughing and singing. Aboard *Revenge*, all hands strained their eyes against the darkness, but the British did not watch as keenly, and the schooner made her way out undetected.

One by one the lights of Norfolk town sank into the black horizon, then the top lights of the British ships. In the blackness, *Revenge* tacked east-northeast, and finally, long past midnight, the lighthouse on Cape Henry winked out and disappeared like a guttered candle.

This was the last Philip Nolan would ever see of home.

INTO CUSTODY

BEYOND THE BATTERIES OF THE FORTRESS AT SAN SEBASTIÁN, THE BAY OF Cádiz was flecked with white, the leavings of a stern *tramontana* that had blown for three days and two nights. The sky above the bay was brilliant, though the sun that rode through it was low, tending to the south and west on a bright and pleasant winter day. To the northeast, beyond the lower reaches of the harbor, light slanted over the delta of the Río de San Pedro. Past the marshland, in stages and switchbacks the road to Seville cut through the rolling countryside of Andalusia, the hills dotted here and there with orchards, vineyards, and round Spanish towers. As beautiful as this was, none of it interested the young man walking along the uncompleted ramparts toward town as fast as his long legs could hurry him.

Frank Curran had seen a white nick on the horizon, a pair of them, in fact, and they were the ships he had been waiting for. He now hurried back to the town, clasping a long glass under his arm and occasionally pressing his hat down on his head when a gust came at him from across the bay. These Curran could almost always anticipate, for they showed first on the reefs below the fort (how the swell broke there), and his sailor's eye was keen enough to notice the changes in the sails shaped by the fishing boats and *barca longas* plying the wide bay. He was, after all, a naval officer, a fact gratefully confirmed by the newly signed commission that crinkled in his coat pocket.

Of all his papers and possessions laid carefully in a cruise box and a pair of seabags back at the inn, the commission in his pocket was the most precious thing he owned. It would embarrass him had anyone seen how he'd studied it by candlelight or reread it a dozen times even this afternoon when he was alone on the point under the battery. He had folded and unfolded it, pretending that he had just discovered his name, Francis Gifford Curran, and the high-flown words placing on him *especial* trust for his patriotic valor, conduct, and fidelity, fairly charging all midshipmen, sailors, and Marines junior to him to render obedience, etc., etc., written in a boldly wielded pen proclaiming him a lieutenant in the Navy of the United States from the date of February 3, 1827—a day that had come and gone not forty-eight hours ago. Even now Curran could feel the unaccustomed weight of the epaulet on his left shoulder, and from the corner of his eye he caught its glimmer now and again, a physical manifestation of his joy.

Curran stretched out his legs and filled his lungs with the fine, crisp air. The day was glorious; as a newly commissioned lieutenant he would have thought it fine if it were blowing a whole gale. On the winding coast road a mounted Spanish officer passed by on his way to inspect the San Sebastián guns, and Curran touched his hat. The Spaniard peered for a moment at the uniform and the tall, sandy-haired young man who wore it, vaguely connecting him to the American ships heading into the bay.

The Spaniard said, *"Buenos, señor,"* as he bowed slightly in the saddle, and then damned his horse in a gush of deep-voiced, lisping Castilian when it threw up its head and tried to caper. Curran could make out a few of the words, excellently chosen, something about horsemeat and the making of glue. Curran suppressed a smile out of military courtesy; the officer was a major, and like most sea officers Curran rode indifferently. In fact, he did not care for horses at all, even though his mother had taken pains about his equitation as she was of an old Shenandoah family that took horsemanship as the mark of a gentleman.

Curran walked on, and when he glanced back he saw the Spanish officer also looking over his shoulder, partly out of embarrassment and partly to reassure himself that the man with a telescope was not after all a French spy. Halfway to town, where the ramparts were highest, Curran stopped again and swept the sea with his glass. At the top of the bay, gliding under topsails, was a frigate, plainly *Constellation*, the Stars and Stripes at her mizzen and her commission pennant streaming from the maintop. She was still several miles in the offing, and he could just make out the officers on her quarterdeck and occasionally the green jacket of a Marine.

Curran turned his glass south, and the wind pushed at his back. From this height his eye commanded maybe fifteen miles of sea, and he could see another vessel coming under reefed courses, tack on tack, off Cape Zahora. A man o'war, by the way she handled. Her hull was too high and wide for a Royal Navy frigate, and Curran could see that she was every bit *Constellation*'s match, and perhaps her better. The ship came about crisply as he watched, but she was beating nearly straight into the wind; her tack presently took her away from the land and toward the bright, rolling horizon.

There were a dozen other vessels in the Bay of Cádiz, but only one was carrying on so determinedly north. Curran held the glass, counting her gun ports, and as he watched, the ship put out trysails very briskly. Without doubt she was *Enterprise*, one of the United States Navy's newest frigates—a crack ship nearly as renowned as her cousin *Constitution*. So similar were they, built off almost identical drafts, that it took an appreciative eye to tell them apart. If anything, *Enterprise* was sharper built, with a longer quarterdeck lending grace to her lines; an elegantly spooned bow rendered her motion in the seaway very much like that of a galloping thoroughbred. Regardless of her beauty, the wind was presently in her teeth, and it would be the better part of the afternoon before she could wear round Punta de San Sebastián and run into Cádiz.

Curran snapped closed his telescope and continued toward the edge of town. He must meet the ships, he thought. Present himself and compliments. Perhaps even ship into his number one rig. *Constellation* would be in the harbor first; he could signal for a boat. But then Curran thought better of clambering aboard in his best uniform just to show away. What a gull he would look. No, he would save his dress blues for going aboard *Enterprise* to present his orders and his commission.

Again, an immense, peaceful joy came up in Curran's heart. He had spent a third of his life at sea, almost all of it in foreign oceans, and every minute of sea time—some of them very anxious moments indeed—had been spent learning his profession and earning the modest amount of gold upon his coat. Though he had yet to experience command, in eight years at sea he had drawn a full measure of responsibility, and there were moments that it still astounded him that the lives of every man on board had depended on his ability to read the stars, sum their courses in the sky, and make landfall on unknown shores.

All of this long process had changed him from boy and landsman to as perfect a nautical creature as ever walked on two legs, but none of this slow transformation compared to the metamorphosis that had altered him wonderfully, almost magically, into an officer. What had really changed in the last forty-eight hours? What made him so different? He had not grown taller, and his gait on land was still that of the rolling sailor. His mind ticked with the same thoughts and his blood coursed with the same desires, but a great longing had been satisfied. He had been made an officer by an act of Congress; he had gotten his step, passed for lieutenant, shipped his swab, and almost nothing in his life had ever pleased him so. As Curran walked into Cádiz he knew this to be one of the happiest afternoons of his life.

Where the cobbles started at the edge of town there were three large bodegas, their doors open and the shade within cool and beckoning. Inside the storehouses Curran could see the round fronts of a hundred oaken solera, and as he went by he caught the smell of oloroso, clove, and almond. Siesta was just over, and shutters were being lifted up from windows and doors of the taverns fronting the harbor. Curran pressed a few centavos into the hand of a little boy and sent him on his way to Tres Osos to fetch his seabags and dunnage. *Constellation* was yet miles off, *Enterprise* even farther away, and there was time to drink a glass of fino and listen to the wind rattle the shutters.

He had timed everything nicely. Curran finished a glass of sack and then another as *Constellation* finally headed up and launched a boat. It surprised him that the frigate did not cast loose her bower. Instead of anchoring, *Constellation* lolled out in the roadstead as her boat pulled steadily toward town. Curran stepped into the street, and above him the wind rustled the palms. Already the whitecaps in the bay were fewer and the wind had veered east a point. The *tramontana* would be over by nightfall. He watched the oars flash and pull, flash and pull.

Behind him in the *mercado* came the rumble of cartwheels, and a high, unbroken voice piping, "*Teniente americano, teniente americano.*" Curran turned to find the boy ploughing straight at him, and behind the child, a man leading a vast, slab-sided oxcart, empty except for Curran's own baggage. The man leading the ox looked exactly like the little boy made larger—an uncle, perhaps. Curran gazed at the cart, a contraption quite large enough to move an admiral, maybe even two admirals, and he started to figure that it would cost him most of the coin he had in his pocket to trundle his things what remained of fifty yards. Again the flash of the gold on his shoulder lifted his spirits—he was no longer a starving, penniless mid. When his commission arrived he'd drawn six months' pay in advance, and there was the pleasant bonus of reimbursement from his date of rank, the sum amounting to almost 112 gold dollars and 75 cents. Curran was richer now than he had ever been in his life, and he simply waved for boy, uncle, bullock, and cart to follow him to the boat landing.

Curran came up to the end of a short pier, whistled at the boat, and held his hat aloft. He saw the officer point his glass toward him and hold. Recognizing the uniform, and by God the glorious epaulet, the coxswain deflected the tiller and the boat came on, threading between the parallel reefs below the star-shaped fort. In a few moments *Constellation*'s number two cutter shipped oars and kissed neatly against the stone wall and the pier head.

The boat's officer came nimbly across the gunwale and onto the quay. He was a red-faced man, a lieutenant, maybe thirty or forty years old. His eyes were narrowed against the sun, and his squint turned up the corners of his mouth. This gave an impression of happiness or mirth; but it was soon apparent by his tone that neither he nor the men in the cutter were particularly happy about anything.

"Is *Enterprise* gone?" he asked curtly.

Curran touched his hat. "I believe she is in the offing. Still south of the cape."

The officer's expression lightened and he took a few steps down the pier. Standing on a piling, he turned toward *Constellation* and waved a white handkerchief in a circle over his head. Curran looked down into the cutter. There were a dozen sailors in working clothes and a pair of green-jacketed Marines holding muskets against their knees. Between them was a man in a faded blue coat. The boat crew seemed uncommonly mum.

The officer came back and lifted his hat. "I apologize, sir. My name is Hancock, third lieutenant of *Constellation*."

"Curran, sir. Honored."

"Are you from *Enterprise*?"

"In transit and under orders," Curran said. "I am just off *Epevier*." He might have added, "and I am a lieutenant for almost two whole days," but that could easily be deduced. Though Curran's uniform jacket had seen sea and sun, the swab on his shoulder was pristine and beautiful. To any seaman alive Lieutenant Curran looked as freshly minted as a new penny.

"My captain is anxious that we might have advantage of this wind, Mister Curran. I trust you will make a transfer for us?"

"I am at your service, sir."

Two canvas sacks were passed up from the boat.

"There is mail for *Enterprise* and dispatches for the Mediterranean Squadron."

Curran watched as the Marines took up the man in the blue coat. Manacled hand and foot, his chains clattered as he was heaved up and onto the quay. From the stern of the cutter a small sailcloth bag was swung up after him. The bag had not been properly tied, and some books, clothing, and papers spilled out. The wind fanned the pages of a worn and thumbed book, and a small tissue stuck through with pins blew down the pier. The prisoner crawled a few feet over to his spilled belongings, but a hobnailed boot came down near his hand.

The tissues floated off, some cut into the shapes of stars and clouds. As the chains dipped between his wrists, the man shoved his books and clothing back into the bag and closed the drawstring. The prisoner took up the small sack and stood with what dignity he could.

Curran said to Hancock, "What is the prisoner accused of?"

"Convicted, sir," answered the officer. "He is a murderer and a traitor."

As the prisoner came to his feet Curran looked him over. The man wore patched duck trousers, loose cut in the naval fashion, but his old blue coat looked like an artilleryman's coatee. The prisoner's face was neatly shaved and deeply tanned, not like a man who had been kept below hatches but like a sailor who had walked the decks of a ship at sea. The man had a strong jaw and an aquiline nose. His age was not readily apparent, probably somewhere between forty and fifty; not quite six feet tall, he was lean and his eyes were deep-set, gray-blue, and piercing. His hair had once been dark but was now mostly gray and drawn back in a queue, as was the custom of officers before the last war.

Hancock took a thick leather envelope from his coat and handed it to Curran. "These are the prisoner's instructions."

Curran took the orders and glanced at the man who was in his custody. His captive did not seem by any measure repentant or abashed, nor did he seem overly concerned about the Marine bayonets leveled at his belly.

"Do you have a pistol, sir?" Hancock asked.

"In my cruise box."

"May I suggest that you arm yourself?"

"Of course." Curran walked to the oxcart and pulled round his sea chest. It took a few moments to open the lock and take his pistol from a tray within. He came back to the quay, and not knowing exactly what to do, tucked the pistol into the front of his belt.

Hancock offered a rusted iron hoop from which dangled a pair of brass pinions. "These are the keys to the prisoner's shackles." From out in the harbor came the banging of a signal gun, and the Blue Peter ran up at *Constellation*'s foremast. "We must be away," said Hancock. "Do you have any questions?"

Curran prepared to open his mouth but was surprised when the prisoner spoke.

"I have a question."

Curran and Hancock swiveled their heads. It was almost as if a dog had suddenly gone up on his hind legs and asked the time of day.

"Shouldn't the pistol be loaded?" the prisoner asked. "I mean, if I am to be prevented from absconding?"

Hancock scowled. Abashed, Curran went to his cruise box again, found cartridge and ball, and thumbed it down the barrel of the pistol. He returned ramming the wad home and threading the ramrod back under the stubby barrel.

"I feel safer already," the prisoner said. The sailors in the boat smirked quietly, and Curran felt his cheeks burning.

"Mind your tongue sir," Hancock said, "or you'll have a thumping."

Hancock and his Marines dropped back down into the cutter. The whole business had passed so awkwardly that Curran felt compelled to speak. "Will *Constellation* be home bound, then?"

At the word "home" the men in the boat seemed to flinch. Hancock took up his place in the stern sheets and mumbled, "We are bound across the Atlantic, sir. Beyond that, I am not at liberty to say." He nodded to the bow and the boat shoved off. "Give way together," Hancock said to the oarsmen, and then he lifted his hat and shouted out, "Good day to you Mister Curran. Good luck."

The boat went straight away, and Curran was suddenly aware of the eyes of a dozen people upon him. Attracted by the landing of the boat, a handful of townsmen stood gaping at the man in chains. Long accustomed to his manacles, the prisoner casually pushed the shackles over his wrists and onto his forearms.

"*Es un hereje para ser quemar?*" someone said from a balcony.

"*Él no es solo un asesino,* él *es un perro protestante,*" opinioned a woman pushing a cart of sardines.

Curran answered in Castilian that there would be no burning at the stake, and that both of them would soon be taken aboard the warship in the bay. Curran noticed as he was speaking that the prisoner smiled at the crowd—his Spanish was as good as Curran's own. The townsfolk moved away, and Curran looked into the offing where *Enterprise* was just now rounding the battery at San Sebastián.

Constellation hoisted the private signal and made her number. *Enterprise* had answered, but neither ship seemed much interested in the other. Curran watched as *Constellation*'s cutter was taken in tow and the frigate let fall her mains and courses. Towing her boat, *Constellation* sailed west into the mouth of the bay.

"If I may ask," the prisoner said pleasantly, "would that ship be *Enterprise*?"

Curran did not answer. In the roads, the ships passed without a cheer or even a hailing from deck to deck, quite as if they were ignoring one another. As *Constellation* groped out of the roads, *Enterprise* hauled down the private signal but left her own number flying proudly.

"A two-decker I believe," said the prisoner. "A fine-looking ship. Very much like *Congress*, I am sure. Perhaps they were built at the same yard."

Curran looked at him with an expression of cold bafflement. The business of a prisoner in a threadbare Army uniform was unusual, and the conduct of the ships was equally puzzling.

The man seemed suddenly to remember his place and said quietly, "You'll forgive me, sir. It has been a while since I have had company."

Enterprise headed up, and as soon as way came off her the frigate's best bower splashed into the harbor; when her yards were squared and the sails had been made fast in perfect neatness, she put a boat over the side.

"Prisoner, can you swim?" Curran asked.

"I suppose I can. It's been a long time since I tried."

Curran tossed him the keys. "You will remove your shackles. Should our boat upset crossing the reef, I'd not want to watch you drown."

Curran looked on as the boy and his uncle took down his chest and seabags from the oxcart. The prisoner knelt and prized open the irons on his legs, and then the manacles from his wrists. With a practiced hand he looped the chains around the top of his sailcloth sack and secured them with a loop and cinch. The prisoner stretched out his limbs. "This is kind of you."

Curran opened his cruise box and shifted into his number one uniform coat. "Do not mistake my manners, sir," Curran answered. "If you try to run, I will shoot you."

GOING ABOARD

ENTERPRISE'S BLUE CUTTER WAS COXED BY A PETTY OFFICER, A BLUFF SAILOR with red muttonchop whiskers. Curran could hear the coxswain and stroke oar joking together as the boat approached. They were dressed in their best shore-going rigs: blue jackets, duck trousers, kerchiefs, and tarpaulin emboldened with the words "United States Frigate *Enterprise*." All were happy, obviously expecting liberty.

"Coxswain, we are for *Enterprise*," said Curran as bow oar heaved a line to the pier.

The sailor at the tiller, Finch, looked at Curran and then at the prisoner and was made instantly solemn. In the cutter the smiles were gone and a dozen oarsmen sat with their heads locked, looking neither right nor left, but exactly at nothing, eyes in the boat. For a few seconds no one spoke or moved a muscle.

"You, sir, in the boat. Do you hear me?"

"Yes, sir," Finch said. "We're here to get you."

Curran's things were quickly put aboard. The coxswain narrowed his eyes at the man in the blue coat, troubled by the chains and shackles draping from his hands. "Sir, would you like me to send out for them leathernecks? We got nothing for arms aboard except a pair of cutlass."

"That won't be necessary," Curran said as he dropped into the cutter's stern. "Directly to the ship, please." Curran sat on his sea chest next to the coxswain, and the prisoner was put forward in the bows.

"The ship it is, sir."

The cutter backed water, came smartly about, larboard holding and starboard pulling, and the men stretched out for the ship. There was only the sound of the trucks in the oarlocks and the smooth pull of water under the sweeps. Curran noticed that the oarsmen on either side of the prisoner took pains to lean away from him as they plied their oars.

In the boat, the man in the blue coat did his best to become invisible. The prisoner had such a talent for silence and self-effacement that Curran soon forgot he was there. For the ninth time in twenty minutes Curran made sure that his papers and orders were in their silk and sailcloth folder, checked again that his number one scraper was firmly lodged on his head, and flicked away a bit of lint from the shoulder of his best dress blue jacket.

Ahead of him, still most of a mile off, Curran could see *Enterprise* riding easily. She had shifted colors and now wore the jack at her bow and the national ensign astern. Curran had so concentrated on the American ships he'd almost failed to notice that the harbor was full of vessels, merchants all of them: Swedes and Danes, Finns and Dutchmen, and lateen rigs of the Med, all in various states of cleanliness and repair. Small boats plied between them and ranged up and down the harbor. There were even a few stranger craft—herring busses, xebecs, and a dismasted hulk being used as a receiving ship. Most shocking of all, a hermaphrodite-rigged poleacre, painted red, black, and white with a lateen sail rigged as a mizzen, a contraption so heterogeneous that it could only have been sailed by men without a notion of shame: Ragusians or perhaps Greek spongers.

As the cutter came into the anchorage, Curran could see that *Enterprise* was busy. *Constellation* had come and gone in silence, but from *Enterprise* came the screech of a bo'sun's pipe and orders shouted from deck to maintop. *Enterprise* was putting over her long boat and both gig and cutters, liberty men in some, working and watering parties in others. Bumboats from the town were already about, offering every temptation of the port, jabbering in the pidgin of half a dozen languages, and deals were being struck for many things more potent and desirable than bottles of blackstrap and *mitad y mitad*.

Close up, Curran had seen *Enterprise* only in the yards at Boston. The ship had seemed impressive then, but from the stern sheets of a 30-foot cutter the frigate seemed so massive and rooted in the water that it did not float so much as jut up from the sea like a cliff. As the cutter pitched in the chop, the tall black sides of the frigate did not move, but conducted the swell down the waterline, showing a band of white and copper as the waves passed. *Enterprise* was renowned, as was her sister *Constitution*, for stiffness in a seaway. She was nearly 210 feet from beakhead to taffrail, 2,200 tons burthen, and of course ship-rigged. *Enterprise* was what the British had come to call a "pocket ship of the line," for they learned that *Enterprise* and her sisters outgunned and outsailed most of what His Majesty's navy called frigates.

This *Enterprise* was the fourth United States warship to bear the name. Laid down at the Boston Navy Yard in 1811, "Easy E" had an enviable reputation as a comfortable ship and was as fast as any man o'war that ever swam. Built from a Humphrey draft, *Enterprise* differed from *Constitution* in that she had a taller rig, an enclosed spar deck (and therefore an elevated poop), and a pair of stern galleries instead of only one. Her masts were raked aggressively, and her bristling rows of gun ports and Nelson chequer gave her a menacing, even predatory appearance. All of this imparted on Curran a sudden sense of wonder, of both the ship and his new place on it, and he was conscious not to stare at the rigging and to make sure his mouth was closed lest someone aboard mark him as a gaper.

Above them from the quarterdeck came the hail, "Ahoy the boat," to which Finch boomed out, "Aye, aye," meaning that there was a commissioned officer aboard the cutter. Curran did not suppress a grin. This was the first time in his life he'd been the object of this small bit of naval courtesy. Finch returned the nod of the officer of the deck, and the cutter passed under *Enterprise*'s towering stern. Curran tucked his orders into his jacket, hitched up his sword and scabbard, and stepped past the prisoner toward the bow of the boat. The painter was tossed to a ship's boy, and the cutter made out to a boom on the larboard side of the ship.

Aware of the eyes upon him from the decks and the rigging, Curran started up the side. Halfway up he remembered the pistol in his waist, made it secure, and came through the entry port onto the quarterdeck. On deck his arrival generated no ceremony. Men passed fore and aft, rolling out hogsheads for the ship's fresh water, mending and splicing, and removing the battens and hatch covers from the hold under the foremast. A lieutenant about Curran's own age had a long glass tucked under his arm, the emblem and principal instrument of the officer of the deck.

A short, tousle-headed midshipman sat on the ladder of the main companionway, glancing around generally and then staring at Curran openly. Curran turned aft, touched his hat to the colors, and then faced the officer of the deck. "Permission to come aboard, sir?"

"Granted. Come aboard."

The smells of the ship were familiar—tar, turpentine, paint, sweat, and galley smoke. "My name is Curran, sir, reporting aboard from *Epevier*."

A smile now, the first one Curran had seen all afternoon, and the officer of the deck held out a tanned, callused hand. "Welcome aboard, Mister Curran. My name is Kerr."

Down from the quarterdeck came a large, broad-shouldered man wearing a short blue coat and duck trousers. Kerr put his heels together and touched his hat. "Good morning, sir." Curran at once guessed this man to be the ship's executive officer, and a taut one despite his working clothes. Curran saluted, though the man in the stained jacket was not covered.

Kerr said, "Mister Erskine, may I present Lieutenant Curran, just reported . . ." Kerr faltered on the foreign word, and Curran quickly covered, "Reporting transferred from *Epevier*, sir."

"Excellent, Mister Curran. We have been expecting you. I'm Erskine, the exec." Obviously a man who trusted his own work, Erskine carried a marlinspike in his belt. He bellowed an order to a pair of sailors working in the mizzen top; at that same moment, a rooster in the coops at the waist chose to crow at the top of its lungs, and a group of caulkers forward started a fine, syncopated hammering.

"Sir," Curran shouted over the din, "I have dispatches for the squadron and mail for the ship."

The word "mail," a single syllable muttered on the quarterdeck, was able to penetrate through the clangor and passed quickly with smiles and winks from maintop to the cable tier.

"Mail, did you say? Well then, sir, you are welcome indeed."

The mail and dispatches were brought up from the cutter, and the canvas sacks were at once taken up by the captain's clerk and a smiling group of sailors. Erskine then noticed the pistol tucked into Curran's waist.

"Was there some excitement ashore, Mister Curran?"

"No sir, I shipped this to guard the prisoner from *Constellation*."

Kerr mumbled a remark about every man aboard *Constellation* being a villain, or at least a degenerate, for there was a great rivalry and even antagonism between the ships. One of *Enterprise*'s old salts sauntered to the rail and looked down into the cutter.

"It's Plain Buttons, sir," said Padeen Hoyle, senior petty officer in the starboard watch, "still on his cruise of the world."

Erskine looked over the rail and said softly, "Poor bastard," and then turned to Curran. "Do you have the prisoner's instructions?"

Curran touched his jacket. "Here, sir." The leather envelope was next to his own precious certificates and orders.

"Mister Kerr, see that Mister Curran's things are brought aboard directly," Erskine said. "Midshipman Wainwright will show you to the wardroom."

When Mister Midshipman Wainwright did not appear instantly, Erskine barked, "Wainwright, goddamn your eyes, you idle lollygagger . . ."

The midshipman sprang like a cat from the hatchway and bounded over to the larboard quarterdeck. He was a thin little boy, almost swallowed up by his round hat. "Here I am, sir."

Erskine's eyes were hooded. "Mister Wainwright, I hope you are not unaccommodated. Are you at leisure, sir? Available for an assignment?"

Wainwright blinked as if he were peering into the mouth of a carronade. "Oh yes, sir. I am quite available, sir."

"Then you will please show Mister Curran below and see that his things are placed in his cabin." Erskine said these words as though he were speaking to a particularly intelligent but untrustworthy monkey. The exec's smile returned when he said, "We'll give you some time to settle aboard, Mister Curran. At four bells, please be so kind as to present yourself to Captain Pelles."

"Yes, sir. Thank you."

Wainwright stepped forward, touching his hat again and again. "Good afternoon, sir, welcome aboard, sir, and this way, sir, if you please."

Kerr rolled his eyes and did his best to stifle a smirk. The after companionway was being used to hoist out barrels, and Wainwright led Curran forward and then below by the forward hatch. As they departed, Curran heard Mister Erskine roar again, "Master at Arms! Marines to the quarterdeck, and lay a guard on the prisoner."

Descending to the gun deck, Curran could feel the heat of the great black camboose stove. The smell of roasted meat came to him, and as they passed down the starboard side of the galley Curran watched as the mess cranks lined up before the stove. Big scoops of lobscouse and wedges of cabbage were being thumped into growlers to be carried to individual messes. Wainwright led Curran aft through the happy jostle, but only half the mess tables had been lowered, owing to the liberty men going ashore.

"Where did you come from, sir?" Wainwright asked. Clearly, the boy's spunk returned when he was out from under the first lieutenant.

"*Epevier*," said Curran.

"She's now homebound," the boy piped. Mister Wainwright was very well informed.

"I was put ashore at Cádiz," Curran answered. "*Epevier*'s been transferred to the Atlantic Squadron."

"Ah, God's own ocean," said Wainwright. "Mind 'yer head, sir. Some of them rammers is kept low."

Curran was already being sized up by the men gathering at the mess tables hanging between the guns. Like the news of mail, the fact that a new officer was reporting on board was already known throughout the ship.

Curran followed past the starboard 24-pounders, all bowsed neatly, their tackle laid just so, the lines faked down, and round shot and bar glistening in their racks. Over each gun was painted a name: "Liberty's Trumpet," "Honey Don't," and "Woolybooger" were a few of the standouts among the midships battery. Curran became aware that Wainwright was talking again; he would soon discover it was something the midshipman almost never stopped doing.

"I wish I was in the Atlantic Squadron, sir," said Wainwright. "Of course, here we're supposed to be chasing Barbary pirates, Ay-rabs, sir, Tripolitans and Algerines. Broke the treaty they had with Mister Jefferson and have been none to kind to Mister President Monroe, neither. But they know better than to sail when we're about. It's lucky for them that what we see is mostly empty water."

That patrols could be monotonous Curran knew already, but aboard *Enterprise* apathy did not seem to be much in evidence. What Curran had seen on deck and below told him that *Enterprise* was a happy ship, her men well fed and content, and her rigging and weapons in as good an order as he'd seen on any flagship. They went down the ladder, Wainwright offering his opinions of both the present administration in Washington, politicians in general, the Navy Department, and Republicans and Whigs, and by then they were aft of the mizzen.

"Wardroom's straight ahead, sir. Compared to the mids' berth, a palace! Your cabin 'ull be fourth down the starboard side. It's just been painted, and two whale

oil lanterns which I supervised bein' put in and squared away. You'll have Doctor
Darby to larboard and Mister Kerr just forward. Both snore, but not as bad as the
gunner. I'll see that your things are put in, sir." The midshipman opened the door
to the wardroom but did not set foot into officer's country.

"Thank you, Mister Wainwright." Curran saw that the wardroom was empty
but for the steward laying a cloth and plates. He turned in the doorway. "Mister
Wainwright, I wonder if you might explain something for me?"

Wainwright blanched slightly. It was only yesterday that the first lieutenant
had asked him the difference between a French bowline and a snatch tackle.
Wainwright's explanation had failed so spectacularly that he had been sent to the
masthead with a cake of soap between his teeth. "A nautical explanation, sir?"
Wainwright quavered.

"A general one," Curran said. "Why was it that *Constellation* and *Enterprise* did
not exchange boats? As far as I could tell, the ships did not even hail each other."

Wainwright became very grave and he said, "Oh." After that, there was a
silence of many seconds.

Curran began to understand Erskine's quick exasperation. "'Oh' is not an
answer, Mister Wainwright."

"You don't know, sir?"

"Do you not find it unusual that two United States naval vessels did not speak
to each other in a harbor three miles across?"

"I thought the whole Navy knew, sir."

Curran managed to say patiently, "Perhaps if you tell me, Mister Wainwright,
the entire Navy *will* know, for I find that I alone have not been let in on this highly
esteemed, perhaps even world-changing piece of information."

Wainwright stammered, "It was that duel, sir."

"What duel?"

"It was in Italy. At Leghorn, sir, there by Livorno. It was our own Cap'n Pelles
that shot off Captain Edmund's nose, over an operatic lady, in the year seven."

THE MARINE OUTSIDE THE GREAT CABIN DOOR CAME TO ATTENTION WITH A
moderate clash of arms, brought his musket vertical, and said with great enthusiasm, "Good evening, sir." Having completed his duty as a human door-knocker,
the Marine stared earnestly into Curran's face until above them both the ship's bell
tolled four times, two strokes and two. The Marine then smartly turned about,
opened the mahogany door, and said, "The captain will see you immediately, sir."

Curran placed his hat under his arm, balanced the sailcloth parcel that held his
orders and certificates, and walked aft. A short passageway led to the well-lighted
great cabin. To starboard was the pantry and the captain's steward standing quietly;

to larboard a sleeping cabin, dark and unknowable except for a lantern burning a single taper. Curran automatically lifted his eyes as he entered the great room, fixing his gaze on the six great windows curved gracefully inward from the stern. The captain's desk was in the far starboard corner, turned at an angle. Four bright lanterns hung from the overhead, and the desk was lit by a green-shaded lamp. The room was quite as glorious as naval hands could make it; the sole of the cabin was covered with sailcloth painted in the Nelson chequer, and on the cabin's partitions were a barometer, three Breguet chronometers, and an engraved gilt and silver inclinometer, all shined brilliantly. The darkness beyond the great windows was not yet completely black, and it framed Captain Pelles, who was standing with a foot up on the leather-cushioned lockers under the stern lights.

As Curran approached, Captain Pelles put a match to a long clay pipe. Curran turned toward the desk and stopped next to a straight-backed chair placed in front of it. He came to attention and said, "Lieutenant Curran, sir. Reporting aboard from *Epevier*."

Pelles turned in a blue waft of smoke. He was nearly as tall as the cabin's overhead, a large man who moved languidly. The left arm of the captain's dress coat was pinned up and empty, and in his lapel button he wore the silver medal of the *Guerrière* action. Curran guessed, correctly, that Captain Pelles had traded his arm for the silver medal and bit of ribbon on his coat.

"Your orders, Mister Curran?"

Standing at attention, Curran still had his orders clamped under his arm. "Yes sir, sorry sir," he said as he removed the packet and placed it on the desk.

Pelles lowered himself into the chair behind the desk. "You may sit down, Mister Curran." Deftly, the captain opened the envelope and spread its contents on the baize-covered table. The pipe clinked into a saucer, and Pelles lifted a small pair of half-oval spectacles and hooked them behind his ears.

Curran kept his head level, as his rank required, but he could see that a pale scar traced across Pelles' forehead and jaw. Pelles was middle-aged, maybe fifty or less, and it surprised Curran that a man this grave and somber could command what appeared to be such a happy ship.

"I read here that you are the son of a diplomat."

"Yes, sir. My father was posted to Constantinople. American consul to the Sublime Porte of Sultan Mahmud II."

"How did you come to be in the Navy?"

This question was not an invitation to enter into conversation, and Curran did not intend to spread canvas with his answer. He knew, and Pelles knew, that his family must have had some influence, political influence, to have gained for their son a midshipman's berth. Pelles wanted a simple, concise answer.

"My father had the honor to do Captain Bainbridge a service, sir, after his capture by the Tripolitans. The commodore was later kind enough to find me a berth with him on *President*."

Pelles digested this perfectly normal transaction and tried to separate any animosity he felt for Bainbridge. Pelles knew Billy Bainbridge to be a hard horse and an unpopular captain; by his peers, Bainbridge was considered both unlucky and a bit too eager to please his patrons in Washington. It was, after all, Bainbridge who had surrendered USS *Philadelphia* so disgracefully to the Tripolitans in 1803.

"You did not choose to stay with Captain Bainbridge?"

"I had no reason to wish to part, sir. It was the needs of the service, and I was transferred to *United States*, rated master's mate, then to *Epevier* whence I have just come."

"Just so. Just so," muttered the captain. There was, Pelles had to admit, some good in Billy Bainbridge—he did redeem himself later when he defeated HMS *Java* while in command of *Constitution*. Pelles' severe green eyes held Curran. "You've seen much service in the Mediterranean. Do you have the lingo, Mister Curran? The Lingua Franca?"

"That, sir, and the Ottoman's Turkish, French, Spanish, and most of the Arabic. Sir."

Pelles grunted and turned his head slightly, lifting the corner of Curran's file as he read. Free to let his own eyes roam for a second, Curran glimpsed a small portrait placed near the quarter galley; it was of a blue-eyed woman with a full mouth. Her small bosom was not fully covered by a diaphanous gown, and there was a gaggle of awkwardly painted ships in a harbor behind her. Curran had a moment to think perhaps this was the operatic lady.

"Captain Gormly informs me that you are a fine navigator and a tolerable seaman."

"Thank you, sir."

"Don't thank me, Mister Curran. I have yet to form an opinion." The pipe came up from the saucer, the bowl glowed, and Pelles let the smoke curl up from his lip.

"You passed for lieutenant when?"

"April thirteenth last year, sir. I was made three days ago, sir. Aboard *Epevier*."

"Well then, I trust the celestial tables are still fresh in mind. You will relieve Mister Kerr as navigator." Pelles picked up the leather envelope containing Nolan's orders. With the dexterity of a card sharp his thumb and forefinger untied the ribbon and drew out a sheaf of papers. "Are you acquainted with our prisoner, Mister Curran?"

"No sir!"

"I did not mean as an accomplice. Are you aware of the circumstances of his confinement?"

"Isn't he to be hanged, sir?"

"Hanged? That would be a great mercy." Pelles puffed his pipe and spread the papers on his blotter, looking them over.

A silence passed and Curran tried eventually to staunch it. "Mister Hancock of *Constellation* said that he was a murderer and a traitor."

"Of murder he is innocent. Mister Philip Nolan, now our guest, was involved in a duel at Richmond; he prevailed, and to my mind when a gentleman shoots a fool, it is not murder. Mister Nolan's crime was his association with Aaron Burr."

Curran tried to think; the western conspiracy and Burr's trial were many years ago, while Curran was just a child. His comprehension was further muddled by distance, for his own boyhood was spent in the Levant and Europe, and the news that reached him was in the form of newspapers, always weeks and sometimes months old. "Wasn't Burr found innocent, sir?"

"The court at Richmond ruled that the charges against Burr were not proven. The big flies escaped—rightly, for all I know. Nolan admitted to carrying messages for Burr—and was found guilty for leaving his post to do so." Pelles sat back in his chair, stuffed an additional pinch of tobacco into his pipe, and puffed it to life. "You and I would have never had any business with Philip Nolan had the trial been a regular one, but it was not. Colonel Burr was a clever man, and he had clever lawyers. He walked free, but an example had to be made. Nolan was a commissioned officer, and it would not do to question the loyalty of the Army."

"How long is his sentence, sir?"

"It is indefinite, Mister Curran."

Pelles handed Nolan's order of confinement across the desk. Curran noted the date and drew a breath; the document was dated five years before the start of the last war with Britain.

Curran read the order silently, astounded and then awed by its simple, terrible severity. "I am surprised, sir, that I have never heard of Nolan."

"He is a ghost—or as close to a phantom as a living soul can be. His commission was rescinded, he was stricken from the Army list, and his name was blotted from the records of the Military Academy." Pelles took the documents and placed them back into their worn leather envelope. "It has been the decision of the Navy Department that the circumstances of his confinement be kept in strict confidence. Likewise his dossier, biographical notes, endorsements, and papers."

Now Curran came to understand the extraordinary conduct of *Constellation*'s boat, and the strained silence about *Enterprise*'s cutter as he and Nolan were rowed to the ship. None of the boat crews had spoken because they dared not.

"As you see, Mister Nolan is a special case. And as it was you who has brought him to *Enterprise*, Lieutenant Curran, it shall be you who will bear responsibility for his custody. You are not at liberty to discuss our prisoner with the officers or sailors of any other vessel, or the persons manning any shore station or office of the American Navy."

Pelles handed the papers back to Curran. He continued, "You will see to it that around the prisoner there is no talk of home or the politics of our nation. You will ensure that no books, pamphlets, or letters come into his possession in which he could read of our country. Should a newspaper be lent to him, first cut from it the words 'United States' even if they appear in an advertisement for a private concern."

"Yes, sir."

"Have the carpenter prepare Nolan a cabin aft of the midshipman's berth. Unless he attempts to escape, he is to have the freedom of the decks during daylight. Once a week he will dine with the officers in the wardroom, and on the second Sunday of each month he will dine with me, in my cabin. At all other times he will take his meals alone."

"Does he receive mail, sir?"

"He does not. Letters addressed to Mister Nolan are intercepted at Washington City."

"May he write them, sir? Letters, I mean."

"He may not write to or communicate with any person without my express permission."

"I understand, sir."

"I won't keep you any longer; I am sure you have much to do."

Curran stood, clasped his hat under his arm, and made a short bow. Captain Pelles placed his fingertips over the scar on his face, a gesture he made when he was tired.

"You'll find that I run a taut ship, Mister Curran. Ensure that my orders are carried out."

THE PLACE THE CARPENTER PREPARED FOR PHILIP NOLAN WAS ON THE ORLOP deck, not exactly adjacent to the midshipmen's berth, but probably closer than a civilized person would care to lodge. *Enterprise* had once carried a chaplain, and it was Captain Garret in 1816 who first had the cabin built; as it was below the gun deck and did not have to be cleared for action, the space had wooden, not canvas, walls and a louvered door. Garret was a bit of a fire-and-brimstone sort and had felt that a man of the cloth berthing in close proximity to the midshipmites might compel them to live a godly life. It did not. Parson Hiedgockle preached daily sermons but left the ship amid whispers of a pederastical connexion with a Neapolitan castrato named Velluti. *Enterprise* never again sailed with a chaplain.

What had been the parson's cabin had been gradually taken over by the carpenter's mates, used as a storeroom and hidey hole, and it was not without some grumbling that they had cleared out their adzes, hammers, planes, bevels, mallets, and pots of varnish. After the Marines had thoroughly searched Nolan's belongings, he was led belowdecks and put in. It was not half an hour later that he was brought a lantern with a candle and could examine the space he had been allotted.

Lifting the light and peering about, Nolan found it to be a dry place, and there was no evidence of rats. Even subtracting the tumblehome of the ship's hull, his berth and the enclosed deck space were just wider than the span of both arms held out from his shoulders. The overhead too was generous, a good three inches higher than his head excepting the places where the frames crossed. Fiddled shelves had been put in fore and aft, and a hinged plank folded down from the forward partition. Though warped slightly, the board had provision for an inkwell, but the tool marks and paint stains on it showed that it had not been used recently as a desk. The carpenters had taken away all of their stores, leaving only a three-legged stool and one shelf filled with dusty Bibles provided for "Seamen, Sailors, and other various Seafarers" by the evangelical committee of an organization called the Brethren of the Nazarene.

It would not have taken long for Nolan to stow all of his things, but he kept most of them in the sailcloth bag. He hung his coat on a dowel and hook he made long ago on *Revenge* and placed his chains and manacles on the shelf next to the Bibles. Nolan sat up from the berth when a Marine brought in his supper—a broken chunk of hardtack and a sharp-smelling tankard of water. Judging from this stingy meal, Nolan was sure he would soon be put somewhere else, and he sat back on the berth and crossed his legs.

The ship rode easily at anchor, and the lantern barely moved on its hook. This cabin, though dark, was a much more commodious place than he had ever been kept, even aboard flagships, and he did not allow himself to become settled. He was used to the games sometimes played on him when he was first taken aboard. In his years at sea, Nolan had been the butt of occasional horseplay, and now he calmly anticipated that the ship's corporal would barge in, tell him to immediately "clamp on his bleeding seabag" and follow him at once to some cramped and damper part of the ship.

For a while Nolan sat listening to the lap of water on the hull (he was six or seven feet below the waterline), and occasionally laughter or an oath would drift down from the midshipmen's berth. Though an artillery officer by training, Nolan had formed an affection for ships and the way they were built. Not an inch of space was wasted on a man o'war, and he marveled at the ingenious construction of the neat tiers of shelves. They were placed up high as possible so that things might be stacked below and a man might work freely at the folding desk. All of the things he owned could be spaced out neatly on just two of the shelves on the aft partition. Nolan had lived so long with so few possessions that he could not imagine what even a dozen sailors could have kept in all the shelves, sills, racks, and drawers.

In the paucity of his belongings Nolan had become very much like the men who were his keepers. In all his years at sea he had never met a sailor who seemed very much attached to material things. Some prized waterproof trousers or grogram jackets, but these were freely lent to other shipmates, often taken steaming off one back coming off watch and given to another going out into the weather. They did all love money, especially prize money, but even that appeared only to represent the pleasures it could be traded for on land—rum, food, and women. Nolan had never heard of one sailor who did well with even a fortune on shore. The concept of wealth or shrewd advantage in business seemed to repel them. Once at sea, a purse jingling with gold quickly lost the magnetism it exerted on land, and Nolan had several times watched drunken sailors skipping dollars across the water, playing ducks and drakes, rather than come back to the ship with unspent money.

At sea it was impossible for Nolan to feel that he was poor. All of the sailors aboard owned about as much as he did—that is to say the clothing on their backs, one jacket that was more or less better than the other, and enough small sundries to fill a ditty bag. The officers—save, perhaps, the most successful and well married—seldom owned more than the contents of a pair of cruise boxes. Nolan could name more than a hundred officers who slept in hanging cots under scratchy wool blankets and spent what money they earned on pistols, swords, or navigational instruments and never a set of curtains. Every man who has ever taken to the sea is eventually bent to this spartan ethos. Enough is plenty; any more is surfeit. Gradually, Nolan had come to embrace the sailors' philosophy, living as much as he could in the present.

Nolan heard the ship creak, and someone said "what ho" to the Marine out in the passageway. Six bells, then seven; Nolan dozed, and he heard the sentry change outside his door. Nolan's Breguet watch had been taken from him while he was aboard USS *Amity* (Lieutenant Papeneau said it could be used to aid navigation in case of an escape), but life afloat was not reckoned by a clock. It was nearly eight bells in the second dogwatch, what a landsman (or an Army officer) would say was 8 p.m. Nolan heard laughter again, the sound of sailors turned off watch, and the hoots and shouts of some going ashore. Occasionally a boat thumped gently against the hull as liberty men came and went. Eventually the decks became silent, and even the midshipmen quieted down. It slowly occurred to Nolan that the relief had been made, the standing orders were in effect, and any new orders had by now been carried out. He might not be rousted out this watch at all, and it was increasingly likely that he would be left in this cabin overnight. The thought astounded him—these were the best quarters he'd had in nearly twenty years at sea.

With a stamp, the sentry came to attention outside the door. Nolan heard the Marine say crisply, "Good evening, sir."

There was a knock, and Nolan rose from the berth. As the door opened, the Marine snapped back to attention, a wonderfully blank-faced and mechanical creature. A shadow moved just on the other side of a lantern, and Nolan made out the silhouette of an officer.

"I came to see that you were settled," Curran said.

There was slightly more light in the passageway than in the cabin, and Nolan answered to a shadow, not quite able to see the face. "I am, most handsomely," Nolan said.

Curran glanced into the cabin and saw that Nolan was still clutching his coat and seabag.

"You have not stowed your things?"

As Curran stepped into the light, Nolan made out the face of the man who had taken custody of him on the pier. To Nolan, the man seemed even younger than he had in daylight, surely not more than twenty-five, though he had nothing of a casual air about him.

"Is this where I am to stay?"

"It is," Curran replied. "Do you have a complaint?"

"No, sir, I do not." Nolan tossed his seabag onto the berth. "If it was you who put in a word for me, I thank you."

"I said nothing on your behalf."

"Well, thankee, at any rate. On *Hornet* I was kept in a scuttle." Nolan upended his bag and dumped his things on the berth. Curran saw that all the man owned did not cover half of the mattress. A razor, a scrap of towel, pieces of wool and cotton cloth, and a set of tissue patterns traced on paper that made Curran think that Nolan made his own clothing.

"Have you eaten?" Curran asked.

"I have been fed."

On the plank table Curran saw a gray-yellow rectangle of ship's biscuit—the corner of it moved as a weevil worked free. A dented can was next to it, leaking a not quite transparent liquid onto the middle of the desk.

"What is this?" Curran said to the Marine.

"It is salt cracker and bilge water, sir."

Curran dropped the biscuit into the pot and handed it to the sentry. "See that the prisoner is fed a full portion from the mess deck. He is to have the regular ration, as well as ship's water."

The Marine was away at once. Nolan sat back on his berth, wary, considering. He said after a pause, "Well, I thank you then, Mister—"

"Curran. Now sir, about the terms of your confinement."

"Ah. I know that I pose somewhat of an imposition. I will try to give as little trouble as possible."

"I would be obliged for that. In return you are to have the run of the ship during the hours of daylight. I will curtail this privilege if you attempt to escape or violate the conditions of your sentence."

Nolan waited for the inevitable "additional modifications," for although every ship that had received him carried out the provisions of his sentence to the letter, some captains piled on amendments to the orders, sometimes for their own convenience, sometimes for their own amusement. Nolan waited for a list of off-limits places—the maintop, the boats, the powder magazines—and a roster of persons to whom he could not speak—midshipmen, the quartermasters, sometimes even the yeomen and clerks.

Curran added no extra conditions, and the pause lengthened. Nolan finally mumbled, "I am free to move about the ship?"

"During daylight, sir. After supper and retreat you may move about below-decks. You are to retire to your quarters at lights out."

In his years in custody Nolan had rarely been granted this much autonomy. He drew a breath and then held it, like a man considering an unexpected move on a chessboard. He looked at the floor of the cabin, thinking. As Curran regarded Nolan, he began to form the impression that during his confinement the prisoner had lost something of the deportment of an officer. Nolan was given to speaking very quietly, often not looking an interlocutor in the eye. Curran wondered if perhaps the prisoner had lost some of his mind. For his own part, Nolan was still uneasy that this might all be some elaborate practical joke. He did not wish to give offense, especially at the start of a new commission, but he did not wish to be made a fool.

"I am to extend an invitation to dine with the officers of the wardroom, tomorrow at supper."

"An invitation to me?" Nolan asked.

"Do not mock me, sir," Curran said coolly.

"I meant no offense, Mister Curran. The circumstances of my confinement, you understand, have varied from ship to ship. I am sometimes practiced upon."

"I am not in the habit of amusing myself at the expense of others, sir."

The Marine returned, his musket slung over his shoulder. In his hands he carried a wooden tray piled with bread and ham, a piece of pale yellow cheese, a dollop of yellow mustard, and a pot of table beer.

"It's the ration, sir," the Marine said. "Old Chick says that there ain't no hash what's still hot, so it's cold pork, soft tommy, and small beer. There's some of that hard Spanish cheese what's just come aboard, too. Same as the watch has for midrats." The Marine handed the wooden mess kid over to Nolan. "Will that do, sir?"

Nolan considered that if this was a joke, it was being played with elaborate and generous hospitality. He said, "Yes, it will do very well."

Nolan took the plate, and Curran saw the prisoner's reserve melt away into astonishment and pleasure.

"Captain Pelles has directed that you dine once a week with the officers. On each second Sunday, should the captain find himself at leisure, you will be invited for dinner in the great cabin."

"Captain Pelles, is it?" Nolan asked. "Well, I am honored. Yes, of course. Thank you again." Nolan placed the tray onto the folding table and stood beside it, moving his eyes to the loaf—soft baked bread made from white flour—and then he looked at the sentry and then to Curran.

"I'll leave you to your supper."

Nolan bobbed his head, said something obliging, and pulled the short stool up to the table.

"Good evening, Mister Nolan."

Nolan shifted a mouthful of ham into his cheek and said, "A very good evening it is, Mister Curran." Swallowing, he added, "Thank you for my supper."

Curran walked aft to the ladder as the sentry closed the door and threw home the bolt.

SHIPMATES

I N LIFE AT SEA CURRAN HAD NEVER HAD A CABIN OF HIS OWN, AND THE SHEER vastness of his new stateroom, all of seventy-two square feet, made him feel every bit an oceangoing raja. His cabin had a standing bedsit supported by stanchions fore and aft. Though he would have preferred a hanging cot, the cabin was an auxiliary surgical space for Doctor Darby, which explained the princely length of the mattress and also why the berth was fixed to the deck. There were two gimbaled whale oil lanterns, as Wainwright had promised, a luxury that gave more than enough light to read and write—again, a coincidence and benefit of the cabin serving in battle as a dressing station.

A hanging brass stove was suspended on a chain from the overhead. In colder climes it would be filled with coal, another luxury for a ship whose home port of Boston could lash her sons with a bitter winter. Behind the hanging stove, an eight-inch scuttle passed through the hull—which in this part of the ship was a gratifying slab of oak all of three feet thick. The scuttle could be closed with an iron baffle so the through-hull could be shipped tight in a running sea. This bit of craftsmanship allowed a generous amount of ventilation without making the cabin parky or wet. Despite the opulence, that night Curran slept fitfully, not yet accustomed to the sounds of his new ship.

Dawn was still an hour away when Curran went on deck to meet Kerr coming off the middle watch. They retired into the master's cabin, and Curran formally relieved Mister Kerr as navigator. Kerr was as happy as any young man released from a great responsibility and good-naturedly countersigned the papers accounting for the ship's several chronometers, sextants, hundreds of charts, and six fat leatherbound copies of the requisite tables. On *Enterprise*, the navigator was accountable for the lead-covered signal books as well as the ship's codes and ciphers, and Curran signed the paperwork acknowledging all sorts of brutal, peremptory, and shameful punishments should he permit, cause, or allow the ship's signals, codes, or papers to fall into the hands of an enemy, hostile power, or foreign prince.

Kerr made introductions to Mister Pybus, the sailing master, and Mister Midshipman Fancher, master's mate. They seemed almost like father and son, both dark-haired and muscular with piercing eyes and the same ready crooked smile. The master had come up through the hawse pipe, serving first before the mast as a seaman ordinary, captain of the maintop, master's mate, then the very man himself.

Mister Pybus had more time at sea than Curran had on earth, and was not the sort of old salt that was much bothered by young officers.

Fancher was the most senior of the midshipmen on board, just twenty, and would sit his examination for lieutenant in the spring. Kerr had told Curran privately that Fancher was a fine hand with the charts and tables, serious, dependable, and certain to be given his step, which was more than could be said for the other midshipmen—Hall, Nordhoff, and Wainwright—who were not only slovenly and lazy but also of no use in naval matters: incorrigible rascals and superfluous chow burners. Curran listened as Kerr disclaimed them, together and individually, as embarrassments to the service and a blight on the nation from which they sprang. Curran agreed to keep a close eye on them but did not forget that three days ago, he too had been a midshipman.

During the pleasant, windy morning *Enterprise* made the rest of her water and provisions were put aboard: great wheels of cheese, hams, casks of wine and beer, two or three lowing cattle, half a dozen piglets, a harem of hens for Chanticleer the rooster, two goats, and a pair of suspicious and troubled-looking sheep. There were also liberty parties passing back and forth, and though some of the men might return to their duties slightly impaired by a night ashore, all hands turned to with efficient goodwill. Erskine was everywhere, above and below, seeing to the shifting of ballast, scribbling with the purser, and even rejecting some of the more decrepit stores himself, making sure the carpenter, sailmaker, and bo'sun received honest value for the items they paid for.

During the second watch Curran met each of the quartermasters, generally a sober set of men; among them was the captain's coxswain, Guild. Also presenting themselves were Kanoa, Finch, and the other senior petty officer, Padeen Hoyle; all were right seamen. Together, out of 400 sailors on *Enterprise*, there were almost 70 Britons, 35 Irishmen, 15 Africans, 10 Scots, 9 Norwegians, a Swede, a Finn, a French-speaking Dutchman, 2 Bugis, an Algerian Jew, and 10 of a boat crew all brought up in the Sandwich Islands, tattooed and proud, one of them a former Nantucket harpooner and blood prince of the island of Moloka'i. Also aboard was a white-faced, black-eared terrier bitch named Beazee. The scarcity of rats aboard *Enterprise* was due to her zeal and industry (she'd been rated an honorary forecastleman), and "Queen Bee" had the run of even the sacred quarterdeck. It was known she had no love for the ship's cats and had driven each of them on occasion scratching up halyards, sheets, and even bare masts in mortal fear of their nine lives. Beazee was much caressed and was said to like nothing better than rattling a Norway rat, slurping a quart of beer, and being turned loose on the deck of an enemy ship.

The *tramontana* expired in puffs and gusts, and as the morning spread on, the harbor became still and flat. During the day, Nolan was occasionally seen on deck, always followed by a Marine. The men set to details and working parties generally ignored him, and he had enough sense of ship's business to usually keep out of their way. A few of the older hands who had seen Nolan in other commissions might simply nod hello, but as far as Curran could tell not one sailor or officer spoke to him all day.

At the end of the forenoon watch Curran joined several of the officers and Mister Erskine on the quarterdeck for the noon observation. Like druids worshiping the sun, half a dozen officers faced out over the larboard quarter, peering through smoked glass lenses, waiting for the precise moment of zenith. At sea, the noon sight was one of the crucial observations for establishing the ship's position. In port it was mostly a ceremonial occasion, and though attended by more formality than necessity, the ritual was an immovable part of the ship's routine. The officers all held their sextants fixing the disk, and when it was as high as it would get in the sky, Curran in his capacity as navigator pronounced, "Mark." Mister Pybus and Mister Fancher concurred, and Midshipman Nordhoff stared at his instrument with an expression of bafflement and heartbreak.

Curran said to Mister Erskine, "It is noon, sir." Erskine walked two steps to the binnacle and said to the Marine and the bo'sun of the watch, "Pipe the hands to dinner."

The glass was turned, eight bells ended the forenoon watch, and as the last of the bell strokes throbbed away, the pipes screamed first "all hands" and then "pipe to dinner." As the notes trilled out, there was a general movement to the hatches and then a sustained sort of crashing belowdecks, shouting, and the banging of pots and tankards.

In the harbor, the men of the returning liberty boat were seen to stretch out at their oars, rowing like heroes so not to miss the meal—or the ration that was just now serving out of the tub forward of the mainmast, a concoction mixed with exacting measure by the bo'sun and the officer of the deck. The spirituous ration aboard *Enterprise* was whiskey cut twice with water and, when stores were aboard, sometimes sweetened with citrus and sugar, as it was today. Rum was used when it could be had in the Caribbean, preferably taken from British merchantmen. American sailors had taken to calling their liquor "Bob Smith" after President Jefferson's Secretary of the Navy, the Honorable Robert Smith, who had decided that monongahela—that is, *American-made whiskey*—was a salubrious and republican beverage more befitting the character and fighting humors of the United States Navy than the Royal Navy's grog, a potion invented by a slab-sided, mincing king-worshiper of a British lord and occasional admiral.

Erskine looked up at the bows, his hands on the quarterdeck railing. Nolan had pressed himself against a gun carriage, making himself as thin as possible so sailors could stream into the hatchways to the mess decks below.

"It isn't noon everywhere," Erskine said.

"I would have hanged them both," sniffed Lieutenant Varney. The Marine's somewhat lurid complexion contrasted awkwardly with the green of his jacket. Varney cleared his throat. "Burr and this cully as well."

Curran watched as Nolan walked to the bow and sat on the larboard cathead looking out to sea. "I have heard the men call him Plain Buttons, Mister Erskine," Curran said. "What does that mean?"

Padeen Hoyle, just presented on watch, put himself forward as an expert. "Beggin' your pardon, sir. It's that coat he wears. It is the uniform jacket of an Army officer. Only he ain't allowed to wear the Army buttons nor epaulets as they bear the emblem of our country."

"His coat has gotten a little thinner over the years," said Erskine.

"Do you know him, sir?" asked Curran.

"No one does, well. Though when I was a mid he was held aboard *Constitution*."

"I know this," Varney said. "He is a bastard, as well as a traitor. He was born in Rhode Island during the occupation, the natural son of Sir Henry Clinton, the British general commanding in New England. His mother was a whore."

Captain Pelles' voice came from the ladder way: "Do you know that as a fact, Lieutenant Varney?" The officers touched their hats as Pelles came onto the quarterdeck. The captain glanced at the log board and then his eyes fell on the Marine.

"I beg your pardon, sir," Varney muttered. "Only I have heard it said around the fleet."

Curran moved to larboard as the captain looked down onto the main deck.

"Perhaps you have also heard that Mister Nolan fought a duel before his court-martial. He shot and killed a pompous militia colonel with a flapping jaw."

"I believe what I heard to be the truth, sir," Varney grunted. "About his mother, that is."

Pelles' expression was glacial. "Then I gather not many have said it to Nolan's face. I do not condone gossip, Mister Varney. I find it a bit feline for a gentleman— and it should be rather beneath an officer."

Varney folded his hands behind his back; he dared say nothing else. Pelles' reputation as a duelist and fighting captain was such that he no longer feared disagreement, much less affront. In a democracy, no mayor or governor or even president wielded so complete authority as the captain of a warship. And no magistrate in any court wielded so complete and arbitrary justice over his subjects. Aboard *Enterprise*, Pelles was judge and jury. His word was absolute, and with the authority of his command came the ability to brook no disagreement.

Pelles looked down onto the spar deck at Nolan. It now fell to him and to the ship's company to administer Nolan's sentence, and Pelles knew that his own conduct, measured in the smallest gestures of courtesy or derision, would shape the behavior of his officers and men. Pelles thought his check of Varney was sufficient; he would not tolerate chatter about the prisoner, not in his presence and definitely not on the quarterdeck. Pelles knew as well as anyone aboard how a crew could create a scapegoat. He would not tolerate cruelty.

The captain looked into the rigging and then at the clouds hanging above. Nothing moved; there was not a breath of wind. "Mister Erskine, the ship will remain one more night in Cádiz and depart with the first ebb. The glass is falling, and we may soon have a Levanter."

"I have noticed that, sir."

"All hands who have completed their duty will be permitted a run ashore, the starboard watch to return to the ship not later than three bells in the first watch, and the larbolines given Cinderella's liberty."

"Very good sir."

Pelles looked out into the harbor. The calm had induced a boatload of whores out into the roadstead. Though they did not approach *Enterprise* closely they did wave and flaunt their handkerchiefs. Pelles looked beyond the bawdy boat and toward the town. An open carriage was passing down the cornice, and it was not hard to imagine a beautiful Spanish *doña* borne by it.

"Have you any additional business in Cádiz, Mister Curran? Should you like an evening on shore?"

"I had a three-day run, sir, after *Epevier* sailed. I have seen all of Cádiz."

All the officers knew, and Curran could now only suspect, that Captain Pelles was quite fond of evenings ashore, particularly evenings at the theatre.

"Mister Erskine, who is the midshipman of the watch?"

"Nordhoff, sir. The youngster."

Pelles seemed to suppress a smile. "Please have him put on a presentable uniform and bring his journals and the noon figurings. He will join me directly in my cabin for dinner." Pelles started for the ladder and said over his shoulder, "Mister Curran, have you checked the noon reckonings of the young gentlemen?"

Curran tried to remember if that had been mentioned as part of his new duties. "No, sir," he said, expecting squalls, "I have not."

Pelles answered, "When we are back at sea, you may wish to have the duty midshipman assist you and Mister Fancher with the noon sights. Before you came aboard, on Wednesday last, Mister Wainwright handed me a reckoning that placed us in a sea of lava very near the center of the Earth. I weep for my country when I think of that young man navigating a warship."

"I will attend to it, sir."

Below, the word was being passed for Mister Nordhoff, who had been found near the after hatchway. His terrified voice peeped up. "Me? Dinner with the captain? Oh Jesus, what did I do?"

Pelles pretended not to hear, and the terrified mid continued squawking, calling for someone to help brush his coat and begging Wainwright to let him just glance at his reckonings. The captain went below, the officers dispersed, and Erskine suppressed a yawn.

"Mister Hall," Erskine asked. "What is playing at the opera house?"

Curran watched as the midshipman removed a folded newspaper from the pocket of his coat. Apparently knowledge of the theater's schedule was a collateral duty. Hall squinted at the paper. "It's Mozart, sir."

"Mozart is dead, Mister Hall; we have been through this before. *What* is playing at the opera house?"

Confounded, Hall narrowed his eyes at the paper.

"*The Magic Flute?*" Erskine asked.

Hall's lips twitched.

"*Die Zauberflöte?*" Curran suggested.

"It's all foreign, sir," Hall mumbled. "Don geo-something?"

"Avast heaving, Mister Hall," Erskine smiled. "I believe the captain will want his gig alongside in an hour. You can arrange that, I am sure."

"Yes, sir," Hall answered. "Right away." Hall stuffed the paper back into his jacket and skipped down the quarterdeck ladder.

"The captain enjoys opera?" Curran asked.

"He is an aficionado," Erskine smiled. "Mister Curran, it might do for you to plot courses from the roadstead tonight, one for an offing and one through the Gut and into the Med. It is our captain's habit to conceal his intentions until after we have raised the hook."

"I will, sir."

Captain Pelles had indeed decided to spend the night ashore, and after the ceremony of his departure Mister Midshipman Nordhoff was sent into the mizzen crosstrees. Though not quite as implausible as the reckonings of his messmate Wainwright, Nordhoff's scribbled calculations had placed *Enterprise* somewhere north of Bay St. Louis, in the Mississippi Territory, hard aground in a pine forest. Curran saw that Nordhoff took a book up with him and permitted him to smuggle a sandwich under his jacket. A few minutes after three bells, Curran followed Kerr and Pybus into the wardroom.

Even a happy ship exhales when the captain is not aboard ("Jehovah is no longer among us"), and in the half hour before dinner the wardroom of *Enterprise* filled with her officers, a content and conversational set of men, all anticipating supper.

It was the first time Curran had seen together all of his mess mates, a dozen of them, plus the two Marine officers, Captain MacQuarrie and Lieutenant Varney. The doors to the cabins adjoining opened and closed as officers shifted out of their working clothes into more presentable dress. The space was generous, especially compared with the cramped gunroom on *Epevier*. Fore and aft ran an oak table ten feet long and all of six inches thick. Punctuating the officers' cabins on either side were two of the long 24s. The wardroom's four guns, collectively called "the Apostles," were bowsed neatly and kept shining with the cook's own plush. All was lit by the beautiful expanse of the stern gallery, the glass polished to perfect transparency, and a padded locker ran the breadth of it, strewn with blue-covered cushions.

The table was set with linen and china, and as this was an in-port rather than an at-sea meal, there were bread barges set in place, with soft tommy fresh from the oven and two rounded ladle scoops of butter on saucers fore and aft. Mister Erskine stood at his place by the head of the table, welcoming everyone by name, and his good humor was on fine display. Most of the officers had blown their gaffs the night before; anyway, Cádiz was not the liberty port of the world, and they were most of them happy now to sip beer and half-water Bob as they smelled dinner preparing in the pantry just forward.

Lieutenant Ward scraped at a fiddle (he was the sort of officer who had curtains in his berth), but he played a creditable version of the Virginia Reel as conversations gathered. Curran took a can of beer from Mister Leslie, wishing him health, and as talk continued, the officers drifted toward their set places at table. To Erskine's right was the Marine captain, MacQuarrie, a thin, boyish man, nevertheless famed as a fighter, and just the person to lead a boarding party or to smash up a battery ashore. There was Piggen, the purser, and MacQuarrie's assistant, Lieutenant Varney, still looking somehow put out, but attending to Ward's music with some satisfaction. Curran listened more than he spoke, trying to make out currents and cross currents of conversations, and he guessed correctly that Varney's hauteur could become tedious on a long commission.

There was the master, the redoubtable Mister Pybus, and the third lieutenant, Mister Fentress. Mister Leslie, the fourth, was a tall, gimlet-eyed Virginian, a native of the Tidewater, who managed to combine courtly manners with a wry sense of humor. All seemed fine people, with Fentress maybe a bit unpolished, and definitely a man who said exactly what he thought. The surgeon, Doctor Darby, was in his black coat, a bald man without even eyebrows, and it gave his face a constant expression of either wonder or delight. Doctor Darby was highly regarded by the crew, though he made them filter every drop of fresh water brought aboard through sand, charcoal, and wood ashes. Darby had also persuaded Captain Pelles to line the number two water tank with beech wood and store in it three hundred gallons of lager, which the doctor swore was the finest antiscorbutic known to man.

Last to join the mess was the second lieutenant, Kerr, who had just signed ship's articles for a dozen British seamen who had swum away from HMS *Melampus* at Gibraltar and come overland to Cádiz hoping to find an American ship. He was still smiling when he came into the wardroom, slapped Erskine on the back, and said facetiously, "God bless King George. Bless him! Two of them were rated gunner's mates, and one a quartermaster. And not one word of foreign do they speak. I shall now replace that damned rascal Sulesi, Solangrutan, whatever his name is, that damned pirate Boogie man as loader of number seven."

Kerr filled a glass and Erskine stood behind his chair at the head of the table. "Gentlemen," he said, "most of you know we've been joined by Mister Curran, who is come over from *Epevier*. He has relieved Mister Kerr as navigator—"

"And I am glad of it," said Kerr.

"And we are safer for it," said Leslie taking up a tankard.

"I hope you will make Mister Curran feel to home."

Nods and bows. The three officers he had not yet met came across and shook his hand saying welcome, and the purser and Captain MacQuarrie made very civil bows across the table. "Your servant, sir," said the purser, but Curran judged him to be like the rest of his profession—calculating and close-fisted.

Curran was asked a few questions about *Epevier*. She was French built, of course, captured by the British off Ushant carrying dispatches from Napoleon himself. Taken into the Royal Navy at once, she sailed for half a dozen years as HMS *Epevier*. MacQuarrie surprised Curran by saying that he had been a lieutenant of Marines aboard USS *Peacock* when HMS *Epevier* was captured off Cape Canaveral, between the Bahamas and Spanish Florida, during the War of 1812.

"I heard it was quite a fight," Curran said. "When I was first aboard there was still a plug in the hull, square in my cabin."

MacQuarrie smiled, for although it had been a desperate fight, things had come out well. "*Epevier* was pretty badly shot up," MacQuarrie said. "The prize crew had the devil's own time getting her back under the St. Mary's battery in Georgia." MacQuarrie did not mention it, but it was his own fine seamanship conning the sloop back to port that had won him promotion. The prize money wasn't bad either. Although *Peacock* had left HMS *Epevier* a battered hulk, Georgia shipwrights had put USS *Epevier* to service as a weatherly and well-found vessel. Kerr and Ward had both seen her in the Atlantic and said pleasant things to Curran about his former ship.

"She is a right basher," Curran said, "and maybe even a bit over armed. Captain Gormly dearly loved to hear things go boom, and we carried sixteen 32-pounders."

"Sure, that's a lot of guns," said Erskine, "for a sloop-of-war."

"It was, sir," said Curran. "But in the Atlantic station we found our enemies pretty well spaced, not many pirates or slavers in the northern station, but our captain did have us shoot targets constantly, and once or twice even at icebergs."

Overhead, the quartermaster began to toll out six bells. By the second stroke, Ward had put the fiddle away. Erskine sat and passed the bread: the meal began. The stewards brought in tureens of turtle soup, and the more sharp set of the officers put their spoons to use. At the exact instant the last bell clanged, there was a rap on the wardroom door. A Marine sentry opened it and revealed Philip Nolan in his best coat and slightly yellow linen.

The appearance of the prisoner immediately brought conversation to a halt. Curran stood and Erskine turned in his chair. In the enthusiastic conversation before dinner, Curran had almost forgotten that Nolan was invited. Erskine had been told (he was, after all, president of the mess), but it had also slipped his mind. Spoons were poised in midair, and faces wore empty looks triangulated somewhere between contempt, indifference, and confusion.

"Forgive me, gentlemen, if I am late," Nolan said. He was in fact, exactly on time, to the stroke of the bell.

Curran said to the table, "Mister Nolan will join us for supper, gentlemen. He will do so every Monday during our cruise."

There was silence, and just as Pelles knew, Erskine realized that the wardroom officers would take their cue from their seniors. He said, "Welcome, Mister Nolan. You will please join us."

Nolan stepped into the room, presuming to look directly at no one in particular, and found the empty seat across from Curran. The steward brought him a bowl of soup, and to Nolan's immediate left Lieutenant Varney stood. With excruciating dignity the Marine said to Erskine, "Sir, may I have permission to leave the mess?"

MacQuarrie looked at his subordinate but did not countermand him.

Erskine said, "If you wish, Lieutenant Varney."

The officer went out, and there was only the sound of spoons against china. Finally Erskine took up the cause. "So, Ward, what tune was that you were playing?"

No one dared say "Old Virginia," and Erskine realized almost at once that he had blundered into shoal waters.

"The name escapes me now, sir. It was just a reel I picked up somewhere."

"It was played very well," said Curran, who knew the name of the tune as well as anyone at the table.

"Ward has much time to practice," said Kerr. "I would too, if I was not so attached to earning my keep or learning my trade."

There were a few snickers. Fentress, who was not the keenest of *Enterprise*'s wags, said, "I have heard it played before. When I was in *Cumberland* we called the tune 'Sweaty Betty.'"

"Perhaps there are different lyrics for different occasions, Mister Fentress?" said Erskine, hoping that Fentress would not sing them a few lurid verses.

"They were quite descriptive, sir." Fentress smirked. "Very informative—"

Erskine gave him a look, and Doctor Darby shook his head. There was silence again for a little while, and one by one empty soup bowls were taken up.

"Mister Nolan," Curran said, "I could not help but notice that in your cabin you have a copy of Epictetus."

"I do, sir."

"If it is in Latin, you need have no fear of me borrowing it," Darby smiled. "I have enough with my medical texts, and have come automatically to associate Latin with all that man must suffer."

"Very true," added MacQuarrie. "Latin and I parted lifelong enemies." He signaled for the steward to take his bowl, asked for the bread barge. "Epictetus. I seem to recall that name, though I don't remember him to be an emperor. I take it the book is in some manner a classic?"

Leslie said, "MacQuarrie, they are all classics. Every bleeding one. I have the switch marks to show for my trouble."

"But I have read a bit," Darby said. "Is he not a Stoic philosopher? Of the second century, I think. Some find him greater than Seneca."

"Seneca?! Not those damned cannibal Iroquois?" asked Fentress.

Curran put in kindly, "Lucius Annaeus Seneca: Seneca the Younger. A Roman philosopher, sir. I believe that the Indian tribes share the name only by coincidence. Though the Indians are most warlike and grim, Seneca himself was a bit of an opulent cove, for a Stoic."

"Have you read Epictetus, Mister Curran?" asked Nolan.

"I have read the *Enchiridion* and his other fragments. My father swore by him. So much so that he taught us grammar from the book itself. Mister Leslie and I probably share the same stripes."

Leslie raised his tankard. "I hear you, Mister Curran. A nasty business that language is."

At this moment the stewards brought out two steaming platters of langoustines, several gallon-sized kegs of porter, and a tray of finely chopped salmagundi. The beer was poured, though Mister Kerr abstained and the purser poured himself a dusty bottle of blackstrap. There was a general crunching as tails were twisted off and shells cracked open. Doctor Darby launched into a story about the relative intelligence of lobsters, as opposed to crabs, which said more about the doctor than any crustacean.

There came soon after a fine paella filled with finger-sized prawns, mussels, chorizo, and five pounds of saffron-colored rice. A curried relish appeared in small ceramic dishes, and Curran was told this was Old Chick's specialty ketchup. Nearly everyone poured the Vesuvian mixture over everything they were served, but Darby stayed away from it, and warned Curran that it was so spicy he wondered how even a hyena could survive swallowing it.

Mister Leslie slathered a dollop over his paella and said, "It only burns twice!"

Doctor Darby was by now in a well-lubricated state and said, "Then, Mister Leslie, it will serve you as a sturdy, perhaps even heroic anthelmic."

"*De gustibus non est disputandum*," Nolan quipped, and Doctor Darby beamed. "Capital sir! Most capital! A glass of beer with you, sir!"

The far end of the table laughed again after MacQuarrie mistranslated Nolan, rumbling out, "You are what you eat," and Erskine raised his glass.

"Where did you come by such prodigious Latin, sir?"

"At Magdalen College. In Oxford."

"England, sir?" sputtered Fentress.

"In 1794. Between the wars," Nolan said. "I first went up as a servitor, a sort of student and knight of the washtub."

"An academic midshipman?" asked Curran.

"If you will, sir," Nolan bowed. "The comparison is apt."

"What did you study, Mister Nolan?"

"Languages, of course, and a certain measure of the classics cannot be evaded. I read history and mathematics."

"I did not know that there were so many—" Curran was plainly stumbling over the word "Americans," but Nolan rescued him.

"There were five of us, sir, six when I started, and almost two dozens of Canadians among the other colleges, particularly at Pembroke."

Fentress blinked. "You found no hostility there, because you was—"

"None, sir. Well, very little. It was, as I said, between the wars."

This was coming dangerously close to talk of country, or at least of nationality, and Curran put his hand on the rudder of the conversation. "I would guess you found the course of study challenging?"

"The winters were more challenging, and the food," Nolan said. "The English boil things that have no business being put into a pot."

"Hear him!" said Kerr. "They are the very Huns! Savages, sir, with the vile things they eat. Soused pig's face. Trotters fresh from the sty's bilges! The most unwholesome offal and fish that even the French would not feed to prisoners."

"They have as a people a vile compunction to eat haslets on purpose," said Doctor Darby. "I believe it is what compels them to extreme bellicosity and dyspepsia."

"And, I would add, a certain want of romantic vigor," Nolan said. The table rang with laughter. Nolan had come quite close to proving himself agreeable company.

Fentress poured some beer. "Now, I know a man who went to Oxford, like you, between the wars. I'd always heard that he was one of them gentleman commoners, like you said. His family, they was plantation owners, and had some sort of timber operation in . . . well, it was west of . . . anyway, they grew trees, as I said, and tobacco and corn of which they made whiskey. What you would call a very tidy operation. This man, his name was Fitzgerald, though was not one of those insolvent, slovenly bog-trotter Micks, no not, by no long shot. A gentleman and an attorney. He was an artillery officer too. Big as a barn."

Nolan's face had brightened as Fentress spoke. "Fitzgerald! Do you mean Wendell Fitzgerald, sir?"

"Why, yes. As I said, I knew him in . . . well, I did not say that. But I knew him well enough. And his wife was the most beautiful thing ever."

"Was Fitzgerald a friend of yours, Mister Nolan?" asked Curran.

"A particular one, sir. I would not have survived Oxford without his help." Most of the gentlemen at the table had been educated at sea, and with the possible exception of Doctor Darby, there were very few of them who would have survived there at all.

Nolan said, "When I first went up to Oxford, I was assigned to wait on Lord Melville's son. A quite ill-mannered drunk, and though he was a friend of my guardian, I found the situation very unpleasant. I was treated little better than a footman. Wendell was a year ahead of me, and he lived in great style. Made no bows to lords or the swell mob."

Leslie, who was a staunch republican, said, "Right he should."

"Just so." Nolan nodded. "I was hungry, and he fed me—a fire in his rooms every night. He was very generous. And big as a cart horse. He actually called out Melville's son—sabers it was, not pistols. Fitzgerald disarmed the scrub in the first pass and then beat him with the flat of his sword—right on the field. He settled the young lord's hash, as we used to say. I had no trouble after that." Nolan turned smiling to Fentress. "It has been years since I have seen him. I hope you last saw him well?"

Fentress shoveled more rice into his moving jaw and spoke with his mouth full. "Don't take offense because you ain't heard from him."

There was a small space of time when the only sound was Fentress chewing. Nolan finally asked, "Why is that?"

"He was killed at Fort McHenry in 1812."

Curran froze at the mention of the battle, and Erskine glowered at Fentress. Oblivious to them both, he continued bitterly: "I served in the naval batteries there. One of them British Congreve rockets arced in all the way from the harbor. Fitzgerald and an entire gun crew was swept right off the parapet and blowed up. I saw it myself."

Fentress fixed Nolan with a particularly icy expression. "Right after your goddamn schoolmates burned Washington City."

———

THE DECK WAS STILL. THERE WAS A FAINT LIGHT IN THE SKY, AND THE HARBOR seemed to glow, indigo and aqua, smooth all the way to the town and the battery. The air was much colder, and the lights coming up on the cornice showed plainly— candlelight in windows, lanterns in doorways and on carriages, and a lumenaria in progress around the theater. Nolan stood by the mainchains, hands behind his back, looking out across the anchorage.

The sentry was nearby, half a dozen steps away, and with him sat the ship's terrier, scratching herself absently. Standing perfectly still, Nolan's mind played through the course of the conversation, working backward from the words that had stunned and cut him. What had made him so misjudge the men in the wardroom? Why had he thought that this ship might be different from all the others that had carried him? Had the small courtesy of a livable cabin led him to hope?

Overhead, the rigging creaked and the masts swayed against the gathering dark. *It would be better*, Nolan thought, *if they were all like the Marine lieutenant— abrupt and open in their dislike.* He could now remember little of the meal except the look on Fentress' face—cold, calculating, intending hurt. Nolan became aware of the sentry moving away from him, the Marine coming to something more like the position of attention. Curran descended the quarterdeck ladder and came slowly across the spar deck.

"Good evening, sir," Nolan said.

"It looks to be," Curran answered. It was nearly dark, and Nolan would soon have to quit the deck. Behind Curran the sentry held back, cradling his musket with his arms crossed.

After a pause Curran said, "That was a hard way to learn about your friend."

Nolan took a breath and put his hands on the bulwark. He said quietly, "It seems amazing to me that he is really gone."

A party of topmen went by carrying lanterns; in their passing light Nolan's face was ghostly.

"How many ships have carried you, Mister Nolan?"

"I couldn't say. Some never even opened the envelope that held my papers. It is more than a dozen commissioned vessels, not counting gunboats and packets. I believe I have been in every ocean of the world save the Antarctic sea. I have seen as much of the planet as any man—just not as much of the earth."

Curran watched as Nolan studied the glittering strand; the lights of people's homes were as far away from him as the stars. After Nolan had left the wardroom, Erskine had coldly dressed down Fentress, letting him know in no uncertain terms that if he ever again violated the conditions of Nolan's sentence, he would have him flogged. Few aboard had ever seen the exec so thoroughly enraged. An evening that had begun with so much promise had ended in acrimony and recrimination.

"I know this evening was difficult for you," Curran said. "I will not require you to attend any other mess nights."

"No, sir. I did not find it unduly trying."

Curran was touched by Nolan's calm and determined smile.

"I would like very much to dine with the officers—that is, if they will have me. I find challenging company better than none."

"Then we will have you, sir."

Nolan made a short bow, a courtly gesture from another era. It was hard not to feel sympathy for this man whose life and manners were trapped in amber.

"If you will excuse me, Mister Curran, I think I will return to my cabin," Nolan said. "Good evening, sir."

"Good evening, Mister Nolan."

The terrier stayed and stretched out her limbs, but the sentry glided below, as close to Nolan as a shadow.

Curran walked aft to the quarterdeck. There was not a breath of wind and the scattered clouds were silver around the moon. In the east, the Pleiades were fully risen; Atlas and Pleione, dim in the left-hand sky, Alcyone, and the rest of the Seven Sisters, clustered together exactly as Tennyson described them—fireflies tangled in a silver thread.

Curran hoped there would be wind tomorrow, wind to get under way, for the lights on the shore seemed now a provocation to him, and he knew that to see them must be worse, much worse for Nolan.

Captain Pelles came on board at first light, or rather sprang aboard very much like a tiger. He went up the side quickly, his body turned slightly sideways on the ladder, sliding his one hand deftly up the forward manrope. He arrived on deck and saluted the colors, then the officers; the Marines presented arms with a shout and crash.

It occurred to Curran that Captain Pelles looked a dozen years younger than the man who'd gone ashore the previous evening. An earnest if somewhat rustic production of *Don Giovanni* had been a pleasant distraction. But if Pelles seemed like a tiger, it was one that had just been fed, for the part of Elvira had been played by an enchanting soprano. Her perfume might still be detected on the captain's best uniform had any of the officers ventured close. It was a smell so delicate that it could never have been discovered through the fug of the waking ship and the pleasant smells of coffee, bacon, and just baked bread.

Pelles looked up at the dogvane above the mizzen. "Mister Erskine, when we have weighed, we shall make all plain sail. This land breeze should help us make good an offing."

Erskine answered, "Very good, sir," quite as though the order had not been anticipated.

Enterprise was already at single anchor, and the capstan bars were shipped. The gig was quickly brought aboard, and the waisters were added to the mass of men standing by on the forecastle.

The pipe trilled "all hands up to anchor," and the fiddler played "The Old Thirteen." A voice called from the forecastle, "Short stay."

Captain Pelles said in a conversational voice, "Heave round, stamp and go." The bo'sun repeated this in a booming shout, and through the hatchway the fiddle could be heard squeaking rapidly. Pelles stood on the starboard side of the quarterdeck; Curran, Erskine, and the other officers to larboard, just aft of the wheel. Padeen the quartermaster and Lachat the sergeant of Marines stood behind the wheel and binnacle, two of the most experienced and surest men of the ship. The music came piping up from below, faster and faster, and as *Enterprise* made good her hawse, the ship was drawn toward the eye of the wind. Pelles looked up at the vane and then back across the harbor as a cat's paw of wind went away past the battery. *Enterprise* yawed slightly as the anchor was broken out from the sandy bottom.

From the forecastle again a deep voice: "Up and down, sir." Then, "Anchor's aweigh."

Pelles watched the work on the forecastle closely, and as the bo'sun thundered "Catted, sir," the captain cupped his hand around his mouth and shouted, "Up the jib and loose topsails." That eponymous sail ran quickly up the forestay. As the jib filled, the bow started to fall off and the ship slowly turned away from the land. The topmen took to the shrouds, quickly scooted out across the stirrups and out onto the yards. Curran watched as the men aloft laid out, and let fall in a body. The topsails fell together, dropping like curtains at the end of a play, and were briskly sheeted home. *Enterprise* gathered way, and there was a rush of water along her sides.

As the ship made the various evolutions of getting under way, Nolan observed from the spar deck. He was not lubberly enough to obstruct either the men heaving or those going aloft, and by the time the swabs and holystones came out at the bow he had moved aft to the mainchains.

Pelles turned his eyes on Curran. "Since you have set an open course, Mister Curran, I gather you have some curiosity as to where we are bound?"

"I do, sir."

"We're down for the Barbary Coast of Africa, gentlemen. The Algerines are used to us in the Mediterranean. I mean to surprise them off the African shore. After we put Madeira behind us we will sail southwest. When the moon is new we will make a coastwise approach. Perhaps we will surprise a few of the villains before the whole continent knows what we are about."

"Very good, sir. I'll see that the course is laid."

Erskine gave Curran an almost imperceptible nod. That a course would be laid for Madeira and then the African coast was soon communicated about the ship, and as *Enterprise* continued to gather way, the singing of the water down her sides was answered by a growing enthusiasm among her crew. Pelles was himself glad to shake the dust from his feet, for though he had spent a charming evening ashore, one that was, in fact, very agreeable, the ocean was his element and he was glad to be back in it. To Curran, Pelles looked completely unlike the silent, brooding man who had read his orders in the great cabin.

The topgallants bloomed, and *Enterprise* was soon making four knots and then six. As all captains are, Pelles was merged with his ship. He knew both her fine points and when she would gripe. He knew the ship's course and her point of sail by discerning a vibration, something very like a musical tone. With the same calculus that he knew the vessel, Pelles also knew his men. Since Nolan had come on board there was added to the composition both a deeper note and a measure of silence. And silence in a crew is something all captains are alert to.

Below the quarterdeck break, Nolan was sitting on a starboard carronade trying to coax Beazee closer with a piece of biscuit, but she was soon away, snapping at one of the insolent tomcats who leaped up onto the fife rail with bristled tail. Pelles stood at the rail, looking on with an expression that was difficult to translate.

The captain drew a breath—for a moment it seemed to Curran as though Pelles was about to give an order, but the expression on his face changed and he said quietly, "Carry on, gentlemen. I shall be in my cabin."

THE WORK OF A SHIP AT SEA COMMENCED. EACH MORNING WAS BRIGHTER AND warmer than the last, and soon *Enterprise* took a fine bone in her teeth, logging 130 or even 150 nautical miles each day under no great press of sail. When they were a few days out of Cádiz the second Sunday came, and Nolan was escorted by a pair of Marines to the captain's cabin at precisely eight bells in the afternoon watch.

Nolan disappeared into the coach and remained during the captain's Sunday supper and for two hours after. The quartermasters later said that they heard laughter through the skylights, but the captain's steward, Grimble, would report only that they ate a pair of fowls in oyster sauce, fried potatoes, and chess pie, and drank two bottles of Latour.

What was to be made of this the lower decks didn't know, but two of the ship's old hands set a parcel of first voyagers straight that night when the smoking lamp was lit. Though he was most of a seaman, Billy Vanhall had harangued a few of the gullible with tales that Nolan had been sent by Burr to assassinate President Jefferson. Sitting next to Old Chick, Padeen Hoyle puffed his pipe and grunted that Vanhall's story was all bull and a crock.

"Plain Buttons and the Old Mogul was shipmates in the Pacific. Would our skipper ship with what you would call a known assassinator? Not by a long chalk."

"Thas' right," drawled Old Chick. "And wasn't Mister Nolan with Porter when he sailed to Tie-heety? Now, would someone like that get to make a cruise to Nuku Hiva, what is a sailor's paradise, mate, and also take eleven rich British whale ships as prizes? Not hardly if he was as guilty as you says, Billy Vanhall. Not hardly."

"Well, he's convicted, was all I was saying," huffed Vanhall. "And I heard him called a jinx, too."

"Like you ain't, neither," said Padeen, narrowing his eyes.

Vanhall stood and hitched his trousers. "Say what you like," grumbled the little man, "but there's a Marine stands sentry at his cabin every night. Why? So's he don't kill us all in our sleep. So there." At this, Vanhall walked aft, smugly put his hands into his pockets, and tripped over a bucket.

For several pleasant days the brisk Levanter drove them west. It was a fine topsail breeze, two points on the frigate's quarter, one of her favorite points of sail. When the wind backed round to the north, Curran laid a downwind leg for Madeira. *Enterprise* set her watches and kept lookouts, but she was making a passage, not yet cruising, and there was an easygoing complacency about the ship. Watch after watch glided by; the log was heaved and her course made good.

Six days out they met a New Bedford whaler, *Libertas*, homebound but ordered to Lisbon to meet one of her owners. When the whalerman backed her topsails and lowered boats, Curran walked forward. Nolan was sitting on the combing of the middle hatch examining a dozen small shrimp he had caught in a cast net. Next to him was a pad weighted down with a piece of bar shot. On it, Nolan had begun a very careful sketch of the creature with colored bits of chalk.

"Good morning, Mister Nolan," Curran said. "I am afraid I must interrupt your drawing."

Nolan looked up from his work—he had been using a magnifying glass, and it took him a second to refocus his eyes. From the quarterdeck he heard the officer of the deck bark through his speaking trumpet, "Larboard manropes!"

Nolan began to gather his pencils. "I gather we have been hailed?"

"We have, sir," Curran said politely. "I must ask you to go below."

When he stood, Nolan could just see over the hammock nettings. The whaler was two or three hundred yards downwind, hove to under the frigate's lee. The bo'sun and his mates converged forward of the mainmast and opened the entry port.

"Forgive me for troubling you, Mister Curran," Nolan said. "I didn't realize she was so close aboard." Nolan gathered up his things as quickly and quietly as possible. He did not want to give the impression of taking liberties, not early in a commission, and not to an officer who had been kind to him. He wrapped up the shrimp in a bit of cloth and put them into a basket.

"I don't think you will be inconvenienced long," Curran said.

The whaleboat was pulling across, and already a few of the men had formed a sort of cordon to screen Nolan from the larboard gangway. As Nolan picked up his papers, an awkward gust came across the forecastle, scattering a few of his drawings. Curran could see the very real stamp of embarrassment under Nolan's tanned brow.

"Allow me, sir," said Mister Wainwright, slouching down to take up a few of the wayward papers. "This way. If you please, sir."

The midshipman crossed the deck in a few youthful bounds, and Nolan was guided after him. As they disappeared into the companionway, Curran took up a sheet of paper Nolan had left under the bar shot. The drawing was of an arc-shaped creature, something between a crab and a shrimp. Under the half-completed drawing Nolan had written: "A nondescript Amphipoda of the class Malacostraca." Red and yellow lines rendered it exactly, depicting its various parts and capturing its translucence perfectly.

Curran heard the bo'sun's pipe and turned. The whaler's captain came up the side, beaming "How do ye" and slapping backs. He was a large, sun-browned man in a faded black coat. He said he was "*dee-lighted*" to see *Enterprise*, knew her right away, and was damned happy to see the Stars and Stripes.

Pelles emerged on deck and was introduced. The whaler captain seemed inclined to gam, and Pelles asked him into the cabin. The whaleboat was veered astern and a man in a tall black hat and red waistcoat came aboard: Mister Conway, sailing master of *Libertas*. Nordhoff and Hall met him at the ladder, and Mister Kerr had a smile wider than usual as Curran climbed up to the quarterdeck to meet their visitor.

"You're the navigator, sure?" said Mister Conway, holding out his hand.

"Curran, sir," he answered, tucking Nolan's drawing into his coat.

"Thankee, yes, yes, and I wonder, Lieutenant, if you might have a moment at leisure?"

Curran nodded.

"As I explained to your midshipmen, I believe I have a problem with my instrument," Conway said, somewhat in an undertone.

"Which I told him we have a physician aboard," said Nordhoff flatly. Beside him, Hall strangled a guffaw. Curran narrowed his eyes at the boys as Conway doffed his hat, reached into it, and removed small wooden box, the sort that held timepieces.

"You see, sir, it's a sidereal matter."

"In that case, I might be of service," Curran said. "This way, sir." As Curran showed Mister Conway to the master's cabin, he said over his shoulder, "Mister Nordhoff, you will take this drawing back to Mister Nolan in his cabin and then join Mister Hall in the mizzen top."

The sidereal problem was not hard to grasp but was impossible to solve. In Mister Pybus' cabin, the whaler opened the box and revealed an Arnold chronometer smashed completely into a handful of silver, gold, and crystal fragments.

"Off the chart table and across the cabin," Conway said. "A wildcat of a night, gentlemen, in fifty-three degrees south. Rolling it was, thirty footers, and then we took one out of nowhere. Big like kingdom come, stole upon us like a thief. We were in five-hundred-fathom water, but it reared up and broke like a comber. I saw it, pitched out with a black shadow in front of it—we was pooped and neared like to founder. The brass repeater in the captain's cabin swept clean overboard when the deadlights bashed in." Mister Conway stirred the wreckage with the tip of his finger. "Lost our best sextant too, smashed t'other, and lost a dozen men when a boat was swept off the davits."

Curran and Pybus were astonished to learn that *Libertas* had made good a course from the Carroll Grounds, nearly five thousand miles, solely on dead reckoning and a sextant with a broken mirror. Pybus and Conway at once set about establishing latitude (which Mister Conway had computed accurately) and, more important, longitude, for without a working timepiece *Libertas* might have made only a very, very rough speculation.

Enterprise had two fine stellar reductions and a lunar from last night, as well as a fresh plot, and the gift of degrees, minutes, and seconds was very gratifying to a mariner with a smashed chronometer.

Mister Conway clucked that it wasn't more than 173 miles out from where he'd guessed. *Libertas* had piled on sail for the last six weeks and had put the heels to a dozen other whalers, mostly Americans, but also one Liverpool ship and a Dane, who were all still lasking up the African coast, a sorry set of buggers.

Libertas was a fast ship, Mystic built, and had carried tea before she was taken into the fishery. Her sailing master seemed as proud of her as he was of his navigation. He might have a right to his opinion, now that they were out of the Bight of

Benin, filled to the gunwales with oil and their backsides covered by nothing less than a United States frigate. A side trip to Lisbon didn't signify—not for a ship that was a hundred miles closer to port than she had reckoned, and not for a crew that had been three years from home.

The sun had become enormous as it touched the horizon. The visitors shook hands all around, then dropped back into their boat. Standing on bowed legs, the whaler's captain steered back to his ship, clamping the stern oar under his arm and turning about to wish a prosperous voyage.

As *Enterprise* made sail, *Libertas* wore ship and yawed north, showing an ornate and gilded stern. In place of an ensign staff the whale ship had a bronze torch held by a carved gilt arm—the hand of the liberty goddess herself.

Curran watched as Mister Conway's top hat darted here and there aboard *Libertas* as her crew shipped an elaborate flambeau atop the torch—a hundred minute panels of leaded glass fashioned into the shape of a flame. A whale oil lantern was hurried to life and put inside the glass, filling it with a pure, gold light.

All of *Enterprise* stared. "It is very grandiose for a stern light," Doctor Darby sniffed.

"I have never seen its like," Curran answered. He wondered how so elaborate a chandelier could have survived a storm that smashed both of the whaler's clocks, battered in her deadlights, and swept a dozen souls to eternity.

Forward, by the bow chasers, Padeen nodded to one of the Bannon brothers. "It would be the two of 'youse that I would make shine that thing."

"How them codfish put on airs," Christopher Bannon said.

His brother Stephen did not take his eyes off the light but was jealously calculating the value of a fiftieth of a single share of a fully loaded whale ship. Disgusted, he muttered, "It's all well to show away and top the nob while it's us that plays the watchdog."

Their observations were cut short by eight strokes of the bell and a long warble of the bo'sun's pipe. *Libertas* and her crystal torch were a fascinating sight but could not compete with the smells from *Enterprise's* own mess decks: a hundred pounds of fresh-caught tunny, fried in filets, a hogshead of rice from Murcia, and buttered okra only two weeks old. As the whaler steered north, *Enterprise's* hands rumbled below to mess between the guns. The tide of men settled down to supper, and Nolan was allowed out of his cabin in the orlop.

He passed unseen up the ladders from the hold, through the berth and gun decks, and by the time he emerged on the spar deck there were only the watch and the lookouts above. The warmth had gone out of the breeze and darkness was quickly lowering. As Nolan's eyes adjusted to the dusk, he saw a bright light moving away to the northwest. Where he thought to see the whale ship's stern, a yellow light came down on a gilded arm holding aloft a bronzed and laurel-wrapped torch. Rising on the swell, the whaler's transom shimmered, and letters of gold presented themselves: LIBERTAS, and below, the ship's home port, MYSTIC. Rippling from the mizzen were the broad Stars and Stripes of an old-fashioned ensign. The glow of the stern light made the flag luminous, iridescent as a piece of sunset. The sight astounded him, and for a few seconds Nolan succeeded in dismissing it as some trick of light—an illusion conjured of memory. Nolan did his best not to feel a pang, but the power of his will was not complete. He found he could not turn away from the light. Nor could he escape the ache in his heart.

The first, bravest stars pricked themselves out against the sky, and Nolan watched until the whaler's sails took on the color of night. The sea between the ships seemed blacker than he had ever seen, and the slender glow that spilled between grew thinner, thinner, and parted at last.

BY THESE STARS

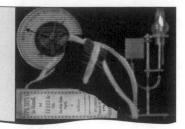

IN BRIGHT SUNLIGHT THE BLUE CUTTER, WITH MISTER MIDSHIPMAN WAIN-wright as boat officer, pushed over the last set of lashed-together barrels; he was assisted in this responsibility by Padeen Hoyle, steady at the tiller as coxswain. As Petty Office Hoyle was a few decades older than his nominal commander, he served also as his sea daddy. Under the old salt's minute supervision Mister Wainwright had been sent to undertake the routine task of laying targets. The blue cutter had crossed *Enterprise*'s wake and worked to leeward, placing in the water five rafts made of beef casks and barrel staves. These now wallowed easily on the swell, appearing on the crests and dipping into the troughs, a perfect game of peek-a-boo. On the last target, Wainwright had made a special effort; a broken piece of stretcher was pointed up among the barrels, and to this was lashed the shattered collar of an oar, making a rude cross. This contraption was crowned by a rotten melon and swathed in a piece of frilly petticoat. A short plank had been nailed to the target on which Wainwright had daubed the words "Maggie's Drawers."

Padeen worked the cutter back to the ship, handling both tiller and sheet so Wainwright had time to admire his nautical scarecrow. "It's just the thing, Padeen. Don't you think?"

"It is, sir," answered Padeen, winking to the stroke oar, Sean Michael Hoyle, his very own cousin from County Sligo. How Wainwright had come by a set of lady's undergarments was a deep and abiding mystery.

The cutter's crew came up the side and the boat was veered astern. A clean sweep had been made of the decks, the lesser cabins dismantled, mess tables slung up, and the garlands and shot racks made full. As *Enterprise* wore round in a broad, easy half circle, the smell of slow match streamed across the deck. Powder was served out to the guns below and those on the spar deck. The lower courses were sheeted, the ship was stripped to her fighting sails, and on deck the sun was brilliant.

Curran stood with his division by their section of guns, 32-pound carronades just forward of the quarterdeck break. Not considered equal to the 24-pounders for range, the carronades were nevertheless called "smashers," and for close-in work they were deadly. Curran's division was known in the ship as Bastard's Alley. Lieutenant Varney had previously commanded this section, but on Curran's coming aboard, that nimble officer had availed himself of the opportunity to take over a less visible section of long 24s on the gun deck below. Bastard's Alley got its name because it was right under the conn, and therefore under the unblinking gaze of the captain. Working guns under Pelles' knowing eye called for nothing less than strict attention to duty, and even perfection. The standard of gunnery on *Enterprise* was very high indeed; the captain placed the ability to load, aim, and fire three broadsides in three and half minutes as the very apex of naval virtue, equaled only by godliness and love of country.

Curran called together his charges: gun captains, loaders, swabbers, rammers, firemen, and those who would be sail trimmers. Padeen had rejoined after his excursion and took his place as captain of number eight. After consulting with Padeen, Curran had shifted a few of the men; he had inherited, in addition to Mister Wainwright, Kungkunhan Sulawesi and his mate Lembeh, both Bugis from faraway Sumatra. The pair were ferocious and eager, but neither possessed much English beyond the words "fire," "swab," "heave," "fuck," and "shit." On the pretext that they could understand each other even if they could understand no one else, Curran assigned them as loader and fireman under Wainwright, thinking that no two jobs could be more obvious than feeding a cannonball into an empty gun or splashing water on a burning shipmate.

"Gentlemen," Curran said to those who could understand him, "I have just come from USS *Epevier*, where I had the privilege of learning the craft of gunnery under Master Gunner James Morell. Mister Morell more than once put a boot up a midshipman's ass to make a point. I will tell you, gentlemen, aboard *Epevier* I learned fast."

There were smiles among the older hands. Most of them had seen a midshipman lifted vertically by the seat of his pants. Curran went on. "It is my intention that you will be the finest gunnery division on *Enterprise*. I will expect you to load, lay, aim, fire, and engage targets beyond six hundred yards."

Only the Bugis were not amazed. Wainwright blurted, "You mean with carronades, sir? That far?"

"That and farther. With shell and canister too."

Curran noticed a few wry expressions. Enthusiasm from young officers was something they were used to, but Curran knew what he was about, and expected fully for his crews to perform to the standard he expressed. "Our nation built this ship. And the guns are the reason this ship is at sea. We serve the guns. You have used carronades for only close-up work, but on *Epevier* we used them for long bowls and made them stick. For this first exercise," Curran went on, "I will lay and aim at the far targets, and I'll teach each gun captain to do the same. We will do this together, as a team."

"On deck!" Pelles barked. "Fore and aft, by divisions, make ready your guns!"

"The far targets, Mister Curran?" Padeen whispered, "them to starboard?"

Curran nodded. "Lay hold."

Padeen spat on his hands. "All right, you swabs! Out tompions! Lay hold and heave! Load powder and ball! Ram home!"

The word "ready" relayed down the deck. Then silence.

On the quarterdeck, Pybus was at the wheel, nursing the ship parallel with the first line of floating barrels, two hundred yards to leeward. Beyond them, barely visible, was the second set, barrels marked with staves and strips of canvas.

Pelles' voice carried across the deck. "The exercise shall be undertaken by divisions. Long guns, the far targets, carronades and chasers the closer sets. From forward to aft, lay fire on your individual targets, and reload and fire until they are destroyed."

Curran saw Nolan standing with the captain by the quarterdeck rail. Pelles reached into his vest and removed his watch. "First division!" Pelles shouted. "Fire as they bear!"

In the bow, Kerr's division opened fire. The first gun, a long 24, went off with a thundering crash. A white cloud gushed out across the water, stabbed through its center with an orange tongue of fire. Another gun a second later, and then two in the same instant; merged into the crashing was the whirr of the outgoing shot. At the first raft the balls struck up twenty-foot splashes of water, the first wide and the second just over. The last fell short, then jagged directly over the barrels, shaving off a foot-long splinter before caroming off the top of a swell and tearing up a rooster tail of foam—a fearsome and beautiful sight. There was a length of silence, seventy or eighty seconds, and the firing resumed; blast after blast, the shattered target hit again and again.

The standard of gunnery was excellent, as good as Curran had ever seen. A muffled cheer could be heard below and forward, but Pelles' expression was blank.

"Silence on deck!" the captain boomed. "Apes, sir! Gibraltar's own apes can chatter when they throw a rock." The captain's voice could be heard through two feet of oak. He yelled, "Second division, fire as they bear."

Directly below his feet Curran felt the thud of the after battery. Smoke boiled out from the ports, and a shock passed up through the deck, making the sails shiver. By the targets solid columns of water went skyward; a loud slapping sound was followed by a howl as another 24-pound ball slammed into the surface and wobbled off into the sky. The guns fired one after another. The period of silence between the salvos seemed shorter, and the target was soon battered and sinking.

Pelles came down the ladder from the quarterdeck, his fist twisted up in his lapel. He walked past Curran's division without a glance and stopped at the mainmast. The guns below were quickly run in and loaded. Forward, Wainwright stood by, almost trembling. His men spat on their hands in anticipation.

"Fire, Mister Wainwright."

Wainwright barked the command, or did his best, but his voice cracked somewhere in the middle of the second consonant. The roar of the guns blotted out his embarrassment. Water went up on both sides of the target, framing it like gateposts. A cannonball punctured and swept away one of the barrels on raft number two, the glory of a direct hit undone by a voice below saying, "Jaysus, they hit the wrong fookin' target."

Varney's division had made the error, and the entire ship knew it. On the last raft, the scarecrow still bobbed defiantly, the petticoat waving in the breeze. Pelles walked back from the mainmast to the quarterdeck ladder, his sea boots thumping on the deck. Curran's ears were ringing, but the silence behind him was even more unsettling.

The captain moved aft to the quarterdeck ladder and said quietly, "Well, Mister Curran. I leave it to you to complete this comedy. You may fire as you bear."

Coming up to the beam was the rippling petticoat, now more than five hundred yards away, opening diagonally and dipping slightly in the swell. Padeen glanced at Curran; the closer set of targets beckoned.

"Cock your weapons," Curran said softly. Locks went back one after another like a series of doors latching. Curran squinted out at the far line of targets. As they rose in the swell, he quietly said to one of the Bannon brothers, "Engage the second line. Left, handsome does it. Three inches. An inch more."

The aimers worked their crows under the carriage and the carronade yawed over.

"The whole battery now, at your crows, the muzzles left. Another inch . . ."

All of the guns were heaved and the trucks squealed in protest. The ship seemed to hold its breath, and it was Pelles who exhaled: "Jesus and everyone else! Before Christmas, Mister Curran!"

Out of the corner of his eye Curran saw Wainwright twisting his hands, but he still did not fire. He whispered to Padeen, "Steady. Wait for the roll . . . up now . . . fire!"

Padeen jerked the lanyard, the flintlock snapped, and number fifteen went off with a thud. Curran moved quickly down the line, taking but half a second to check the lay of each gun before shouting, "Fire!"

Round shot whirred past the close targets. Traveling low and close to the surface, they seemed to hang in the air. Every man who had expected the nearest row to be struck now blinked in disbelief; a splash came down in front of the most distant target, skipped once, and then struck square. On the raft, the melon atop Wainwright's scarecrow was swept away in a green-yellow puff. A second ball hit the target on the fly. The oar shaft splintered into a thousand tiny bits and dashed up the water like gravel thrown into a pond. The third ball went home: a direct hit. The barrels exploded, splinters and cooper's hoops caterwauling up into the air. Each of the remaining four shots struck the same spot, one huge splash on top of another six hundred yards out—twice as far as any hand on board had seen a carronade brought to bear. The target barrels disintegrated, and the petticoat was sent twenty feet into the air, slinging water in crazy circles. The pillars of water came down with the sound of a rainstorm, hissing and buzzing, and then a blasted tatter of underskirt floated to leeward and was swept behind a wave without a sound.

"Cease fire," Pelles said, his eyes gleaming.

From below and then above came cheering, whoops, and yahoos. Men stuck their heads out of gun ports, craning their necks to look up and see what magic had laid the guns.

"Mister Curran, I have hope for our country yet. You may secure your guns, sir. Well done." Pelles raised his voice. "For the rest of you, an example has been set. By divisions, make ready your guns. It will be a long day for the awkward!"

The Bannon brothers congratulated each other, and the Bugis embraced and then salaamed. Padeen stepped forward. "Better shootin' I never saw, sir. Never in me life have I seen the equal. Not to be impertinent, like."

As the other guns were run out, Curran's men swabbed out theirs, reloaded, returned the tompions, and bowsed them fast. Curran looked up as the captain mounted the ladder. Nolan was standing near the railing at the quarterdeck break. As Curran watched, Nolan looked down at Bastard's Alley, smiled, and lifted his hat.

IN HIS FIRST WEEKS ON BOARD NOLAN WORE A MASK EVERY MOMENT HE WAS not alone, assuming the part of a quiet, cheerful, observant man. He asked no favors of the men charged with his custody, and he took no liberties. He ate what he was served, kept his cabin immaculate, and took his daily turn on deck. When he appeared on the quarterdeck, Nolan took pains to do so in his best clothing, always wearing his round hat and a plain black cockade. He did not interfere with the officers or men at their duty, neither initiating conversation nor avoiding it if it were offered. He never declined when asked to help a sailor with a task of reading or adding sums. He was touchingly grateful for scraps of canvas, broken needles, or bits of thread from the sailmaker. To all hands, Nolan was unfailingly polite and graciously thankful for even the smallest courtesy. Not quite a member of the ship's company but familiar, ever respectful to them all, Nolan was now treated as part of the ship, if not as a member of her crew.

Curran began to feel himself more of a fixture in the watch schedule and in the wardroom. In particular, Doctor Darby was good company—slightly eccentric, very widely read, and occasionally even witty. Leslie and Kerr showed themselves every day to be hardworking, optimistic, and well respected, even loved, by their men. MacQuarrie too was a fine shipmate. His Marines were crisp in their green wool and leather jackets, pipe-clayed and shined to perfection, and were run like a clock by Sergeant Lachat.

But Curran found a few of his messmates to be less than genial company. There was Fentress, who was always brusque and perhaps even inconsiderate; what others weighed before they spoke, he fired double-shotted into conversation. He was incompletely informed on some matters but held his opinions firmly. If he was corrected or contradicted at table, he would look the matter up in Doctor Darby's copy of the *Encyclopaedia Britannica*. To his credit, when he was wrong, Fentress would quickly come over to the truth. Though he would readily cede his former opinions, when armed with fresh information Fentress would hold forth with the evangelism of a convert, a cardinal, or even a pope. Varney was another to be wary of. Curran learned he had a habit of demanding satisfaction over small insults. A stiff-necked, belligerent appreciation of his own self-worth made the Marine too vain by half. Varney had shot dead a midshipman in Syracuse and wounded a brother Marine officer ashore in Beyrut. Affairs of honor had quite gone into the past, and were strongly condemned by the Navy Department. It might have occurred to Varney that his interviews were among the several reasons he was still a lieutenant.

Yet by and large, the ship was good-natured; taut but not overly strict. The tone set by Erskine in the wardroom was collegial. The officers, to a man, knew the ship and their duty. It was only Piggen and Varney who seemed to have formed any sort of clique. As Curran came to appreciate this he joined the rest of the mess in patiently humoring them.

Nolan's second wardroom supper passed without incident, but it was also without much joy. Varney, of course, absented himself, and Leslie was on deck; any meal without Mister Leslie was likely to be less witty. Fentress, still smarting from Erskine's stern rebuke, also asked to be excused, and the empty chairs made everyone careful in speech and precise in etiquette. Nolan arrived in the wardroom as he had before, exactly at the stroke of six bells. Curran noticed that he wore the better of his two jackets, a swallowtail no longer exactly Prussian blue, with lapels and facings more rose colored than crimson. On deck, Nolan wore duck trousers and a thin linen shirt without a waistcoat. His buttons were of unadorned brass, and though Nolan did his best to polish them with ash from the stove, they did not glitter. His stock was leather, the same sort that the Marines wore, a bit old-fashioned but durable, and it was tied precisely.

Curran welcomed Nolan, as did Kerr, Erskine, and Doctor Darby. Nolan came into the wardroom carrying two books: the *Enchiridion* by Epictetus and a thin volume of Sappho, half of the library Curran had seen in his cabin.

"I have come to do some horse-trading," Nolan said. "I have two books to loan and would be thankful for anything you might have to read."

There was an awkward pause. Erskine considered what might be offered in exchange, what in the wardroom cases might be safe, but Curran took the books from Nolan and covered bravely. "I have books," he said, and he went to the case and took out a copy of Shakespeare's plays and a novel by Maria Edgeworth; Curran knew both to be safe enough. Shakespeare never once wrote the word "America," and Edgeworth cared for Britain more than any other place. Curran could tell at once that Nolan had often had the Bard palmed off on him, but the Edgeworth was new.

"I am an old hand at Shakespeare," Nolan smiled. "But thank you for the novel. I will return it directly."

Erskine was glad the incident had been handled and was anxious to start the meal. Mouths stuffed with supper were less likely to make mischief. Nolan again took a seat across from Curran, acknowledging the several empty chairs and taking their message. As pumpkin soup was served out, Nolan was polite but slightly reserved. The conversation at this second meal was generally very tepid, dealing first very completely with the weather, and Nolan had as much to add as any man who had been so many years at sea. He agreed that dawn in these waters was probably the most spectacular any human could ever witness, and even though the glass had been rising, the high, ragged clouds above promised continued fair sailing.

The soup bowls were taken up and supper was brought in from the pantry: colcannon, as hot as it could be made. It was not as pleasing to the eye as paella, but it was a much-loved sea dish and put to good use the remains of the fine loin of veal that had been served at dinner. As is often the case in ship's messes, the conversation drifted into a technical discussion of naval architecture, the state of the rigging, and the relative merits of different sail plans and the rigs of warships that the members had sailed in. Nolan ate quietly, knowing that any comments he might make would be taken, per force, as those of an amateur.

As the ship had entered warmer waters there had been many flying fish about, and Curran was relieved when Darby turned the conversation to them.

"I have noticed that several of the less unintelligent species of flying fish were in the rigging this morning," Darby said, helping himself to a bowl of peas.

"Which ones are the smart ones, Doctor?" asked MacQuarrie with a smirk. Darby often expounded on intelligence as the principal force that animated nature, and MacQuarrie knew how to goad his friend.

Darby returned archly, "I am sure that even the Marines have noticed that it is far less likely to find a four-winged fish aboard a vessel at daylight, stranded, than it is to find a two-winged fish. This obviously says something about their native state of wariness."

"You speak of *Cypselurys heterurus*, sir?" asked Nolan. "The Atlantic four wing?"

"Yes, precisely," smiled Darby. "I am surprised you are conversant in the Linnaean nomenclature, sir."

"There was a copy of Linnaeus' *Systema Naturae* on my last cruise. I had time to read it from cover to cover," Nolan said.

Curran smiled. "I find the pictures more edifying than the Latin."

"It's only a matter of practice, I think, Mister Curran," said Nolan. "My tutors made it very clear to me that my skull was thicker than a Roman milestone."

"Linnaeus does not say much of the genus *Cypeslurus*, though there is, I understand, a separate species, equally intelligent, that inhabits the Pacific Ocean." Darby said this as he elbowed Mister Piggen and pointed to the jug of cider.

"Off the coast of Alta California, Doctor, I have seen the four wing."

"You've sailed in the Pacific, Mister Nolan?" asked Ward.

"I have sir, aboard *Essex* and *Holyoke*."

Curran saw Erskine pass a look to Mister Leslie—*Holyoke*'s rakish sail plan had been a topic of discussion at a previous meal—and it was Captain Pelles himself who had once been her first lieutenant. Nolan had not mentioned either ship when the officers had argued about their studding sails.

Doctor Darby returned to his fish. "Have you found, Mister Nolan, that the fish most likely to come aboard are *Cypselurus melanurus*, the two-winged variety?"

"I have seen both come aboard, sir."

"One more than the other?"

"In roughly equal numbers, I reckon, though I could not say precisely."

"It's my opinion that the four wing is the more intelligent of the two. Fewer seem to come through gun ports or come to grief in the hammock netting come morning."

"Might they be less blind or merely less stupid?" Kerr grinned.

"Maybe them four wings just fly better," said Piggen.

Nolan smiled. "Admirable hypotheses, gentlemen." He raised his glass, sipped, and then said to Doctor Darby, "I'm not a trained anatomist, Doctor, as you are, but I have observed that both species are much alike in their eyes and what little there is of their brains."

"Have you dissected them, sir?"

"Well, after a fashion, and only with my pen knife. But I have eaten probably thousands of them, of both species. I've become familiar with their organs and such."

Silence jolted across the table. If Nolan had said he had eaten musket balls it might have been less of a shock.

"I have heard they are eaten in the Leeward Isles," said Curran. He did not add the words "because people were starving."

"It was in the Leewards that necessity forced on me the experiment," said Nolan. "But I had also the encouragement of the cook on *Hornet*, who assured me I would not perish from the attempt. He was a Barbadian, a wonderful artisan with the camboose."

"A liberated Negro, no doubt," said Piggen.

"He was a white man, sir. Jemmy Witherspoon, one of the distressed class of the island who are called Red Legs on account of their sunburns. Irishmen they are, in the main. Witherspoon told me he had eaten them as a child, and I was persuaded one morning to eat a freshly caught specimen."

"How are they eaten, Mister Nolan?" asked MacQuarrie. "The fish, I mean; are they any good?"

"An old one is not very savory. But a fresh one is very delicate, especially if you are lucky enough to have a lime in your pocket. As I said, I have had occasion to dine on flying fish, both intelligent and unintelligent, for the last several years."

Nolan had a greater familiarity with both species than he admitted. On several of his voyages, flying fish had been a principal source of his food. He was used to gathering them up from the decks at dawn, and when the ship's cook was sympathetic, having them fried for his breakfast. On *Hornet*, where he had been denied ship's rations, he had occasionally resorted to eating them raw, which he found was possible if sliced very thin and dusted with a pinch of powdered mustard.

Another somewhat embarrassed silence followed, and Nolan was gracious enough to staunch it. He stood and placed his napkin on the table. "Gentlemen, I thank you for supper and for the books. The meal and your company were first rate." He bowed to Mister Erskine. "May I have permission to leave the mess, sir?"

"Of course, Mister Nolan. A good evening to you."

As Nolan took his leave, Curran and the others felt a small jolt of pity but a more pronounced feeling of relief. Even though the conversation had ultimately taken some interesting turns, talk at supper had to be kept away from the most natural topics—letters from family and home.

"An interesting gentleman," said Darby. "He is very well informed."

Erskine narrowed his eyes, thinking. "Mister Curran, you were in the Atlantic Squadron—who commanded *Hornet* in 1815? Was it Biddle?"

"Sir, it was. It was him that took HMS *Penguin*."

Darby huffed, "Penguins and peacocks. And HMS *Peacock* became USS *Peacock*."

"And USS *Peacock* took HMS *Epevier*, which became USS *Epevier*," smiled MacQuarrie, who'd had a hand in that dashing action.

Curran raised his glass to MacQuarrie. "A fine afternoon's work, sir."

"Damn me if it don't seem we should just rent ships from the British," said Darby. "For now they sail HMS *Chesapeake* and HMS *President*. It is a right merry-go-round."

"*Chesapeake* and *President*, bah. Let us not mention those vile, unhappy ships, sir," tutted Piggen. "It is bad luck. Worse than whistling on deck."

Erskine was still considering *Hornet*. "Did you know Captain Biddle, Mister Curran? Was he a bit of a hard horse?"

"I met him several times. He was very cordial, sir, very accommodating. An ardent officer, though."

"I wonder that Nolan had to eat flying fish while aboard, and not Christian food. I wonder if he was not treated harshly."

Curran wondered too, for like the others he'd heard that only the Spanish—the cruel Spanish—and sailors starving and adrift in lifeboats ate flying fish.

"I think I know the reason," MacQuarrie said. His rank entitled him to express his opinion freely. "It did not occur to me until just now, but when I was in the Atlantic Squadron I heard it from scuttlebutt that *Hornet* had a prisoner aboard, some sort of traitor. I am certain now that person was Nolan. *Hornet*'s first lieutenant was a man named Hansen."

Erskine nodded; he had served with Hansen on a previous commission. "John Hansen?" he asked.

"The same," MacQuarrie said. "His family had been killed and his house burned at Hampton when the British came up past Norfolk in 1812. It was, as you might remember, on their way to burn Washington City. It was a very, very ugly affair."

No one at the table had forgotten: "Remember Hampton" had been a rallying cry during the War of 1812. After being repulsed from Norfolk the British had shelled and rocketed the town of Hampton, brushing aside a company of local militia. They landed forty boats of troops; a regular British regiment, the 102nd Foot, murdered American prisoners of war and then ran riot in the town, raping and burning.

Erskine said quietly, "Knowing what I do of Hansen—he was a very zealous cove, a right tartar—I am ready to believe that when he had custody of Nolan, flying fish was all that Nolan had to eat."

"Sure, there is a reason Nolan is treated so," Piggen said. The purser was particular friends with Lieutenant Varney and had absorbed his prejudices. "The man is an enemy to our nation. A traitor who should have been hanged. It shows how merciful is the government that he was not hung up on a gibbet."

Curran said nothing to Piggen, but he was coming to the opinion that Nolan had not been shown mercy, but quite the opposite.

After the cloth was drawn, Curran went on deck to take the evening's observation. It was one of the rare nights when an officer's watch schedule allowed a full night's sleep, and after the sight had been reduced and the chart pricked, Curran stretched out on his berth. He found Nolan's copy of Epictetus and pulled it into the circle of lamplight. A similar volume had been Curran's grammar when he was a boy, Latin on one page and English opposite, four slender books out of eight of the philosopher's famous *Discourses*. Alive in the second century AD, Epictetus had been a Roman slave banished to Greece for speaking of self-reliance. The great man himself wrote nothing, and might even have been illiterate. What there was of his work had been compiled by one of his students. Curran recalled that even the philosopher's name was suspect, *epiktetos* in Greek meaning "acquired"—less likely a man's name than a line from a slave dealer's ledger.

Nolan's copy of the *Enchiridion* was worn and obviously treasured. Betrayed by the binding, the book fell open to a place where the ink seemed eye-worn. "You are exiled. You must die—but must you die groaning too? What hinders you, then, but that you may go smiling, and cheerful, and serene?" Sixteen hundred years ago these were the philosopher's words—a man unbroken though deprived of his liberty, made a slave, and cast on a foreign shore. Curran turned the pages of the familiar text and found another passage marked in pencil: "For our country and friends we ought to be ready to perform or undergo the greatest difficulties." At that place Nolan had written in the margin, "What is one man but an atom of his nation?"

Curran turned a few pages and read: "When you are insulted, or provoked by taunts, remember that it is your own judgment that goads you. Be not quick to answer. For if you gain time and respite, you will more easily command yourself."

Tucked into the end of the book was a small scrap of newspaper, an old tatter long ago gone yellow. It was from the topmost portion of the *Columbia Centennial*, a Boston paper frequently sent to sea with the packet boats. The name of the city, the date, as well as the Federalist eagle on the paper's masthead had been cut away with scissors. Curran lifted the scrap and read a column under a short black border:

> DIED—In the Osage country, WHITECHAIR, the principal Chief of the Osage Tribe of Indians: After an illness of short duration. Upward of 100 Osages have gathered since July and are of the opinion that something supernatural caused his death. Word is about that they must kill one of the Pawnee nation to appease his ghost—

The piece ended in mid-sentence. Almost expecting the obituary to continue, Curran glanced at the reverse of the page. There, the torn paper neatly bordered a short item in single column:

> VISITORS OF DISTINCTION—Doctor Andrew Graff and his bride have arrived in Town of yesterday. Doctor Graff will speak at the Harvard University Medical School. On Saturday morning last, Doctor Graff was married to Miss Lorina Rutledge, in the city of [the word "Philadelphia" was inked out]. After lectures, the couple will take ship to Lisbon and the Continent for an extended tour.

The scrap had been placed among the final fragments of the *Enchiridion*, the newsprint putting down a yellow smudge that spilled into the gutter between pages. Curran could not imagine that the death of an Osage chieftain or a lecture at Harvard could have been of much interest to Nolan. There was no date visible on the scrap of newsprint, rendering it timeless. If Miss Rutledge had been a sweetheart, it was a cruel bit of paper for Nolan to have read—and much stranger for him to have kept. On the page marked by this sad tatter Curran read:

> A man needs but little, and no chains are heavier than those wrought by frustrated desire.

The ship was quiet, and Curran could hear the steady creaking of falls and blocks in the tiller room as the helmsman made a thousand small corrections to steady the ship. He replaced the sad piece of newspaper, carefully aligning it to the stain.

Curran turned to the front of the book and opened the flyleaf. There, in blue ink, a jagged hand had written: "*Illae stellae, docebit vos.*"

There is something about a language taken up in childhood that puts words so close to thought that translation is no longer necessary. Curran had been reading Nolan's book now for most of the last watch, and his Latin grammar had returned in full gallop. The words written on the flyleaf burst fully and directly into comprehension—not Latin or English, but a voiceless, emotive language pitched directly into his heart: "These stars will guide you."

On the facing page, the same pen had scratched a dedication:

Given to Philip Nolan,
aboard USS Holyoke *off Valparaiso, Chile,*
February 6, 1814
with friendship, Arthur Pelles.

THE AFFRONT

To KNOW THAT A MAN MARKED PASSAGES IN A BOOK MEANT LITTLE—THE *Enchiridion* was a sprawling bit of philosophy, and like any great haystack of words there was much to pick and choose. Besides humility and forbearance, Epictetus urged complete self-confidence; the great Stoic said paradoxically that a man should live like a lion in the mountains and at the same time never contend with others. Taken as a whole, the *Discourses* were nearly as baffling and inconsistent as the Bible or the Koran. Yet a trace of ribbon and a forgotten scrap of newspaper had put down a track through this heaving sea of words, marking a general current of thought. Taken together, the marked passages revealed more about Philip Nolan than he could have ever imagined—much more than his quiet dignity would have wanted known.

During the mid-watch Curran returned to the locked box in the chartroom and opened the leather envelope that held Nolan's dossier and papers. The detail assembled in the prosecutor's files was staggering; some of the facts had been taken from Nolan's military records, but there were other particulars that could only have come from someone who knew Nolan well—very well indeed. Curran was surprised to read biographical summaries dated well after Nolan had been sentenced; a dozen pages more, written in a close, dense copperplate with their paragraphs numbered. Someone among Nolan's friends must have spoken with the government; Curran was left to wonder who and why.

Philip Clinton Nolan was born at Newport during the British occupation of Rhode Island, in the second year of the American Revolutionary War. Nolan's widowed mother, Hester Bryne Nolan, was the mistress of Sir Henry Clinton, the British general in command of Royalist forces in New England. That liaison produced two children, Philip and a sister who died in infancy. When the British withdrew from Newport, Mrs. Nolan took the infant Philip and his older half brother, Stephen, to New Orleans and eventually to Texas and Mexico, where the Bryne family had commercial interests.

Philip spent his boyhood in San Jacinto, where his mother's acquaintance with the Conde de Castella Deidra Vigo yielded the family a tract of land on the Arroyo Nogal in east Texas. Fourteen years older than Philip, Stephen Nolan set about building a pueblo on the land and eventually trading in cattle and working as a *guía del terreno*. His labors prospered.

As a child Philip had been amused by a number of tutors at his mother's villa and her apartments in New Orleans. He was precocious and glib, but when it was discovered that beneath his fluent babbling the boy was *illiterate* in both English and Spanish, and ignorant of sums, remainders, products, and quotients, it was decided to put a finer point on his studies. At the age of thirteen Philip was put aboard a ship bound for England, it being thought that he should begin the serious part of his education with his father's people.

This brought Philip Nolan to the Harrow School. His father arranged for Nolan to be boarded with old Mrs. Leith in her ramshackle house near the village chapel. Neither Harrow nor Philip Nolan was to make much of an impression on the other. Mrs. Leith's was a disorderly, decrepit place filled with grasping, unctuous, uncouth, and ignorant boys, from whose example Philip did not profit. These boys soon found Philip to be the very epitome of misconduct, and he led them to new depths of anarchy. For his sundry acts of rebellion, Philip was repeatedly caned. He responded to discipline by running away three times, and his last escape took him as far as Portsmouth. At the docks he attempted to stow away on an Indiaman and sail to Madras. The captain knew Nolan's father and detained the would-be sailor aboard.

Had Philip succeeded in this attempt to run away to sea, the story of his life would have been vastly shorter—for the Indiaman he had tried to join, *Halsewell*, was wrecked a week later, foundering in a blizzard off St. Alban's Head.

Fortunately for Philip, Sir Henry had been nearby at Bath. Unfortunately, his father arrived promptly and with his fury intact. Sir Henry had little time to coddle a wayward child and had Philip sent back to Harrow riding on the outside of the London mail coach; eighteen hours in the wind and cold were intended to remind him of his manners. Half-frozen, Philip returned to school just as word of the *Halsewell* disaster spread through the city.

At Harrow it somehow came to be understood that Philip had *survived* rather than merely *avoided* the shipwreck. This macabre celebrity put Nolan beyond the ken of his peers and outside the wrath of the older boys and many of the masters. His newfound reputation (and Sir Henry's great authority) eventually reconciled Philip to his studies. Nolan had a certain amount of classical history and even Latin whipped into him. His learning—if not his manners at table—was eventually considered sufficient for him to go up to Oxford.

At Magdalen College, Nolan blossomed, taking refuge in history and mathematics. A very modest stipend was enough for Nolan to continue his studies, and he carried on for three semesters, though sometimes with a rumbling stomach. This was a fond, golden time for him, and until his last days Nolan would warmly remember the place of his intellectual awakening.

When Sir Henry died at Portland Place in London, Philip was not invited to the funeral. As he expected, at the end of term a letter came, written by Sir Henry's solicitor. It said that as his lordship had not formally acknowledged Philip's birth, the estate regretted that no further provision could be made for his education. All of the whereases and therefores educed the fact that there were to be no further remittances for tuition or board, and Nolan was to withdraw from university.

Without prospects and without his degree, Nolan took ship for Savannah and rode overland through Alabama and the Mississippi Territory. Nolan arrived to find the country of his birth vastly expanded. The Spanish, fearing the unrestrained migration of American settlers from Louisiana into Texas, had broken diplomatic relations with the United States. The quibbles of nations are frequently the ruin of families, and Nolan arrived at last in New Orleans to find his mother bereft and their family's Texas ranchlands confiscated by the Spanish. Worse, much worse, was the news that Nolan had lost his much-loved stepbrother. After leading a party across the Brazos, Stephen had been ambushed by a squadron of Spanish cavalry. The skirmish would remain obscure to history, but it was cruel enough. Stephen Nolan was shot through the heart and the settlers in his charge were put to the bayonet. Their possessions were sacked, their livestock driven off, and their wagons burned. By way of warning, Stephen Nolan's corpse was lassoed and hung from a white oak.

It was Philip's painful duty to return to Texas, gather his brother's bleached and broken bones, and bury them on the sandy banks of the Arroyo Nogal. Back in New Orleans, Nolan's mother surrendered to grief and laudanum. It was these heart wounds that turned Philip Nolan from a carefree if somewhat studious young man into a soldier.

An appointment to the Military Academy at West Point was arranged. Mrs. Nolan's acquaintances and connexions were of the highest quality; one of the letters written in support of Nolan's appointment was written by the Marquis de Lafayette, and another by Albert Gallatin; both had been friends of Madame Nolan before the war in Paris. No one was surprised when Philip Nolan graduated, two years later, at the top of his class.

A brief posting to Washington City followed, where Nolan endured a sort of ornamental clerkship filing maps at the War Department. General Dearborn happily discovered that Nolan was one of the few officers who had intimate knowledge of the lands between the Brazos and the Rio Grande. What the young officer knew of that country was rapidly wrung out of him in a series of map corrections, synopses, and reports. The quality of this work gained him some attention, and one afternoon Nolan was summoned to the executive mansion to speak to Captain Meriwether Lewis, who was then putting together a reconnoitering expedition grandly called the Corps of Discovery. Lewis had been directed by the president to lead a picked band of men to find the headwaters of the Missouri River, cross the continental divide, and descend via the waters of either the Colorado or Columbia River to the Pacific Ocean. Arrangements were being made in strictest secrecy as portions of the territory to be crossed were claimed by Spain and Britain. Nolan listened to the captain's plans eagerly and volunteered on the spot.

Nolan threw himself into preparations for the expedition, scouring the capital for maps and navigational instruments for Captain Lewis and attending to an unending train of commissary and equipment requirements. Captain Lewis found Nolan's efforts gratifying, but he had need of only a single assistant, and eventually the position of second in command of the expedition was granted to his friend William Clark.

Nolan's disappointment was allayed by a fresh set of orders confirming his commission as a second lieutenant of artillery and engineers and returning him to West Point with assignment to a course of surveying and military fortification under the supervision of Major Jonathan Williams. On completing his course, Nolan was dispatched west, first to Fort Green Ville, and then to Fort Massac on the Ohio River. Then came the fateful, wicked day that he shook the hand of Aaron Burr.

Facts about Nolan loomed, points in a curve, portraying a history but failing to fully illuminate his character. Nolan had traveled much as a child, and though his mother's relations with men were somewhat unorthodox, Madame Nolan could hardly be called outré; Dolley Payne Todd, later the wife of James Madison, was a girlhood friend. Both the Bryne and Nolan families had been well to do, and several prominent and even famous persons were happy to render for Mrs. Nolan and her sons what services they could, Nolan's admission to Oxford and West Point being but two examples.

Yet nothing could have been easy for Nolan; the illegitimacy of his birth opened him to calumny and even disrespect. Ironically, President Jefferson, a great begetter of bastards himself, had a lifelong animus against men of illegitimate birth. That may have been the reason he was left behind by Captain Lewis—the Corps of Discovery was, after all, Jefferson's project. Curran read that Nolan had fought a number of duels, beginning at Oxford and continuing at West Point. He always prevailed, sometimes by the expedient of obtaining apologies, but more often by taking the field, though his last outing had been very nearly fatal. Even now, Nolan's manners were cordial but quite unbendable; he was not a person to be trifled with. Though he was open and pleasant to the people he liked, his sense of personal honor was keen, perhaps even bristling. In these traits he was very much like Captain Pelles. They were much of a type, Pelles and Nolan, both of them from the age when a gentleman's honor was more important than his life.

Curran tied up Nolan's dossier with its black ribbon and opened the naval files; they were nearly as thick. On the back of Nolan's sentence were the endorsements of a dozen American warships: *Revenge* and *Wasp* in the Atlantic, *Holyoke* and *Essex* in the Pacific, *Peacock* in the Indian Ocean, *Independence* and *Intrepid* in the Mediterranean, bomb ketches like *Aetna* and *Vesuvius,* ignominious little gunboats (numbered instead of named), sloops, packets, humble store ships, and illustrious frigates that had sailed in seas of glory: *Essex, Constitution, Constellation.*

Nolan's previous friendship with Captain Pelles was surprising, but it might have been deduced. Only the captain had authority to permit Nolan to walk

Enterprise's quarterdeck. There was also the incident when Pelles had pulled Varney up short for a hint of gossip mongering. It was not surprising that neither Nolan nor Pelles chose to have their friendship advertised. In Nolan's case it would have been both indecorous and presumptuous to claim familiarity with the commanding officer. For Pelles to acknowledge a particular friend among the ship's company would have been equally untoward.

The dedication in the book had been written during the two-year cruise of USS *Holyoke* in the Pacific. When exactly Nolan was put aboard was not recorded but was likely during a rendezvous between the supply ship *Tom Bowline* and *Holyoke* off Valparaiso, Chile, in the middle of March 1813. It was not possible that Nolan and Pelles ignored each other for long in a 140-foot gun brig, and the gift of Epictetus, and its compassionate dedication, spoke of a respectful and solid friendship.

All those years ago, when he was aboard *Essex* and *Holyoke*, even the most fervent of Nolan's detractors must have thought that one day an official letter would come and he would be set free. But that never happened. Perhaps they had already decided in Washington that Nolan's sentence was to be open ended; maybe it had become simply a matter of *non mi ricordo*, but no orders came changing his status. As Nolan was passed from sea to sea, no officer took it upon himself (or his career) to bring him back.

Orders did eventually come for Pelles, and he was transferred from *Holyoke* to the North Atlantic Squadron, an executive officer's billet aboard USS *President* and a brush with both death and glory. When Arthur Pelles and Philip Nolan parted on a bright morning off the coast of Brazil, neither knew when, or if, they would ever meet again. Nolan was transferred to USS *Peacock*, bound for the African cape; from that ship he went into *Hornet*, and then on to a dozen more.

For all its grandeur, a warship at sea is a fragile, temporary conveyance, an imperfect machine made by mortal men. No ship swims forever, and no sailor takes to the sea in perfect peace or safety. For nearly two decades Nolan had ploughed the world's most variable element with indifferent companions close, and the nation's enemies always over the next horizon; a prisoner suspended between a six-inch plank and briny eternity. Exile to the Bastille, a Tower dungeon, or even Siberian banishment would have been more humane.

Curran retied the prosecutor's papers and folded them back into the leather envelope. He replaced the tattered sheet of newsprint into Nolan's book and lined it up carefully with the marks on the page. Curran said nothing to his messmates about what he had read, of the marked passages, or of Pelles' dedication, or the scraps of newspaper. He placed Nolan's copy of the *Enchiridion* on the shelf in the wardroom; the book remained in the mess for several days, there for any officer to read, but no one touched it. As far as Curran knew, no one ever even opened the cover.

A week after it had been loaned, a polite and decent interval, Curran returned the *Enchiridion* to Nolan and awkwardly thanked him for the chance to work on his Latin. Nolan, pleasant and sincere as ever, thanked Curran for the loan of the Edgeworth novel.

Curran had seen grief touch Nolan when he learned he had lost a friend at Fort McHenry. Philip Nolan was flesh and blood, after all. Had his shipmates seen Nolan watching the lights of the departing whale ship, had they seen how his eyes were fixed on the torch and the golden word beneath it, if anyone had seen the look of quiet misery on his face, they would have thought Philip Nolan very much more human still.

AT SEA, TIME IS NEVER SERVED OUT IN JUST PROPORTION. THERE IS ALWAYS TOO little or too much. Weeks may pass in tame, pleasant sameness, and then, without warning, a doldrums of routine can be replaced by shocking panic. In moments of danger, time seems to elongate. A hurricane, a sea battle, or the fall from a topmast—all stretch out in time and resonate in the witness' soul; every life-threatening moment at sea has about it this curious trait. Aboard a ship, pleasure and safety leave almost no mark at all; a routine sunny day is almost instantly forgotten. And it was routine that *Enterprise* settled into. In pleasant days the crew gradually became used to Nolan's presence and his habits. The older hands told the younger ones what his confinement was all about—that he could not be spoken to about the United States and that he could never return. But no one seemed to know exactly *why* Nolan had been exiled. This added, of course, to the mystery surrounding him, and while it could not be helped that some hands disliked him, others instantly held Nolan in a sort of awe.

Even those who shunned him had to admit that Nolan was a decent and courteous shipmate. After so many years at sea, he knew that his company could be an imposition. Sailors talk very often of family and their homes; it might be their favorite subject next to the wind and the state of the sea. Nolan was always careful not to stand too long with any group of men lest his presence put a check on their conversation. A second problem was that of his rank. Even though he was no longer an officer, he was not one of the hands. Aboard a man o'war, what might be said on the mess decks could not be said on the quarterdeck. It was the crew's right to gripe, but it was not their place to do so in front of their officers. Their talk was always constrained when Nolan was about, and he knew it. For this reason he was mostly alone on deck, and it was in these moments that he was likely to be approached by a midshipman flummoxed by a word in *Falcon's Marine Dictionary* or stumped by a page of trigonometry. The mids were a group that economized in everything (including the labor of thought), and they soon came to depend on Nolan's explanations of arithmetic, mathematics, and algebraic processes. These functions were vital to their mastery of celestial navigation and pilotage. The mids were ever mindful of the captain's wrath, and so it was not uncommon to see two or three of them gathered around Nolan before the noon reckoning, hunkered at the main hatchway with books upon their knees. Nolan could always be counted on to supply a trigonometric proof with a gracious smile. He was never patronizing, and even the mysteries of running fixes and axial progression did not discourage him.

Gradually, Nolan became part of a reading circle of midshipmen and officers. Aboard ship it was a common enough way to get rid of time. People took turns reading aloud and others came and went, listening, more or less, while they chewed tobacco. When Nolan was included or nearby, the books did not involve the forbidden topic. That left a wealth of material not published in America—or alluding to it. Nolan had a fine, strong voice, and he read very well. He was especially good at plays and poetry, and his voice was capable of expressing fine emotion. When he read *Macbeth*, his audiences became so rapt that they would hush the fiddler, and even dancers from the forecastle would come aft to the mainmast to sit and listen. One afternoon, while Curran was below, it happened that Nolan joined a circle of mids and several officers. Lieutenant Varney was nearby, chewing, and Mister Piggen joined them, submitting a volume of Walter Scott to the books going round the circle.

The Lay of the Last Minstrel was then in its fifth edition, and though many had heard its praises, few aboard the frigate could say honestly they had read it. Thought to be about Highlanders and Scottish gallantry, the book was considered a safe enough topic. On top of that, the poem was set a full century before America had been discovered. Perhaps the words were not so famous then as they are now. It was certain that neither Nolan nor the listening sailors knew what was coming next—but Varney and Piggen did. They had made sure the book went into Nolan's hand when it was his turn to read. Nolan went peacefully enough through the fifth canto, then turned the page and read aloud:

> *Breathes there the man with soul so dead*
> *Who never to himself has said,*
> *This is my own, my native land.*

The listeners, to man, were embarrassed for Nolan. Discomfited, some wished they could turn the pages forward or magically change the book in his hands to something else—anything else. Nolan began to blush even as he continued; the letters swam before his eyes, and he felt himself losing his presence of mind. His voice hitched, and he skipped ahead, hoping to find a stanza that would not sear him so—but what waited in that poem was worse still:

> *Despite these titles, power and pelf,*
> *The wretch, concentered all in self*
> *Living, shall forfeit fair renown*
> *And doubly dying, shall go down*

To the vile dust from whence he sprung,
Unwept, unhonored and unsung.

With a pained, astonished look, Nolan dropped the book onto the hatch cover. Looking past the silent ring of faces, he turned away and staggered aft, reeling over the deck like a man punched in the gut.

Varney stepped in front of him and said, "Pick that up."

Nolan lifted his eyes. "What?"

"I said pick that up. Are you deaf?"

Behind Varney, Piggen's sallow, pocked face took on a look of base delight.

"That book is my property," Varney barked, "and I'll have you treat it so."

Nolan made a move to walk away, saying, "Please pardon me, sir."

As he tried to pass, Varney put out an arm, jolting him bodily. Nolan's expression changed from sorrow to perplexity, and then to fury.

"Take away your hand," Nolan hissed.

Varney took a quick step back, lifting his fist. Nolan stood still and said softly, "Touch me, and I will beat your brains out."

Piggen glowered, but had enough sense to take a step backward.

"I will not tolerate being handled," Nolan said to Varney. "You will apologize at once."

The deck was as silent as a grave. Varney kept his fist cocked but dared not throw the punch.

"Who are you to tell a gentleman what to do?" minced Piggen.

"Have you trained a puppy to speak for you?" Nolan turned his gaze back on Varney. "Apologize."

"I will not," said the Marine.

"Then I expect to hear from you. Perhaps your greasy friend owns a pencil?"

Piggen made a noise in his throat. Nolan took a step toward Varney. "Now stand aside, you braying jackass, or I'll put you over the hammock netting."

Varney did step aside, but only because he was too furious to form a thought in his head. Nolan turned to the others in the reading circle and bowed slightly, "Good afternoon, gentlemen."

Below the waterline, silence thrummed with the vibration of the passing sea. Curran went down the passageway, past the sentry and toward the open door of Nolan's cabin. A light burned within.

"If you would give us five minutes, Gerrity?" Curran said to the Marine on duty.

"Aye, sir," the sentry said and went forward.

From inside the cabin, Nolan's hand reached across the keeps and opened the door the rest of the way. "Thank you for coming, Mister Curran. I would not have asked to meet you here, but I did not think it would be appropriate to speak on deck." Nolan gestured to the cabin's single chair. "Please," he said, "come in and sit."

Curran ducked into the small compartment. Nolan adjusted the lantern overhead and pulled a three-legged stool from under the folding desk. It was the first time Curran had been in the cabin since Nolan had come on board. He was struck again at how small it was, small but immaculately clean and orderly. Nolan's clothing was hung on a set of triangular wooden dowels, his linen folded and stacked, and his several books put into the fiddled shelves above his bed. He had put a dustcover over the dozen Bibles from the seaman's society—his hat, gloves and belt were placed on top of them.

Nolan cleared his throat. "I regret there has been an incident that may affect my confinement."

"What sort of incident?"

"I have been challenged to a duel." Nolan took up a paper from his desk and handed it over. Curran at once recognized Piggen's spidery scrawl. It took him a few moments longer to comprehend what had been written. The purser, assuming the role of second, was communicating a demand for satisfaction from Lieutenant Varney. For all its quibbling form and strained politeness, the letter was in deadly earnest.

Nolan spoke calmly. "I'll not bore you with my version of who said what, but I will admit that I used some crude expressions."

"Why?"

"I was accosted."

"Were you struck?"

"It was more of a shove. I was inclined to ignore it, but Varney persisted. And when I asked him to apologize, he refused."

Curran looked at the paper and shook his head. Nolan's expression was hard to see in the lantern light, but he did not seem overly concerned.

"Of course, I will need a second," Nolan said, "and I would be honored if you would oblige."

Curran leaned back in disbelief. "I can't allow you to fight a duel, Mister Nolan."

"Am I not still considered a gentleman?"

"You are."

"Then you know this cannot be ignored. Not a shove. I was in my own rights to beat Varney where he stood—but I did not. Out of respect for you and Captain Pelles, I was willing to let the matter drop. I would have." Nolan shrugged at the paper. "It is Varney who has seen fit to call me out. In any case, he is a bully, and if I do not stand up to him his conduct will only become more offensive."

"A few incautious words are a small enough matter."

"They were underlined by a shove, which no gentleman can tolerate, and I suspect the entire incident was deliberately staged." Nolan lowered his voice. "This ship is my entire world. There is no place else I can go." He looked into the shelves above Curran's head. "I would not play Varney's victim in any case. You see, whatever small amount of honor I still possess is precious to me."

"There can be no duels on this ship."

"I will consider a withdrawal of the challenge should he reconsider it, or a simple apology should he come to his senses," Nolan said. "Otherwise, I must insist on the interview going forward."

Curran drew a deep breath.

"I will require a second, Mister Curran, whether or not there is a fight." Nolan paused. "Will you do this for me?"

Curran stood. "You are in my custody," he said. "I am responsible for you. Though I will tell you, sir, I think dueling is a wicked nonsense."

The ship creaked, the note underscored by the droning of the sea around them. Nolan turned his face upward. "Do you think that honor is ridiculous?"

"I do not."

"Then we might agree that it is fragile."

"I've never fought a duel, Mister Nolan, and I do not consider myself less of a gentleman for not going out."

"I do not think less of you either, sir. My ways may be the old ways, but they are mine. If Varney comes to his senses and apologizes, I will happily let the matter drop."

"And if he does not?"

"I am a gentleman, sir."

On the way back to his cabin, Curran thought to order Nolan confined to quarters but reconsidered at once. The challenge had been formally delivered, and the fight would be formally conducted. There was very little chance of the two gentlemen flying at each other on sight, but this was a grave and serious business. Whether he liked it or not, Curran was now functioning as Nolan's second. It was not unusual for seconds to come up with a diplomatic solution, but that took a great deal of intelligence and a flexible mind, two things his counterpart, Piggen, did not possess. Also looming over the matter was the fact that Curran was responsible, militarily responsible, for both Nolan's care and his conduct. Curran did not want to see him hurt, nor could he allow Nolan to harm Lieutenant Varney—no matter what he thought of the man personally.

By the end of the mid-watch Curran had anguished sufficiently over the problem. As he came down into the wardroom, he saw that a light was on in Erskine's cabin and knocked.

"Yes, come in." Erskine smiled as Curran opened the door but saw at once that his expression was a bit more tired than might be expected even of a man who'd just finished an all-night watch. "What's the matter, Mister Curran?"

"I'm sorry to bother you, sir. I need both your opinion as a gentleman and your guidance as an officer."

Erskine listened to the circumstances as Curran knew them, and then read the challenge written by Mister Piggen. He rubbed his eyes. "Jesus Christ," he grunted.

"I realize that these matters are supposed to be kept confidential. But I saw a conflict between what is my clear duty and what might be my obligations as a gentleman."

"You did the right thing to bring this to my attention." Erskine tossed the paper on his desk and pushed the door closed with his foot. "Is there anyone else who knows of this?"

"Piggen, of course, and Varney. I have told no one. But I am sure several of the men witnessed the incident. I thought it best not to make a general investigation."

"Just so."

Curran leaned forward in his chair, placing his elbows on his knees and gripping his hands together. "Do we tell the captain?"

Erskine leaned back in his own chair and cocked his head. "That's the rub. We are obligated to inform the captain of everything that could affect the conduct of the men or the ship. But this is a personal matter, an affair between two gentlemen, even if Varney is a donkey dick."

"I wonder if it all might be ignored. Like a child's tantrum?" Curran said.

"They have a much better way of settling these things before the mast. Nolan would have punched out Varney on the spot. Done and done."

"I have no doubt that Nolan was sorely provoked," Curran said. "He has ignored a dozen slights that I know. Some of them very hurtful."

Erskine nodded. "I have known him off and on for more than a dozen years. I sailed with him on *Brister* when I was just a yonker. He has always been a perfect gentleman. And that is what compounds the problem."

"The captain is cut from the same cloth, isn't he?" Curran observed. "I mean, a fighting sort."

"He is," Erskine nodded. "The Old Mogul is quite particular about points of honor. If he were to get wind of this, I'm sure he'd steer the ship to some desert island and let them play at cutlasses. I don't care very much about Varney, but I care very much about the reputations of our captain and our ship. An intramural duel would be a disgrace."

"Might we find some sort of compromise?"

Erskine shrugged. "From what you tell me, it is not Nolan who is the problem. He would accept a simple apology, and it is his due. The problem is Varney."

"And Piggen."

"That honking fart," Erskine muttered.

"Perhaps, sir, you might have a word with Captain MacQuarrie?"

"He is a decent sort." Erskine put the paper into his desk. "He might be able to talk some sense into Varney." It would not help that MacQuarrie was everything that Varney was not—calm, brave, and dignified—but Varney might at least listen to a superior who reminded him that shooting a prisoner was, at best, not good for a career.

"We might also be able to put this thing about if we transfer one or the other of them off the ship," Erskine said.

Curran thought about the moment he first saw Nolan in Cádiz, rowed to the pier by a silent boat crew. "I'd not like to see him put off for this," Curran said. "It was Varney who started it."

"Varney has friends in Washington. Nolan has none."

Eight bells, and from below came the sounds of reveille, bo'suns roaring, and the ship coming to life as the sun came up.

"You will speak to Mister Piggen?"

"Yes, sir." Curran did not need to add his own opinion of the man. He could hardly better Erskine's assessment. "Perhaps I can make some progress," Curran said, though he was not hopeful.

The executive officer stood; the meeting was over. "God damn me," Erskine yawned, stretching his long arms over his head. "Is that bacon I smell?"

BREAKFAST WAS ALWAYS A SKETCHILY ATTENDED MEAL AS THOSE OFFICERS WHO had been on night watches usually preferred to grab an hour's sleep. On this morning, exhausted from his duties, Curran did exactly that. Navigational chores filled the rest of the morning, and Curran was hungry when the hands were piped to dinner. In the wardroom, he could already feel a diffused sort of grudge lurking under the conversation. At the far end of the table Varney was his usual complacent self. The Marine might even have considered himself a little more charming than usual, joking with the purser and expounding on the new triggers he had put on his pistols. He drank a fair share of the doctor's lager and put away a pair of ham-and-cheddar sandwiches; the prospect of a duel had not affected his appetite in the least.

Each time Varney filled his mug with beer he got louder. Piggen was, as usual, playing Sancho Panza to Varney's Quixote. Curran could see measured glances pass between Erskine and MacQuarrie. They were the two most senior officers in the mess, and it was obvious to a knowing eye that they had spoken. From Darby's scrupulously polite treatment of Piggen, Curran guessed that Erskine might have told him as well. That would not be surprising, as Erskine and Doctor Darby had long been shipmates. It was an awkward meal, and Curran knew that the situation would become increasingly unpleasant until it was resolved.

After dinner, Curran asked Piggen if he might have a word. Showing a mouthful of yellow teeth, the purser answered that he might be able to do so at four bells. The delay did not bode well for their discussion. The postponement was a snub; it was well known that Piggen generally napped after his midday meal.

During the early afternoon, Curran and Pybus went through the navigational fixes, marveling at Nordhoff's and Hall's more outlandish calculations, and at four bells Curran went below. Bleary from the long night, Curran washed his face and shaved. This had the effect of both refreshing him and allowing him to be slightly, but not insultingly, late for his appointment. Reminding himself to be polite, he arrived at Piggen's small office in the after end of the berth deck. It was a low, dark, and cramped part of the ship. Curran knocked and opened the door.

"Oh, there you are," Piggen exhaled, "I was just about go on deck." This was communicated with a straight face, even though the purser was sitting behind his desk in a nightshirt.

"I know you're busy, Mister Piggen. With your permission, I'll get to the point." Curran pushed a box of pen quills to the middle of the cabin and sat.

The little man smirked. "When shall we schedule the interview?"

"I had hoped that we might drop the entire matter."

The lantern winked off the lenses of Piggen's tiny glasses. "That would be impossible without a formal apology. A written apology."

Curran felt his teeth grind. "Piggen, *you* wrote the challenge."

"I did," he said with a vapid sort of pride.

"Are you very familiar with the code, sir?"

"I am," he fibbed.

"It is you who have laid the challenge. It is not Mister Nolan's place to offer an apology. Only an explanation."

"Of course, that is what I meant," Piggen said.

"This is a deadly business, sir. An exacting one."

"You need not inform me of my duties, Mister Curran," Piggen sniffed. "I am a gentleman."

Curran said evenly, "I have read the challenge. I wonder if you might tell me what happened?"

"Lieutenant Varney was insulted."

"I gather that. What were the circumstances?"

Piggen sat back in his chair. "Nolan was reading aloud from a book, and went into a passion. He threw it down and stormed off. Mister Varney merely reminded him that the book was not to be thrown on the deck."

"Were you present?"

"I was. I saw it with my own eyes."

"Whose book was it?"

Piggen made a blank face.

"Who owned the book?" Curran asked.

"I loaned it to Lieutenant Varney."

Curran folded his arms across his chest, studying the man behind the desk. "Mister Piggen, you are aware that Nolan is being kept in a unique, confidential type of custody?"

"Everyone knows it."

"I am responsible that he not read of the United States at any time he is aboard this ship. Nor may he discuss our country with any member of the crew."

"He probably deserves worse for what he done."

"That is not for you to decide, and it is my responsibility to see that he is kept in accordance with his sentence."

"The book had nothing to do with America."

"No. Strictly speaking it did not."

"There. See? It makes his conduct all the more—" Piggen faltered, "well, ungentlemanly like."

"I think, Mister Piggen, that some joke was being made of Nolan. A sort of prank at his expense."

"That's not true."

"Have you read the poem?"

"Yes, I have."

"Perhaps you could have guessed that it might be provocative?"

Piggen shrugged.

"That it might be wounding to a homesick person?"

"You can't be trying to defend his conduct?" Piggen sneered.

"No. But I don't see that you and Varney are without blame."

"Blame? How could that be?"

Curran let a second or two pass. "It would be in the best interests of all of us, and in the best interest of the harmony of the ship, if this challenge were to be withdrawn."

"A gentleman never withdraws a challenge," Piggen huffed.

"He does, sir, when he was mistaken in delivering it," Curran said calmly.

Piggen's face was growing red. "Nolan insulted a commissioned officer, in front of the crew. He threatened to beat him."

"After he was shoved by Lieutenant Varney."

"Well, it was not really a shove."

"Did Varney *touch* Nolan?"

"He might have. I couldn't see."

Curran knew this line of inquiry would go nowhere. Piggen did not know his way very well about affairs of honor; Curran had at least a firm knowledge of the code duello. He had not been out, but he had served on three occasions as a second. Twice he had helped to adjust the disagreement, putting the matter to rest; the third time he had carried a bleeding friend from a dew-covered meadow. Curran guessed that Piggen had never seen a man shot through the face.

"So," Curran said, "we are at an impasse."

Piggen smiled. "I reckon we are."

Curran chose his words carefully. "As you know, sir, if a doubt exists as to who first gave offense, the decision rests with the seconds."

"Of course," Piggen said, though he was anything but firm on the details.

"As a blow was involved—"

"A shove."

"As you will, a *shove*," Curran conceded, "the code does not allow for any apology."

This seemed to delight the purser. "Then Nolan must fight."

"It would seem so," Curran said. "Are we agreed, then, that the matter should proceed strictly in accordance with the code?"

"I am for it, firmly," Piggen said.

"I was hoping you might say that, Piggen. I counted on it."

Piggen bent from the waist, making a sort of sitting bow.

Curran said, "Seconds are considered of equal rank in society . . . " The purser nodded happily. He understood the concept of rank. "And, of course, as we support our respective sides in this affair, we may choose to become involved on the field," Curran said.

The bliss started to evaporate from Piggen's face. "Involved, sir? How do you mean?

"As participants," Curran said pleasantly. "We have the honor, as seconds, to join our principals on the field."

Piggen looked shattered. "The disagreement is between Varney and Nolan."

"And you and me," Curran said, "as seconds. We are at an impasse, are we not?"

Piggen belched nervously. Curran was applying a rigid interpretation of the *Irish* code (the one used in the wild places of Antrim and Sligo), and while it was true enough, it was much more a Hibernian than an American tendency for the seconds to fight alongside the principals.

"I am sure you took up your duties as a second fully informed of these obligations," Curran said. Piggen did not answer. "And, according to the code, as you and I cannot agree, we may resolve to exchange shots ourselves at the same time as the principals. At right angles, of course, and after the principals have fired their first volley."

"I am no pistolero, sir. I don't even own a weapon."

"We can provide you one," Curran said. "You won't need it long."

"But I have no quarrel with you, Mister Curran, no sir-ee," Piggen winced.

"I'm not taking it personally, Piggen. Not at all. It is the code, you understand. Since we can't agree on the particulars of the first offense, we shall fight when the principals do."

"This seems very irregular, sir."

"There is a copy of the code duello in the bookcase in the wardroom. Please, if I am mistaken, only tell me." Curran put his hand on the cabin door. "Now, I'm sure you know that this matter must be kept strictly confidential, especially now that it has become, shall we say, expanded?"

There were two wet spots on Piggen's blotter where his hands had rested.

"Mister Nolan will have to be smuggled off the ship in order to conclude this business, so I'll need some time to make arrangements."

"You need not fight me, Mister Curran." Piggen's face had gone from yellow to gray. "We have no quarrel, do we?"

Curran had no intention of fighting anyone, or of allowing anyone to fight, but Piggen didn't know it. Curran said with all the sincerity he could muster: "Piggen, I regret that I must discharge my duty in this affair. We are both gentlemen and are bound by our obligations. Since we cannot agree, we will exchange two shots, like our principals. Of course, if the matter should resolve itself without us resorting to bloodshed, I would be only too happy. Shooting you once or twice would be a sad way to end our friendship." Curran touched Piggen on the shoulder. "Please pass along my best compliments to Lieutenant Varney. Good day to you, sir."

THE WAIF POLE

IT WAS NO SECRET ON *ENTERPRISE* THAT THE CAPE VERDE ISLANDS WOULD BE the next landfall. Though no announcement was made at quarters, every sailor aboard knew their course, west by south, and some of the brighter ones could even work out a dead reckoning. The Cape Verdes were a logical turning point for a vessel trying to work back to the African coast; besides, the groaning arithmetic from the midshipmen's berth could be heard on the mess deck as far forward as the butts. Even factoring in the preposterous calculations of Mister Hall, most of the crew expected the ship to make Isla Alegranza in the Canary Islands by the end of the week. The weather was agreeable, plain sailing upon a sapphire sea, and no one who had shipped long with Captain Pelles worried much about his destination. He had told them in Cádiz that they would have a cruise against the Barbary pirates, and the Old Mogul knew what he was about.

South and west of Madeira there is no land, only rolling blue ocean a thousand fathoms deep, so it was a matter of some curiosity in the afternoon watch when the masthead reported breakers two points off the starboard bow, at a distance of three miles. Both lookouts confirmed seabirds in profusion over a gray-dark mass that seemed to draw the bottom from passing swells. Waves broke on the mottled form exactly as they would on an isolated rock or ledge, and to the keenest eyes there seemed to be pale strands of kelp drawing back and forth as the sea passed over. A glass was sent aloft, and the lookouts reported an empty boat drifting to the west of the rocks. On the quarterdeck, Captain Pelles lifted his hand against the glare and stared out at the patch of whitened sea.

Now and again a small fountain of water would leap up as though a wave had broken, and the distant boat lifted its prow as the swells passed under. Two hundred feet of painter connected the bow of the boat to the place the waves surged. This increased a sense of mystery, for though the boat was empty, the rock, or whatever it was, could hardly be considered big enough to hide a person. It was very unlikely that even the most fearless African fishermen would be tempting fate in this empty quarter of the sea.

Curran and Mister Pybus were called on deck. Both seemed a little discomfited, for either this phantom reef or the frigate itself was vastly out of place; one or the other was not where it should be. Curran was as sure of his position as Mister Pybus was certain that there were no rocks or islets, charted or uncharted, between

Ilha Deserta, now 150 miles behind them, and Isla Alegranza, the most northerly of the Canary Islands, still 100 miles to the south.

Curran watched as Captain Pelles lifted his glass and studied the breaking waves and the pitching boat. There was a crooked pole set upright amid the surging whitewater, and even more implausibly, a brass lantern swayed back and forth from the top of it.

"What should I make of this, Mister Curran?"

The quarterdeck was silent. The helmsman, the Marine sentry, the officer of the deck, the lookouts, and even the midshipmen were mute. Pelles' question had life and death in it; for a ship to come unexpectedly on a reef was a mortally serious business.

"There is no reef or island on the charts, sir," Curran answered.

"And it would seem we have found one, marked by a lantern, and moored to it is some fool's boat." Pelles lowered his glass.

"I sailed the Atlantic for twenty-five years, sir," said Pybus firmly, "and I ain't never heard of no shoal or foul water south of Funchal."

Pelles again fixed his eye to the telescope, studied the place a while longer, and then said, "You are right."

The entire ship seemed to exhale as Pelles handed the long glass to Curran. "It is not a rock, gentlemen," Pelles said. "It is the carcass of a whale."

Being the most junior lieutenant, Curran was put in charge of the red cutter and sent to investigate the whale and the mysterious empty boat. Nolan was given the captain's permission to go along, and he appeared on deck with his nets and sketchbooks and pencils.

The main yard was backed, the sheaves whirled in their blocks, and the cutter was swung over the side. As the crew dropped down onto the stretchers, Doctor Darby asked to accompany them, as much to see the whale as to assist any distressed mariners who might be in the boat. Curran agreed readily and handed down the doctor's case. Winks passed between *Enterprise*'s old salts, and as the cutter splashed down some wag asked if they might bring back some dandelions since they was goin' ashore on liberty. These exchanges took longer than was strictly proper, and finally Erskine bellowed, "Away the goddamn boat!"

Padeen put the tiller over and the cutter pulled off straight into the eye of the wind. Curran stood in the stern sheets, shifting his weight from one leg to another as the cutter was lifted by a long, even swell. Darby, alive as ever on the sea, named a few of the birds skittering in a white-and-gray helix above breaking waves. As they rowed, the sky took on an eerie copper color and the sea became intensely green. Nolan turned and looked back at *Enterprise*, now under easy sail half a mile to leeward. Behind the ship were the stately domes of three towering thunderheads piled layer upon layer, each gray below, their luminous and white spreading tops touched by the color of sunset.

Between the rollers, the cutter was taken into a series of green troughs, wide as valleys. In these bewitched, silent places cloud scudded above and the sea tilted ever shifting. Padeen held their course true as the oars dipped and recovered, and each time they breasted a swell the twisting cloud of seabirds rose up before them. The cutter would fall again into a trough, the gyre of birds would again disappear from sight, and all that could be seen was a bronze sky supported by pillars of jade-colored cloud. As they pulled within a cable's length, the whale's vast carcass looked even more like an island. The flesh beneath the combing swells was a dull, mottled gray, and the waves went booming over it quite as though they were breaking upon a thing rooted to the ocean floor, sturdy and unyielding as granite.

A trio of whale irons jutted up, stuck fast into the quarter acre of the creature's back. The harpoons held aloft garlands of line tangled like a cat's cradle. Near the whale's head, a long bamboo rod waved back and forth; a lamp fixed to the pole's end wagged like a bell that had lost its tongue. As Nolan watched, the vast, bowed back of the whale seemed to quiver, and water whipped up and over the dappled flesh. Now and again there was a gray or light brown triangle to be seen in the whitewater, and a drumming series of thumps was transmitted into the cutter.

"Keep us to starboard, Padeen," Curran said.

Peering over the gunwale, Nolan could make out the shapes of dozens of sharks in the clear green water, turning onto their backs as they gnawed out chunks of blubber from the side of the whale. The empty places they left were perfect hemispheres, sharply white against the sun-blasted skin of the whale. Each bite was the size of a child. Whatever greed and frenzy was visible from the surface, there was much, much more violence below. In the foam sweeping over the whale's back were smaller sharks, some four and five feet long, somersaulting madly to escape the jaws of others twice and even three times their size. A slick of blood and fat spilled away to leeward, and in its iridescent spiral a dozen more fins curved like scythes, slicing and circling back on tatters of blubber drifting like rags. As the sharks gnawed the carcass and each other, a seabird would occasionally dart toward the water. Nolan watched as one of these birds snatched a bit of flesh from the surface and was suddenly clamped over by a bright, ragged set of teeth. Both the daemon's jaws and the screaming gull vanished in the same instant.

They were close enough.

Curran had only to glance at Padeen, who at once put the tiller over, steering the cutter away from the spattering frenzy and toward the abandoned boat. Double ended, shallow draft, clinker built, it proved to be a whaleboat, painted buff under a dark blue gunwale. Up close, it was plain that the boat had been peppered with musket fire. A dozen holes showed through the thwarts, and her stern was shattered, put through with a 2-pound ball. The name *McKendrie Evans* was painted on the starboard quarter along with the numeral 3. A bit of bloody shirtsleeve fluttered from the gunwale, and under it was painted the name of a home port: Point Judith.

Curran cupped his hands around his mouth. "Ahoy the boat!" When no voice answered, he said, "Put us alongside, Padeen, if you please."

"Give way, starboard. Port side, ship your oars."

The cutter bumped against the whaleboat. Darby skipped over, moving with sureness, for he had been a long time at sea. Curran stood next to Nolan in the stern; from this vantage both could see down into the whaleboat. A foot of blood-tinted water splashed about under the thwarts. The harpoon lines were still made fast to the loggerhead and ran forward through the stem, but every other thing of value had been taken out: the oars were gone, the water casks, line tubs, spades, and lances; the compass and steering oar were absent, as were the men who had worked them.

"Empty," Darby said. "And I cannot tell if the blood aboard is that of man or beast."

Only pirates could have turned whale hunters into prey, and the oarsmen in the cutter deliberately found other places to look—a lost boat and blood spilled by pirates being perhaps the most unlucky things a sailor could gaze upon. Darby's weight had caused the shattered whaleboat to settle, and the sea began to spill into the shot holes, wave and retreat, bloody water out and seawater in, as though the stricken boat was pumping away its lifeblood.

Darby stood on one of the few unbroken seats, looking at the blood on his stockings. Nolan leaned over from the cutter to offer Darby a hand, and a change of color in the water between the boats made them both look down. Nolan thought at first that it must be the shadow of one of the thunderheads—a trick of light. The space between the boats was no longer the deep emerald of the open sea, but was slowly eclipsed by a flat, drab shadow. This visible darkness extended under the entire length of the whaleboat and beyond it forward and aft. With no percepti-ble movement, the shade had taken position between the cutter and the battered whaleboat. It did not seem possible that it could be solid until a swell went over and glittering ripples played upon a surface that seemed suddenly like green-dark velvet. Nolan staggered back when he realized that the phantom below him was the enormous, wide back of a hammerhead shark, nearly twenty feet in length.

Curran and Darby perceived the shark a second after Nolan. Darby had sense enough to sit quietly back down on the whaleboat's centerboard and remain com-pletely still.

"Lord, that is a big fish," he said quietly.

There was a four-foot gap between the cutter and the thwart of the whaleboat, and in this space the hammerhead rolled onto its side, lifting one of the wings of its head three feet out of the water, a great, scalloped arc topped with a yellow eye the size of a pocket watch. The shark's pupil was an oval void centered in blazing cabochon. Its cold, myopic gaze fixed Nolan. Just under the surface, the wide cres-cent of the beast's mouth gaped open, rows of knives above and below. The creature moved in regal formality, sinking back again under the whaleboat and hovering there, its towering dorsal and tail brushing against the keel in a series of careless, hissing thumps. Darby looked down in amazement; the width of the shark's back was half again as broad as the beam of the whaleboat.

The sight of the creature had put rigid attention into the oarsmen, and even Padeen Hoyle, nephew of Neptune himself, had a hard time appearing unimpressed.

"I suppose you should like to rejoin the cutter, Doctor?" Nolan said.

"When you find it convenient, sir," said Darby stiffly. The whaler had begun to settle noticeably, and blood-tinted water washed up around the doctor's shoes. It was one of Darby's firmly held beliefs that the hammerhead shark, having such a capricious headpiece, was the most intellectually endowed of all sea creatures. It stood to reason that so intelligent a creature was quite capable of having preferences about its food. Darby did not share these reflections, but the anxious look on his face made his thoughts fairly obvious.

"Port side, lay your oars across the gunwales," Curran said.

"Handsomely, lads," Padeen added in a hoarse whisper. "Don't make a fuss."

The oars went over, gunwale to gunwale, and Darby clutched at the blades and then the shafts, pulling the whaleboat toward the cutter's side. Darby crawled toward the oars, now forming a bridge between the two boats, and as he pulled himself over, a resounding crack thudded into the whaleboat's keel. The violent jolt knocked Darby off his feet and back into the bilge with a splash.

There was another thump, this one accompanied by a great gush of water thrust up between the boats. As the bubbles cleared, Curran could see that the shark had smashed the whaleboat's keel with its tail. The first blow had unseated the centerboard trunk, springing it from the sole of the boat. Darby had come back to his feet but was upset again when the shark turned and rammed its head into the iron-edged centerboard, shearing it from the whaleboat's keelson. Ripped from the boat, a five-foot section of mahogany fluttered into the bright green depths. The hammerhead moved its tail once and spiraled down in pursuit. In the time it took to blink, the massive fish went out of sight a hundred feet below.

Padeen passed over a line, and as the boats kissed together Darby sprang aboard.

"*Sphyrna zygaena*," Darby muttered, as though a mouthful of Latin might be a charm against becoming a meal. "Would you say the creature was twenty feet long?"

The cutter was all of twenty-six feet, and the shark was every inch as big. "I'd have to agree," Nolan said solemnly.

As the oars were taken back into the cutter the shadow returned, and again one of the great hammers lolled out of the water, massive as a gatepost. The glimmering eye passed over the empty whaleboat, then angled to have a slow look at the men in the cutter before it slid back, unblinking, into the depths. To even the least superstitious it seemed that the shark had cast a yearning, hungry eye.

Curran said firmly, "Ship oars, Padeen. And step the mast."

The hands turned to quietly and Nolan and Darby peered under the foundering whaleboat. Its gunwales were now awash, and its strakes and planks were creaking as the waves began to work the vessel apart. The shark appeared on its starboard quarter, moved deliberately around the whaler, and then turned belly up, striking the boat amidships and heaving it up a foot. The blow transmitted a shock through the water that made the cutter rattle like a tin cup.

"Saint Brendan, help us," said one of the Bannons.

"None of your bad-mouthing, Christopher Bannon, you *mahu!*" said Kanoa firmly. Another of the Hawaiians, Waipahu, chucked Bannon behind the ear.

"What's wrong with you?" the big man hissed.

It was easy enough for the Hawaiians to be disgusted. Kanoa was a prince of royal blood, and from birth he had feared no thing that swam in the sea. Every son of Moloka'i knew, even if the sons of Erin did not, that a man who did not cower would never be harmed by a shark—even a hammerhead the size of *Enterprise* herself. Had Bannon kept silent, Kanoa's own protection would have been granted to the entire boat. The Hawaiians did not fear for their own lives, but mumbled among themselves that they had shipped with a right awkward set of buggers.

"Pipe down you, mokes," growled Padeen. "You heard Mister Curran; rig the damn boat."

The mast swayed up and the stays were made fast. Pillars of light flickered in the opalescent infinity below the cutter, and Nolan looked for a long time where the darkness spread. Nothing moved in the depths. It is one thing to have seen a monster, it is quite another to know where it has gone.

"Ready, sir," said Padeen.

Curran replaced him at the tiller. "Haul away." The mainsail rose and the jib was sheeted home. Curran let the cutter fall off to windward, away from the cursed, foundering whaleboat. The wind was now dead astern, and Curran let the mainsheet out across his knees. The sails billowed as the cutter gathered way.

Nolan and Darby sat in the stern, next to Curran, looking aft. Nolan's expression changed, and as Darby pointed mutely Curran turned around. The shark broached behind the distant whaleboat, this time showing all of its frightfully shaped head, fully six feet across, gray above and milky white below. Water streamed from its cavernous mouth as its head-planes cast a rectangular shadow over the water.

To Nolan, the shark was so gigantic that its movements seemed braked in time. The transom of the whaleboat disappeared into the creature's maw; planks and nails, thwarts and beading wood exploded as the teeth slammed together. As the stern piece splintered, the shark lifted itself up with a second great sweep of its tail. Flailing back and forth, the great rectangular head crashed through the gunwales, shredding the boat like paper. For a moment the wreckage seemed to tremble, then the bow was driven down, the shark's massive back arched, and the stricken craft slipped under in a gush of red, oily foam.

Darby cleared his throat. Curran expected some witticism, but none came. Everyone in the cutter had seen the whaleboat torn to pieces, and most feared they would be next. Curran put the cutter's head around and sheeted home. The ship was a mile to leeward, and between it and the cutter was the whale carcass, surrounded now by an even greater number of sharks. Nolan saw that there was no part of the great whale that did not have a set of jaws fastened to it. The sea around was flecked with constant thrashing, above and below.

A mile to leeward, on the quarterdeck of *Enterprise*, Pelles had seen the shark destroy the whaleboat. A score of others had watched as well, and few believed their eyes. No one in the ship had ever seen a shark of this size. The watch was gathered on the frigate's larboard rail, looking on in dread. Pelles again put his glass on the boat, his lips pressed together in a firm line. As he watched, Curran drove the cutter for all she was worth, up the backs of the swells and skittering down the front. Pelles called for all hands to make more sail.

At the top of each of the wide crests the cutter's sails billowed out, and water hummed along the sides and splashed away from the bow in a pair of fine coils. In the troughs, the wind fluttered to a whisper and the sails went slack; the boat slowed and the tiller became heavy. Curran looked back and cursed out loud; the shadow that dogged them was faster still; winding right and left it came steadily on, wind or no.

Another swell gathered behind the cutter, translucent toward its peak and bottle green at its base. Just as the sails began to fill, the colossal hammerhead rushed from the deep onto the clear, pitching water of a crest. Banking, its fins perpendicular, the shark dashed across the inclined face of the wave; ripples dappled strokes of lightning across its broad, spiteful head. In the apex of the wave, the shark was illuminated in the face of the swell, a shaft of sunlight holding it fast like the glory around an angel. For a moment the shark hung above the cutter's sternpost, its head arced and its wagon-sized back rippling with banded muscle. In an instant it turned, vanishing into one wave then surfacing and turning toward them on the next.

Clinging to the thwart, Nolan drew a breath and held it as the slanting shape swerved back at them. Five feet of dorsal hissed up, cleaving a translucent wake; the tail beat again, and the shark slid headlong against the advancing swell, closing with an appalling burst of speed. The sails shivered as the wave and the menace within it heaved up; the glittering crest touched the transom, and the shark rolled onto its back, extending its lower jaw. In that second, Curran jerked the mainsheet and pulled the tiller toward his chest. Surging forward, the cutter twitched like a startled animal. The stern yawed away from the shark and the swell passed under the transom. In the churning wake Nolan saw the jaws clamp together with a sound like a pistol shot.

"Padeen," Curran bellowed, "start the water!" The big man clutched at the leather straps that fixed the water keg to the thwart. He curled his fingers under the barrel, and Nolan helped him wrestle the ten-gallon firkin over the side. The keg splashed into the wake and the fin scythed toward it. Again the mouth gaped open, and wood splintered as the jaws slammed closed, crumpling the hoops and blasting the head off the barrel with a pounding thump. The shark thrashed its head, scattering the pieces, then dived straight down out of sight.

Curran passed the tiller to Padeen and clawed open the stern locker. "Keep us on a beam reach," he shouted.

"To the ship, sir?"

"Toward the whale, Padeen. Back to the whale and lay us alongside."

Padeen shook his head but steered where he'd been told. In the stern locker Curran did not find what he was looking for. Instead of the standard musket and pistols, there was only a musketoon, an ungainly and clumsy thing, and though there was a powder horn, the cartridge box was empty.

"There is no ammunition." Curran cursed himself. It may have been someone else's duty to place the weapons in the boat, but it had been his responsibility to check them. Curran tossed the weapon back onto the locker in disgust. Behind the boat the shadow rose again. Nolan watched the dorsal rip through the crest of another wave as the big animal circled back for the cutter's wake.

"Is there powder?" Nolan asked.

"In the horn," answered Curran.

Nolan picked up the musketoon, clamped it between his knees, and reached into the locker. He poured a double load of powder down the muzzle.

"We have no shot," grumbled Curran.

"We have these," Nolan answered, plucking the buttons from his round coat and dropping them one by one into the muzzle. Nolan clamped the ramrod between his teeth as Curran tore at his shirt collar for cloth to make a wad. Ahead, fifty yards to starboard, was the whale; below it, a thousand teeth were flashing like sparks. As the cutter came near, several smaller sharks threw themselves at the bow. One of them, a six-foot whitetip, flipped completely out of the water and rebounded off the stem. A lightning slash from Kanoa's hatchet split open its head.

Nolan rammed the patch, buttons, and powder into the barrel. He handed the musketoon to Curran as the cutter dipped into a trough. Curran cupped his hand, poured a pinch of powder into the pan, and snapped the frizzen closed over it.

Curran braced himself against the gunwale. "Take us about, Padeen!"

The helm went over, and the cutter turned instantly, brushing its stern against the carcass of the whale. A dozen smaller sharks scattered just below the surface, and Curran saw Nolan point. In the next instant, jaws and teeth and burning eyes came hurtling over the sternpost in a nightmarish leap. Nolan tumbled backward into the thwart as the mouth gaped outward, a convex horror of interlocking teeth. Curran swung the muzzle over Nolan's head and pulled the trigger.

The flint struck steel, the powder in the frizzen crackled, and Nolan had time to think that the powder had been wet and that they were now lost. Then the weapon went off with a thud and an ear-splitting crack. The concussion of the

point-blank explosion above Nolan's head was stupefying. The shark's great rectangular head twitched back, consumed in gun smoke. Nolan opened his eyes to
see that four of the buttons had opened holes under the shark's mouth and a long
gash had been ripped into the animal's back. The ramrod had been driven through
the shark's right eye like an arrow shot through to the fletch; the creature's blood
was astonishingly red. Shaking its massive head side to side, the shark lurched off
the stern and sank back into the wake. In an instant it was set upon by the others,
struck above and below and ripped to pieces.

A DOZEN STRONG, EAGER SHIPMATES HELPED RECOVER THE CUTTER, AND THE
crew came aboard. Nolan had somehow managed to strike his head as he tumbled into the bottom of the cutter. Though he had doused his face in saltwater
and Darby had mostly staunched the bleeding, much of Nolan's exposed skin was
stained like rust. His uniform coat was crusted with parts of shark, and a few of
the more squeamish averted their eyes even as they congratulated him. Up close,
Curran could see that Nolan's wound, though spectacular, could easily be put right.
He offered his hand. "Well done, Mister Nolan."

Nolan looked pale, but extremely alert. "We are better than the fish," he
grinned. Nolan did not notice that Varney and Piggen had gone below, but Curran
did. They alone among the ship's company had not cheered when the shark was
killed. Pressed by concerned crewmembers, Curran walked aft to give his report
to the captain.

"Welcome aboard, Mister Curran," Pelles said from the binnacle.

"I am mighty happy to be back, Captain."

"Whose boat was it?"

"*McKendrie Evans*, sir, out of Point Judith. Her sides were chewed with grapeshot, but there were no bodies aboard."

"Very well. When you have cleaned up and are at leisure, please join me in my
cabin."

"Aye, aye sir."

As Nolan went below with the doctor, he heard himself saying more than once
that he was fine, that it was a small cut and that he felt good. In truth, his skull
was pounding, and as he pushed the matted hair from his eyes he noticed that his
hands were shaking.

Before the crew was piped to dinner, Doctor Darby prescribed for himself
three ounces of monongahela to rectify his humors and then drew out a quart of
lager for Nolan. Sipping from the can, Nolan winced as the doctor pricked a dozen
catgut stitches into his scalp. Galvanized by the adventure, Darby laughed and
talked. It was perhaps the first time in his life at sea that death had come for him
personally, and his escape had made him almost giddy.

"A knowing and cunning animal, Mister Nolan." Darby lifted his beer in salute.

"Certainly he was," answered Nolan. "And I am glad to say that we were a little bit more intelligent."

"Oh, a trifle more, certainly. You are a nacky cove, Mister Nolan, I declare. I'd have not thought of my buttons in a million years!" Darby took another sip. "The completest thing I ever saw!"

Later on deck the cutter was repaired by lantern light. There were knowing whistles as the carpenter's mates pried thirteen thumb-sized teeth from the counter and stern. One was given to the captain, and one to each of the oarsmen except the Hawaiians, who refused them on religious grounds. The watch had witnessed the chase from start to finish and now listened as the crew of the red cutter narrated a long version of their adventure.

It had been the biggest shark in the world. None as wicked except in the Red Sea. Would have eaten us and been happy for more. As the hyperbole mounted, the Hawaiians stood aloof, arms crossed, assuming the attitudes particular to their heroes of battle. "It was no big thing," Kanoa said.

For the Hawaiians, the ordeal in the boat had not been a close call, but a test of faith. Never in a hundred lives could a pious prince of Moloka'i be harmed by a shark, and the hatchet used to bash the whitetip was handed about as proof. With the forecastle suitably awed, Kanoa then led his countrymen in a fierce, stamping hula, damning the hammerhead and every other skulking thing in the sea.

Six teeth were given to Nolan to replace the buttons on his old round coat, and the armorer promised to mount them with bits of wire. The Irishmen, a bit more impressed, drew crosses on the ones given to them and promptly threw them overboard, muttering in Gaelic, "Saints between us and evil."

CURRAN'S STEWARD BROUGHT BACK HIS UNIFORM COAT, PUT AS RIGHT AS FRESH water, pipe clay, and a stiff brush could make it. In the wardroom, Curran took his supper with the congratulations of his messmates, though the mood was soured slightly when Piggen handed him a docket for six dollars and twenty three cents, the cost of a Springfield armory blunderbuss, with flint, ramrod, leather strap, brass fitting buckle, and cartridge box marked USN.

At six bells Curran met the captain, Pybus, and Erskine in the great cabin. A chart of the Cape Verdes was spread out on the table and weighted at the corners with volumes of merchant ship registers and tide tables for the coast of West Africa.

"Come in, Mister Curran," Pelles said, glancing over the tops of his spectacles. Kanoa rapped on the door behind him and entered in his best blue jacket, carrying a black, lacquered hat under his arm.

"Reporting as ordered, sir," Kanoa said, fixing his eyes someplace beyond the stern lockers.

"Petty Officer Kanoa," Pelles said, "please stand at ease. I understand you were once in the whale fishery."

"I was, too, captain. A harpooner and mate." Kanoa stepped into the circle of light around the chart table.

"Outstanding. What do you know of *McKendrie Evans*?"

"I never sailed on her, but I saw her sometimes on the grounds and in port, too. She hailed from Point Judith, but she was owned by some haoles from Connecticut—meaning no disrespect, sirs. They was Quakers, and a bit close with their money. Kind of an old lady, sir. Meaning the ship, not the owner."

"Was she well found?"

"She was old style. Had a tiller made of whalebone. Ship rigged, 120 feet, maybe 500 ton. Until now she was a lucky ship. And fast. Not like a frigate, sir, but fast enough; and for a whale ship, a right galloper."

"Would *McKendrie Evans* have been homebound?" Pelles asked.

"No, sir. I last seen her twelve month ago, in Narragansett. She was just back from a cruise and only starting to fit out. No way she made her stake by now. I guess she only left New England three, maybe four months. She's probably bound for the Horn by way of the Carroll Grounds. If she was clean—light loaded, sir—she might have peeked in round Cape Verde for some fish."

"This is a chart of Cape Verde, Kanoa," Erskine said. "Where might a whaler have touched?"

Kanoa did not look down at the chart. He navigated between his ears. "She wouldn't make no landfall, not yet."

"Not even for water?" asked Curran.

"She got a year's worth of water stored up, sir, and four years' pork and beef. They'd go nowhere except for whales."

"Obviously they found one."

"And then someone found them," Curran said.

Pelles leaned over the chart, his eyes searching. "Did *McKendrie Evans* carry any cannon?"

"Not hardly, sir—why, nothing but maybe a couple of swivel guns. She had gun ports painted on the side, but that wouldn't fool most people."

"They would not have left a whaleboat adrift?"

Kanoa shook his head. "Never, Captain."

"How many boats did she carry?"

"Four. If they lowered, they probably put 'em all out."

Erskine asked, "Would they have lowered for a whale at night?"

"No, sir. No master I know would. They just started to cruise. No point to be desperate so early. Besides, the best whaling grounds are in the Pacific. They might have come on some right whales for practice, like. Since they was down bound and light, maybe they'd put out. But that whaleboat, Skipper, it hung out a waif pole—that lantern—but for sure they struck their fish in daylight. They were over the horizon, lost the ship temporary like, and tried to ride out overnight."

"The boat was badly shot up, sir," Curran said.

Pelles stared at the chart, calculating distances as well as wind. His dividers tapped places a swarm of pirates might have come from, pirate *boats* being spawned in different places than pirate *ships*. "In your experience, Kanoa, do you know of any whalers that have been attacked and taken by small craft?"

"Maybe in Sumatra, or by Maori off'n New Zealand. It takes brass. There ain't no pirates in the Atlantic, hardly. And no way off no place Portagee, what with they already have slave ships to make money."

Pelles put his elbows down. "Thank you, Kanoa."

The Hawaiian touched his forehead. "Yes, sir."

When he had gone, Pelles rubbed his eyes. "Since they were still made fast to the whale, we can assume the boat's crew was taken by surprise. Had they sensed danger they would have cut loose the fish and sailed away."

"Them whaleboats are right weatherly, sir," Pybus said.

Erskine agreed. "Not many ships could catch them, not going close to the wind. They would not have let a pirate get so close."

Curran remembered the blood washing around in the scuppers and the shattered mass of the whaleboat's stern, sprayed with grapeshot. "Then *McKendrie Evans* is taken, sir?" Curran asked.

Pelles nodded. "I think the whale ship was in pirate hands and sailed right up to the boat and snatched her up. Using false signals she could have recalled all her boats and taken them in turn."

"Why, sir?" asked Pybus. "Why would pirates mess with them little boats if they already had the ship?"

"They can ransom the men," Curran said quietly. "Or sell them as slaves."

"If *McKendrie Evans* has been captured," Erskine said, "it was by a corsair ship and not a gaggle of fishing smacks."

Pelles stood and stretched his right arm behind his neck. "If it is the Sallee or the Algerine, they will try to make for the Gut of Gibraltar. In either case they will have gone north."

Curran noticed a predatory gleam in the captain's eyes.

"Plot a course back to Jebel Musa, Mister Curran; there is not a moment to be lost."

WHAT SHIP?

ADASH OF A PENCIL LAID DOWN A COURSE IN THE MASTER'S CABIN, THE
ship was put about briskly, but the winds were not so easily put in train.
Through the middle watch, *Enterprise* piled on all the sail she could
carry—topgallants, royals, and even topgallant studdingsails—but when dawn
came, she still had no great way on. As the day broadened, the lookouts strained
their eyes, but the horizon revealed only thunderclouds and Venus fading in the
western darkness.

Eight bells, loud and clear; the crew came on deck and stowed hammocks,
most peering up at the masthead lookouts. Judging by their calm silence it was
quickly known that the horizon was empty of ships. A half-hearted thunderstorm
came up, and Nolan sat with Beazee under the companionway, watching the water
run off the luffing sails.

The air about the ship seemed charged, not so much with impatience but with
a general sort of cheerfulness. All hands knew that *Enterprise* was on the hunt,
and breakfast was punctuated with gusts of laughter. It was Thursday, make-and-
mend day, and by the time the sun came fully up the spar deck was crowded with
sailors carrying bundles of slops, ditty bags, pea jackets, and laundry. Some hands
mended, others washed. Younger hands gathered about the old salts, learning basic
stitches and the fine embroidery required for the bowls, legs, and serifs of letters to
be embroidered on hat ribbons.

Almost all the officers were in their oldest working uniforms, some even wearing red liberty caps. The captain himself came on deck in trousers and shirtsleeves,
taking his turn on the holy windward side of the quarterdeck. Pelles leaned over the
hammock netting, sipping coffee and glancing from the horizon to the lookouts with
a calculating expression. Laundry hung about on lines put up between the masts.
This naturally gave the ship a slovenly, disordered appearance, and though it was
a necessary part of shipboard life, there wasn't a hand on board who cared for his
frigate to be seen with drawers, nightshirts, and stockings festooning her decks.

Pelles' eyes narrowed as he watched the general milling about. During a second
cup of coffee he gestured for the officer of the deck, Mister Leslie, and said something quietly. Wainwright, overhearing, grinned with frank delight then bounded
down the quarterdeck ladder. Scooting around piles of clothing, Wainwright ran
down the main hatchway and at once into the sailmaker's cabin. Sailors looked up

and grinned as the boy loped by, his excited happiness passing from man to man like kindling taking light.

Curran came up the main hatchway fresh from a collision with the high-velocity midshipman.

"I have never seen Wainwright move so quickly," said Nolan. "Has he been threatened with death?"

"He ploughed into me on the ladder way, the creature," said Curran. He had been belowdecks and had heard Wainwright squeak to the sailmaker, "The Old Mogul says we are going to ship the mirkins!"

There was laughter aloft from the lookouts, a rare breach of discipline that was quickly corrected by Mister Leslie.

"The crew is very much amused," Nolan said.

Curran smiled. "I think we will soon be amusing the enemy."

Nolan and Curran watched as mending and making were gradually forsaken and every man of the first division went forward and helped carry a series of large, folded sheets of canvas up from the hold. The word spilled up on deck, bringing more laughter and winks with it. There was a good deal of merriment and a rude comment about cookie dusters and the bo's un's daughter's whiskers.

Nolan, at a loss, said finally, "If 'mirkin' is a nautical word, I am not sure I've heard it before."

"It is a word, to be sure. But it's not nautical. Not in its usual usage. It's fairly apt in this case, though, and the crew obviously is delighted in pronouncing it."

"Pray, what does it mean?"

"I am almost embarrassed to say, Mister Nolan. A mirkin is a wig, a sort of distaff toupee that is used to . . . I am not sure I know how to put it."

"I was a soldier once, Mister Curran. You need not be delicate."

"Well, then, it is a hairpiece, used to adorn a woman's pudendum."

Nolan raised his eyebrows. "A wig, sir?"

"Exactly. Hussar's whiskers, as it were."

"Are you practicing on me, sir?"

"I am not. Have you not heard the crew tittering the ridiculous word?"

Captain Pelles called from the quarterdeck rail: "Mister Erskine, we will strike topgallants and stun'sails, and secure the booms. Then furl everything but topsails and fore staysails. But I want it done in a lubberly manner. Gaskets like a rat's nest, and a loose bunt."

"Aye, sir, a mess it is."

On a man o'war, deliberate squalor was unthinkable, but the order was carried out with delighted zeal. Set among the yards and tops, the crewmen who scrambled aloft were eager with a sort of conspiratorial glee.

"Shipping the mirkin is a bit of seagoing wit," said Curran, "and one, I believe, that is peculiar to the crew of *Enterprise*. I would not have known what it meant had I not been run over by Mister Wainwright as he went forward."

Nolan stood with his arms crossed, looking forward in a noncommittal way. Aloft, the yards were set conspicuously askew, and port and starboard men set about hanging the strips of canvas over the side and lacing them into place.

"Pray go on," said Nolan.

Curran continued, "I believe that a mirkin was used to make a certain body part appear more . . . shall we say, eligible. I was told belowdecks that this evolution is one of a number of stratagems, or even pranks, the captain plays upon his adversaries."

"Am I to think this is all some sort of ruse de guerre?"

"It is. They are rigging the cloth over the side to cover the gun ports. Merchant ships often hang painted canvas on their sides so that they might be mistaken for men-of-war—or at least vessels more heavily armed than themselves. See the folded bundles of sailcloth they are rigging forward? They have been painted to almost exactly match the color of the hull. I say 'almost exactly' because the bo'suns have taken great care to mix the paint so that it does not quite match. See it is of a lighter shade, actually gray-blue, using indigo instead of black to match the hull . . . "

"Why would we assume such an obviously transparent disguise?"

"That is the point. They are being hung slightly off the plumb. It is meant to be obviously . . . well, fraudulent."

Nolan looked about. Now that topgallant booms were stowed and the cloth pulled almost neatly across the gun ports, *Enterprise* had taken on a casual, slovenly air. Laundry and scuttlebutts were scattered about the deck, and the sagging clotheslines completed the transformation of a warship into a fat, lazy merchantman.

"Then our disguise is that of a merchant *pretending* to be a frigate?"

"Just so. That is why the colors of the canvas are so obviously wrong—within reason, but not quite the thing. Faded, mind you. It is not likely we would meet a pirate who would willingly take on *Enterprise*, at least not in single-ship combat. But a China ship—especially one homebound—well, for a pirate I reckon that would be almost irresistible."

"I am astonished."

"Mister Nolan, I am too."

In her tattered camouflage *Enterprise* continued north by west. Though her yards were askew she was conned with the greatest attention, her sails trimmed exactly, and aside from the circus on deck, the ship continued to function with exact naval precision. At noon the crewmembers mustered by divisions, presented their clothing and persons to be inspected—freshly scrubbed and in good order—and then were piped to dinner. The watch changed; the midshipmen sweated over their noon plots, and supper came at six bells.

In a saffron-colored dusk the lookouts and even a few volunteers went aloft, but the sea around the ship remained stubbornly and most emphatically empty.

AN UNEVENTFUL NIGHT, THEN DAY, AND NEVER A SAIL ON THE HORIZON. THE watches were called and changed and night came on again. The sun slipped under as a red gibbous moon rose in the east. *Enterprise* ghosted along under all plain sail, the wind having veered in the first dogwatch. To the south, lightning grumbled and crashed below a glowering thunderhead. The ship was quiet. Belowdecks the starboard watch snored away, and above the rigging whispered softly. The ship sailed on, glass after glass, the watch touching neither sheet nor brace.

Curran walked the quarterdeck, scanning to windward with his night glass. It was a hazy darkness, very black under the storm clouds and mottled where the moon shone through. Now and again a streak of lightning went through the gloom, pricking the eyes of the watch and revealing Mister Wainwright dozing on one of the aft carronades, his hands deep in his pockets and his chin on his chest.

In the yellow-orange light of the binnacle, one of the Bannon brothers steered the ship. Beside him, a Marine stood as still and silent as a bollard. At four bells, Curran roused Wainwright and had him toss the log: three knots and two fathoms; steerageway and not much more. Curran considered setting more sail, but with a squall booming away to the south it did not seem worth putting men aloft just to send them up again twenty minutes later to reef. Water whispered down the side, and Wainwright returned to his spot on the gun carriage. Curran resumed his steady pace to and fro, and when he had gone three times from taffrail to helm he stopped.

Stephen Bannon noticed the officer's short halt at once, and while the Marine remained stationary, the quartermaster inclined his head. Curran glanced to windward and then walked to the empty larboard hammock nets. The wind came in short, irregular puffs, occasionally west of north. Curran turned and his eyes found Bannon's. He said nothing but his expression formed a question mark.

Curran looked aft and said, "Mister Wainwright." And then again: "Midshipman Wainwright." A shadow stirred on the carronade slide, mumbling something that sounded like a girl's name. The Marine of the watch stepped out of the darkness and came back toward the wheel, propelling the midshipman as respectfully as possible by his collar.

"I was just coming over, sir," Wainwright yawned. His face was pink in the binnacle's light.

"Mister Wainwright. Please give the captain my compliments and ask him if it would be convenient to join us on the quarterdeck."

Wainwright's eyes and mouth became a perfect set of Os. "What for?" he sputtered. Curran gave the boy a withering look. Wainwright quickly assembled his sleep-numbed wits. "I mean, is there anything wrong?"

"If there was something wrong, Midshipman Wainwright, I am certain that you would be the last person aboard this ship to apprehend it."

"Why do you want to wake the skipper?"

Curran was scanning the horizon again with his glass. The Marine made a warning face at the midshipman, but Wainwright was too sleepy to see it. "Mister Curran, I don't see why—"

"Mister Wainwright, would you care to spend the rest of the watch towed behind the ship on a hatch cover?"

Wainwright scooted down the companionway three steps at a time. At the wheel, Stephen Bannon stole a glance out to windward. Lightning bloomed, illuminating the sea almost to the horizon. Then all returned to black and gray. Curran held his glass on a point to windward.

"What is it, sir?"

"I don't know, Bannon."

In a moment Captain Pelles came onto the quarterdeck, barefoot and dressed in a nightshirt. The left arm of his gown flapped in the breeze, making him look like a specter. The captain went immediately toward the binnacle, peered into the compass dome and then ran his eyes over the log board.

"Who is the officer of the deck?" he asked.

"I am, Captain." Curran stepped forward, touching his hat. "Good morning, sir. I am sorry to have disturbed you. I know this may sound unusual. I have not made a sighting, but I am pretty sure there is another vessel about."

"Are you clairvoyant, Lieutenant?"

"No, sir," Curran paused. "I think I smell something."

Standing behind the Marine, Wainwright's face went gray.

"When I was a boy with my father in the Levant, off Smyrna—I never forgot it. I never will forget it," Curran said. "A blackbirder, sir. A slave ship."

All of them could sense it now. What before had been an unknown, slightly unpleasant impression was suddenly, very plainly, an odor. Shit, sweat, and misery wafting toward them from somewhere in the dark. Pelles turned to windward and stood for a few moments, his steel gray hair flowing around his head. Off to starboard, thunder made a guttural rattle out in the dark. Pelles called for his night glass and had the running lights extinguished.

Above *Enterprise* the sky was pitch, but ahead the moon poked through the clouds, thrusting down shafts of weak, colorless light. The captain laid his telescope over the empty hammock netting and scanned the horizon, concentrating on the dark sweep of sea to windward. Lightning tore the skies again, branch and bough, and the sea around the ship jumped up emerald green.

In the tops, the lookouts had kept a keen watch and a voice came out of the wind: "On deck, there is a light on the larboard bow."

The captain's voice easily reached the lookout. "Where away?"

"Three points forward of the larboard beam, sir," said the disembodied voice. "Now there's topsails, sir. I can just see them on the rise."

Curran stood beside the captain, straining his own eyes, and in a dull, far-off flicker of lightning he caught sight of a pyramid of silver—a ship-rigged vessel under plain sail. The stranger's stern lights winked white and yellow as she ploughed on, dead north. *Enterprise* was approaching from her starboard quarter. Curran knew, as Pelles did, that on this dirty night *Enterprise* might get very close indeed before she was ever seen.

"Orders, Captain?" Curran said.

Pelles rubbed his face then snatched up the flapping, empty arm of his nightgown. "Rouse the starboard watch, Mister Curran. We'll come to quarters. Have the gun cloths removed, but quietly, no drums."

"Aye, aye, sir."

Pelles handed his night glass to Wainwright. "Be so kind as to wake my steward, Mister Wainwright. I think I'll be wanting some trousers."

Within five minutes the starbolines were turned out of their hammocks, some still frowzy with sleep, but all of them willing. Now Pelles' firm leadership showed its splendid power. The hammocks went into the nettings and the guns were quickly manned. Puddenings and dolphins were sent aloft. The master assumed the conn, the decks were damped and sanded, shot garlands and splinter netting were laid just so, and canvas screens were placed over the magazine hatches. It was a marvel to Curran how efficiently the frigate went from slumber to readiness for battle; in the span of a few minutes *Enterprise* had gone to general quarters in near perfect darkness, with no fuss and almost no noise. The captain's steward helped Pelles into his second-best uniform coat, the one the crew called his "fightin' duds." Erskine came onto the quarterdeck, found the captain in the light of the binnacle, and said, "All guns manned and ready, Captain."

"Very well, Mister Erskine. You may go forward and see to your division. We may have some excitement yet."

"One can hope, sir," the executive officer said. With a bow to Curran, Erskine tromped down the ladder and below.

Above the maintop, Saturn showed briefly through the murk. Around the smudged glow of the planet the sky was thick; to the north, a lump of moon hovered above within a hand's breadth of the horizon. *Enterprise* went on under courses and staysails.

Lightning struck the top of a far-away crest, framing the chase in silver. Curran could see that the stranger was nearly the size of a frigate, with a pale, yellow hull and a crimson band along her gun ports. As *Enterprise* passed downwind, her decks were swept with the reek of the distant ship. Sometimes the smell that came to them was like that of a barn—sometimes it was the more pungent reek of human filth. In the gloom, it was possible for a few of the keener noses to tell the bearing of the chase by the power of the stink.

A rain squall descended, hissing and smoothing the swell. Standing from them on a larboard tack, the stranger was close-hauled and made changes to neither sail nor course as the rain came down. Her gun ports remained closed, marking her as supremely confident, or utterly foolish. When the squall lifted, a pair of gilded stern lights and a gaudy top light loomed out of a lifting curtain, not six hundred yards to windward.

Leaning over the rail at number fourteen, Billy Vanhall smirked, "And she looks like a Baltimore whorehouse." Two or three of his shipmates thought, *You should know*, but only one said it aloud, judging his volume so the crack did not reach the quarterdeck.

"Mister Pybus," Pelles said, "wear, clew up topsails, and we shall catch her wake. Lay me within pistol shot."

The sail trimmers sprang from their guns; courses, topsails, and jibs were quickly put right, and the frigate went about in a smooth, sure arc. The few visible stars turned overhead as *Enterprise* crossed the stranger's wake, her bow surging deep and coming up sharply as Pybus put the helm over. Tack after tack, Pybus pointed her up as far as she would go, nursing every inch to windward. Willed on by four hundred predatory souls, the frigate closed on her prey, pouncing from cloud shadow to squall line, sure and silent.

"Stand by the clew lines," Pelles said. "Gunners, prime your pieces."

The order was repeated in hoarse whispers. *Enterprise* continued to close: a hundred yards, and then fifty—still no hail.

"Let fall!" Pelles called out. The topsails bloomed, the frigate surged deep into the furrow of the stranger's wake and closed hard on the stranger's quarter. By the time Mister Pybus eased the helm *Enterprise* was within fifty yards, and finally she was seen.

Aboard the chase, there was consternation; one of the stern lights went out, and then the other. The chase made to hoist some sort of flag—it went halfway up and fouled in the halyard. Curran could see the ship's gun ports opening in ones and twos, some darkened, some lit, and there was a disorganized waggling of lanterns on deck. Trying to signal was a fool's errand; *Enterprise* was ranging fast on the starboard quarter, now only twenty yards away.

As *Enterprise* crossed the ship's wake, the frigate's towering sails ate the wind out of the stranger's canvas—the mains and courses of the chase flapped and luffed, suddenly slack and dismayed.

Pelles pulled himself onto the quarterdeck rail and threaded his right arm through the mizzen shrouds. Aiming the speaking trumpet he bawled: "What ship is that?"

An answer came back, "What ship is that?"

Pelles jerked the speaking trumpet. "*Enterprise*! What ship is *that*?" There was no response.

Gloomy shapes flitted across the stranger's decks. Curran could make out a circle of men gathered in the glow of a binnacle; the shadows seemed to be arguing. The ships continued parallel, twenty yards apart. Spray flew on board from waves redoubled between the hulls.

Pelles snarled into the trumpet, "If you do not give me a proper answer, I shall put a shot into you."

Again the voice came out of the darkness: "If you fire, we will return a broadside."

Atop the hammock netting, Pelles went rigid with fury. He roared, "For the last time. What bloody fucking ship is that?"

"His Britannic Majesty's ship *Donegal*. Send your boat aboard . . . "

Curran could now plainly detect an accent—English was not the speaker's mother tongue.

Pelles jerked his head toward the conn. "Mister Leslie, give them a rocket."

The flint clinked, and tinder caught under the fuse. With a screaming howl a flare ripped out of the signal rack and tore into the darkness. Dragging a trail of sparks, the cone ignited and came down smoking under a scrap of linen.

What the flare revealed was no British frigate. Two-thirds the length of *Enterprise*, the yellow-hulled ship looked like a slattern—cargo strewn about, guns half-manned, confusion in the rigging aloft. Looking down on her decks, Curran could see crewmen frozen in postures of duty or panic—bewildered as the flare light pinched their eyes.

"Run them out, Mister Erskine!" Pelles barked.

Enterprise's gun ports flashed open; the frigate's entire larboard battery thrust out and thumped against the side. The muzzles of fourteen 29-pound cannon scowled down at the squalid foreigner.

Pelles took aim with the speaking trumpet. "This is the United States frigate *Enterprise*, Captain Arthur Pelles commanding, and I will be goddamned before I send a boat aboard any piss-pot blackbirder." The flare hissed scorn, and *Enterprise* threw rectangular shadows over the twitching sea. "Send a boat and your papers aboard me at once, or I will blow you out of the water."

THE YELLOW SHIP WAS NAMED *AZÓLA*, A SHIP-SLOOP BELONGING TO KING JOÃO VI of the United Kingdom of Portugal, Brazil, and the Algarves. Her appearance and readiness did not do His Christian Majesty any credit, but *Azóla* managed to put a boat over without delay after she had heaved to under the frigate's lee.

An officer came up the gangway briskly, and MacQuarrie's Marines presented arms with precisely measured insolence. Curran was surprised when the officer removed his chapeau; though he had come up the side like a boy, he was a gray, wizened man of sixty. On his red coat he wore a pair of heavily embroidered epaulets and the blue-and-white star of the Military Order of St. John. Pelles did not return the officer's salute, deeming the Marines' courtesy sufficient. Looking about with somber, intelligent eyes, the officer bowed and said in a melancholy voice, "*Je m'appelle Don Diego Paulo Sula, capitaine de la frigate* Azóla. *Votre servant, capitaine.*"

"Don, is it?" Pelles muttered.

Captain Paulo Sula replaced his hat and touched a sailcloth envelope tucked under his thin arm. The old man went on a bit in lisping, accented French. Pelles understood only English and enough Italian to support a love of opera. He was never impressed by flattery, and looked at Curran impatiently for a translation.

Between the accent and the man's wheezing, scratchy voice, Curran could understand only a few pleasantries and the word "*papiers.*" "Captain Paulo Sula regrets that his English is poor. He expresses his compliments and asks if he might present his ship's papers."

Pelles inclined his head as though considering a fly in his soup. "You may speak to him below, Mister Curran. I am to be told at once if there is the least irregularity in his documents."

Don Paulo Sula bowed, apparently not comprehending, and Pelles returned a tight-lipped frown. The Portuguese officer was led down the main companionway, not to the great cabin as he expected but into the wardroom. As the door was opened, Captain Paulo Sula saw the dining table and realized at once that the captain would not receive him. It was an offense to both personal and national pride that he would be quizzed by a junior officer—but there was nothing to be done. He placed his envelope on the baize-covered table and stood until Curran bade him sit.

In the glow of the wardroom lanterns Paulo Sula looked even older. His uniform was long past glory, and the old man did not fill even half of a wardroom chair. From behind one of the cabin doors, Darby snored and farted in his sleep. The captain folded his hands and looked at Curran with what little dignity he could cling to.

Curran poked his head into the pantry and whispered, "Chick, some sherry and cookies. Make it snappy, and put out word I need a hand who speaks Portuguese."

"I thought you talked foreign, sir?"

"Sherry and cookies, and find me a Portuguese speaker. On the double." The wine came in and was apologized for—it had traveled the width of the Atlantic and back—but the shortbread was fresh and made with Irish butter. Curran made small talk, careful to steer the captain into ordinary phrases that he could understand, and after a few pleasantries Sergeant Lachat tapped on the door.

"Enter," Curran said.

"Beggin' pardon, sir. The only hand aboard that can speak good Portagee is Guapo di Silva sir, larboard watch—and he ain't so easy on the eye." The sailor in question had lost most of his lower jaw to a British musketball and had a truly menacing appearance. Lachat continued, "Mister Nolan heard us puttin' out the word and said he spoke the language. He asks if he might be of some help."

"Send him in," Curran said. A moment later, Curran stood as Nolan entered. Captain Paulo Sula sized up Nolan's coat and figured him to be some sort of soldier in undress uniform. He would have been depressed further if he knew Nolan was not an officer but a prisoner.

"Mister Nolan, thank you for coming. Captain Paulo Sula is the master of the ship to leeward."

"Just so," Nolan said. Like everyone else aboard *Enterprise*, Nolan had smelled the yellow ship and knew she trafficked in misery. "Do you wish to examine his commission?" In his cabin, Darby continued to rattle, and Nolan was at once aware of the captain's embarrassment.

"That is the captain's wish," said Curran. "And as he has declined to join us, I hope you will make our guest feel . . . "

"Of course." Nolan made a civil bow and said in excellent Portuguese, "Captain, my name is Philip Nolan. Lieutenant Curran has asked me to assist as interpreter."

Nolan's Portuguese was perfect, without a trace of the grammarless honk of a Verdean or Brazilian colonial, and some of the gray went out of the captain's face.

"It is my pleasure to meet you, *senhor*." The little captain bowed.

THE PORTUGUESE OFFICER EMERGED ON DECK, FOLLOWED BY CURRAN AND Nolan. *Enterprise* still had her weapons manned, and gun crews remained poised near their pieces. Pelles was standing by the quarterdeck break next to Lieutenant Varney and a party of Marines. Their bayonets glittered in the moonlight; had the interview gone badly, three squads of leathernecks were prepared to board.

"Are the ship's papers in order, Mister Curran?"

"They are, sir. Captain Paulo Sula holds a regular commission."

"Does he not carry slaves?"

"There are none aboard now, sir. He has come from Senegal, and he did transport one hundred slaves to the port of Madeira. He has shown me his Portuguese license and the bill of sale."

"An officer with the king's commission was trafficking in slaves?" Pelles huffed.

"I believe it was a bit of a private venture," Curran said. Pelles clenched his jaw and Curran added quickly, "Mister Nolan was good enough to help me make conversation, sir."

"What else have you learned, Mister Nolan?"

"The captain informed me that he saw a corsair ship this morning," Nolan said, "an Algerine. It was sailing in the company of two smaller vessels."

"Was one a whale ship?"

"I asked, sir," Nolan answered. "He said he only saw the others from a great distance. The corsair sailed close but went away when *Azóla* showed Portuguese colors."

There was an arrangement between His Christian Majesty and the Barbary pirates. If *Azóla* had been spared, it was more out of regard for tribute money than respect for the force of Portuguese arms.

"What course was the pirate steering?"

"North sir; north by east."

The two commanders were separated by language but were perfectly fluent in the expression of authority. Paulo Sula slumped in his overlarge uniform and Pelles stood in remote formality. Obviously disgusted, Pelles said coldly, "Mister Curran, he may go."

Captain Paulo Sula touched his hat. He started for the quarterdeck ladder but turned. The words he put together in English were heavily accented, slow, and considered. "Captain Pelles," he said, "you must be aware that we did not see you until you were close aboard." If Pelles was surprised that the man had suddenly learned English, he did not show it. Paulo Sula continued: "We did not answer your hail so we might gain time to man our guns. When you came upon us, I thought you were the corsair come back to attack us."

Pelles said nothing.

Paulo Sula's voice was respectful but unapologetic. "And although, sir, you might find my transportation of Africans to be distasteful, I am permitted by international treaty to engage in the trade. My license is recognized by your government, and it is your own country that is the principal market for enslaved Negroes."

Pelles answered coldly, "I will thank you to leave my ship."

Curran cleared his throat, but Paulo Sula was already walking to the ladder. The Marines presented arms, again with calculated derision, and the small man dropped into his waiting boat.

The Portuguese had left behind him an awkward and lengthening silence. Pelles watched without expression as the captain's gig pulled back to his ship.

"Mister Nolan," Pelles said at last, "I am obliged for your help."

"You're very welcome, Captain."

"I believe that you are still officer of the deck, Mister Curran?"

"I am, sir."

"After we have put about you will please double the lookouts. When we are away from this despicable son of a bitch have the gun crews stand down and replace the canvas over the gun ports." Pelles looked up, considered the rigging, and said, "You may set topgallants while we have both watches on deck. And get us out of this vile stench."

THE THUNDER

NOLAN CREPT INTO HIS CABIN AFTER THE MID-WATCH, PITCHED OFF HIS uniform, and crawled into his cot; he remained under the blanket, watching the slow turn of the lanterns in their gimbals and sensing the easy motion of the ship. Nolan thought of the Portuguese captain, that sad, wizened little man; shame had wafted from him like the reek of his ship. Nolan thought on the nature of guilt; of crimes committed and sins inherited, and eventually the pain returned, quite as fresh as ever.

Nolan hoped he might be forgiven in the next world, but he had accepted that he would never be set free in this one. Christian virtues he retained (charity and forgiveness, the ones chiefly denied to him), but over the years of his sentence the practice of Christianity slipped away from him. Given away were his scapula, rosary, and missal, and put out of mind were the memorized prayers, paternosters, Ave Marias, and the Act of Contrition. Nolan took up Stoicism as his armor, and it had proven its worth for daily living. As a substitute for faith, he found that it kept him from anger and fatal self-pity. Though he was no longer an optimistic man, he started each day as if it were a gift, and the only thing he knew to be eternal was the sea. Nolan did not blame his keepers and did not hate them, not even the brutal tyrants who starved him aboard *Hornet*. He no longer felt animosity toward the military tribunal that had judged him or the nation whose retribution had made him a stateless person. Was this not what he had asked for? The world was his prison, the wind and sea the fortress that kept him. The vastness that daily surrounded Nolan, sometimes the very empty vastness, made the passage of time seem utterly abstract.

Stoicism inoculated Nolan against grief, disappointment, frustration, and jealousy during his waking hours. But there was still one place he was vulnerable—a place where sorrow and anger still taunted him. Nolan's dreams were like an unending train of squalls, haunting and reproachful. Sometimes he had nightmares of lost things, things that could hardly be named, an unending career of suffocating guilt, shameful recriminations, nights of twitchy, sweaty sleep shot through with fearful shadows. In these dreams Nolan's armor melted off him like wax and the arrows of misfortune pierced him. He could see the people and places he loved, but they did not see him. He was a phantom, a shadow that could not speak or touch or love. But these dreams, too, Nolan learned to endure.

He surfaced to the trill of pipes and the roar of the bo'suns down the ladderways: "*Up and at 'em! Out or down! Hit the deck, bright-eyed and bushy-tailed.*" For a long moment Nolan did not know where he was, or on what ship. The noises of a nautical reveille were universal, the same throughout the fleet. Slowly he shook off the dull coils of sleep and remembered. He was aboard *Enterprise*. On the mess decks above he could hear the clatter of plates and the sound of someone singing in the bread room. Nolan blinked himself awake; it would have taken a more abstemious soul to ignore the aroma of coffee, bacon, and oatmeal streaming back from the galley stack.

Nolan dressed and went quickly on deck. As dawn brightened, a purple sky gave birth at once to blazing sun. All of the officers and most of the crew were about, and many were aloft, crowding the tops to look sharply about the edge of the horizon, east and especially north. But the sea was empty.

Soon after reveille everything was made ready for the command that would bring *Enterprise* to bear down on an enemy. The gun crews had minutely examined the vent aprons, locks, and touchholes of their pieces. The cartridge boxes that would serve the long guns and carronades were stacked and ready to be filled with powder. Pikes and boarding axes had been ground to razor edges, and Marines had filled bandoleers and grenadoes. But the hours passed without a shout from the masthead. The sea stretched empty in all directions.

Noon came, and as the hands were piped to dinner it was difficult not to feel that an appointment had been missed. The long day passed. Lookouts spent the afternoon scanning with shielded, half-closed eyes; the blazing, sunlit water showed nothing. Beazee sought out the shade of a carronade slide and sat against it, her tongue lolling. Nolan took up his papers and pencils and sketched her half-heartedly, bracing his pad on his knee against the long, even swell. The watch changed, the log was heaved, and when Wainwright piped "Six knots, sir" in his uneven quaver there were smiles on the quarterdeck.

The sun was slanting in the sky when a call came from the mizzen top, "Sail ho, two points on the starboard bow. Topgallants, just on the rise."

It was echoed almost at once by the foremast lookout, repeated and amplified, "On deck, there, two sail. Belay that. Three of sail. Two close and another astern, lateen rigged."

"Where away?" said Pelles, bouncing up the ladder in trousers and round coat.

"Starboard bow, sir, two points and three points off. Four leagues, maybe more. They are all just coming hull up."

Pelles lifted his glass and the other officers did the same. A dozen keen and learned eyes studied the three white specks on the northwest horizon. One was ship rigged, carrying on under plain sail and courses. She was painted black over red, a large ship, perhaps 800 tons burthen. Next to her, close by, was a snow, two-thirds her size with a broad spanker aft. The third vessel, the farthest away, showed herself only on the rolls. As lateen sails made themselves visible, some took her for a felucca, though no one had ever heard of so frail a rig so far from the coast. She was struggling behind her companions, making heavy weather of it, and as she clapped on more sail she revealed a square-rigged mainmast, a genoa forward, and a vast, patched lateen aft—a shabby xebec, her hull streaked brown, with ochre painted gun ports.

The others had reduced sail, allowing the lateen to catch up. The larger ship was handled creditably, almost man o'war fashion, but on close inspection she did not appear to be a frigate. Eight ports pierced her sides, but she seemed broad of beam, and her stern was a bit pompous for naval tastes, flashily painted like a Company ship.

"What do you make of them, gentlemen?"

"They aren't likely to outrun us," Erskine grunted.

Enterprise not only had the sun at her back, she had the all important weather gauge. The wind was on her larboard quarter and her chases were to leeward, allowing *Enterprise* to initiate contact or break and run as she chose. Pelles gave orders to put the helm down and strip *Enterprise* to her fighting sails.

The three vessels continued to stand north. *Enterprise* could be seen now, even to a lazy, casual lookout, and Curran watched the trio of vessels, expecting them to signal. If they were men o'war or sailing in convoy, it would have been the first thing to be done upon spotting a strange sail. But no flags ran aloft. No signal guns puffed. That they did not communicate spoke of an informal association—and that itself was suspicious. When Curran lowered his glass he saw Nolan come up the ladder. He was dressed for his turn on deck in his plain blue coat and canvas trousers. He went to the leeward side of the quarterdeck, standing away from the other officers and allowing them to do their duty.

"I gather we have company," he said when Curran came closer.

"We have. Would you like to look?"

Nolan took Curran's glass and studied the horizon. "They are a bit shabby."

"So are we."

Enterprise still wore the canvas over her gun ports, and Pelles had ordered at dawn that the yards again be set haphazardly. From this distance *Enterprise* looked as disreputable as art could make her. Nolan's brow lowered behind the eyepiece. He studied each of the hulls and their sails then handed back the glass. The farthest vessel had revealed herself to be a xebec, somewhat curiously rigged but almost certainly a corsair's ship.

"Am I wrong to think that none of them is a whalerman?"

"The snow is too small and the ship-rigged vessel is too large," Curran said. "And I know of no xebecs in the fishery. I believe it is more of a Mediterranean sort of conveyance."

Nolan had sensed the eagerness in the crew, heard their whispers, and during breakfast he had listened as two of the older forecastle men, both Rhode Islanders, swore that the Old Mogul would find the pirates that dished out the whaleboat, and that payback was right as rain.

Lieutenant Leslie came onto the quarterdeck followed by one of the starbolines. "Beg your pardon, Captain, but there is a man in my division who thinks he knows one of the ships."

A red-faced Dutchman, Schwimmerhorn, came up the ladder. "I know them, your honor," the man said, taking off his cap. "The ship rig is a Dutch East Indiaman name of *Ameland*. Used to be, anyhow. A Company vessel, latterly was just a-tradin' in the Med. She was captured by the Arabs last year off Tripoli."

"Captured by pirates? Are you sure?"

"Damn sure . . . er, sir."

"That would make her a lawful prize." Pelles scanned the horizon. None of the vessels yet showed an open gun port, though on the xebec there was an unseemly amount of running about.

"A former Company ship would have carried two dozen 18-pound cannon. Plus carronades," said Pelles distractedly. Aboard *Enterprise* every creature with a pair of eyes squinted hard at the black-hulled ship. Her sides were steep and her gunwales solid, but no weapons were visible on the decks.

Erskine considered for a moment and said, "If the Sallees took a Company ship, sir, they might have put her long guns into the fortress at Tripoli."

Curran stared at the long row of closed gun ports. "She rides low for a ship not bearing arms."

"She does indeed, Mister Curran." The ship and her consorts stood on with no change in sail.

"He would have come about if he thought we were one to be plucked," Pelles grunted. Despite her clever gun covers and the canting of her spars, *Enterprise* had not been mistaken for a harmless merchant. "Off the gun canvases, Mister Erskine, and fire a gun to leeward," the captain said.

Number fifteen went off with a deep thump, and a veil of powder smoke roiled across the sea. In response, the ship that had been the *Ameland* hoisted a red ensign quartered with white stripes.

"Danish colors, sir," said Erskine.

"Dane, my ass. Now the dance is a masquerade." Pelles lifted his chin and boomed out onto the spar deck. "Number two, put a round across her bow. On the roll . . . fire!"

From below, one of the long 24s went off, a deep resonating bang. There was the hiss of the outgoing shot and a splash three quarters of the way toward *Ameland*. The ball slapped into a rolling swell and tore up a furrow before disappearing to the north. Heedless, the three ships went on for a minute, and then the xebec fired a gun to leeward, the bulge of smoke rolling away from *Enterprise*.

Such a display might have been an acknowledgment—a leeward gun was also a sign of surrender. This was neither; it was a signal, and as the smoke shredded away, the brig and then the xebec put their helms down and wore downwind away from *Enterprise*, spreading as much canvas as they could.

Pelles had all the confirmation he needed. "Beat to quarters, Mister Erskine."

The Marine drummer snapped into a long roll, the *générale*, but none were alerted and no one had far to move. All hands had been at general quarters for the last half hour, and the ship had been ready since dawn. *Enterprise* was a mile from the black-hulled ship and a mile and a quarter from the xebec and the snow. Though they were sailing off, it was plain to all hands that the smaller ships had no hope of running away.

Aboard *Ameland*, the Danish colors were hauled down and topgallants were set neatly. From her bowsprit a flying jib was sheeted, brilliant red on its top half and saffron colored below, the colors set off by a startling zigzag. She had yet to show an ensign or pennant, but the dazzling red-and-yellow foresail marked her as an Algerine.

Enterprise went about in a smooth, slow turn to starboard as the snow and the xebec scrambled off. As Nolan watched, a pair of stern ports fell open on the Algerian ship. No guns were run out, but the message, like the jib, was unmistakable. The black ship that had been *Ameland* was a man o'war, and willing to fight.

Pelles looped his telescope around his neck and walked to the quarterdeck rail. "Shipmates," his voice rumbled, "you see that Indiaman. She is a lawful prize, a Dutchman taken by pirates, and even if she shows a national ensign we are bound and in our rights to take her. The other two flying from us are either her prizes or likewise they are pirates and we will have them, too. As for the big Algerine, you can be sure he will fight, and I can be sure you will fight harder."

Around the guns there were growls of assent, and someone belowdecks said, "Damn right, Skipper."

Pelles went on, "This is likely the villain who did our whale ship. So, first we will dish him out, as that is our simple duty, and then we will snap up his prizes, because the money will jingle sweeter in your pockets than in his nasty petticoats." A cheer went up and there were a few hoots; Pelles' speech had strummed the crew admirably. "Now, stand by your guns, lads, and when you are told, ply them briskly. Knock off these three and then I'll pipe you to supper."

There was another cheer, and Pelles motioned his officers to join him at the windward rail. As they converged, Nolan stood off to the side, his hands clasped behind his back. "Mister Erskine," Pelles said in a conversational voice, "I don't care very much for piratical sons of bitches, and I do not care to spill our own blood for no reason. The corsair will likely have sent men away to man their prizes. The ship will be short of hands even if it is long on brass. I doubt that they can man their guns and make sail at the same time. It is my intention to outmaneuver this scoundrel and engage him, both sides, under sail."

"Yes, sir."

"See that the larboard guns are also made ready, and the sail trimmers stand by to go aloft. If a sheet or tackle goes adrift, no man will go wrong clapping on or helping to heave and trim.

"Captain MacQuarrie, we'll launch the red cutter and the gig. They will be veered to larboard as we approach. A platoon of Marines and a few howitzers in the boats should put you right. Would you like to take a carronade or two?"

"One, sir, if you could spare it. In the gig."

"You'll have it. And plenty of canister. Mister Leslie will accompany you. Stay outboard of *Enterprise* and out of sight until I give the signal, then go for the xebec and the snow."

MacQuarrie's delight was transcendent. The only thing he liked better than handling a boat under sail was combat on an enemy's deck. Of the other officers and midshipmen, some wore careful looks, some were slightly pale, but all of them listened intently. Curran had been in action several times, but he did not pretend to be habituated to combat. He could not help but wonder what the afternoon held for him.

"Division officers. See that your guns are elevated fully. I want the corsair crippled, not shot through the hull. Be ready to reload with bar and grape when ordered, and put your shot where it will do them the most evil. If we should come to a general engagement, make certain no broadside is wasted. There is no ship afloat that can stand up to our guns if they are well laid. To your stations now, and Mister Curran, I will have a word with you."

The officers dispersed. Erskine went forward to command the gun deck and chasers, Kerr to the waist, the others and Lieutenant Varney below to the gun deck and their divisions. Fine in their best green jackets and pipe-clayed flawlessly, a quartet of handpicked Marine sharpshooters slung their Kentucky long rifles and took up stations in the mizzen top.

Enterprise was on a larboard tack, with the wind just aft of her beam. Mister Pybus himself was at the helm, steering carefully to pass astern of the Algerine, who also kept a larboard tack, still the best part of a mile to the north.

"Mister Curran, from what you can see of her transom, does that ship have a name?"

Curran lifted his glass and squinted at the gaudy work on her stern galleries. He was finally able to pick out a rivulet of Arabic script carved around the nymphs and tritons that had been the pride of the former owners. "*Ar R'ad*, sir," Curran said. "She calls herself 'The Thunder.'"

Pelles allowed himself a small smile. "A snappy name. Most martial."

"It is also religious, sir. *Ar R'ad* is a sura of the Holy Koran."

"I am delighted for them. I wonder if they carry a parson?"

Steadying himself against the belfry, Pelles pulled his sword belt around on his waist. "Mister Pybus, one point to larboard. I intend to approach on their quarter and cross their wake at three cable's lengths."

"Aye, aye sir, larboard a point, and cross at three cables."

The barge and cutter were made out to the boat boom, and the first platoon went down into them, Marines and sailors packed together, guns and bayonets bristling.

"Guns are run out of her stern ports, sir." This from Mister Hall, on the quarterdeck. He was the signal midshipman.

At the starboard rail, Nolan watched as *Ar R'ad* glided to the top of a low swell, two long guns jutting from her stern galleries. The guns fired just before the top of the roll—white clouds shot through with orange and black. Two seconds later came the noise of the cannon, a double bang, and then the whirr of the incoming rounds: 12-pounders from their high-pitched hum. The first ball came down a hundred yards to starboard, a shot fired wide but with some correctness as to range. The second ball whizzed overhead, higher than the topgallants. It went past with a crackling hiss and threw up a column of spray far, far astern.

With an artillerist's eye Nolan watched the fall of both shots, one only halfway of use to fix the target, the other thrown away, and he attended to the manner *Ar R'ad* ran in her guns to reload them. The test would be how soon again she ran them out, and how well the fire would be adjusted.

Pelles lifted his speaking trumpet, though his deep bass hardly needed it. "Forward on deck . . . Mister Kerr, you may try a ranging shot with the starboard chaser."

This order had been anticipated; the gun had been pried round and minutely kept on target for the last ten minutes. As Mister Kerr made final adjustments, Pelles turned to Hall. "Midshipman Hall, the national ensign, if you please."

The Stars and Stripes was broken out and lifted high into the mizzen. Curran could not help but notice that Nolan took his eyes from the horizon and watched the flag sputter and snap up to the top of the halyard.

In the bow, number two went off with a gratifying thump, a report that sent a slight twitch through the deck. As the smoke went away to leeward, a keen eye could just make out the speck of the 24-pound ball flying flat and true. It disappeared as it approached the gaudily painted stern of *Ar R'ad*, and there was a gray-blue puff from the starboard quarter galley as the frigate's ranging shot tore into it. The damage to *Ar R'ad* was trifling, a glancing hit that shattered a stern light and took off one of the mermaids, but the first shot had gone home true at over 1,300 yards.

There were yeehaws and cheering forward and looks of envy from the gun captains along the spar deck. *Ar R'ad*'s stern guns answered within the span of three or four seconds. The first ball struck fifty yards off *Enterprise*'s bow, and a pillar of water dumped down onto the forecastle. The second ball came diagonally across the deck, passing ten feet above the main chains. As the ball grazed the mizzenmast, a bayonet-sized splinter ricocheted over the taffrail. Everyone on the quarterdeck flinched, everyone except Pelles and Nolan—a fearless pair.

Curran's hand went instinctively to his face—a blur had gone right past his nose. He turned to see his best scraper rolling across the deck, a gaping hole blown through the cockade.

"Mister Curran, are you all right?" Pelles asked.

"I am, sir," Curran answered, "but my hat is ruined."

Pelles smiled brightly—wit under fire was his favorite sort of humor. He turned to Nolan, who alone among the officers on the quarterdeck seemed to know that trying to dodge a cannonball was a pointless impulse. "This will soon turn brisk, Mister Nolan. For your own safety, you might wish to go below."

"I wouldn't mind a little air, Captain."

Pelles bowed slightly and walked to the larboard rail. Nolan plucked up Curran's tattered hat from the deck and put his finger through the hole; the prospect of standing before an enemy's guns seemed to delight him. Nolan was smiling, grinning actually, and seemed suddenly ten years younger. "It seems they have aired out your hat," Nolan said, handing it back.

"See that they don't do the same to you, Mister Nolan." Curran managed to smile, but the hat gave him the impression that he had used up his luck for today.

At the larboard rail, Pelles looked down and called down to cutter and gig. "Away the boats!" MacQuarrie saluted from the gig and called back, "Good luck to you, sir."

The gig and cutter tacked away and quickly crossed *Enterprise*'s wake. A lookout aboard the snow caught sight of the Marines and gestured wildly at the masthead. Until now, the snow and the xebec had stayed as much as possible under the lee of their protector, narrowly balancing escape and cover. As the Marines closed, it was obvious that they would now have to fight or fly, and they were prepared to do neither. Aboard the xebec there was a fracas as her crew tried to set a flying jib, only to blow out a boltrope and yaw away far to starboard. The gig and the cutter both came about, moving to cut off any chance of escape.

From the conn Pelles said, "Corporal Gerrity, you may send the others aloft." A dozen green jackets climbed upon the gunwales and over the chains fore, main, and mizzen, carrying with them grenadoes and kegs of powder for their swivel guns. Like spiders they went quickly up the shrouds and into the tops, joining the sharpshooters.

Pelles kept his glass trained on the enemy's quarterdeck. Closer study revealed that the Algerine was spilling his wind. Neither main nor fore courses were carefully set, and it was preposterous that he had not manned his fighting tops. The mystery was doubly perplexing as it was the Algerine who had opened the engagement. To every other appearance the corsair seemed prepared and even eager to fight. "Mister Curran, you may join your division. We'll soon have need of your fancy shooting."

Curran went down the ladder to the spar deck and his guns at Bastard's Alley. As he ducked under the splinter netting, Padeen lifted his knuckle to his forehead.

"All primed and ready, sir." The guns were trained forward; loaders, rammers, and swabbers ready; the slow match smoldering in the tubs in case the double-flinted gunlocks should fail in their duty.

Ar R'ad now seemed to be changing course, falling off the wind a point or two. Curran watched over the top of number fourteen as *Ar R'ad* began a languid turn. It was not a tack, not even half of one, and for a moment it appeared that she had missed stays, intending to wear ship and fire a broadside but failing, putting her helm over in time.

At the wheel, Pelles murmured to Pybus, "Ease your head, Master. Steady as she goes."

The master let the helm down gently, and *Enterprise* almost instantly began to slow. *Ar R'ad* remained in her apathetic turn and the distance between the ships continued to close slowly. Pelles leaned on the starboard rail, eyes fixed on the strangers. Why would *Ar R'ad*'s commander now dawdle away his advantage? There was nothing to do but let the seconds pass. On the quarterdeck, Nolan stood with the other officers at the leeward rail, listening to the hum of water down the ship's side.

Forward of the quarterdeck break, Curran's division comprised carronades—shorter-range guns—and he knew that he would not be called on to fire until the ships were fully engaged, perhaps even yardarm to yardarm. The sun was now lower in the left-hand part of the sky. He fixed his telescope on the three ships across the darkening water.

The snow and xebec had showed their heels but soon began a series of ineffective, random shots at the gig and cutter. From the snow there was a clumsy popping of musketry, answered at once by a compact, well-fired volley from MacQuarrie. In the gig, the carronade fired, skipping a ball through the xebec's mainsail.

Ar R'ad continued her unhurried turn, and finally her yards bent round as she came beam-on to the wind. For a moment she hung, poised either to come to the aid of her consorts or turn to fight *Enterprise*. As Curran watched through his long glass, *Ar R'ad* wavered then sheeted home, settling on a course that would pass *Enterprise* within eight hundred yards—a long go for carronades, if she intended to use them.

But she did not.

Curran watched through his telescope as the master on *Ar R'ad*'s quarterdeck began rapidly spinning the wheel. Drawing a neat arc, the big ship tacked to starboard, making her turn briskly. Four long sections of gunwale toppled down, revealing the decks forward and aft of the corsair's mainmast. The segments fell like trapdoors, exposing several thinly manned carronades of various types, all more or less pointing at *Enterprise*, but what grabbed the attention of all hands was a pair of rectangular objects placed between the hatches.

Standing next to Captain Pelles, Nolan stared at *Ar R'ad* but could not believe his eyes. On either side of the mainmast a long, tapering cylinder projected from a three-sided iron box, like a furnace with its smokestack set horizontally. Each was the size of the tryworks of a whale ship, rectangular, impossibly huge things. Nolan slowly realized that they were guns, grossly out of scale and borne on equally unlikely pivots—long-tailed, wheeled Gribeauval carriages. Slabs of iron riveted together shielded the guns. Nolan had only seen this arrangement on casemate guns in coastal defense artillery.

As *Ar R'ad* went over a swell, Pelles could look onto her decks. Each of the guns' trails was heaved round by the brute strength of almost sixty men.

"I believe that those are siege guns, Captain," Nolan said quietly. "Forty-two pounders."

Pelles narrowed his eye behind his telescope and grunted. Aboard *Ar R'ad* the splinter nets were triced up and the loaders were scrambling away from the guns. Pelles had seen pivot guns before, but he had never seen weapons this large; nor ever in his time at sea had he seen guns shielded by metal plates. This was heavy artillery, ordnance that had no right to be afloat. Through his glass Pelles could see a tall, black-turbaned figure atop each of the rectangles, persons he took to be the gun captains, shouting and urging their crews on with blows from a rattan.

A gigantic cloud of smoke jetted from the space between *Ar R'ad*'s masts. A pear-shaped tongue of fire belched from the gun; this happened in silence. White-water splashed along the Algerine's quarter, and then came a mighty, gut-churning thud. The discharge of the weapon set a concussive shock through sea and air that twitched *Enterprise*'s jib and main.

At the quarterdeck rail, Pelles called out: "All hands! Flat on your faces!"

Before the first round could arrive, a second thunder-crack broke over the corsair ship. Peering over the hammock netting, Curran saw the flashes and a massive roil of white-gray powder smoke. "Down!" he yelled, taking Padeen by the elbow and pulling him into cover behind number fourteen.

There was a sputtering, a nasty hiss, like a sail tearing aloft, and a whirling shadow crashed into the bow. For an instant Curran's brain tried to apprehend the staggering shock and gust of darkness. The deck beneath his feet pitched up violently, as though *Enterprise*'s keel had run up on a reef.

The first ball smashed into the starboard anchor, tearing the flukes with the noise of a shattering bell. The clangor merged with the hoarse, choking scream of a dozen men as the forward guns were enveloped in a cloud of murder. Hot shards of iron hissed across the deck and cracked through the rigging. The loader of number twenty-one tumbled headlong down the companionway; his leather powder bucket tore open and a ruptured bag of fine best cylinder rolled across the deck. Curran scrambled forward and kicked the deadly charge overboard as a second salvo smashed into *Enterprise*.

There was a two-note sound, almost like a cathedral's organ, and then a horrifying double explosion. The bow of the frigate twitched like a shying horse; a massive, soul-churning jerk went through the deck, and Curran was driven to his knees. A swarm of red sparks skittered across the forecastle and the crew of number one was felled as though a scythe had been swept under their knees. Lieutenant Kerr was blasted over the side in pieces. Badly mangled, two Marines were thrown into the foot of the mainmast. Behind the conn, both Pelles and Nolan had been staggered by the impacts. Pybus remained upright only by managing to hang on to the wheel. Others, including the captain's clerk and the signalmen, were knocked flat. Nolan helped Pelles to his feet. Both men did what they could to conceal expressions of bewilderment and awe. *Enterprise* had been knocked back on her heels.

Nolan knew precisely what a 42-pounder could do to a block of houses, and now had an idea what it could do to a floating wooden object. In a lifetime at sea, Pelles had never seen such damage done by a single salvo. Forward, the smoke was clearing to reveal a chaos of twisted wreckage. The heads were smashed, two gun carriages were overset, and a dozen men were down. In the bow, the beakhead had been blown to bits and what was left of the best bower anchor pendulumed from the smoking stump of the cathead.

Pelles shouted, "Steady now, lads. Steady and hold your fire. We will pass astern, and give him a raking! Stand by your pieces!" Along the spar deck the officers readied their crews, and on the gun deck below, muzzles inched back, trained on the enemy. In a more conversational but still firm voice Pelles said to Mister Nordhoff, "Lead a party forward—cut the cable and cast off the anchor. Quickly, boy!"

Enterprise continued to close, and *Ar R'ad* rolled out her 9-pound chasers. The noise came quickly after the white clouds: thunder and flash closer together. Both shots were clean misses. The first ball fell wide and the second wobbled harmlessly overhead. Compared with the deafening noise of the 42-pounders, the long 9s seemed subdued, even harmless.

The wounded were carried below, and the dismounted cannon were griped down on deck. At his station, Curran balanced his glass on the hammock netting. On the deck of *Ar R'ad* he saw the big guns rotated to centerline. The jostling crowds working the carriages heaved, and the dark muzzles again trained upon *Enterprise*. The crowds surrounding the huge weapons performed the evolutions familiar to any naval gunner—swabbing, loading, ramming home—but on a gigantic scale. And they were slower. As the guns dwarfed the men, the work dwarfed the crews. Especially laborious was the loading of shot into the muzzle—it took four men to lift the massive ball in a stretcher, and six men to serve the rammer that put it home. Three minutes had passed since the first rounds had struck *Enterprise*, and Curran guessed it would be at least three more minutes before the second salvo would be ready to fly.

Every eye on the starboard side watched the two ships close. Every brain considered the positions and calculated the distances. Aboard *Ar R'ad* the loaders were moving away from the guns. Curran glanced over at Wainwright, who stood behind his midship division. The boy's mouth was open.

"A fine day, Mister Wainwright," Curran said. "You are about to see us put a full broadside to use."

"I am looking forward to it, sir," the boy said. He cleared his throat. "I only hope we will do it soon."

A bullet spanged into the gunwale six inches from Curran's head. A splinter of wood went sailing into the air and the bullet twittered off, punching through a leather bucket behind number twelve. Curran jerked around and his eyes fell on the enemy's quarterdeck—*Ar R'ad*'s captain was lowering a miquelet rifle. Even at four hundred yards Curran could see that the shooter was a large man dressed in a heavily embroidered jacket and vast purple trousers. As Curran watched, he handed the flintlock to a sailor in a red skullcap, who quickly set about reloading.

"He is taking potshots, the creature," Curran scowled. He then said in a louder, firmer voice, "Sargent Lachat, you may send their captain my compliments." Lachat walked over to the hammock netting and laid his Kentucky rifle across. He licked his lips, let out a long breath, and squeezed the trigger. A second later, a bullet spanged off *Ar R'ad's* binnacle and Curran watched the red skullcap skip and caper and fall.

"On deck," Pelles boomed. "Starboard batteries, stand by. When we put about, fire on my command. Pour it into him, then we will round to and give him the other side."

"Ready your locks," Curran said. Along his division, the gun captains snicked back the flintlocks and cupped their hands over the vent holes. Pry bars heaved the carriages around, making small corrections. They were now within two cable's lengths, and the ship beat with a single heart. Finally, *Enterprise* could give instead of get.

"Port hard, Mister Pybus."

The frigate's bow went around more quickly than Nolan could have imagined, and the starboard battery came across *Ar R'ad*'s quarter, ranging it exactly. Aboard *Ar R'ad* there was confusion, then dread.

The Algerine had expected *Enterprise* to wear, not tack, and Pelles knew he had caught them on the wrong foot. *Enterprise* had bought herself another precious ninety seconds as the great guns were trundled around to face the opposite direction. The frigate went quickly under the stern of *Ar R'ad*, passing close enough to count the mermaids and tritons carved onto her brightly painted galleries.

"Fire as they bear!" *Enterprise*'s starboard guns went off in a rippling paean of thunder. Midway through the broadside, *Ar R'ad*'s gunners brought their muzzles to larboard, aimed to meet *Enterprise* as she emerged from her turn.

The great guns went off one after another; at close range the concussion was astounding. As *Ar R'ad*'s aftermost gun fired, a shock twitched through the frigate, wrenching her from tuck to keelson. The concussion seemed to have temporarily stunned the wind. Muzzle blast merged with the howl of the incoming shot, putting the sails back and ringing the frigate's bell.

Nolan saw a deadly shape tear across the forepeak, and the blue cutter, all thirty feet of it, leapt from its cradle and disintegrated into a maelstrom of splinters.

The huge shot continued aft, trailing death behind it. Creasing the mainmast, the ball ploughed though the crew of number seventeen. Smashed from its carriage, the carronade was blown up and end over end, its lugs and trunions gone to pieces. Men fell in gory, twitching heaps—rammers, swabs, and pry bars still clamped in dead hands.

Through the appalling mayhem came Pelles' voice, strong and calm. "Sail trimmers, away! Hands to the lee head braces and jib! Stretch out! Stretch along the weather braces!"

In chaos, training replaces thought. Aboard *Enterprise*, in battle, the crew functioned like a creature of a single instinct and being. On deck the crews went about their duties impervious to the slaughter around them. They cleared away wreckage where they needed to work, every man finding his place and performing a task. Anticipating that the larboard guns would now be brought to bear, *Enterprise*'s gun captains scrambled across the wreckage in the waist. Working in fine, concise movements they primed the guns and prepared the locks. Marines slung their rifles and helped heave and tally.

Enterprise went round again, the smoke drifting to leeward. From the quarterdeck, Nolan was the first to see the damage done to *Ar R'ad*. Maneuvered onto the corsair's quarter, *Enterprise* had hit *Ar R'ad* with a murderous, raking fire. Every gun had sent home a round, and each shot had traveled the length of the corsair, killing, maiming, and destroying. The frigate had taken six rounds; *Ar R'ad* had absorbed two entire broadsides. Both times, Pelles had slapped the corsair as she started to rise. *Ar R'ad*'s stern galleries were utterly destroyed, a shambles of smashed wood and shattered glass. Her mizzen boom was shot through, and a dozen holes were gouged diagonally along her copper. Blood ran down her sides and dribbled from her scuppers, but she still showed a long line of teeth.

Pelles was aware that the great guns could fire through a wide arc to port and starboard, but could not be trained less than three points off the bow or stern. *Ar R'ad*'s after guns thundered, and a volley of grapeshot swept the quarterdeck, killing a Marine and smashing the signal locker. Pelles kept *Enterprise* in a position to pour a raking fire into the enemy's quarter—exposing the frigate to the return fire of the stern chasers and carronades but trying desperately to avoid the deadly guns perched amidships.

Enterprise discharged two more unanswered broadsides into *Ar R'ad*. Now within biscuit toss, Curran saw the helmsman on *Ar R'ad*'s quarterdeck frantically turning the wheel to starboard, but it was Captain Pelles who comprehended the danger. *Ar R'ad* was preparing to fire her after great gun directly through her own stern.

Pelles joined Pybus at the helm. "Ready about!" he barked.

Together they put the frigate's rudder over. As the frigate paid off, Pelles' voice rang across the spar deck: "Lay down!"

Close aboard, *Ar R'ad* came about like a cutter and the corsair's midship guns were inched around *Enterprise*. There was a pair of closely spaced thunderclaps as the big cannon gushed two improbably symmetrical cones of fire: one firing across the beam, one through the stern gallery. But the huge guns had been fired a second late.

The first round passed astern of *Enterprise*, howling past with a noise like a tolling bell. The second struck the water immediately behind the rudder, cleaving the surface with a deafening crack. The impact drove up a fifty-foot column of water and lifted the frigate by the stern. As *Enterprise* came down there was a heaving jolt; the ship's stern settled, and the geyser fell back for ten seconds with the snarl of a waterfall. Had the rounds struck the ship they would have swept away the quarterdeck and unshipped the rudder—a mortal blow.

Both of *Ar R'ad*'s principal guns had been fired, and it would be six minutes at least until they could bite again. In six minutes, Pelles intended to lay his enemy to waste. "Larboard guns, fire!" A dozen 28-pounders went off in a rippling broadside, a nearly simultaneous blast that ripped *Ar R'ad* from stem to stern. The smoke coiled to windward, stalling in an opaque bank on the corsair's deck. Pelles called again for sail trimmers, who backed the yards as musket fire snapped among the rigging. *Enterprise* wore again, bringing the fresh starboard batteries into action, and Curran led his gun crews to the leeward side. As he laid hold of number thirteen, Curran glanced forward at Wainwright.

On the boy's shoulder was a pry bar, and he was heaving with all his hundred pounds, marshaling his crews in a shrill pipe. "As they bear . . . smartly now," he yelled. "Prime as she comes around!" Incredibly, Wainwright still had his hat placed squarely on his head.

Again from *Ar R'ad* came the deafening eruption of one of the big guns. It had been loaded, trained, and fired quicker than any could have imagined. The ball struck the hull directly below Bastard's Alley, sending foot-long splinters in every direction. Curran had time to lift his arm in front of his eyes as the explosion swept over him. The back of his head was splashed with something scalding, and from belowdecks he could hear a long, inhuman wail. The ball had been fired diagonally, passed under the guns of his division, and swept destruction the width of the gun deck. Two port lids were beaten onto one, a dozen feet of bulwark was shattered, and a storm of splinters and iron and fire struck down Varney and the Marine crew of number nine. On the spar deck, a bo'sun's mate named Jones was cut in half and thrown overboard; a rag doll spinning in circles.

Curran slammed into the deck, and Wainwright and his crew were felled by a whirlwind of fire. After a numb, incoherent gulp of breath, Curran lifted his face. Padeen knelt next to him, frozen with a rammer in hand. Curran shouted at him to reload; the command was automatic, but the big man did not move. He pointed and blinked. The crew of number nine was gone, the bulwark aft of the gun was hung in a crimson curtain of gore. The crew of number ten was ripped into pieces, but their gun, incredibly, was upright and still primed. Tumbled under a fife rail,

Wainwright had been blown mostly out of his uniform and was bleeding from his nose and ears. As Curran watched, the midshipman rolled onto his knees and took up the lanyard of the gun. Around him smoke and some sort of flesh-colored vapor seemed to hang like a halo. Wainwright jerked the dowel as he toppled forward and the carronade fired. The recoiling gun bucked up and jerked against its breeching, the skeet missing Wainwright's forehead by a fraction of an inch.

A second after the report, a hard, rending crack issued from the haze of smoke engulfing *Ar R'ad*. Cleaved by a 32-pound ball, the foot of the corsair's foremast swayed forward and went by the bitts. A tangle of sails, spars, and blocks crashed down on the forward gun, smothering it and its crew in a tumult of debris.

Wainwright collapsed onto his side, his eyes open, his pale face streaked with powder. Curran willed himself toward the boy, but his limbs would not answer. He seemed to be moving underwater. Finally, his fingers closed around the blasted collar of Wainwright's jacket and he pulled him closer. Curran was aware of a shadow moving behind him. Oddly, he could hear the crunch of splinters against the deck. The footsteps were plain, but the rest of the world moved in a kind of painful, throbbing silence. Curran saw the smoke part and watched as Nolan and Padeen strained to lift a section of shattered gun carriage and push it aside.

"Surgeon! Surgeon!" Nolan bellowed.

Wainwright looked up, astounded. "By Jesus," the boy said, "I have lost my hand."

Curran saw the boy's arm laying on the deck, cut off below the elbow, the wool sleeve without a smudge and even the linen cuff about the wrist still white. Nolan removed the belt from a dead Marine and cinched it around the stump of Wainwright's arm. The boy's eyes wandered back in his head and he gently slumped over.

Nolan shook him by the collar, "Kevin! Kevin!" Wainwright snorted, exactly like a child falling asleep, and Padeen took the child from Nolan's arms, bundled him up, and turned for the hatchway. Curran lurched over to Nolan, still kneeling in the youngster's blood. A bullet smashed though the rail and whined away somewhere aft.

At the sound Nolan lifted his face. His eyes narrowed, as though he did not know where he was, and he came unsteadily to his feet. Aboard the corsair a trumpet was blaring and kettledrums throbbed. There was a fire burning on her foredeck, but her carronades were still firing briskly. Nolan staggered blankly past Curran and bent at one of the shot racks. Curran saw that Nolan's hands were trembling as he lifted one of the deadly soldered tin cylinders and hefted it to his shoulder.

"Now, lads," Nolan said, "let's have a go at them. Now as they're loading." Nolan's voice was calm, but its deep tenor carried to the men around him. He waved to the powder boy. "Here, Mulherrin, give us that cartridge. Handsome does it, handsome now." He took the powder charge from Mulherrin and shoved it with his own hands into the mouth of the gun. One by one the survivors of Wainwright's division gathered around him.

"Help me ram home, Vanhall. You too, Parnin. Double-shotted now, a double whiff of canister for these nasty sons of bitches." Nolan took up a round of case shot from the rack and tossed it to Guild. "Reload handsomely, boys. Load and run them out!"

Along the larboard side, the gun crews came together, shoving away fallen tackles and prying around the carriages to bring their muzzles to bear.

Nolan laid number eleven and shouted, "From forward, as you bear . . . fire!"

A staggering barrage slashed into *Ar R'ad*, pelting her sides and sweeping her decks. There was a great, reverberating clang, and the aftmost of the two swivel guns was shaken by a fiery explosion. The loaders around it were consumed in a crackling like a lightning strike, and a gunpowder fire started to burn under the carriage.

Nolan could see the captains of the corsair's big guns scramble for cover behind their plate armor. Out of the din came a new sound, the sharp report of Marine howitzers firing down from the frigate's tops. A swarm of grape scythed through the crew of *Ar R'ad*'s forward gun, leaving not a soul standing. A dozen of the corsairs scuttled away from the aft gun and tried to run belowdecks. A second howitzer banged from the frigate's maintop, and a puff of canister tore them to pieces.

Ar R'ad's starboard guns fired by pairs; their reports were followed a half second later by a huge crash forward and a long, grunting scream. The wind had shifted and now was driving the smoke of *Ar R'ad*'s guns across *Enterprise*'s deck. Bleeding heavily, Ward was carried past. Through the haze, Curran caught sight of Nolan pulling Fentress from beneath an overturned carronade. Forward of the quarterdeck break, three gun ports were smashed together; dead and wounded lay on the deck, and the upright crews were functioning on instinct alone. The engagement was general now, each gun fighting on its own hook, firing nearly point-blank into the corsair's starboard side. Assisted by the quarter-gunners, Nolan supervised the reloading of his division. Sword in hand, Captain Pelles was on the spar deck, pointing guns, pulling men together, standing like a monument in a maelstrom.

Carrying a round shot, Nolan looked over his shoulder at Pelles. "I am showing them how we do this in the artillery, sir."

"I see that you are, and I thank you, Mister Nolan," said the captain. "I shall never forget this day, sir. And you never will."

Pelles bellowed back to the conn, "Lay us alongside!" The master put down the helm, and the frigate made a slow turn to starboard.

Pelles came forward through the drifting smoke. "Mister Curran, you look spry enough."

"I am in one piece, sir."

"And I commend you for it. Serve out cutlass and pistols. Your division will board."

"Aye, sir." Curran hitched on his scabbard and barked over his shoulder, "First Division, arm up!" He moved to the center of the boarding party, wedged now between carronades loading with double case shot. They were ordered compactly: Marines first, then those sailors armed with pistols and cutlasses; behind them, in a pressing throng, came the Bowie knife and hatchet men. Fiercest among the boarders were Kanoa and his tattooed cousins, armed with *pāhoa* war clubs, shaped like spades and lined with jagged spirals of snow white shark's teeth.

Enterprise sailed into the bank of powder smoke and closed on *Ar R'ad*. Grapnels sailed through the air and the spar deck carronades erupted, overlapping the corsair with a point-blank skein of hissing canister. In the tops, Lachat's Marines gave wing to a flock of grenadoes. Trailing arcs of smoke, they tumbled onto the enemy's decks and went off like a series of hammer blows. The noise deafened, and the stuttering explosions blinded. Rifles fired from the tops, and the boarders were shouting—this was the chaos in which Curran drew his sword and pulled himself up onto the hammock nets. "Marines and boarders! Prime your pieces!"

Curran considered the distance between the ships: two cliffs coming together over a heaving, debris-strewn blackness. Sword held in his right fist, Curran drew his pistol with his left. He felt the hammock nets dip as Marines and sailors pulled themselves up behind him. Below, the water closed into a narrow band, the ships crashed together, and Curran shouted: "Enterprises! Follow me!"

HELL AFLOAT

GRAY-WHITE, CLINGING LIKE FOG, A PALL OF POWDER SMOKE HUNG OVER the deck. Curran had expected to land in a welter of musketry and slashing steel; instead, he was greeted by silence and ruin. Smoke eddied through overturned carronades, tangles of line, cut-through blocks, and shattered spars. The mainmast stood crookedly, but both foremast and mizzen were gone, blasted through at the bitts. Through a wavering blur Curran could see the implausible, black-painted hulks of the great guns. Even dismounted there was menace in them. The forward gun was canted over, engulfed by the ruin of the foretop. Flesh was intermingled in the wreckage.

By the dozens, boarders came over from *Enterprise*. No one spoke. The silence was breached only by the clump of Marines' boots and the softer knock of sailors jumping down onto the deck behind them. Weapons clicked and rattled, but found no enemy to slay. Curran turned aft, holding his pistol and sword at the ready. The light was failing, and below the shattered hatches the corsair's lower decks oozed a gloomy, mournful darkness. Though the boarders had weapons of a dozen different types, no one had come across with a lantern.

One of the Bannons came aft, carrying his musket over his elbow like a fowling piece. "The forepeak's empty, sir. There was irons and shackles, like they had prisoners, but no one's there."

"Why would they fight us if they were in ballast?" asked Padeen. "Sailin' empty is nothing to die over."

Sergeant Lachat pointed his musket down a companionway and stirred the darkness with his bayonet. He saw nothing, but pulled a grenado from his belt anyway.

"Belay that, Sergeant," Curran said. "Padeen, take the second division down the forward hatch. Work aft and check the other holds."

"Them holds *below*, sir?"

In his life at sea Curran had learned that Irish sailors had no fear of the living but often possessed an over-scrupulous respect for the dead. "Yes, Padeen, *below* decks," Curran grunted. "I believe that musketoon will preserve you from evil. Get along now, or there will be no light at all."

Muttering a Hail Mary, Padeen went down a broken ladder, followed by a grousing, sullen gun crew.

"Sergeant Lachat, come with me."

The sergeant reluctantly put away his grenado and directed Corporal Hackman and his squad to mount the quarterdeck. The Marines lowered bayonets and moved aft, fingers on the triggers of their muskets. The terrier Beazee had come aboard, either carried under an arm or having jumped clean over when the ships came together. She now scurried before the advancing search party, her hackles up and her stub tail twitching with anger. Low, jagged shadows grew longer around the smashed parts of the ship.

The after great gun was turned to starboard, away from *Enterprise*, and pointed skyward. A cannonball had entered though the exposed back of the gun, struck a trunion, and ripped the pivot from the deck. Parts of a green *shemagh* wafted from one of the cheek plates, and a black pool of gore meandered from under the carriage to a broken scupper. Somewhere under the hulk, a fire smoldered, producing a nauseating, greasy smoke.

The slaughter was biblical. *Ar R'ad*'s crew had been visited with more than death; they had been destroyed, and where they fell, their bodies had been churned up by shell and splinter. No hand who went aboard that devastated ship would ever forget what he saw—or what would happen next.

Beazee had scratched to a stop by the after hatch, rigid and trembling, shaking the way her kind did when they had a varmint cornered, one front paw lifted and her head cocked. What she heard was soon buzzing in the ears of the men. The noise was comprehended first as an undertone, a sort of groan, increasing in volume as it descended in pitch. It lengthened into an awful, mournful howl. To Curran, it seemed at first to be a trick played by battle-deafened ears, the buzzing echo of cannonade and musketry. The faces of the Marines around him became incredulous and then appalled.

"What in the hell is that?" In the stubborn smoke, it was impossible to determine the origin. It was first believed to be behind them, then above. "The hull is settling," someone cried out. The noise seemed to be everywhere, like the bass note of an organ in a cathedral: inherent, fundamental, and defining.

"It isn't the ship," Curran said.

From below came a rhythmic pounding—a crash, knocks, and thuds—then plainly the sounds of shouts. A hatch cover bucked up and was flung onto the deck. Curran stared as twenty African men and women clawed over the combings and out of the hold; they were mere skeletons, with bloated bellies and yellowing hair. Their eyes flashed and blinked with jaundiced terror, and their skin was ulcerous with the product of the lash and tar brush. Another twenty of these specters tumbled up, then another dozen, children scrambling among them, most naked, some in irons, all of them filthy and closer to death than life. Their lips were peeled back in gaunt, desperate faces, teeth ghastly white. They had been held in darkness so long that even the fading light of dusk seemed to blind and startle them.

The living were turned loose among the dead. *Ar R'ad* had been made into a charnel house, and now perfect chaos was set loose in the midst of it. Slaves scuttled up fore and aft, propelled through the hatches by ever more wretched souls pushing up from below. The first group gained the ship's waist and caught sight of the Marines. Terrified by white faces, the mob winced backward, heaving over bodies and debris. Some climbed the stumps of the masts, others darted onto the wreckage of the ship's boats or sought refuge behind the overhang of the shattered guns.

Curran shouted, "Friends! Amis! Amigos!" to utterly no effect.

A shout went up in answer; it was magnified into the panicked jabber of a dozen African tongues. There were shoves and punches; members of both the boarding party and freed slaves were knocked down and trampled. Curran tried to slow the stampede.

"Easy there! Friends." His voice was lost in the gabble of a tide of humanity. To prevent being bowled over, Marines used the butts of their rifles, roaring, "Back off!" and "Pipe down!" Words that brought instant compliance aboard *Enterprise* did no magic here. The deck was filling with people, and still more came up from below.

"Sir! Mister Curran!" Curran could barely hear Padeen over the commotion. "She's holed through amidships, Mister C, taking on water, bad. And a hundred more of these poor bastards is down there, still in irons!"

Curran turned to a Marine, "Hackman! Hail *Enterprise* and tell her we will need some help! You others, help me lift this hatch cover!"

Belowdecks, the darkness was nearly opaque. At the bottom of the companionway was a pile of corpses—a Gordian knot of limbs, carnage, and flesh. *Ar R'ad*'s wounded had been first carried below; later, as the engagement turned, the dead had been tossed down the ladderway. They lay now in a chest-high pile, the seeping, fetid detritus of battle. In the half-light Curran pushed past the mound of bodies. Water swirled up from the bilge and orlop, mixing with the things on the deck, making a vile, tepid brew that came over the tops of his boots.

Curran had to crouch as he moved away from the blood-splashed ladder. The deck above was sagging and the deck below buckling up, as though the ship were being pinched by a giant hand. Thirty-two-pound balls from *Enterprise*'s carronades had raked *Ar R'ad*'s lower decks, ploughing through both of the pivot gun's supports. Sergeant Lachat peered through the shattered timbers, straining his eyes against the darkness of the hold below. He pushed his bayonet through a canvas screen and tore it back. With this motion, a new sort of stench jolted through the air around them: a fug of sweat, grief, and filth—the quintessence of misery.

"Here, sir," Sergeant Lachat choked. "There's people here. Jesus, look at these bastards."

At first, Curran could make out only shadows. He heard the sound of a child and a word, *"A'tana,"* sobbed out over and over. A weak shaft of light fell into the compartment from a hole in the deck. Lachat kicked down the rest of the partition, revealing a low, elongated space filled with slaves. Long iron rods were secured fore and aft, and almost a hundred people were shackled to the bars. More were stacked on pallets bolted to the sides of the ship. At the sight of Curran and Lachat, some struggled against their chains. Others prayed and covered their faces.

Water was rising steadily, and Curran could see the tops of waves washing into the shattered stern galleries. The ship was settling fast. He put his sword back into the scabbard at his waist. "Marines!" Curran shouted. "Find some pry bars! Quickly!"

Lachat put his bayonet under one of the bars and heaved. It came away from the deck with a sharp clank, but the rod was held down with a thick Spanish padlock. Curran waved him back, drew one of his pistols, and put the muzzle against the lock case. He pulled the trigger, but the weapon only clicked and sputtered. Curran tossed the gun as Guild arrived with a pry bar. Petty Officer Guild was the captain's coxswain, the biggest man on the ship, bigger even than Padeen, and had boarded *Ar R'ad* armed only with a ten-foot pike. He doubled up the weapon and the crowbar and slipped them both under the lock's hasp.

"Damascus steel and a Springfield pike, sir. This will do it. Or I ain't a bastard in the navy." The strongest bastard in the navy, he might have added, for the big lock shattered and came from the deck planks with a resounding twang. Guild applied the crow and pike to three other bars as Curran and the Marines helped slaves doff their shackles. The dead were mixed thoroughly with the living. Several lifeless bodies had to be dragged off the bar before others could be freed. Still chained together, the corpses were tossed among the dead piled by the ladder.

The water was higher now—knee deep. A last iron shackle was pried away from a stanchion, but none of the people came to their feet. Curran bent down, sliding the bar out of the loops of chain. A mother with a ten-year-old child in her arms, half a dozen young men, and a middle-aged woman—all were dead. Curran put his hand out, steadying himself, and a shadow coalesced in front of him. It was a huge man, a Mozambequean warrior, a giant half again as big as Padeen. In the blink of an instant the shadow grabbed Curran by his uniform coat and thumped him against the bulkhead.

"You! Portagee!" The big man smashed Curran back against the pallets, then pinned him against the overhead. "I'll kill you, Portagee dog fucker!" The huge ebony fists clutched at Curran's lapels.

Curran managed to rasp out: "You speak English?!"

The big man's teeth flashed in the darkness, an evil set of filed triangles. "Enough to kill you!"

The giant swung Curran around, thudding him against the foot of the mainmast. The blow was staggering. Curran blinked back unconsciousness and finally choked, "We're not Portuguese! We're Americans."

A pair of thumbs pushed down into Curran's windpipe, extinguishing his voice. The hands closed completely around his throat, the fingers interlacing at the back of his neck. Curran reached for his sword, drew it, and smashed the pommel across the bridge of the giant's nose. He might as well have struck a granite post. The pressure increased on Curran's throat. Darkness rose behind his eyes. As Curran started to pass out, he heard the distinct click of a gunlock. In the demi-light Curran could see that Padeen had a horse pistol leveled at the warrior's ear. The Irishman palmed back the hammer. Padeen's voice was death. "Let him go!"

The warrior moved his thumbs away from Curran's throat but held tightly to his shirt. "Let him go," Padeen hissed, "or I'll blow off your fookin' head."

The black man shoved Curran away. Gasping, sputtering, Curran flew across the water-slopped deck. He splashed into the bilge, and a gallon of bloody crud went over the top of his collar and soaked his shirt. Curran coughed and finally gasped down a lungful of air.

Padeen held the pistol steady but inwardly doubted he had enough weapon. The man standing before them was almost seven feet tall and easily three hundred pounds. It seemed improbable that a .50-caliber ball, even fired point-blank, would kill him all at once.

"Now what?" the giant grunted.

Curran retrieved his sword and pointed to a cage set in the after hold. "Help us free these people."

The giant shook his head and scowled: a jagged leer.

"Help us," Curran said again.

The giant did not deign to answer. He sauntered over to the iron cage and peered into it. There were a dozen children, brown and black, tumbled together inside. They blinked in awe as the warrior grabbed the bars and pulled. There was a rending screech as rivets were popped and screws jacked out of solid oak. The Mozambequean jerked one side of the cage and tossed the bars into the orlop. Squalling, the children rushed out of the hold and away from the rising water.

"There," the big man said. He sauntered past Curran and Padeen, mounted the ladder, and went up on deck.

Curran put his hand to his throat. His collar was ripped and he could barely swallow.

"Jaysus." Padeen blinked. "I hope they only have one of him."

On deck was bedlam. People yelling, jabbering, crying, and laughing. The giant lumbered aft and shielded his eyes from the last faint light of dusk; he looked around at the destruction and lifted a lip. When he saw *Enterprise* lying close by he said, "Good." Then, looking at Beazee, he mumbled, "Good, good dog."

Gaining the deck, Curran was pressed upon by a dozen people, each yammering thanks and shouting questions. Padeen and Lachat had to push back a few of the most earnest supplicants. "What are they saying, sir?"

"I don't know. All the languages of Babel."

Guild brought forward a young man in rags, a Krepo with ashy black skin. "This one was speakin' Port-a-geeze, sir. Talking the lingo. I heard it plain—and I'm from Rhode Island. We got the Portuguese there."

Guild's Krepo was effusive. "That's Portuguese, ain't it sir?"

Curran knew that Krepo people sometimes worked aboard slave ships, and he called to the giant. "You, there!" Curran pointed at the Krepo with his sword. "Is this man a pirate?"

The big man sneered at the Krepo, plainly an inferior species, and scowled, "Ha! He's no pirate. He is a Krepo—if you eat 'im he wouldn't make a pirate's turd."

Enterprise had sheered off to prevent the riot from spilling over, and Captain Pelles hailed the deck. The brass speaking trumpet lifted his impatience by a quarter tone. "Mister Curran, are you having a county fair?"

"I can't talk to them, sir," Curran shouted back, "There's one who speaks English and nothing else . . . I have one who might speak Portuguese."

On *Enterprise*, Pelles sent Nordhoff to find Nolan. When he came onto the quarterdeck, Pelles removed his hat. "Mister Nolan, we are very grateful to you today. You've become one of us, and done duty beyond any expectation. If I could impose upon you for a bit more of your time, I would be grateful."

A smile crept over Nolan's powder-streaked face. He pressed the captain's hand and stammered, "I am the one who is grateful, sir."

A plank was put across, and Marines kept the way around it clear. Nolan was helped up onto the gang board, jumped across, and dropped onto *Ar R'ad*'s deck. The stricken corsair was now fully three feet lower than when the boarders went over. Water washed in and out of her shattered stern, and the wreck was listing markedly to starboard.

"Nolan," Curran said above the tumult, "see if you can calm them. Tell them they are free."

Nolan's eyes fell on the giant. "I gather this one is in charge?"

Curran nodded. "Completely. But he claims he does not speak Portuguese. Nor is he interested in the others."

Around them were shouted a dozen languages and dialects, from Hutu to the croaking of Beledeljereed. Nolan said a few words in Portuguese, basic words, and the young Krepo man translated, shouting into the crowd. An Ashanti translated into Bantu, a Bantu into Zulu, and a Ghanese woman called out in Mala. There was a gasp, a moment of disbelief, and then yelps of delight.

Questions were shouted to Nolan and translated, more or less, into Portuguese. Nolan interpreted: "This man says he paddled to Fernando Po to find a doctor and that the slavers captured him within sight of his home." Nolan's voice became thick. "These people say that they were led from their country by a Sunni imam. He bid them settle near a fort to be nearer Allah, and they were thrown into shackles."

Nolan struggled with these translations, each tale of woe deeper and more heart-breaking than the last. "This woman," Nolan choked, "has not heard a word from her child in more than a year, and she was locked up in an infernal barracoon." Nolan's face became pale. "This one says he had not seen his family in three years. This one saw his parents killed and his home burned." Nolan felt as though his heart would burst. His agony was so plain that even the giant could see it.

Nolan ached to hear how much home meant to these people; even as death clutched them, they wanted not life but home. Each time Nolan recounted the death of a loved one or the breaking up of a family his voice faltered. The burden of these words seemed almost to make him swoon.

Half a dozen lanterns came over from *Enterprise*. In the light of the first of them strode Captain Pelles. The Marines presented arms with a clap and stomp, which silenced the deck.

"This is a goat fuck, Mister Curran."

"It is, sir. We are trying to restore some order."

Pelles surveyed the material aspects of the ship, subtracting human elements both dead and living. He frowned as he looked over the masts, hull, deck, and what remained of the guns. The corsair was a wreck.

Nolan gathered himself. "Sir, they are asking what will be done with them."

"Done with them?" Pelles said. "Why, they are free!"

The giant tapped Pelles on the shoulder. The captain glared about, looking for the person who had the temerity to lay a hand on his person. Pelles' eyes widened as he looked up.

"Free, you say?" the giant grunted. "What does that mean?" The warrior pulled himself up to his full height, as tall and broad as a pair of shot lockers.

"Who is this man, Mister Curran? Is he a corsair?"

"Portuguese bastard," the warrior hissed. "I am Mozambequean."

Curran was certain that no living human had ever called Pelles a bastard and survived. He could not be sure how long the captain's patience would last. Curran said quickly, "He was chained below, sir. One of the captives."

Pelles marveled at the man's pointed teeth. They were brilliant in the lantern light. "How is it that he speaks English?"

"How does a dog bark?" the warrior snorted.

A smile pulled up the corner of Pelles' thin mouth. "How did you come by your language, sir?"

"Pssssh," the big man scoffed. "I learned from British missionaries. Same as you."

Pelles' booming laugh ignited smiles around the deck.

Nolan said, "Captain? What do I tell them? They want to go home."

"Tell them I will take them all to Sierra Leone," Pelles said. "They will be safe there."

The Krepo jumped onto the wreckage of one of the guns and bawled out the news at the top of his lungs. The crowd thronged around Pelles, practically ecstatic, and a baby was waved under Pelles' nose.

"Captain's pardon, sir," Padeen broke in. "But they ain't going anywhere on this ship, sir. I got some holes shored, but she's filling fast and there ain't no pump."

Pelles was already convinced that the ship was doomed. "Do what you can to keep her afloat until we can transfer these people aboard the xebec."

The ship gave a long, shivering groan. It was going to pieces under their feet.

"Mister Curran, see that the irons are knocked off the captives. And let's have some food and water."

The darkness about them was total. Pelles lifted his lantern and peered around. By the shattered binnacle, the corsair's captain lay dead, cut through with a cannonball. *Damn me*, Pelles thought. *This has been a nasty business.*

THE DEADLIGHTS HAD BEEN REMOVED FROM THE GREAT CABIN'S WINDOWS, evening had fallen, and the wide, curving parabola of glass reflected back the scene within. Pelles sat in duck trousers and a cotton chemise, a small cut on his scalp shaved and stitched, his shoulders hunched, and his empty sleeve pinned to his shirtfront. He leaned over his desk with blotter squared, best paper, inkwell, and a steel pen just at hand. A whale oil lantern burned on the table, and another lolled sullenly on an overhead gimbal.

Enterprise was heaved to a mere half a degree from where the sea fight unfolded. The hands had been piped to supper ten minutes earlier, and the decks had quieted. Pelles was tired, nearly exhausted, but long training and an implacable sense of duty made him sit to write down the facts of the engagement before their details could be forgotten. He threaded his spectacles behind his ears and placed a shade upon his forehead. His eyes burned from powder smoke, but he dipped his pen and wrote neatly:

> Officer Commanding,
> United States Frigate *Enterprise*
> At sea, 18th May
>
> The Honorable Benjamin Crowninshield
> Secretary of the Navy
> At the Capitol, Washington City
>
> Sir,
>   On the 16th instant, being in latitude 31° 24' N, longitude
> 20° 48' W, the frigate *Enterprise* under my command encountered

an abandoned boat belonging to the American whale ship *McKendrie Evans* of Point Judith. The whaleboat was found to be damaged by grapeshot and musketry, with no hands aboard.

Taking precautions, *Enterprise* proceeded north, and in the afternoon of the 17th three of sail were discovered from the masthead bearing east by north. The ships were revealed to be a former Dutch East India ship, *Ameland*, taken by pirates off Algiers. This vessel, renamed *Ar R'ad*, had been fitted for cruising and made into a frigate mounting 24 cannon as well as two 42-pound pivot guns. Sailing in consort with *Ar R'ad* was a prize, the brig sloop *Courier*, of Marseilles, and a xebec store ship of 320 tons, *Yunis*.

At 3:50 p.m., *Ar R'ad* hoisted Algerine colors, viz. a foresail painted in the livery of the Dey of Algiers. *Enterprise*'s barge and cutter, manned and armed, then parted and began to chase the consorts.

At 4:50, at 1,400 yards, *Ar R'ad* opened the engagement. At 4:54, at 1,300 yards, *Enterprise* returned fire and struck *Ar R'ad* in the stern. The engagement now became general. The ship *Ar R'ad* was armed with a pair of 42-pound siege guns mounted on swivels. These weapons did terrible execution, and after being struck several times, *Enterprise* was maneuvered to avoid the arc of their fire. At length, *Ar R'ad*'s masts went by the board. I directed Mister Francis Gifford Curran, the fourth lieutenant, to lead a boarding party. At 5:45, he gained the deck. It is to Mister Curran's credit that he was able to locate and free 167 persons, taken as slaves aboard *Ar R'ad* and confined in the lower hold. In the space of forty minutes, after evacuating the captives, *Ar R'ad* set down by the bow and foundered. Captured aboard *Ar R'ad* were ship's papers, which will be translated and sent forward under separate cover.

A Marine detachment, sent in the ship's boats, captured both of the corsair's prizes, the brig sloop *Courier* and the store ship *Yunis*. In this action Marine captain Douglas MacQuarrie distinguished himself, carrying both vessels by main boarding after tenacious resistance.

The men I have the honor to command fought with great courage and tenacity. I bring to your notice the exemplary conduct of Philip Clinton Nolan, late a Lieutenant of United States Artillery, and now a prisoner held aboard *Enterprise* per standing orders of the Department of the Navy. Though not compelled to fight, Mister Nolan willingly and conspicuously put himself in the enemy's line of fire, commanding a gun and then a division of sailors after several of my own officers became casualties.

Although the Africans freed from the corsair place a burden on the ship's stores, it has not been judged prudent to put them ashore in the Portuguese islands, as it is likely that they would again go into bondage. I therefore intend to land the liberated captives at the British colony at Sierra Leone then proceed to the flag at Cádiz to adjudicate the prizes.

Of *Enterprise*'s complement, seventeen were killed and thirty-seven wounded. Among the dead are Mister Kerr, Third Lieutenant, Mister F. R. Leslie, Fourth Lieutenant, and Lieutenant Marvin N. Varney of the U.S. Marines. Seriously wounded were Lieutenant D. K. Erskine and Midshipman B. Kevin Wainwright. Twenty-seven corsairs were captured aboard the brig sloop *Courier*. The enemy aboard the ship *Ar R'ad* fought and died to the last; counted on her decks were two-hundred-forty-three corpses.

I have the honor to be, &c.
Arthur Pelles, Commanding

Pelles finished his letter, sanded and blotted the page, then gave it to the ship's clerk to be copied fair. When the messenger had gone, he stretched out on the lockers in the great cabin. Rolling onto his side, Pelles closed his eyes for the first time in forty-eight hours. He exhaled, sensing the slow roll of the ship, a motion soothing and familiar to the depths of his soul.

After a moment of warm darkness, a woman's name came to him, and then the soaring notes of her voice, "*Sperai vicino il lido.*"

Italian was a language Pelles almost never spoke; he had learned it as an adjunct of the music he loved, an idiom fundamental to melody itself. For Pelles, it was almost a secret language, a grammar of emotions, inextricable from song. Pelles heard the orchestra, and a pure soprano embroidered note upon note, trill and tremolo, beyond any beauty he had thought possible. It was thirty years ago, and he remembered perching in a theater balcony, one soul among two hundred watching enthralled. Before him, he saw the gentle curve of her neck, her hands floating, bone white and as small as a child's. Her name was Edita, and Pelles was beguiled.

As abruptly as a squall, the music gusted and the angel's voice suddenly threatened, the cadenza sweeping all before it, heaving the sea into mountains and avalanching whitewater. Pelles felt her fingers trace the scar on his brow, and he tasted her kiss.

Pelles opened his eyes. The cabin was dark now; Grimble must have extinguished the lamps while he dozed. Pelles placed his hand on his forehead. He heard only the creaking of the ship. The reek of cannon smoke and the tang of blood wafted from his clothing. Valletta was a thousand leagues away and infinitely distant in time. The voice was gone; the notes evaporated into the pale moonlight streaming in through the stern window.

Gone was that perfect creature. And gone, too, was the young midshipman waiting in a balcony for something never to be had.

THE LETTER OF MARQUE

THE EMOTIONS OF BATTLE DO NOT READILY LEAVE A SHIP AFTER COMBAT. The wounds of the crew are the wounds of the ship—harm one and the other is injured also. A soldier might serve in a dozen campaigns, but he will almost never fight in the same place twice. A sailor's battlefield is invariably his own ship; the memory of combat is near as a man's skin, and sorrow for fallen shipmates always as close as an empty hammock.

Aboard *Enterprise*, surgeons and messmates bandaged and tenderly nursed the stricken, even those whose wounds were mortal. When death came, the survivors' pain was like the grief of families. *Enterprise* had received a dozen cruel blows, but her masts and hull were sound. Aside from the terrible cost in blood, the damage was confined mostly to the spar and gun decks, and none of it was structural. Of more immediate concern were the ship's boats. The blue cutter had been smashed to pieces and swept over the side. The gig and red cutter had both suffered on their expedition against *Ar R'ad*'s prizes; only the barge had come through without a scratch.

Though the pirates aboard *Courier* had let their sails fly in signal of surrender, those aboard *Yunis* had used her swivel guns and fought until the last. As the Marines attempted to board, grapeshot and musketry spattered into the red cutter, wounding Corporal Hackman and several others. MacQuarrie's leathernecks then stormed aboard, and in a sharp, desperate action took the xebec. Aboard *Yunis*, fighting had been hand-to-hand. MacQuarrie himself led a party belowdecks and grappled with a black-turbaned fanatic who was attempting to set off the ship's magazine. The *sayyid* managed to stab MacQuarrie before being chopped down by the cutlass of an equally zealous Marine. Later examination showed that a firing train had been laid and tinder prepared throughout the hold. In addition to a cargo of 42-pound cannon balls, *Yunis* carried 150 kegs of finely corned French powder. Had the magazine been fired, the ship would have been blown into the sky.

During the long day after the battle, *Enterprise* was heaved to and her prizes lolled under her lee. The frigate rang with the thud of caulking hammers and the hails of boat crews plying between the ships. Those of the slaves who were not wounded were put aboard *Yunis*. Water and ship's biscuit were served out, along with small stores, Guernsey frocks, and duck trousers, for most of the slaves were mother naked. One of the surgeon's mates set up a sickbay under an awning and fed porridge, boiled eggs, and barley water to a dozen reed-thin children.

Aboard *Yunis*, Padeen had been placed in charge of the working party, mustering the former corsairs with scowls and blood-curdling Gaelic curses. Passed man to man, the cargo of 42-pound shot went overboard in a series of deep, chunking splashes. If the corsairs were not right quick about their duty, Padeen was sure to hurry them, starting them with a fast-moving boot. Most of the cannonballs were cast of iron, but many were carved from single pieces of dark marble, and though they were beautiful objects, they were of little use to *Enterprise* except as souvenirs for the gunner's mates. But the powder was another matter; most of it, in kegs still marked with the French imperial eagle, was carried over and put down into the frigate's magazine.

As *Yunis* was offloaded, the freedmen mostly ignored their former captors. The newly liberated did not care for anything beyond fresh air, clean water, and ship's biscuit. Only the Mozambequean warrior (whose name was Fante) took any interest in justice. It was he who pointed to a shame-faced Syrian and said, "This fuck—he is the one who owns the cargo."

Padeen was not over-gentle when he clapped the Syrian into irons and sent him aboard *Enterprise* to be questioned.

———

IN THE ORLOP DOCTOR DARBY WORKED LIKE AN AUTOMATON. WITHOUT PAUSE or rest he amputated arms and legs, extracted bullets, trepanned skulls, splinted bones, patched and sutured. This labor gradually winnowed those who could be saved from those who could not. For two days and nights he and the surgeon's mates treated the wounded and moved those who could survive the trip into an expanded sickbay on the berth deck. On coming back aboard, Nolan joined Darby in his surgery, helping to bandage and carry stretchers. Those less gravely hurt were carried up onto the spar deck, as it was Darby's opinion that wounded men needed air and light, two things in short supply in the cockpit of a frigate.

Below, in the dim glow of lanterns, half a dozen sailors and two Marines swung in cots, clinging to life or preparing to slip the coil. As Darby worked, Nolan went about with a bucket and swab, mopped blood, and gathered up discarded arms and legs. When he had finished scrubbing, Nolan tended those most gravely hurt, spelling a tourniquet where needed and dispensing datura and blue tincture of morphine under Darby's supervision. This work left them both spattered and exhausted.

One cot hanging in the sickbay was smaller than the others. Under a dim lantern Nolan sponged blood and powder from the forehead of Midshipman Wainwright. The boy had been in and out of consciousness since the cautery of his arm, an agony he bore with heart-rending bravery. As valiantly as Nolan had fought on the gun deck he now struggled for Wainwright's life. He sat all the night at the boy's side, watching as Darby checked his pulse—pounding some moments, weakening dangerously in others—wiping his brow, holding his arm as the shattered limb was re-splinted and bandaged fresh. Wainwright's breathing was normal and slow, but what encouragement Nolan could take in this was shaken by the other symptoms: a deathly, waxen pallor, obvious paralysis below the waist, and a persistent drenching sweat. The morphia made him doze fitfully, and sometimes his lips would move, but he did not speak.

When most of the critically wounded had been taken care of and moved onto the berth decks, Padeen came and sat with them, his eyes brimming and his big, rough hands laced together. In the flickering light Padeen looked at Wainwright and then at Darby. His eyes posed the question, but the doctor returned to his instruments, wiping each against his apron and replacing it in a velvet-lined box. The doctor had done what he could; it was not enough and he knew it. When Padeen left the sickbay and the door closed behind him Darby let his head droop and wiped his eyes.

Curran came at once from the quarterdeck when they sent for him. Wainwright's face in the flickering light of the surgical lanterns was both wan and luminous. Curran sat with Nolan by the hammock, and after a long moment the boy swallowed heavily and his eyes stayed open. Curran had to look away when he saw that Wainwright's pupils were dilated unevenly, one wide and black, the other like a spot on a dirty mirror.

Nolan wetted the sponge and daubed across the boy's forehead. Wainwright seemed to concentrate and then said hoarsely, "Mister Nolan?"

"I'm here, shipmate."

"Good." Wainwright let go of the blankets. His hand flopped across his chest and then closed over Nolan's. The fingers squeezed together weakly, and his palm was clammy. Curran lifted his hand, taking both Nolan's and Wainwright's into his own, locking his fingers and holding firmly.

Wainwright's voice was a whisper wrapped in the murmurs of the ship. "I'm glad of your company, gentlemen," he said.

The hammock rocked slowly on its clews. As a lantern shadow went across Wainwright's face, his eyes fluttered and closed slowly, first the right, and then the left. A sigh came from his pale lips, his forehead relaxed, and his jaw trembled. After this, he was still. So gently did his soul go free from the shattered little body, it was almost as if Kevin David Wainwright had been peacefully unborn rather than died.

THE SYRIAN SENT ABOARD BY PADEEN WAS BROUGHT AFT AT THE END OF THE morning watch. He was led first into the wardroom and then into Curran's freshly scrubbed stateroom. The prisoner was a tall, sharp-featured man with dark eyes. Under a prominent nose he had a weak, almost dainty chin. This, surmounted by a wispy, close-cut mustache and beard, gave an impression of youth, though the man was older than Curran by a dozen years. The Syrian's clothes were dirty but well made, as were his sandals.

Curran's expression showed little, though he was tired, depressed, and angry. He allowed the prisoner's shackles to be removed but had the Marine stand close behind him.

"What is your name?" Curran asked in Lingua Franca, the bastard French of the Levant. The man smiled thinly and shook his head. Curran asked him again, this time using Italian verbs, and the man answered.

"Abdur Rahman."

"Who is your father?"

The man answered that his people were Zurand and al Kharsah.

"And how do you earn your bread, Abdur Rahman al Kharsah?"

"I am a sailor," came the answer, improbably combined in French, Arabic, and Italian. Curran had seen the man praying on the spar deck at noon. The prisoner had been given water for his ablutions and had made a great show of religious fervor.

"You are a pious man?"

"I am."

"Where is your ship from?"

"From?"

"What port is home?"

"Sidon."

"You are four thousand miles from the al Sham," Curran said. "Show me your hands."

The man lifted his palms.

Curran now spoke in perfect, lilting Arabic: "You are a liar, Abdur Rahman. You say you are a sailor, but your hands are like a woman's. Your clothing is finely made and you have leather on your feet. You are no mariner, or you might have had an idea what was east and what was west instead of waving your ass at the Holy Q'aba." The man was astonished. Curran went on: "And though you claim to be a true and orthodox Muslim, I find that you have sailed in a ship filled with Shiite heretics. As Christians, we are not over-concerned with what is correct in a Muslim. Our opinions of piracy, however, are very much more stringent."

"Surely the effendi does not think I am a pirate—or a Shiite?"

"As you bear the name of the same angry creature who slew the gentle Ali, you are not likely to be Shia. Whether you are on the right path I know not, but several of the men aboard *Ar R'ad* were *sayyids*, fierce Shia partisans, and their black turbans could not have escaped your notice."

"I am from the Levant, Effendi. I have learned to live at close quarters with all manner of nonbelievers and apostates—Shiites, Copts, Jews, Maronites, even Druses and Alawites. I cannot be blamed for what others believe."

"Who took the French ship?"

The merchant shifted on his feet.

"Understand me, Abdur Rahman. I don't care very much what happens to you. The ship you were on was a French merchantman. We have her papers at hand. You and the others are not her rightful owners."

"I am a humble merchant, Effendi."

"You are a liar, and you are no seaman. Since you are not a sailor, you cannot exactly be called a pirate. Not *exactly*. But I see no merchandise aboard the ship you occupied other than a French cargo, which is the fruit of piracy, and powder and shot, which are the tools of the trade." Curran put his arm over the back of his chair. "I require information," he said. "And I will get it one way or another. The man in the green jacket behind you is a United States Marine. They are our own *sayyids*, very enthusiastic creatures, perfectly zealous. Their religion is victory, and they worship precision in all things. They spend days dreaming of battle and would rather crouch upon the desolation and ashes of their enemies than lie down in cool gardens. You see, they are much, much more ferocious than normal men, rather more like bulldogs who serve the Devil. Perhaps you have noticed the point of his bayonet? And the cutlass he wears? They do not get paid, or fed, unless they kill a dozen men a month."

"Pray, Effendi, what are they fed that makes them so grim?"

"The flesh of swine. And prisoners."

Rahman searched Curran's face for a trace of mirth. Certainly he was being made the butt of some Frankish joke. But it chilled him when he turned and the Marine met his eyes with fearsome indifference.

"Who owned the slaves aboard *Ar R'ad*?"

"I realize, Effendi, that I must tell you the truth. Each fact exact, precise, and true. So I am grieved that the manifest was thrown over when we sighted your ship. How I am ashamed."

Curran opened his desk, removed a pair of iron-covered ledgers, and tossed them on the desk. They landed with a clang. "Then we are lucky that duplicates were kept aboard the flagship."

The Arab crossed his arms.

"The slaves were your property and were being transported for a fee of ten parts percent, payable to the captain bey. Is that not the truth?"

"It is, Effendi."

"What happened to the American whale ship?"

"It was taken by *Ar R'ad*."

"And also *Courier*?"

"Yes." Abdur Rahman al Kharsah was indeed a merchant from Sidon in the Levant. He claimed, despite the heresy of his shipmates, to be a very good and pious Sunni, and he knew a very great deal about *Ar R'ad*. The merchant had embarked six months ago from Aleppo, trading west, exchanging precious metal and gemstones for rifles, agricultural instruments, and cheap brass manilas. Upon reaching Tripoli, Abdur Rahman embarked with his money chests on *Ar R'ad* and was aboard her when she touched at Bou Regreg in the Maghreb. It was at this notorious port that *Ar R'ad* took on her vast 42-pound cannon, and the ship was fitted for cruising.

"Why would the Dey of Bou Regreg allow a pirate vessel to be fitted in his port?"

"I do not know what the dey knows, Effendi."

"Certainly you knew *Ar R'ad* was no merchant ship," Curran said firmly.

"The effendi knows I am no sailor. I knew only that they had taken aboard cannon. I was happy to be on a ship blessed with such an abundance of protection."

"Where did the guns come from?"

"They were a gift from His Majesty the King of Portugal to the Dey of Bou Regreg. Does your country have a king, Effendi?"

"We do not."

"You are bereft of a guiding hand, a person chosen by God. Does that not leave your government curiously adrift?"

"Tell me about the cannon. How many of them were there?"

"Four. I saw myself as they were unloaded from a Portuguese ship of battle."

"You do not mean a ship of the line?"

"I am not a creature of the sea, but it was a ship bearing cannon, nearly as graceful and warlike as your own, Bey Effendi.

"It was a frigate?"

"Yes, that is the word, that most warlike of ships. The Portuguese vessel bore the name of a place, a beautiful place, in that kingdom."

"*Azóla.*"

"The effendi is all-knowing and wise. That is exactly the name. The Portuguese frigate delivered the guns and assisted as they were put aboard *Ar R'ad* and fitted. There was much work to put them into iron boxes on the deck. Two of the guns were put aboard, and two others were mounted on a pair of great, oaken tumbrels and left the city with a squadron of escort."

"Go on," Curran said coldly.

"There came also aboard in Bou Regreg two hundred of the dey's bodyguards, among them *sayyid* learned in both the Holy Word and the artifices of artillery. We had also the pick of a battalion of Mameluks."

"The dey's bodyguards? I know of no Mameluks who would serve a Shiite commander."

"They are lately come, Effendi. I swear it. They were in the service of the Algerine, Mustaffa Mohamed. He had lately made such an onerous peace with the British, forswearing privateering and cravenly renouncing tribute, and even manumitting all English captives. The Mameluks refused to serve under so unmanly a leader. They went together across the desert to Bou Regreg."

"Even if they were renegades, why would Janissaries, who are Sufis, serve a Shiite imam?"

"I need not tell the effendi that the Mameluks, mostly being converted Christians, do not always grasp fine points of theology. War is their trade, and I heard it said that the dey offered to pay them in gold."

"The dey made no secret of fitting out *Ar R'ad* as a cruiser?"

"He did not have it widely known, though those in the waterfront saw it. Each cannon was the size of a great oven."

"You went willingly aboard *Ar R'ad*, knowing that she would attack American ships."

"By your mother's eyes, I did not. None of us did—none, perhaps, but the *sayyid* or the Mameluk officers. I arranged passage and embarked with my merchandise as a paying passenger. Three days from Sao Toma, the captain bey read the proclamation that we were to cruise upon the infidels."

Curran frowned.

"Pardon, Effendi. I do not number you, so learned a man, among the unknowing who shall burn forever. You are rightly guided and certainly al-Kitab, a person of the book, peace be upon you."

"Go on," Curran said, drumming his fingers on the desk.

"To return to my account, the fatwas were read, and to my wonderment I found myself aboard a ship under orders to engage the enemies of the dey, wherever they might be found. You can imagine my shock when we came upon the American whaler the following week off the Canaries."

Curran grunted. "Where is *McKendrie Evans* now?"

"A person, Effendi? A friend?"

"The whaling ship."

"That vessel was sent back to Bou Regreg, also to fit out as a cruiser."

"And her crew?"

"All safe, Effendi. They were taken for ransom." Rashid then added, "All those who were not killed."

This confirmed what Curran had learned from the ironbound ledgers. One page, written on parchment and swaddled with seals, was a commission from the Dey of Bou Regreg for *Ar R'ad* and the xebec *Yunis* to cruise against His Majesty's enemies, to include merchants of those Muslim states who had capitulated to the Royal Navy. The fatwa, sanely enough, forbid taking British, Spanish, or Portuguese ships, which were deemed protected. This left the American and French merchants as lawful prey. The commission enjoined the captains to cruise upon the

Atlantic but send their prizes all the way round through the Gut into the Mediterranean port of Arzeou. There, in the Maghreb, an accommodation had been made with the dissolute Bashaw of Arzeou and a Ladino banking house. Ships taken in the Atlantic would be sold in the Mediterranean, and pleas for ransom from captured sailors would come from Arzeou rather than distant Bou Regreg. These stratagems would confound those seeking to punish the guilty and screen both the Dey of Bou Regreg and the Bashaw of Arzeou from suspicion.

"I hope that I have been of assistance," the Syrian purred.

"If you have spoken honestly, you may count upon a just and even prodigious reward."

A graceful hand poised on the dainty chin. "Then, Effendi, I wonder if I might in all delicacy raise the subject of compensation for my property?"

The merchant was surprised to be clamped back into irons. The bulky, hard-eyed Marine hustled him through the wardroom and onto the gun deck. The tubs and growlers were being stowed away, and only the gunner's mates and a dozen Marines remained hunched at one of the mess tables. Heads turned as the merchant was dragged forward. There were whistles and catcalls: "Who's the gawkey, Timmy?" and "There goes a nice set of curtains!" Though Abdur Rahman could not understand the words, he understood their tone.

At the far end of the mess deck, Rahman caught sight of Old Chick at the camboose stirring up a sooty cauldron of gumbo. The odors of shellfish and other things *haraam* made the Syrian uneasy; and when he noticed a Marine pushing through the round bone in a ham steak he felt very bleak indeed.

THE AFTERNOON SUN BEAMED THROUGH THE STERN WINDOWS, THROWING moving arches of light onto the captain's desk. *Enterprise* rolled agreeably in a southwest swell, no longer sluggish now that she had been pumped and patched. Pelles' long desk was set in sunlight, and spread before him was Curran's report with abstracts of the papers and ledgers found in *Ar R'ad*'s shattered cabin.

"This document, this commission, it amounts to a letter of marque?"

Curran answered, "It does, sir."

Pelles ran his eyes over the parchment with its seals, ribbons, and wafers of gold leaf. "One sultan says they may cruise upon the Atlantic, and another allows them to sell prizes in the Med; the spoils are divided by Hebraic moneychangers in a Barbary port. It is as neat a bit of treachery as could be imagined."

"If I may be so bold, sir. Wasn't this to be expected, sir, by President Monroe? Surely he means to strengthen the Mediterranean Squadron?"

"Mister Monroe has inherited Dolley Madison's navy," Pelles said. "And I am afraid our president may not find it sufficient to support either his grievances or our glory."

"Would it not be a simple matter to patrol the strait, sir? To prevent prize ships from being sent to market? Couldn't our squadron do that?"

"We have no ships of the line in the Med, and only three heavy frigates. If their aggressions were open, the Barbary States could be dealt with one by one. But the squadron has to safeguard shipping through the entire Mediterranean, from Marmara to the Atlantic. Were we to concentrate our forces in the Gut, our merchants would be vulnerable for the entire length of the sea."

"Have we allies?" asked Curran.

"There is peace, but we have few friends. The British have made their treaty with Algiers and are not about to burn their powder for our cause. And many of them are still smarting over the last war—Jackson's victory at New Orleans still rankles them cruelly. As for the Portuguese, you have seen what they are capable of."

Pelles touched the bell on his desk. When the cabin door opened he said, "There you are, Mister Newsome. Have these reports fair-copied as fast as a pen will move, and double-wrap them in silk and sailcloth. They are to go to Commodore Jones at once in the flag."

"At once, sir," said the clerk, hurrying out. He was met in the doorway by Mister Fentress, looking pale and somewhat top-heavy with his head wrapped in several feet of linen bandage.

"Reporting as ordered, sir." On the quarterdeck the ship's bell tolled out seven strokes.

"I am fond of punctuality, Mister Fentress. Is your head fit for navigating?"

"It is prime, sir. Thank you."

"Outstanding. A dispatch is being prepared by Mister Newsome. As soon as the ink is dry, you are to gather up Finch and eight prime hands, go aboard *Courier*, and take the message to Commodore Jones. You will find him in Cartagena. Stay clear of the Sallee coast, and make your way through the strait at the dark of the moon. You are to fly as fast as ever the brig will bear you. Do not spare the rigging."

"Direct to the Flag, sir. Stay clear of the Sallee and pass through the Gut with the new moon."

"And be certain you have *Courier*'s manifests. With any luck you might have the prize adjudicated before we join you."

"Yes, sir," Fentress smiled. Even with a bandaged head he could work out that his one-sixth of one-eighth's portion of the value of *Courier* would be a pleasant bit of coin. He spun on his heel, and as the door closed he could be heard in the passageway calling for the captain's coxswain.

Pelles looked at his desk and rubbed his eyes. Moving slowly, he stood up and walked across the cabin to the quarter gallery. An arc of light followed him, and over his broad shoulders Curran could see the portrait of the operatic lady. He had a moment to consider her as the captain threaded the ribbon of the *Guerrière* medal through a buttonhole of his best uniform coat. She was as beautiful as ever, maybe more so, her skin radiant and her bosom graced by a strand of tiny pearls. Studying her face, Curran thought that she might be a Pole, perhaps a Silesian. Her eyes were arresting—almond-shaped and as blue as heartbreak. During the fight with *Ar R'ad* a musket ball had found its way into the cabin, ricocheting through the skylight, and had split the picture frame in the right-hand corner. The captain's prize possession had been repaired and set right, as had every other part of the ship. The gilt frame had been stitched together with fancy line and a double-reefed bentinck that would have done the bo'sun proud. Pelles lifted his coatee from its dowel and came back into the cabin, putting the stump of his arm into the jacket and then holding out his hand.

"Please help me into my coat, Mister Curran," he said. "We shall rig church presently."

ENTERPRISE WAS PUT DIRECTLY INTO THE EYE OF THE SOUTHWEST TRADE. THE ship was in irons, as unmoving as anything could make itself on the surface of the sea. Her courses filled but drew weakly, and her topsails were laid carefully back. Halyard and sheets, always precise and taut, had been set cock-a-bill, as custom demanded, and the entry port on the starboard gangway was left open. All of these little faults amounted to the seagoing equivalent of widow's weeds, for *Enterprise* was mourning her dead.

Pelles stood behind a shot locker covered in signal flags, as was the carronade immediately before him; these served as podium and pulpit. Drawn up before him were the ship's divisions, scrubbed, shaved, and in their best uniforms, brass buttons shined, linen as white as saltwater could make it, their black, tar-lacquered hats in their hands. Messmates supported the walking wounded, and a dozen more seriously injured sailors and Marines watched from hammocks slung under the forecastle rail. Behind Pelles stood the officers: Mister Erskine on crutches and Captain MacQuarrie, who had a hundred stitches across his arms and chest, held up by Doctor Darby. Nolan stood in the better of his two shabby blue coats, the swallowtail, with his round hat in his hands. Along the quarterdeck rail, the Marines were mustered in martial glory. Somewhat battered physically, they were turned out in their immaculate green jackets and leather stocks, brass polished and webbing pipe-clayed exactly.

The ship was silent. Arranged by the starboard gangway were seventeen canvas hammocks. All were sewn tightly, and each had one of the beautiful marble cannonballs from *Yunis* stowed at its foot. Under their hammock-shrouds the dead had arms and legs bound with sheet linen, and each body was closed into its funeral veil with a last stitch run through the nose. All, save two: Lieutenant Varney, whose head had been swept away, and Mister Wainwright, for there was not one of the midshipmen who washed and prepared him for burial that could bear to put a needle into him.

Pelles lowered his eyes to the prayer book and looped his spectacles behind his ears. The only sound was the wind in the rigging and the gentle ruffling of the main topsail. "Lord, thou hast been our refuge," Pelles said. "From one generation to another, before the mountains were brought forth, before even the world was made." His finger touched the well-known page. "Thou art mighty in heaven. For a thousand years in thy sight are but as yesterday, and a man's life is past as a watch in the night."

Behind the officers, the midshipmen wept openly, and among the crew many had eyes that were bright with tears. Curran stood next to Nolan, both swaying automatically with the roll of the ship.

"We therefore commit their bodies to the deep, looking for the Resurrection on the last day, and the life of the world to come, when the sea shall give up her dead; and the corruptible bodies of those who sleep in her shall be changed, and made glorious in Your majesty. Amen."

Three hundred whispered "amens" answered Pelles. He closed the prayer book, stepped back from the locker, and put his hat on. The bo'sun lifted his pipe, and a long, shrill melody spilled up. The boards were tipped and seventeen shrouds went over the side. Splashes would be their only monuments.

Pelles turned as Erskine hobbled forward. "You may dismiss the ship's company, Mister Erskine. I am very pleased to find that the frigate is in remarkable order. She has been turned out as good as the day she was launched." Pelles did not often give compliments, and he was pleased to see the look of honest pleasure on the faces of the men around him. "I believe you may splice the main brace."

The order providing a double tot of whiskey would normally have been met with a cheer, but the crew went below without much talk at all. As the formation broke up, Nolan offered condolences to Mister Piggen, but the purser walked past him, pretending not to hear. Without Varney, his goad and guide, Piggen looked forlorn indeed.

Pelles looked over the taffrail. *Yunis* was still heaved to under the frigate's lee, and *Courier* was already going away to windward. Fentress, for all his bombast, was famous for his superstitious dread of funerals, and now he was running *Courier* away like a scalded hound. "Mister Curran, you will go aboard the xebec with a prize crew and transport the captives to Sierra Leone."

It took Curran a moment to comprehend. "I am to take command of the prize?"

"Are you gun deaf, Mister Curran?"

"No, sir. Thank you, sir. But I don't know Sierra Leone. I have never been there."

"You are a navigator, are you not? Freetown harbor is north of Cape Palmas, and I am sure it has not been moved. Mister Newsome has prepared letters of marque and reprisal commissioning your vessel so you may defend yourself at sea. When you are prepared to get under way, *Enterprise* will follow."

Curran touched his hat. "Yes, sir. Thank you, sir."

Pelles turned to Nolan. "Mister Nolan, I understand that you were aboard USS *Cyane* when she was stationed in the Bight of Benin. You were present when she put ashore freed African colonists at Perseverance Island, were you not?"

"I was, sir. With Captain Spence. I learned my Portuguese from one of the freedmen, João Ballinada."

"Would you recognize the landfall?"

"I would, sir; I helped Mister Dashiell with his survey."

Pelles nodded. "And I am happy to tell you that your name is still on the charts. I will have you go aboard *Yunis* as well. Should Cape Palmas have gone adrift, you might help Mister Curran find it. And as the freedmen seem to find you amusing, perhaps you can persuade them to be orderly."

"I shall do my best, sir."

There was no one else with them on the sacred starboard side of the quarterdeck, and Pelles spoke candidly. "Mister Nolan, your conduct yesterday was highly creditable. I want you to know that you have been named in my dispatches."

Nolan's expression showed very little. "I am honored, sir."

"I hope you understand that without authority I cannot alter the circumstances of your confinement. But you may be sure that I will write a letter to the Secretary of the Navy."

"Captain, you need not mix your good name with mine."

"What do you mean, sir?"

"I thank you, sincerely, for your notice of me. But others have written. To the Navy and to the War Office. It does no good, and I am sure it would hurt your interests."

Pelles shook his head. "My interest is the men who sail with me, Mister Nolan. You could have stayed below and counted quills as Piggen did; instead you put yourself in the line of fire. I will make that fact known in Washington. Now grab up your seabag; your boat will soon be away."

RECKONING

ELIEVED OF AN UNGAINLY CARGO OF POWDER AND SHOT, *YUNIS* PROVED
to be a lively and well-found vessel. Her foremast was canted charmingly
over the bow and supported a huge lateen and even a trysail. In his years at
sea Curran had never sailed such an eclectic rig, and it took one of the older hands,
once a Maltese fisherman, to show him the workings of the brails, martinets, and
bowline tackles. Once their mysteries were comprehended, Curran found that his
new command steered, tacked, and went to windward like a charm.

Yunis had been purpose-built as a privateer. Her entrance was narrow and her
beam was wide, making her hull roomy enough to carry a large crew and a generous cargo of loot. An old-fashioned stern castle gave her a benign, even obsolete
appearance. Even in her present ballast she could be steered within three points of
the wind, and her innocent looks and dash were the perfect attributes to combine
in a corsair ship. Yet for all her sprightliness, *Yunis* could not hope to match the
frigate's towering pyramid of sail—but in light airs, or sailing on a bow line, *Yunis*
was a match for any ship that swam.

As they neared the Bight of Benin the sea became increasingly green and shallow. The charts of the coast were nothing to swear by, and the strain of Curran's
first command coupled with exacting navigational calculations made him a bit
more quiet than usual. He had aboard twenty hands from *Enterprise*, including
Padeen and Kanoa, but he also had a hundred freed slaves to care for and twenty
prisoners to watch. This made the decks crowded. Nothing hampers a ship like
spectators, and the milling about made it difficult to simultaneously work the ship
and keep an eye on the prisoners. It had been Nolan's idea to ask *Enterprise* for a file
of Marines, and they proved invaluable for keeping the prisoners apart from their
former captives.

At night, Curran and Nolan slung their hammocks in the xebec's great cabin.
The space would have been called rectangular had it not curved in a pair of smooth,
converging lines to the ornately engraved gallery. In the aftermost part of the cabin,
a padded locker arched below the five inward-sloping stern lights. The carriages of
a pair of 4-pound brass cannon flanked the locker. These were fine, British-made
chasers, fitted to Royal Navy carriages. Like the thick Persian carpet under their
trucks, the guns were the proceeds of piracy.

Well after midnight, Curran came below to work out a sight and mark the chart. Through the stern windows the wake glowed green, lighting the cabin in a pale, wan light. Nolan was in his hammock and stirred as Curran put away his night glass.

"How goes it?"

"I didn't mean to wake you," Curran said. He put down a two-candle lantern on the table and opened his notes. "I have a few jottings to make."

"I wasn't asleep," Nolan yawned.

"I never met a man who said he was," Curran smiled. He unrolled the chart and held it down with the lantern and the case holding his dividers.

"I did a bit of poking around the cabin this afternoon," Nolan said. "I found some flags in the stern locker, satin and silk. They are very grand and make capital blankets. I put one on your hammock."

Curran glanced over. The wake and a band of moonlight made the cabin seem lit by a low fireplace. There was a red piece of silk draped across his berth: it was bisected by a wide green stripe, also of silk: the merchant ensign of the Ottoman caliphate.

"Thank you. I have never had such a blanket."

"Mine is a bit more morbid," Nolan said. His was also of silk, but deeply black, possibly the darkest thing in the ship. "Am I wrong to think this is some sort of badge of piracy?"

"Some might agree, even among the Muslims. It is one of the flags of the Prophet—the al-Uqab. In western eyes, the black flag was flown by buccaneers and signaled no quarter. For the corsair, that is only a happy coincidence. The black flag is an object of piety. Though I must say it pleases the Arabs that a symbol of their belief should strike terror into the infidel."

"The infidel?" Nolan considered the word. "Then I reckon I am one of those."

Curran rubbed his eyes—he did not know what he was. But more pressing, he did not know exactly *where* he was. Before the clouds covered the moon he had taken sights on Arcturus and Deneb, and had added to them a decent series of lunar altitudes. All of these data had to be ground through the requisite tables, calculated, and plotted onto the nautical chart. Once separated from the mind-boggling cosmic principles, it was a relatively simple twenty-two-step task of transposition and arithmetic calculation.

Nolan watched Curran open the thick volume of celestial tables, flip through a couple of pages, and then close the book on his finger. Curran closed his eyes for a moment.

"I hope you'll not think I am being presumptuous, but if you'd like, I might be able to help with the calculations."

"Help me?" Curran asked. "How?"

"This may sound odd, but I can reduce a celestial sight. I am not as versed in the use of a sextant—taking the actual observations—but I can do the calculations and the spherical trigonometry. I can also plot courses and offsets."

Curran might have been less astounded if Nolan had said he had learned how to make gold out of olive pits. "How did you come by your skill?"

Nolan shrugged. "I learned mathematics as an artilleryman. Though most of it was parabolic and statistical, I found that I had an interest. Aboard *Holyoke* I became friends with the navigator."

Curran leaned into the chart table, his weight on his elbows. "You knew Captain Pelles," he heard himself say. Had he not been so tired Curran would have checked his tongue and not simply blurted what he knew.

"I did," Nolan answered, "Lieutenant Pelles, he was then. We shared an interest in calculus. Pelles used to call them 'infinitesimal problems.' He wrote a paper on them. We talked a lot about infinity. I guess all young men must, and I was interested in the stars. It was not considered proper for me to be seen using a compass or sextant. It might have been interpreted as preparations for an escape, but I learned very well how to use the tables and make calculations. And also to draw and plot a survey chart. When one of the master's mates was swept overboard at the Horn, I was allowed to check the plots and eventually even reduce them myself. For a while I had my own dividers and parallel rulers, given to me by the wardroom."

"Poor Mister Pybus has had an ally all along," Curran said. "He never knew he had help in the computational line."

"I couldn't exactly tell the master that I could navigate. He would surely have asked how I learned. In any case, no one asked, and there was no occasion to mention it."

Curran looked across the desk at the pile of tables and scraps of paper. "It would be a great help to me if you could assist in reducing these plots. I find I have all I can do on deck. I am not at all familiar with this rig. It is . . . "

"Exotic."

"I am still almost baffled by the lateen forward."

"Then I will be happy to help." Nolan pushed back his covers and dropped out of his hammock. "There is cheese and biscuit for midrats," he said. "Soft biscuits like the angels eat. Gubbins brought wheat flour aboard and a great wheel of cheddar. If you would care for a bite, I will plot these while you eat."

Curran did not remember when he last ate. "Midrats would be capital," he said. Curran stood and offered Nolan his hand. "Thank you. I will go and eat something."

Nolan returned Curran's grip and slid behind the chart table. "Don't thank me yet. We may still bump into Africa, but if we do, it will not be because I have failed you arithmetically."

Curran did his best to smother a yawn.

"Get some victuals," Nolan said, taking up a pencil. "You can check my plots when you have eaten. Then it will be dreams wrapped in the banners of the righteous."

WHEN DAWN BROKE ON THE MORNING OF THE FOURTH DAY, *ENTERPRISE* WAS hull down in the south-southeast, a white nick in the darkness. Aboard *Yunis*, Nolan went forward to the elm-tree pump in the bow to wash his face. Thunder had been grumbling and crashing since the middle watch, though not a drop had fallen aboard. The sky in the east was saffron, and widely strewn thunderheads put up oblong towers between the last fading stars. To the west, a silver piece of moon drifted low on the horizon. At sunrise, Nolan usually stood in line to use the pump, but this morning he found himself alone. Ordinarily, a dozen believers crowded between the fore and main masts to pray, but the forecastle was empty.

Nolan sensed a mute restlessness among the Africans on deck; to this were added the shifty, hostile glances of the prisoners, who were gathered in a knot by the foremast chains to starboard. As he shaved, Nolan heard whispering and the distinct clink of metal from the forepeak. There were murmurs in Portuguese, which he understood, and orders given in Arabic, which he did not comprehend. Pulling his shirt over wet skin, Nolan calmly folded his razor into his towel and walked back to the quarterdeck.

Curran was at the taffrail, looking into the wake at the boat towing astern.

"Good morning, Philip," Curran said.

"It may not be," Nolan answered quietly. "The slavers are preparing to take back the ship."

Curran glanced forward. On deck, the freedmen were clustered around the mainmast, but the usual orderly line for breakfast had degenerated into a sullen clutch of bodies. Crowded into the bow were a dozen of *Yunis'* former crewmen, the slavers, none of them looking aft, a few of them incongruously wearing cloaks. In the middle was the Syrian merchant, Abdur Rahman; on his head was a voluminous black turban. Curran was suddenly furious with himself; he had underestimated this man completely.

"There are a dozen on deck," Curran said. "Where are the others?"

Nolan calmly tucked in his shirt. "I noticed that they have gained access to a compartment in the forepeak. I think it may be some sort of hidden armory, or a cache of weapons overlooked in our search. Several have slipped their leg irons."

The thunderheads rumbled distantly and echoed off the hull. It was just then four bells, the middle of the watch, and the sand turned out of the glass. Curran said to the quartermaster, "Bannon, strike eight bells."

"Eight, sir?"

"Calmly and deliberately, Bannon."

Bannon did as he was told, striking twice as many strokes as required, and as Curran expected, half a dozen Enterprises came up from below looking to see what was wrong and who it was on watch that had idiotically mistaken the bell.

Curran's ominous expression quickly caught the eyes of Padeen and Kanoa. On deck, neither the slavers in the bow nor the freedmen lined up for breakfast had recognized that an alarm had been sounded. Curran watched as Abdur Rahman continued to harangue the men on the bow.

"What gives, sir?" Padeen hissed.

In a conversational tone Curran said, "Mister Nolan has discovered a plot to retake the ship."

The Irishman looked appalled, but calm, and Kanoa grinned crookedly. "Padeen, please go below and have Corporal Hackman send his Marines to the quarterdeck break. You may serve out pistols and cutlasses to the men below. Gather every man who can fight and put yourself forward of the fireplace. Make a barricade up of hammocks and tables, and do not under any circumstances let the slavers pass aft." Padeen started away. "And Padeen," Curran said, "please send Mister Nordhoff to the quarterdeck."

"Aye, sir."

Curran turned to the Hawaiian. "Petty Officer Kanoa, do you have your club aboard?"

"How come I wouldn't?" he replied, smiling.

"You will arm yourself with it and join me at once."

The skylight opened from the great cabin and Padeen handed up a pair of pistols and cutlasses. Curran armed himself and passed a pistol to Nolan.

"You remember how to use those things?"

Nolan clicked back the pistol's lock and checked the frizzen. The weapon seemed heavy and alien in his hand. "I might," he said. Memories came back to Nolan of the duel at Bloody Run. He remembered the bullet that skittered past his ear, and the one that struck down Colonel Bell. The death of his antagonist and his own wounding seemed to be events from a distant age. Padeen handed Nolan a battered hanger and a second pistol; putting them on, Nolan seemed suddenly abashed, almost shy. "I think my fencing might be a bit old-fashioned."

"Good enough for the likes of them, sir," said Padeen confidently.

The youngster Nordhoff tromped up the ladder. He'd been told what was afoot and carried in his hand a large cutlass. The weapon dwarfed the boy.

"There you are, Mister Nordhoff. I have a job that requires a brave and discerning hand."

Nordhoff looked forward. The boy was barely as high as the quarterdeck rail and had to lift his chin to see over it. He was smaller even than Wainwright had been—not a hundred pounds or anywhere close to it. Curran knew that although Nordoff was resolute, the child would be of no use in the man-to-man fighting to come.

"I want you to relieve Stephen Bannon at the conn," Curran said. "There will soon be a bit of business forward."

"I know that, sir." The boy's words clicked in a dry mouth.

"And I know you are not shy, Mister Nordhoff. But I will need the muscle of Bannon and the others. For us it will have to be all at once, and the first time or

never. We still may have some small modicum of surprise, which will make up for
our reduced numbers and the confusion on our decks."

"Yes, sir."

"Very well. You understand. Take the helm. You will do us a great service to
hold the ship steady until such time as the prisoners attempt to fire a volley into us.
Then you must jink the helm and upset their plans."

"I understand, sir."

"I know you do; now steady up."

The Marines arrived on deck. Silently and eagerly they fixed their bayonets. It
was time. The boy took the tiller under his arm.

"Easy does it," Curran said. "And watch is the word. When the time comes, we
will need an earthquake, Mister Nordhoff."

Nolan nodded and said, "You will be our Jehovah and smite our enemies."

The boy tried to smile. "Jehovah it is, sir." Nolan and Curran went down the
ladder and Hackman ordered his men forward.

On deck, the Africans sensed instantly that violence would soon spill over
them. Some scurried below or cowered next to the guns, but many others, indeed
most of them, surged back toward the quarterdeck. As the foredeck cleared, the
assembling slavers made their move. A hatch opened in the forepeak, and a dozen
scimitars and matchlock muskets were heaved up into the conspirators' hands. It
was obvious that their plan had been accelerated, for though they now had miquelet
rifles, only a few of their matches had been lit. Until they had fire, the corsairs' rifles
were good only as clubs.

Curran and Nolan moved forward, one starboard and one larboard, with the
Marines arrayed between them. Nolan drew his cutlass, transferred it to his left
hand, and then drew a pistol. Crowded before the foremast were about a dozen sick
women and children. They could neither retreat nor advance, so the slavers pushed
among them, lifting them by the arms and shoving them in front as shields. Mixed
in now thoroughly with women and children, the slavers surged aft.

In front of Nolan there was a general clash, stab, and thrust, but Corporal
Hackman yelled repeatedly, "Bayonets, bayonets," and the Marines held their fire.
If the leathernecks would not be provoked, Kanoa showed he could be. Driven to
rage, or pretending it flawlessly, the Hawaiian waded through the hostages, shoving them down and swinging the *pahoa* through the air. He beat down one of the
slaver musketmen, and then another. The corsairs parted before the shark teeth on
the club, reeling backward and falling. In a short span of time Kanoa had clobbered
his way all the way to the foremast, and Nolan had to pull him back before he could
be surrounded and cut off.

Passing a match between them, the corsairs could only fire haphazardly, one
after another; bullets fired high and wide hissed across the deck, cutting through
a pair of lines and punching a hole in the brass lantern atop the binnacle. Pistols

answered back, and one or two of the Marines fired when they had clear shots: none of them missed.

Nolan caught sight of a corsair dragging a female captive by her hair. The sight enraged him, and a violent sort of revulsion burst in his breast. He hacked his way toward the woman, beating her assailant back: a quick pass, parry, and then a *balestra* disarmed the slaver. As the corsair's scimitar flew away from his hand, Nolan's blade went home point and shaft, as deep as the guard. Nolan kicked the dead man from his blade and waded deeper into the fight.

Thrust and riposte, slash and stab, Nolan had by now lost control. A blinding, all-consuming fury devoured him. Decades of sorrow and frustration now exploded in a tantrum of lethal violence. The deck was filled with bellowing, struggling men—black, white, and brown—a furious battle fought mostly hand to hand. One of the corsairs jumped upon the hammock nettings and made it to the quarterdeck break. As the slaver lunged for Nordhoff, Nolan turned and fired. The bullet struck the corsair in the back, and Vanhall brought the wounded slaver down with a Bowie knife.

Nolan ducked a slicing cut and tumbled backward, tripped up by a child darting behind his heels. As he fell, Nolan fired a pistol and his attacker disappeared in an opaque jet of smoke. Nolan clambered to his feet as the child scampered away from him, confused and bawling. A scimitar flashed down, and Nolan lifted his cutlass; there was a grating of metal, a shout. The shaft of his sword shattered at the fuller and the pommel was ripped from his hand.

Disarmed, Nolan crabbed backward against the mast. He ducked another cut as a dark form leaped forward—the child's mother, pouncing like a tiger. Nolan watched as the woman clawed at the corsair's face with her bare hands. The man looked astonished, and as he threw her off, Nolan put his head down and charged, toppling the corsair onto the main hatch cover. Grappling, they tumbled together, fighting hand over hand for the hilt of the scimitar. The corsair's strength was astonishing; Nolan could not wrest the sword away, so he quickly latched onto the man's wrist, holding on and twisting for all he was worth. In an instant, dozens of freed slaves appeared on all sides, shouting, screaming, and armed with whatever had come to hand: belaying pins, sweeps and boat oars, even buckets and swabs. They beat the slaver on every exposed point, but the corsair shrugged off their blows.

Out of the throng, Padeen struck with his cutlass, the blade ripping through the corsair's open mouth. It went through as far as the jaw joint—an appalling wound—but the big man did not fall. Turning quickly, Nolan kicked out with both feet, toppling the corsair from the hatch cover just as Hackman lowered his shoulder and plunged forward with his bayonet transfixing the slaver to the bulwark.

At the mainmast, Curran's uniform had made him a conspicuous target; for a long while it was almost impossible to reckon time in such a struggle. Finally he was able to cut across a parry; Curran lunged, his point went home, and the corsair fell. Before he could turn upon his second opponent, Kanoa's club, in a perfect helix, cut the slaver across the throat and then lay open his abdomen.

By the main hatch Nolan was again on his feet; he armed himself with a corsair's sword and moved toward the bow. The fight was swirling but beginning to turn. Three and four deep the Marines shoved back at the corsairs, stepping over the bodies of the fallen.

As Curran went forward, he saw that a dozen corsairs were poised in the bows, leveling their weapons and preparing to fire a deadly volley. Previously lacking lit matches, they had only been able to fire at random. Curran's eyes found Nolan's. Were the corsairs to succeed in laying down a volley, they would sweep the deck with lead. Nolan turned his head and whistled loudly.

Through the smoke, tumult, and clanging came a high, peeping shout in answer—Nordhoff's voice cracking with exertion: "Jibe ho!"

The English speakers had a vital instant to prepare for the great heave and pitch. The deck staggered up as Curran and the Marines grabbed shrouds, pintles, and gammons to stay upright. Nordhoff shoved over the tiller and *Yunis* lurched like an upset cart. The corsairs did not anticipate that the ship would suddenly roll, and half were thrown down. The corsairs in the bow fired, but their bullets went astray. The freedmen fell on them instantly, beating at them with belaying pins and swab handles.

Overhead the sails beat wildly, topsails gone aback, the great lateen banging like a judgment drum. The corsairs tried to re-form, but the Marines aimed and fired their own volley, each shot aimed true. Ten of the slavers went down, and one tumbled over the rail into the sea. The Marines charged, driving the corsairs into a compact mass.

Curran tossed Nolan a loaded pistol, raised his cutlass, and advanced on the leeward rail. "At them!" Curran yelled. "Once and they're done!"

When *Yunis* paid off, Nordhoff again jagged the tiller, bringing the ship around on her heel, again making the deck a treachery for the slavers. Their weapons fired to no purpose; they now tumbled together in the bow. As Curran and Nolan led the Marines forward, a guttural noise like the bellowing of a bull came from the main hatchway. Fante lumbered onto the deck through a nimbus of powder smoke. The huge black man appeared even more terrible when it was seen he was dragging the beaten and bleeding Abdur Rahman up the ladder by his hair. Within a minute, Nolan and the Marines had shoved the last of the slavers below, and the fore hatch cover was pushed down. Curran ordered the pumps manned and a hose put into the scuttle. Water soon doused the slavers, and their plans and powder.

In the brawl Fante and Abdur Rahman had been forgotten, and when Curran turned he was appalled to see the Arab being hoisted skyward. Fante had looped the black turban around Abdur Rahman's neck and was hauling him to up to the yards on a halyard. Kicking and twitching, the Syrian was purple by the time

Curran slashed the line. Abdur Rahman fell to the deck in a heap, gasping and choking. Panting, Nolan made no move to stop Fante from exacting his revenge.

Curran stepped between the Mozambican and Abdur Rahman, yelling, "Let him go!" But it was only the threat of a bayonet that restrained Fante from stomping out the man's heart.

"The son of a dog! Why protect him?" Fante panted.

Curran shouted, "I will decide who gets hanged on this ship."

Hackman came forward and Abdur Rahman was dragged into the bow. The hatch was pried open and the ringleader thrown into the hole.

"Nail it shut," Curran said. As corsairs were dragged forward, Curran turned to Nolan and saw that he was bleeding. "You have been cut."

Nolan put his hand to his arm and was astonished when his fingers came away red with blood. "I hadn't noticed." Nolan again touched his fingers to the arm of his shirt. "It is a trifle."

Curran, looking closely at Nolan, saw that he was gasping and his eyes were wild.

Enterprise had by then come alongside; the gunfire had carried clearly, and Pelles had put about in an instant. The red cutter hooked onto *Yunis'* main chains, and twenty Marines swarmed over the rail armed with carbines, pikes, and tomahawks. They were dejected to learn that the fight was over.

From *Enterprise*, Pelles pointed the speaking trumpet at *Yunis*: "I gather you are in one piece, Mister Curran?"

"I am, sir. The former owners attempted to take back the ship."

"Did you hang them?"

"I tried," Fante bellowed. "This child would not let me."

"Go below at once," Curran growled.

Fante opened his mouth, but the look on Curran's face brooked no disobedience. Scowling, Fante made his way down the companionway, muttering as he went past, "Nancy boys."

Pelles barked from *Enterprise*: "Where are the prisoners?"

"They are nailed into the forepeak, sir. About a dozen of them. I don't think they will be any more trouble."

"What are the casualties?"

"Fourteen of the slavers are dead, sir. We have a few wounded."

From *Enterprise* came Pelles' disapproving voice: "I hope this has taught you something about keeping prisoners. Now, if you are finished with your little mutiny, we shall continue on to Sierra Leone."

"Yes, sir."

"We have been lucky," Curran said quietly to Nolan.

Nolan made an absent nod; it occurred to him that he had expected to die, and now felt slightly let down that he had not. Curran went forward to see to the placing of fresh guards and arranged for one of the surgeon's mates to tend the wounded. Nolan made his way aft and stood on the quarterdeck with Nordhoff, who still clutched the helm under his arm. The boy was unharmed but had somehow been spattered with gore.

Nolan heard himself say: "You did very well, Mister Nordhoff. Just the thing."

"I thank you, sir. It was nearly run," the boy swallowed. Then in a half whisper he said, "To tell you honest, Mister Nolan, I was scared to death."

"To tell *you* honest, Mister Nordhoff, so was I."

Nolan felt suddenly exhausted, and although he had said differently, his arm hurt him very much. He walked to the scuttlebutt on deck, dipped the ladle, and drank deeply. When he had had his fill, he sat back against the combing of the main hatch—the same place he had just fought for his life. Oddly, where there had moments ago been rage and tumult, the wind now blew gently. Nolan ripped a strip of linen from his shirt and bound up the gash on his arm, tying the last knot with his teeth.

A hose was played on the bloody decks, and the freedmen helped to throw the bodies of slain corsairs over the side. Around Nolan the victors, white and black and brown, smiled and chattered; the differences that existed between them before had now vanished. They had no language in common, barely half a dozen words, but together they had shared danger; now they laughed and joked and congratulated one another for their bravery and survival.

Sitting apart and alone, Nolan wiped the sweat from his eyes and breathed deeply, his thoughts heavy as clay. This morning, when the slavers came aft, Nolan had given battle with the fury of a wild animal. That violence and his own ferocity now astonished him. He detested the corsairs for the misery they had brought to those they enslaved and for killing Wainwright. But never in his life had he fought with such loathing and hatred.

The fight aboard *Enterprise* had been different. The technical requirements and standard commands used to direct a naval battery in combat placed ritual between act and execution. A gun was served by almost a dozen men, all of whom played a part in making it ready, laying it in aim, and initiating fire. When the gun fired and the ball went home, all of them shared equally in the moral responsibility of what they had done. Whether a ball had taken out a mast or a round of canister swept enemy riflemen from a top, the gun's crew, together, shared both glory and guilt. But the fight on the deck of *Yunis* was different. There were no rituals of command. No teamwork refined by practice. From its opening seconds the fight with the slavers had been a life-and-death affair—a battle that offered only two options: success and life or defeat and death.

When he entered the mêlée, Nolan fought not only to prevent the slavers from taking the ship but also to destroy them. Parry and riposte, cut and thrust, Nolan had taken a full measure of revenge for the death of Wainwright. He had aimed each shot deliberately and placed each cut to do maximum harm. Now, as he watched the dead being cast over the rails, he felt no sense of triumph, only an aching sort of emptiness. He'd expected no quarter nor would he have given any, and now the slain were nothing to him, merely broken and bloody bits of debris. *What had made him so callous?* Why had he taken pleasure in killing? As he watched the last, bloody, limp corpse splash over the side, Nolan was stirred at last by a nagging sense of conscience—he had watched Fante's attempt to hang the Syrian with flat apathy. That he could have observed a deliberate act of murder with such indifference now shamed him. How impenetrable was the boundary that separated him from other men? *What had he become?*

When Nolan at last glanced up he saw a little child standing close to him looking solemnly into his face. For a long moment they stared at each other. There was a sore in one corner of the child's mouth, and the dark little eyes that looked back at Nolan expressed almost no emotion. There were no thanks in them and certainly no joy, nor was there judgment or reproof. Nolan wondered what horrors the child had already witnessed, what sorrows the eyes had beheld. He reached out his hand, but the child fled, bare feet pattering on the wet deck.

The pain in his arm came again and he stood. Looking over the rail Nolan was amazed to find the sun still low in the left hand of the sky and a sliver of moon perfectly visible in the west. It seemed equally preposterous, but the thunderheads that had crowded around the ship at dawn had suddenly vanished, and likewise the clouds that had stretched to the horizon. *Enterprise* was just away to larboard, her towering stern rising and falling in the swell. Above the frigate and above *Yunis* the morning was suddenly blue from rim to rim, quite as if the fight had occurred on some other morning and in some distant age.

THE LOFA RIVER

GRADUALLY, CAPE ST. ANN COULD BE PICKED OUT, THE MEASURELESS emerald-dark continent piled up in stages behind it, the coast thickly verdant, fringed by dull white sand and overarched by tree canopies choked with vines. Just ten leagues south of the cape mount, several high-prowed canoes came out from the mouth of the Lofa River, and *Enterprise* signaled *Yunis* to heave to; this was the Krepo country, and aboard the largest pirogues were several persons of consequence. Perhaps the consequential people recognized *Yunis*, or perhaps they decided to parley with the largest ship, for the canoes ignored the xebec and converged with smiles and waving, open hands on *Enterprise*. Now and again the sound of Pelles' voice came over the water as he bargained and wheedled with one of the headmen until at last a hoist of signals broke out at the mizzen. Curran ordered the lateen hoisted, and *Yunis* came under the frigate's lee. Curran stood on *Yunis*'s quarterdeck looking across and up at *Enterprise*.

"*Yunis*, ahoy," Pelles called, "I believe you have aboard your ship a Krepo named João."

One of the freedmen came aft to the quarterdeck, his face beaming. It was the same man Nolan had spoken to on the smoldering deck of *Ar R'ad*. "I believe this is your man, Mister Curran," Nolan said.

Curran cupped his hands and called back, "I have him, sir."

"These are his people," Pelles said. "His father is the chief man hereabouts. You may let him leave the ship."

As Nolan translated into Portuguese, the man's smile expanded until it shone. In an instant, the Krepo kissed Nolan and Curran, bounded three steps toward the taffrail, and threw himself over the side. His dive was so outrageous and agile that no one could think to stop him. In a smooth arc the Krepo cut through the air, splashed deep, and popped up like a duck. Nolan and Curran watched as the swimmer heaved aboard the closest of the canoes. It was moving to see the tears and embraces of friends who welcomed him back as though from the dead.

"Remarkable," said Curran. "That man swims like a garfish."

"It is," Nolan assented. "In these parts the Krepo are called shark men. They are bred to the water from birth."

Two canoes came toward *Yunis* with paddles flashing. There was another splash beside *Enterprise* as a hatch cover was thrown over the side. With much joyful laughter, men on the largest of the canoes took it in tow.

Pelles' voice droned between the hulls. "Mister Curran, I have arranged with these people to relieve you of your prisoners. They have agreed to convey them to shore."

"Oh, God," Curran said. "I would have hanged them if I thought they would be eaten."

Nolan smiled wryly. "They are more likely bound for the seraglio than the stewpot. The Krepo are not cannibals, nor do they keep slaves. They do, however, participate in the trade."

"What do you mean?"

"They are a rigidly commercial people. They work as guides and coastal pilots for slave ships, and when they can, they serve as brokers, arranging the sale of prisoners taken in war or captured upriver."

"Now you are practicing on me, Philip."

"I am not. The Krepo will not keep an African in bondage. But they do not feel bound to protect a slave taker who finds himself in reduced circumstances."

"What will be done with them?"

"If any should be wealthy, they will be ransomed. The Arab corsairs will be sold to the Portuguese, or perhaps the Brazilians, but certainly to the next slave ship to call here for water. There is a pronounced appetite for light-skinned eunuchs in the *harims* of the Nijad."

"You astound me, Nolan."

Hackman and his Marines opened the fore hatch and the slavers were yanked out on deck. Smeared with soot and shame, they stood blinking in the nearly vertical sunlight. The canoes were then alongside, and the Krepo climbed aboard the xebec in dozens. Singing and grinning, the tribesmen pitched the slavers off the forecastle and over the side.

Those that were nonswimmers flogged the water and went gasping below the surface, but no matter to what depth they sank, they were pulled up by divers and dragged to the hatch cover. Abdur Rahman and a few others who could swim tried vainly to avoid capture. The Krepo children took a special delight in swimming them down, climbing onto their heads, and dunking them into surrender. Beaten with paddles and jabbed with fish spears, the last of the slavers were soon clinging exhausted to the hatch cover.

In the largest canoe, the headman waved a flywhisk at *Enterprise* and shouted, "*Bom!* Good!" as the canoes towed the hatch toward the river mouth. The slavers had now been made slaves.

"Our captain has an exquisite sense of irony," Nolan said.

Beside Nolan, Curran looked vaguely contrite. "The noose would have been mercy."

A heavy, dangerous surf was pounding on the river bar, but the Krepo paddled toward the combers with flippant disregard. They were at home among the waves and as nimble as otters. Curran could see a shared expression of dread on the faces of the slavers, and even after the desperate fight for the ship it was difficult not to feel sympathy for them. Stroke after stroke brought the castaways closer to the surf booming on the bar, and soon the small crowd on the hatch cover was pitching between the swells.

As the canoes came into the break, men in the sterns crouched and hallooed, piloting their craft over the sandbar and skittering down the giant waves. A child dived from the transom of the largest canoe, and a flashing knife cut loose the hatch cover. At once a wave loomed up behind it, blocking out the sun. The slavers crouched together as a wall of breaking water peeled off and smashed over them. Hatch splinters and passengers disappeared into a chaos of foam.

Aboard *Yunis*, Curran turned away from the rail. The scene might not have been without some element of justice, but it was terrible to watch.

"Prepare to get under way," he said to helmsman. "Petty Officer Kanoa, you have the conn. I will be below."

The Krepo and their canoes went in through the surf effortlessly, passing the floundering, gasping, expiring corsairs. Nolan remained on deck, looking at the river bar. One by one, the slavers were consumed by the breaking waves and smashed upon the sand. Most, unable to swim, thrashed helplessly as they were drawn up and pitched over by the gigantic combers. Now and then a hoarse, panicked shout came out to the ship.

Riding the breakers, the Krepos' canoes were run neatly onto the beach, and the tribe gathered to see what would come out of the surf. One head appeared amid the tumbling whitewater, then another and another. These were the chosen. The Krepos knew that their gods would select the living; that was their wont and will. The surf was their winnowing basket.

In a vicious reversal of fate, the drowned were lucky and the living cursed. For the Krepo, the iniquitous were meant to suffer and the righteous to drown as free men. Nolan watched as those the gods had cursed were rolled upon the beach, dragged to a fire pit, and branded as property. The wicked would enter a hell beneath the palms—the others, drowned in the sea, went at once to their reward. For the Krepo, there was no joy or triumph in this, or even a token of revenge. It was simply the business of the world.

NOLAN STOOD BY THE GANGWAY IN THE BRIGHT SUNLIGHT, AND BEAZEE PANTED at his feet. The harbor of Freetown, Sierra Leone, enclosed a moderate number of merchant ships, mostly British, some Dutch, and a few rather disreputable French and Portuguese brigs. Though the forest had been beaten back in places, the hills of the peninsula remained heavily wooded. To the southeast, the brown tidal flats of the Bunce River wound away into dark, apparently primeval forest. Almost a hundred stone-and-timber houses were visible in the cleared part of the land, a dozen or so of them four or even five stories, framed and gabled. *Yunis* was anchored in six-fathom water, on the Middle Shoal grounds, the mouth of the Sierra Leone River just to larboard, Kortright House off the bow, and Aberdeen Point just south of west, all triangulated to Curran's satisfaction. *Enterprise*, at single anchor, rode in the fairway in front of Government House.

The morning was hot, without a breath of wind, and already the sun was beating back from the water's surface; it would be hellish by afternoon. For all the commotion on deck, Nolan could still hear cheers and laughter drifting across the harbor from *Enterprise* as the last of the freedmen were rowed across the harbor and put onto the beach under the terrace of Government House.

Every one of the frigate's boats and *Yunis'* own launch had been put into service to transport the freedmen to shore, and they were welcomed happily. Only about twenty freedmen remained aboard *Yunis*, watching as the skiff came back alongside for the last load of passengers. One after another, departing men and women came up to Nolan and pressed his hand to their foreheads. Nolan was humbled and moved by their joy and gratitude. The last dozen passengers (mostly women and children) required careful handling down into the boats. Padeen and Kanoa were everywhere, urging sailors to clamp on and shut up, and directing the passengers firmly but politely to get over the side. As the launch pulled away, Nordhoff jumped down from the poop and pulled his newly bought sennit hat from his head.

"Beg pardon, Mister Curran. Signal from *Enterprise*, sir."

Curran looked across the harbor. The frigate was simultaneously winding her anchor and recovering her boats. Half a dozen colored flags wafted from *Enterprise*'s halyards, emphasized by a windward gun. Before Curran could even think of cracking a codebook, Pelles' voice came across the harbor, literally echoing back from the walls of the English fortress. "Mister Curran! Is this going to take all damn day?"

"One more boatload, sir, and we'll be away," Curran called back.

The debarkation had not started until nine in the morning; there had been some miscommunication between the port admiral and the governor, and though things were now proceeding smoothly, Pelles had been increasingly short tempered.

Another signal hoist went up on *Enterprise*: "Prepare to get under way"—this even though most of the boats were still engaged with passengers.

"The captain is in a hurry," Nolan said.

"I swear, it is the mere presence of the British that aggravates him," Curran said quietly. "He had a bee in his bonnet ashore and hardly even spoke civil to the port admiral, though he seemed a pleasant man and quite willing to help."

The Old Mogul had spent most of his life fighting the British, and though he was thankful that the governor of Sierra Leone had agreed to take the freedmen, he did not want to linger. Pelles had been Stephen Decatur's exec aboard *President* when she was defeated and taken by a British squadron off New York. He had argued vehemently with Decatur before he struck to the British, and the event still rankled twenty years later. *Enterprise*'s officers could scarcely credit Pelles' ill temper to the sight of the Union Jack; in fact, it had the same effect on him as a red cape on a peevish old bull.

Now the captain's voice boomed across a hundred yards of water: "We are under way at once for Cartagena. Recover your boats, sir!"

Curran lifted his hand in acknowledgment as Padeen came up to the ladder to the quarterdeck. "Begging 'yer pardon, sir," he said, touching his hat, "but there's one of 'em that won't go."

"Who is that?" asked Curran.

"The big one."

Curran saw Fante standing beside the mainmast. With his arms crossed over his chest the Mozambequean looked like a monument made of onyx.

"Philip, will you speak to him? If we don't get these boats recovered and the anchor shipped, we shall likely be roasted and sold in Ma Komba."

Nolan went forward, stepping over the anchor cable as it was hauled aboard and stowed.

"There he is, Mister Nolan," Padeen jerked his thumb at Fante. "Watch it, now, he's stronger than a bear."

Nolan addressed the big man. "I am told you won't go ashore."

There was a silence of about ten seconds, and then the big man sniffed: "Why would I?"

"You are free, sir," Nolan said. "Why won't you go home?"

"Why don't you?"

That was more question than Nolan could answer, and as he considered a response he placed his hands behind his back.

Fante jerked his thumb at the shore. "This is no place for a man. It is where ants live."

"Where is your country?" asked Nolan.

"Beyond all the continent. The Angoche in Mozambique. The nation of the Ekoti."

"This is as close as we can get."

Fante's eyes burned. "Bah, that means nothing. My home is gone. Not just far away. Gone. When the Portuguese come, my people fought. By the Powers, we fought. Women and boys too. All murdered. My villages. Burned. All. It was my dishonor to be taken prisoner. Taken half dead after they split my head."

Nolan listened, his mouth slightly open, his face reddening.

"I am dishonored in my nation," Fante said. "I can never go home."

Nolan was speechless. Fante could not read the look on Nolan's face, and took it as a mere dismissal. The big man said, "Do you have honor?"

"I do, sir," said Nolan softly.

"Then you understand what it is to be a man without a country."

The words hit Nolan like lightning. It took him a long moment to ask, "What is your name?"

"Fante Nampula Mabu'wase, *abdahun*—headman—of Ekoti and Enes."

Nolan stopped Padeen as he headed forward. "Padeen, there is an extra jersey and spare trousers among my kit. Will you please see to it that this man has them?"

"Ain't he supposed to go ashore?"

"I will speak to Mister Curran."

"As you wish, sir. This way, my man." Padeen led Fante belowdecks, the companionway ladder sagging under their combined weight. Nolan turned to find Curran standing directly behind him. The expression on his friend's face indicated that he heard it all.

"I have no authority in this ship," Nolan said. "And I have offered perhaps more than I can give. But I would ask you, humbly, if this man be allowed to stay. He has no place to go. No place left . . . I will bear responsibility for his conduct and feed him from my own ration."

"That won't be necessary," Curran said. "He may sail with us."

MOTHER OF SORROWS

FANTE'S FIRST DAY AS A MEMBER OF THE UNITED STATES NAVY WAS NOT an unalloyed success. At more than three hundred pounds he was too big to send aloft, and though he was enthusiastic, he did not know a becket from a bowline. As a result, it was nearly impossible to bid him to his duty, at least not using the correct names for things. Having been ashore all his life, Fante could not be made to understand starboard from larboard, no matter how loudly it was shouted into his ear, and it did not help that he was so bold as to ask why sailors couldn't just say right or left when that was what they meant. But once the big man was started, it was just as difficult to get him to stop.

Though his grammar, and even his diction, was superior to that of many of the petty officers, Fante did not comprehend the words "avast" or "belay," much less the concept "easy does it." When he took up a line and was made to pull, the Mozambequean went at it with a will. When *Yunis* got under way, he was assigned to the fore halyard, one of a dozen hands designated to set the massive lateen foresail. Ignoring the trill of the bo'sun's pipes and the sincere entreaties of his shipmates, Fante shouldered aside the other crewmen, took hold of the halyard, and pulled on it hand over hand. The warrior prince did this, sweating and grunting, until he had raised the twenty-five-foot-long boom from the deck to the foretop. This exhibition had single-handedly put a five-hundred-pound spar thirty feet into the air.

His shipmates were so astonished that none noticed that Fante had continued to pull even after the halyard had been made fast. Thinking that the mast had to be held aloft during the whole voyage, Fante kept such a tension on the line that he eventually bent the iron bit of the cleat up from a three-inch plank.

Yunis rode a pleasant land breeze into the offing, and by the end of the afternoon watch she was into the first puffs of a soldier's wind, full out of the southeast, as fair as could be hoped. The ship had been generously provisioned by the tradesmen of the port, and supper was a lemony seafood stew thick with okra and chorizo. There was bread and haricot beans, and for dessert a custard made of wild apricot and banana. The meal helped staunch the grumble of the more superstitious members of the crew, for *Yunis*, of necessity, had gotten under way on a Friday.

Without a hundred passengers pressed belowdecks, the ship seemed spacious, even hollow, and there was room to stretch out. Fante had been issued with Nolan's spare clothes, a straw hat, and a spare hammock and mattress. The pants required expansion, but Fante was able to use Nolan's long nightshirt as kind of short blouse. The Mozambequean had no other possessions but did not seem to want for anything. As the coast of Africa went out of sight, Fante was one of the few who did not linger at the rail to watch. Instead, he went below muttering, "Pshhh, so what."

Just before lights out, Fante took his new hammock to the forecastle. He was too proud to ask anyone to help him hang it, and anyway, he'd watched as the other sailors rigged theirs. By copying those coming off watch, Fante managed to get one end of his hammock up and then the other. Crouched beneath the low overhead, he realized that putting himself into the sack would not be as easy as the sailors made it look. He lowered the slings almost to the deck, figuring that if he were to fall, a short trip would be better than a long one.

As Fante worked, Billy Vanhall came down the main hatchway and unrolled his hammock. He glared at the black man. "What do you think you're about?"

Fante did not answer.

"Hey, I'm talking to you. Don't you go tryin' to hang your hammock in here," Vanhall huffed. "I ain't berthing with no Africans!"

From out of the darkness a voice said, "What's the problem, Stumpy? Last night you slept with two hundred."

"They was cargo. This here is differn't." Vanhall glanced over and spit a chaw of tobacco. "Listen, here, Congo. You sleep on deck, not with the white folks, sabey?"

Fante continued unrolling his hammock. "I am sleeping here," he said. "Despite the fact that I dislike white people, and you mostly, because you smell bad. You sabey?"

Across the berth deck, Guild burst into laughter. The mirth was general now, delighting Fante and enraging his antagonist.

"I ain't sleeping with no niggers," Vanhall spat. He skipped furiously over to midships, pulled out his Bowie knife, and started to cut down Fante's hammock.

As Fante moved to prevent this, Vanhall's blade flashed up. Fante blocked the knife, cocked a fist, and drove it home under Vanhall's nose. The sailor tumbled back and a crashing grunt burst from his lips. The knife clattered across the deck.

Fante filled his hands with the front of Vanhall's jersey and slammed him against the bulkhead. His teeth clicked, "What does that word mean . . . *nigger?*"

Vanhall croaked out something and tried to wriggle free, but Fante pushed him harder against the mast. "Speak, you fairy's turd!" Fante hissed. "What does it mean?"

Nolan appeared on the ladder, shining a lantern into the compartment. "Stop this at once!" he shouted.

Faces peered silently from their hammocks. Nolan saw the knife lying on the deck, and he came quickly down the ladder. "Fante, what is going on?"

"Oh, this one is teaching me English," Fante said.

The commotion had been communicated quickly through the ship, and Kanoa arrived from the forecastle carrying a rattan switch. "What's a matter, you goddamn swabs?"

Fante shook Vanhall again, banging his head off a lantern hook. "What does *nigger* mean?" Fante rasped.

"It means a small or worthless person," Nolan said. He put his hand on Fante's shoulder, pulling him back. "Now put him down."

Fante did not comply. Nolan barked, "Let him go, Fante, at once!"

Kanoa waved the end of the rattan. "Do like Mister Nolan says."

Scowling, Fante shoved Vanhall aside. The sailor scuttled backward toward the hatch combing, wheezing and choking.

Fante said to him, "From now on, you will be *my* nigger."

Curran appeared from aft, Padeen close behind, carrying a musket. Curran quickly took in the scene; Vanhall was a troublemaker, and it didn't take a great deal of insight to know what had happened.

"Get up, Billy Vanhall," Curran said.

The sailor came to his feet. "That cannibal attacked me. Everyone saw it."

Hoots and catcalls cascaded from the hammocks and bystanders. Someone said, "Vanhall cut his self more than he could chaw!" There was laughter again, and Fante joined in it.

Curran looked at Vanhall. "Will there be any more trouble?"

"I ain't sleeping here."

"Then you may sleep on the weather deck," Curran said icily.

Shaking with embarrassment and rage, Vanhall plucked down his hammock and rolled it under his arm.

"All right, pipe down and turn in, all of you," Curran said. "We'll be watch on watch until we pass Gibraltar. You'll need all the sleep you can get."

Nolan started to say something, but Curran touched him on the elbow. "Square this matter away, Padeen," he said, and guided Nolan up the ladder.

When they had gone, Padeen gave Vanhall a swift kick in the ass. "Ain't it fine, Billy Vanhall, celebrating the accident of your birth?" Padeen growled. "No one made ye king of the world, to be looking down at us all."

"You talk tough with a rifle in your hand, you Mick bastard."

Stephen Bannon dropped out of his hammock and landed like a panther. "Ye little mincing Dutch bugger. Should ye care to learn some manners, here's a Mick happy to oblige." Bannon cocked a fist, but Fante came between them.

"Let him be." Fante gently pushed Bannon back. "I can fight for myself."

Kanoa pointed the rattan at Vanhall. "We ain't never had no trouble on the Easy E, and you'll stop that gob, Billy Vanhall." Kanoa narrowed his eyes. "Or I'll kick your haole ass."

FIVE, TEN, FIFTEEN DAYS OF SUNNY WEATHER, AND THE MODERATE, RELIABLE trades square on their quarter; day and evening barely touching sheet or brace—delightful sailing, 120 miles often made from noon to noon, topgallants aloft and the days passing in perfect naval exactitude. Aboard *Enterprise* and *Yunis* the routines were the same: reveille and hammocks stowed, the decks sanded, holystoned, and flogged dry, watches called and the hands piped to breakfast, then divisions, the morning watch set and relieved, the young gentlemen working up their noon figurings, dinner, divisions again, the dogwatch, supper, then the music of a fiddle and sometimes dancing on the forecastle, the second dogwatch, hammocks piped down, and as the stars turned above, the first and middle watches conned the ship, and at dawn reveille came again. Time passed in a smooth, gentle rhythm, the wake lengthened, and the sea was beautiful each day; a glorious run.

Aboard *Enterprise* Gustavo Gubbins had been Old Chick's assistant, and now, detailed to cook for *Yunis*, he ruled his own camboose and came into his own. Now sailing in ballast, *Yunis* carried not much more than thirty hands, and the prize crew ate like lords. Gubbins was from Charleston, a freedman who'd cooked for the Boykin family until a misunderstanding over a silver punchbowl found him relocated to New Orleans; and there he had joined the Navy during the last war. Gubbins was much admired by the crew for his orange fritters and potent chicory coffee, which he would serve out, gales only excepted, to any sailor come off watch, night or day. There was soft tommy, too, while the flour held out, and *pain perdú* with treacle syrup on Sundays after quarters. Gubbins could be counted on to put on a good feed even when the ship was down to salt pork. Not one to merely steep it and sling it, Gubbins insinuated shredded bits of the stuff into caldrons of red beans and simmered them together for two whole watches, along with onion, celery, and green pepper, adding more soaked beans as their predecessors dissolved into a creamy, sumptuous gravy. By this alchemy was rendered one of the ship's favorite suppers, served out always on Monday evenings over fluffy white rice and slathered with flecks of incendiary peperoncino in vinegar. It went down well with a can of beer or a tot or two of three-water Bob. And it was to this same meal that Nolan and Curran sat down at the narrow table in the great cabin. A cast-iron skillet filled with beans and a beaker of rice were carried from the galley and served with a long white loaf (almost a real baguette) to wipe their bowls. They ate for a while, spoons clinking, and Nolan said, "The humble bean has been raised to ambrosia. This will make me abandon Stoicism and become an epicure."

"It is a simple, honest meal," Curran said, breaking off some bread and pushing it into his bowl. "Gubbins, that worthy man, has composed a magnum opus."

A sad smile came to Nolan's face. "I remember that this was young Wainwright's favorite food."

"He was as brave as a lion, that little boy."

They fell to drinking alternate sips, and for a moment the ship seemed full of ghosts.

"Have you seen many fights?" Nolan asked.

"A couple," Curran nodded. "But that was the sharpest and the bloodiest. I was knocked down twice, and each time thought I was dead." Curran listened to the creaking of the ship and said, "You have seen your own share, Philip."

"Some on land," Nolan nodded. "We chased Tenskwatawa and Shawnee prophets about with horse artillery. And in the end defeated them with a scrap of paper. At sea, I have seen not more than a dozen fights, I reckon." After a pause he continued, "When I was with Porter in the Pacific, naval warfare seemed like a game. We would fall upon a British whaler, fire a leeward gun, and they would surrender."

"Porter was not always so lucky," Curran said. "Nor was *Essex*."

"She was not. I was no longer aboard when *Essex* was cornered and taken at Valparaiso. And that was a sharp fight, surely. But I had been taken off by *Holyoke* before then, and we were luckier. By the time the British converged on *Essex* we were well to the northwest. Aboard *Holyoke* we had an eventful cruise, but even when we fought privateers, I had only near misses. A whiff of grapeshot once took off my hat but left me unscathed. I came to think of myself as impervious."

Curran remembered Nolan's sangfroid during the fight with *Ar R'ad*. He and Pelles had seemed rooted to the deck like a pair of oaks.

Nolan said quietly, "When I was put aboard *Constitution*, the second time, Captain Stewart was very firm about my sentence. He kept me in the brig, larboard side, below the gun deck. I was aboard twenty-six days when we came upon HMS *Cyane* and *Levant*. On *Cyane*'s first broadside, the space was struck square with a 32-pound shot. I was caught up in a tornado of splinters and iron. The blast killed a thief Captain Stewart had placed in there with me, a man named Webb. I was turned upside down by the blast—quite like I had been caught in a whirlpool. I was made unconscious, and when I first came to I had no idea if I was alive or dead. The explosion had blown the jacket off my back. I pulled myself up and saw the rest of the fight through the hole punched in the side. It was a black night, but I had been in darkness so long I could easily see. Well, everything that could be seen from the larboard side. I watched as *Cyane* was dismasted. I saw her strike her colors, and I watched as *Levant* was run down and taken."

Nolan became thoughtful, and he said slowly, "*Constitution* took all the British prisoners aboard, and I was mixed in with them. They told me, 'It don't signify, Jonathan, you have snatched us up, but we have burnt your president's house.'" Nolan drew a breath. "I am ashamed to say that part of me hoped it to be true. I was still bitter then." In the silence that followed Nolan said at last, "Now, when I think of that little boy killed, Wainwright . . ."

Curran poured out two more cans of Bob and lifted his in silent toast. Nolan picked his up, touched it to Curran's, and said, "To our departed shipmates." They drank and stared out at the wake, grown luminous now that the moon had set.

Curran said, "For every terrible thing I have witnessed at sea, death and blood and battle, I've seen a hundred miracles."

Nolan took a sip. "A sunrise over Nuku Hiva, and the glory of the blue Indian Ocean."

"I have seen the aurora burning over a gale in the North Atlantic and even the Saint Elmo's fire."

"What landsman could even imagine those things?" Nolan asked. "Lightning striking a rolling green sea, or the little silver drops that skitter across the surface before a bow wave, so perfectly like stars."

Curran nearly said, "We are lucky," but he knew Philip Nolan was not lucky; not lucky or fortunate or anything like it, and to say otherwise to him would be cruel indeed.

"Come in."

"Pardon me, sir," Nordhoff said. "*Enterprise* has hoisted two blue lights and a red. She wants a parley."

Yunis came under the frigate's lee, and Curran looked up at Pelles standing at the quarterdeck rail. His voice came over the speaking trumpet in an almost conversational tone. "Mister Curran, it will not do to have *Yunis* accompany *Enterprise* through the strait, and especially following behind, like a prize. The whole world will know she is a taken ship, and she'll be of no more use to us than a portrait of Mister Madison."

"Yes, sir," Nolan called back.

"*Enterprise* will depart company, and you are to join the squadron in Cartagena. Keep your wits about you as you pass through the Gut, make sure to darken ship, give the Sallee a wide berth, and join us at the soonest."

"Aye, aye, sir."

"Carry on, Mister Curran. Good night to you."

IT WAS FROM THE MAINTOP THAT THEY FIRST SAW CAPE SPARTEL, THEN THE broad back of Jebel Musa, the southernmost of the twin Pillars of Hercules. North, past the cape, through a dull African haze, was the coast of Spain, the Strait of Gibraltar, and the shining Mediterranean. They'd lost sight of *Enterprise* in a squall two days ago but had a glimpse of her at dawn, a nick on the horizon cracking on toward the cape and turning east for the Gut.

At five bells in the afternoon watch the strait opened silver and gray on the starboard bow. The day was by turns bright and hazy, and north of the strait the swell had about it an odd, restless lift. Holding course first north by east and then north-northwest into the Gulf of Cádiz, Curran intended to remain in the Atlantic until nightfall, appearing as much as possible to be a vessel upbound for Portugal. *Yunis* beat north, the larboard rail buried and a fine white wake trailing behind for a mile.

With a long glass Nolan could pick out the shapes of a dozen corsairs sheltered under Cape Malabata, but none came out. During the long afternoon they sighted a square-rigged ship to the north. It turned out to be a Finnish brig, *Panu Vesterinen*, 500 tons, with a deck cargo of lumber and tar barrels out of Helsinki. *Yunis* attempted to hail, but the brig opened her course and piled on sail.

Collapsing his telescope on his chest, Curran said to Nolan, "She does not care for the cut of our jib."

"Nor should she," Nolan answered. "We look more wolf than lamb."

Curran turned his eyes toward the cape again and said, "That might help us yet."

Deception and stealth were all that *Yunis* could count on; there was not likely to be any help if the corsairs under Malabata decided to come out. Though the Spanish based a squadron of the line at Algeciras, Curran could not hope for its protection. Exhausted by decades of war and defeat, Spain was not much inclined to police the strait. Like Portugal, Spain paid tribute money to the Barbary potentates, using purse rather than powder to safeguard the vessels of its fleet. Though it might be possible for an extraordinarily rich and valuable ship to bribe the Spanish to convoy her, it was unthinkable for Spain to provide escort for a prize vessel— especially a prize taken by a power as far away and feckless as the United States. It would make no sense for Spain to accommodate a far-off nation, even a friendly one, when it had enemies so close at hand. Close by, Morocco was the least aggressive of the Barbary States, yet still the port of Tangiers teemed with corsairs, and any Arab plying the strait was likely to turn pirate if the occasion offered.

The sun went down without color, but off the larboard quarter a low, black band stretched across the horizon. Nolan came up from the great cabin to report that the glass was falling, a sure sign that the Levanter would falter in the next several hours. High above, the sky was streaked with wisps of silver. *Perhaps a tramontana*, Curran thought, *and a welcome thing, though it might make for a wild night*.

At dusk, Curran put the ship about, passed Trafalgar, then took Tarifa close to larboard. He would try the strait before moonrise. Running without lights, and with the Blessing, they would be past Algeciras and Gibraltar by the end of the middle watch. The final leg would be a reach along the coast of Málaga into Cartagena and a rendezvous with *Enterprise*.

Curran ordered a big supper for the men, the last of the goats from Sierra Leone served in a peppery curry. That, cornbread, fritters, and a full measure of Bob Smith made the mess deck a happy place. Aboard *Enterprise* a good feed was always served if there was the possibility of action, and those who knew Pelles suspected the same of his protégé. During their meal, Kanoa told Fante that if the corsairs tried to take the ship back, there would be a tussle. Fante's response was to pick his teeth and say he didn't care, Portuguese or Arab—if they came to *his* ship he would cut off their ears. Few disbelieved him, and none were surprised when the long roll of the drum brought the ship to quarters after supper.

The galley fires were extinguished, the guns manned, cutlasses and muskets were served out, and the lookouts doubled. The wind had clocked round to the north, gusty and growing brisk. There had been almost no twilight as the clouds lowered, and the sky and sea were soon closely matched shades of black.

Nolan stood on the quarterdeck and watched as Padeen lit the lamps in the binnacle. The rigging sang as the *tramontana* pushed them toward the strait at better than ten knots, the starboard rail buried in a luminous torrent of foam.

"It is as dark as a closed mouth," Nolan said.

"The Gut," Curran answered. Without stars or landmarks, *Yunis* was feeling her way by dead reckoning. On their approach Curran had taken bearings on Trafalgar and Tarifa, a running fix to approximate their position. In Curran's head spun a mathematics of time, speed, distance, and another, ineffable component: instinct.

Padeen was at the helm, a sure hand, and Kanoa was also on deck, standing just below the quarterdeck break, watching the sails and the vast darkness alternately. Though Curran and Padeen steered according to compass, the Hawaiian's navigational skills were those of old Molokaʻi. Kanoa could tell the ship's distance from the European and African coasts by the smell of the water and the feel of the cross-swell passing under the bow. Kanoa, a prince royal, was son, grandson, and great-grandson of navigators: he was born upon the sea and raised from childhood for a life in it. Peering into the ink-black night, Kanoa knew where they were as surely as if he had a chart laid before him. A navigator of the Occidental school tells his way by compass, clock, and stars, a Polynesian by never forgetting whence he came and thinking constantly of where he is bound. Even in this moment, on a dark night threading the Pillars of Hercules, Kanoa could turn and point the direction home to Newport, Norfolk, or either way back around the world to Molokaʻi.

As they passed the Sierra de la Luna, the wind came from the cliffs in stuttering gusts. Curran tacked again, steadying on a course north and east. The sails luffed and rumbled but the ship steered true, and after they passed the tower at Guadalmesi, Curran fell off two points, anticipating the headlands of Carnero and Europa fifteen miles ahead in the darkness.

Curran bent into the glow of the binnacle and looked at his watch. There was plenty of night left, but also many miles to make until they were beyond Gibraltar. He walked to the quarterdeck rail and said down to Kanoa, "I would like to put a reef in, before we pass Carnero."

"I 'spected you would, sir," Kanoa said. The topmen were already lined up by the shrouds; at his whistle they now scrambled aloft.

White horses filled the Gut, and below the headland the Las Perlas thudded with a great and booming surf. At midnight the lights of Gib opened to the north, scattered like fire sparks beneath the hulking mass of the Rock.

"Gibraltar, Mister Nolan."

"And I would hardly know it on such a night. I was there for two months aboard *Independence* just after the peace, and was never ashore."

"You didn't miss much," Curran said. "It is more like an English village than a Mediterranean town."

"Mister Cass was the surgeon aboard *Independence*," Nolan remembered. "And he was constantly patching up midshipmen."

"Were they awkward fellows?"

"They had a knack for trouble. And seemed not to be able to steer clear of their British counterparts. They tangled with them almost daily until the commodore restricted the mids to their ships."

"Mister Fentress was one of them, was he not?" Curran asked.

"He was. As a mid he was quite umbrageous, and his personality lent itself to confrontation."

It was not British midshipmen to be feared tonight, but rather a south wind. Eight miles to the south, along the African coast, Curran could see combers battering Cape Leona. Beyond it, connected by a low shore devoid of lights, the promontory of Almina was gathered like a fist on the edge of the dim horizon.

Attaching himself to the binnacle, Curran said to Padeen, "We'll not have this 'norther long."

"I'm of your opinion, sir. With these squalls a'playin', we'll soon have something out of the west. That's certain."

Padeen was superstitious enough not to mention the possibility of a wind from the south. A westerly might speed them on their way to Cartagena, but a wind from Africa—or worse, a flat calm—would do them no mercy. Anything less than a topsail breeze would leave *Yunis* prey to corsair galleys—heavily armed, oar-powered warships. Some of the galleys carried 32-pound smashers—handled by right seamen who worked together in packs. Even now, any number of these rapacious machines might be riding out the gale under the headlands on the African side.

Nolan watched as Curran paced the quarterdeck, lifting his glass now and again and scanning the African darkness. Thunder announced a third squall, and a curtain of rain spun at them, flattening the swell around the ship. The squall also reduced visibility to a stone's throw, a comfort against enemies real or imagined.

At five bells, almost at once, the wind went from north to west, from off the larboard beam to dead aft. Padeen put up the helm and Curran ordered the watch to ease the sheets. Now put before the wind, *Yunis* settled into near-perfect silence, floating with the breeze rather than beating through it. The transformation was astounding. The smallest whisper could be heard on deck, as could the low, constant rush of water along the side. The swell no longer jostled the bow, and the ship seemed to be flying through still air instead of sailing upon the ocean.

Kanoa's hand found Nolan's shoulder. "We're through, sir," he said.

The wind was astern and *Yunis'* bow pointed straight at Cartagena, a mere two hundred miles away. There was not much Nolan could do on deck, and as Kanoa seemed to relax, Nolan thought his own anxious vigilance added little to the safety of the ship. His cloak was soaked through, and after bidding Curran good morning he went dripping into the main cabin.

Nolan toweled himself off as best he could and lay in his hammock listening to the wind and the sea, and wondering, as an artilleryman might, if the priming of the guns had been soaked through. He heard Curran's voice through the skylight telling Kanoa that they would pipe to breakfast at six bells, and then he fell asleep.

The squalls scudded away, and the dawn was pure and brilliant. *Yunis* opened the coast of Marbella, and the day widened under scattered clouds. Curran congratulated himself as the morning bloomed, the wind freshened, and the clouds lifted and became whiter.

"Mister Nordhoff," Curran said just before eight bells, "you are a welcome relief."

The boy had little comprehension of how dangerous the straits had actually been, and this blithe optimism had permitted a good night's sleep. Vanhall relieved Padeen at the helm, and Curran gave orders for the ship to continue north by east.

The wind remained dead astern: a midshipman's dream. Nordhoff chalked the new heading on the slate, saw to it that the bells were rung and the log heaved, and wished Mister Curran a pleasant morning and a good, if late, breakfast. Curran yawned and rubbed his eyes. The smell of coffee, fritters, and oatmeal came up from below, and he followed it down the companionway and aft into his cabin.

Yunis surged along, her lateens set wing on wing and her deck as level as a dance floor. It had been an uneventful but trying passage, and the crew remained in a state of relief even after a sail was sighted in the east. Guild had called down to the deck when the stranger was no more than a smudge on the horizon. The sea was dappled with whitecaps, and the sail difficult to make out, for in the broadening dawn it was within a hand's breadth of the rising sun. The stranger eventually revealed herself to be square rigged and laboring hard to windward. She made heavy weather with her courses, tacking southwest and northeast, sailing much but gaining little. By the time she was two or three leagues off, her broad, round bow marked her as a merchant, and the few who watched her did so with a pinch of condescension. That the distance closed at all was because *Yunis* was sailing before the wind, closing rapidly with her lateens spread like wings.

Nordhoff was not much experienced as an officer of the deck, and on this bright, pleasant morning he made two small but self-multiplying mistakes. First, he took for granted that the hail from the masthead could be heard all over the ship. This wrongly presumed that both Curran, acting as captain, and Padeen, the acting master, were aware that a sail was in sight. Second, Nordhoff assumed that since the corsairs used lateen-rigged vessels, any square-rigged ship was more likely to be friend than foe.

At two bells in the forenoon watch, the stranger was seen to add sail and turn onto a larboard tack. As she closed it was plain that she was a whale ship; her sides were studded with davits, and she had a broad deckhouse aft. More discerning eyes might have noticed that though she seemed every strake and plank to be a whaler, her davits were empty and she towed no boats. The stranger came on, and would have gotten closer still had not Padeen happened on deck, and Kanoa behind him.

"Christ Jaysus," Padeen cried, sprinting up the quarterdeck ladder. "Sodom and Gomorrah, have you been struck blind, Billy Vanhall?!" This as he ran past the baffled Nordhoff and took the tiller himself.

"What are you about?" bawled Vanhall.

Padeen put the helm down, veering away from the stranger and calling out for all hands on deck.

Vanhall scoffed, "Ain't she flying a Nantucket pennant?"

Padeen had now taken over the tiller. "Ya blockhead, there ain't no Yankees hunting whales in the Med!"

Nordhoff felt his guts turn. He had been the first to spot the Nantucketer's pennant and the Stars and Stripes at her mizzen; the possibility that they might be a ruse de guerre had not occurred to him. Padeen ordered the drummer to beat to quarters. Below, in the waist, the deck filled with hands. Kanoa was mustering the topmen and arguing with Fante about where he might station himself.

Curran and Nolan were on deck in an instant, saw the whale ship to leeward, and were astounded.

"That there is *McKendrie Evans*, sir," Kanoa said. "Or was."

Nolan looked out across the narrowing band of water. "The taken whaler?"

"I got no doubt," Kanoa said. "Look at her davits, all swingin' empty. And she was never one to fly the flag if it was not of a Sunday."

Curran put his glass on her. "It is sure he knows who *we* are." At a distance of two miles Nolan could see that the whale ship's decks were full of men and that she was preparing to wear ship. The whaler's brick tryworks were gone, and in their place was a pair of massive guns. One was on a Gribeauval carriage, like the weapons aboard *Ar R'ad*; the other, aft, seemed to be mounted on a more traditional naval carriage.

Curran handed the glass to Nolan. "What do you think?"

Nolan saw that neither gun had the elaborate iron plate shielding seen on *Ar R'ad*, but both looked deadly just the same. "The forward gun is a 40-pounder. The one aft is much shorter, a carronade, but a huge one, I am afraid. Maybe a 50-pounder."

The stranger's yards were shifted and her spanker brailed over. As her helm was put down, the stern came around, revealing a freshly painted transom. Curran took back the glass and put it to his eye: the whaler's stern had been recarved and freshly painted. Below a crescent moon were chiseled the Arabic words *Um Qasim*: Mother of Sorrows.

Nordhoff said, "I am terribly sorry, sir. I had no idea she was a ship-of-war."

"Nor could you have, Mister Nordhoff," answered Curran. "Please be so kind as to run into my cabin and retrieve the Ottoman ensigns. Since our friend is flying false colors we shall as well."

"Yes, sir." Nordhoff was away at once. Nolan glanced at Curran; they had both known commanders who would have torn the boy apart. It would serve no purpose now.

A mile and a half to starboard, *Um Qasim* was shivering her main yards and settling downwind. Curran considered the set of his own sails, wing on wing and a glorious sight, but not the most efficient point of sail. Padeen was at the tiller, wringing every knot from *Yunis'* sleek, shallow hull. All hands were at their stations, and every eye was on Curran. The stranger settled now three thousand yards astern and parallel. There was no hope in engaging so well-armed a foe. Curran's only choices were variations on a theme of prompt and precipitous flight. For the next few minutes there was a narrowing opportunity to try to work to windward. A bold, perhaps even foolhardy maneuver—but if successful it would surely get *Yunis* clear.

Curran watched as *Um Qasim* set royals and sheeted home smartly. Standing at the starboard rail he was barely aware of Fante approaching, and of Nolan waving him back. Curran felt suddenly and irredeemably alone. In all his years at sea this was the first time he had ever been in tactical command. For the first time in combat he would not wait for orders but give them. In the next three minutes Curran would either have to run downwind or put about and try to maneuver under the corsair's stern.

An attempt to flee to windward would expose them dangerously to *Um Qasim's* great guns: a doubtful endeavor. A xebec could sail close-hauled better than any square-rigged ship—but where would they go? West, back into the narrowing strait? If there were another corsair off Gibraltar (and there would surely be at least one), he would instantly join the chase. On the other hand, were Curran to tack to larboard, turning north, he would soon come against the coast of Málaga. He might open the distance temporarily, but to no purpose. The corsair would have him trapped against an ironbound coast, his choices reduced to capture or shipwreck.

The men were silent, and the wind, dead astern, seemed not to be stirring at all. Curran had a few more seconds to work out the probabilities in his head: relative velocities, sail areas, weight of broadsides—some factors in his favor and others decidedly against him. Even well laid, Curran's own armament was worth little: a dozen 8-pounders and pair of long 12s in the stern. He would never be allowed close enough to use them. *Um Qasim's* great guns could destroy him in an instant, but they took a full six minutes to reload. They were big, damned awkward things, as was the whale ship herself. Though a runner for her type, *McKendrie Evans* was not a frigate. And she appeared to be heavily laden. Curran knew his craft was faster, quicker too in stays, but frail as a flower. He could not hope to fight, nor could he blindly run. To survive, Curran had to both outsail his pursuer and remain in a position where he could not be taken under direct fire. His only choice was to remain on course downwind, trusting that a lighter, smaller ship could outfly a larger and heavier one.

Nordhoff came on deck, breathless, dragging both the Ottoman merchant ensign and the jet black al-Uqab. "Which flag should I hoist, sir?" the boy piped.

"Both," said Curran. "Fly them both."

The red-and-green banner went up on one halyard, and the black rectangle of the al-Uqab on the other. Curran had little hope that the enemy might be deceived, but he might be induced to doubt, just as Curran had when he saw the Stars and Stripes. It would have to be enough to answer a lie with a lie.

The moment to work to windward had passed. It would be a chase, and presently there was nothing else to do. "Steady as you go, Padeen," Curran said.

Curran consoled himself that a stern chase was at least a long chase, and everything depended now on speed. Speed and vigilance, for *Um Qasim* had now to be watched for the slightest indication that she was preparing to yaw and fire her massive pivot guns.

"Mister Nolan," Curran said, "what should you think is the range of a long 42?" Curran addressed these words to his friend but intended them to be heard by every man on deck. Nolan understood and formed his answer accordingly.

"It is a preposterous great thing to have afloat. Most unwieldy and difficult to train. For their Long Tom, I should think perhaps four thousand yards would be the far end of an effective range." Nolan spoke confidently, but every hand aboard *Yunis* had seen what similar guns had done to *Enterprise*, a Boston-built frigate nearly three times their size.

The deck waited for Curran to answer, and from *Um Qasim* came the boom of a chaser. The distant report twisted itself into a howl, and a ball skipped across the water and splashed down far to leeward. It had not been a ranging shot but a signal. Curran watched as *Um Qasim* hauled down the American flag and replaced it with the yellow-and-red-striped ensign of an Ottoman warship.

Curran shook his head. "And that is nonsense, too. He is no more Turk than we are." He walked to the quarterdeck rail. "Petty Officer Kanoa, we will throw the deck guns overboard, forward to aft, if you please. But retain the powder and shot."

"Aye, sir." Kanoa went to the bow with a dozen hands and cut away the tackles of number one. With glum expressions they shoved it to the edge of the gun port, put pry bars under the carriage, and pushed it through on the roll. The gun went over with a splash that echoed dully through the hull. So it went, port and starboard, and as *Yunis* was lightened she quickly gathered speed.

"Mister Nordhoff, have you a day glass?"

"I do, sir."

"Go into the maintop. Though this pirate is pretending to be a man o'war, he has fanatics aboard instead of gunner's mates. Firing tends to be a bit of a theatrical event. I will have you call out their preparations so we may anticipate the fall of their shots."

"Yes, sir."

"Go aloft. Vanhall, take a rifle and go with him."

Nordhoff slung his telescope and went directly up the ratlines. Had Curran told him to swim to the bottom of the sea the boy would have obeyed with the same alacrity. The day was bright, and the wind seemed to be building.

Curran said to Nolan, "Would you care to help fight the ship?"

"I would, very much."

Curran smiled. "Take your pick of the gunners. We shall retain the two 12-pound guns in the great cabin. I would appreciate it if you commanded the battery. You may double or treble shot if you think best, but when the corsair comes within a thousand yards, open a steady fire. Though I doubt we will impress or deter him, we may have the luck to knock away something."

"Am I right to think you will jibe and tack to keep us out of the line of fire?" Nolan asked.

"For as long as I can."

"And if we should be holed or dismasted?"

Curran said quietly, "I do not intend to strike or be captured."

"Plain enough," Nolan said, and he held out his hand. "I'll see you for supper, then."

Curran shook hands. "Supper. Somewhere."

Nolan went below and Curran called for Hackman. "Corporal, there you are. How are you fixed for grenadoes?"

"About twenty, sir."

"Excellent. When I was down in the hold I noticed that the previous owners stored powder in demi-casks."

"Near a dozen, sir, at least."

"And I believe there is a barrel of pitch forward. I would like you to make some stinkpots. They will be most efficacious if we should close with the enemy."

"Yes, sir." There was a bit of doubt in the corporal's voice, and he was not the only one within earshot to wonder how they would be delivered onto the enemy's deck. Like grenadoes, the incendiaries had to be thrown by hand.

"You will have time, I believe, to make a dozen or so," Curran said.

"Aye, aye, sir."

"And I believe we may serve out the remaining rifles and tomahawks."

"Yes, sir," Hackman nodded his head obediently, but as he walked away he narrowed his eyes. "Tommyhawks and stinkpots, damn my guts," he muttered to himself. "Us against all the Turks of the world."

Kanoa came aft carrying his *pahoa*. "The guns is overboard, sir."

Behind Kanoa, the deck was a long, empty sweep punctuated by slashed breeching and unhooked tackle. "Very well. Start the stores and water over the side, then the anchors. You may keep the kedge and skiff."

"Yes, sir."

A steady series of splashes went up on either side of the ship as casks, crates, and various stores came out of the hold and were tossed over the side. Curran pointed his glass at their pursuer, now hull up and steering in their wake. There was some activity aboard *Um Qasim*, a bit more scrambling about than was quite proper aboard a man o'war. Soon, studdingsail booms appeared low and aloft.

The sails were let fall, nearly doubling *Um Qasim*'s canvas, and the wave before her bow spread wider and dragged far astern. Curran held his breath and studied her, but *Um Qasim* was not gaining. *Yunis*, now lighter by several tons, was plain flying before the wind.

"How does she steer, Padeen?" Curran asked.

"Like a dream, sir. Light as a feather." Padeen shot a glance back at *Um Qasim*, still a mile and a half behind. "We might make Cartagena yet."

"On deck," Nordhoff's voice came out of the maintop. "On deck, there. She's limbering her guns."

Curran lifted his glass. *Um Qasim* had her gunwales rigged on hinges, like those of *Ar R'ad*. Her wide gangways, used to cut in and work on whale carcasses, had been screened with pieces of canvas, and these were now drawn back, revealing the long, tapering barrels of her twin guns pointed over the larboard beam. Curran could just make out the men heaving at the wheels of the gun carriages, swinging them about.

"On deck," Nordhoff sang out. "They are training the forward gun."

Now would come a test, not only of marksmanship but of seamanship. Curran knew as well as anyone that this first shot would tell a tale.

From the top: "They have fired, sir!"

A huge, gray-white cloud bloomed in front of *Um Qasim*. To Curran's surprise, she had not turned to starboard as far as he had expected. Her forward gun, the long 42, had been pivoted forward and fired narrowly across the bows. As the smoke gushed, the whale ship's entire suite of sails shivered with a concussive ripple. The water in front of *Um Qasim* was whipped into foam, and a shudder went through the sea, reaching *Yunis* a good two seconds before the report of the gun, a deep, resonating, and incomprehensibly loud thud. The booming was followed instantly by a tearing noise, a screech that increased in pitch and volume. The ball struck the water three hundred yards astern, caromed off a swell, and splashed down a hundred yards farther on, trailing a lopsided rainbow.

Ten seconds later, *Um Qasim*'s after gun fired over the larboard rail. The report was less sharp and the explosion less grand, but the incoming round was louder, a noise that was part whistle and part rumble. This ball slammed into the wake less than a hundred feet astern, far closer than should have been possible. The shot went to pieces as it slapped the water, and the air was filled with a sputtering buzz. A hundred tatters lashed the wake, and splinters tore into *Yunis*' rigging and transom, shattering the glass in her sternlights. The round had gone to pieces, either destroyed in flight or fractured in the barrel. Big drops of saltwater pattered down, and among them shards of razor sharp black stone.

In the cabin Nolan bent to retrieve one of the pieces—the cannonball had been made of marble rather than iron. He realized that the corsair's gunners must have double-primed the guns to extend their range. It was a small consolation that if *Um Qasim*'s gunners persisted in overloading, their marble shot would continue to disintegrate. With any luck they might eventually burst a gun. But even as Nolan hoped for the enemy's misfortune, *Yunis* suffered one of her own.

There was a crack from the maintop, and the xebec seemed to lurch forward. On deck Curran was standing between Padeen and the starboard rail when he heard a shout from above. At his feet, a shadow fluttered across the quarterdeck; he did not have time to discern its source before the mainsheet had parted at the block. The line twanged back, whipping across the deck and casting the block up and then over the side. As the block went over the side, the huge triangular mainsail warped uncontrolled around the bowline tackles. The lower half of the lateen swept aft across the deck and crashed into the break of the quarterdeck, narrowly missing Fante.

Sixty feet above, the opposite end of the spar whipsawed around the masthead. In an instant, both Vanhall and Nordhoff were swept out of their lookout and cast into the air. Vanhall had been struck by the spar behind his ankles; the impulse threw him upward, head over heels, and then over the cap. Tumbling through the air, Vanhall thudded off the starboard rail and disappeared in a bloody splash. He was followed by the compact shape of Nordhoff, somehow put into the air upright and remaining that way as he fell through an arc fifty-seven feet. Curran clearly saw the boy's face as he slammed into the wake—his eyes screwed shut and his teeth bared in a terrified grimace.

Fifty yards back in the wake Nordhoff surfaced, head and shoulders, followed by the inert body of Vanhall. Aboard *Yunis* three men sprang to the rails and shrouds to point at their position. They saw Nordhoff swim over to Vanhall and turn him onto his back. The sailor's face was crimson with blood, but a moving arm demonstrated that he had survived. An empty basket was found on deck and heaved over the side, and a barrel went after it, each as much marker as lifebuoy.

On the quarterdeck, Curran had an instant to act. Already *Yunis* was steering wildly, the boom and mainsail flogging themselves to pieces. "Let go the foresail!"

Instantly, the way came off *Yunis*, the prow squatted down, and the wave before her sputtered out. Though she was still moving through the water, the xebec settled by the stern and began to wallow.

Curran cupped his hands around his mouth, "On deck! Be ready to clamp on the mainsheet and make it fast." That line was now a ragged end wriggling through the air like a convulsing reptile. "We shall put about in a moment, and you must be ready to splice the sheet."

Kanoa shoved the few uncomprehending hands out of the way, and Guild and a dozen others readied lines to make the sail fast. There would be only one chance to perform the necessary evolutions.

Behind them, *Um Qasim* was coming up fast. Should Nordhoff and Vanhall be picked up by the corsair, their fate would be slavery—or worse. If they were left to the mercy of the sea, their deaths might be more noble but equally torturous.

There was one more second to reconsider and continue to flee, but Curran did not hesitate: "Ready about!"

On deck, Fante and Guild moved into position to collar the out-of-control boom as it came around. Kanoa held a line and marlinspike clenched in his teeth, prepared to splice or knot the mainsheet the instant it could be plucked out of the air.

Curran took one more look into the wake. He could see Vanhall but not Nordhoff. Then he saw neither of them.

"Put up your helm, Padeen," Curran said. "Put us about."

Padeen shoved on the tiller, pushing it toward the starboard rail. Instantly *Yunis*' bow banked around. In slightly more than her own length she came about, changing direction as nimbly as a cutter.

As the bow went through the wind, Fante and Guild threw themselves on the end of the spar, wrestling it against the quarterdeck break and pinning it there. Kanoa found the clew of the sail and the cut-through mainsheet. The decks bucked and pitched as the ship went round, first beam-on to the swell and then through it. Spray flew over the rail, the canvas boomed, and the spars banged against the masts. Even as the ship seemed to beat herself to death around him, Kanoa tied a pair of water knots into the mainsheet. Knotting, if not splicing, made the sheet whole again, and Guild quickly made the bitter end fast to a cleat.

The other sails were tended round without a word of command. In forty-five seconds *Yunis* was again under control, had reversed course, and was heading back toward the men in the water.

"Who has the swimmers?" Curran shouted.

"Two points off the starboard bow," shouted one of the lookouts. "A cable's length, no more."

Leaning through the shattered sternlights Nolan caught a glimpse of them going up on a swell: Nordhoff's small, white face and the bloody lolling head of Vanhall. Beyond them, *Um Qasim* had reset all her studdingsails and looked very formidable indeed—a white tower. The ships were now closing on each other with a combined speed of more than twenty knots. Kanoa and Guild were rapidly stripping log line from its reel and lashing together a pair of boat hooks.

The men in the water were now fifty yards away. *Um Qasim*, their destroyer, the doom of them all, was a thousand yards distant and closing in great bounds. *Why doesn't he fire?* Nolan wondered. *Why doesn't he heave to and give us a broadside?*

"Ready about!" Curran heard himself say. The words had come from him automatically.

"Call it, your honor," Padeen whispered.

"Wait. Wait." And then in a stern voice Curran called out: "Helm's alee!"

Yunis answered instantly, her bow swinging round like a cutting horse. The xebec turned, and Nordhoff and Vanhall passed within six feet of the starboard side. The boy was holding the sailor up by the collar of his jersey, kicking with all his might.

From the deck, Kanoa thrust a boat hook at them. Nordhoff's hand went for the shaft, missing it by a desperate inch. Vanhall did not move, but only slumped back into the water, his blood spreading in an oily sheen around them both.

"Let go the sheets," Curran called. With a great thunder of luffing sails *Yunis* again went dead in the water. This would be the final, desperate measure to get the men aboard. Another line was thrown, but neither could catch it.

"Swim! Swim!" came a dozen shouts.

It was now apparent that Vanhall was either unconscious or paralyzed. "Swim, boy! God damn you, swim!" But Nordhoff would not leave Vanhall.

Nordhoff pedaled his legs but kept both hands on Vanhall's collar, holding him up. Desperately pumping his legs the midshipman could only make slow progress toward his rescuers. From the masthead came the croaking voice of one of the Marines, "On deck, she is striking her stun'sails, sir."

Curran looked back. *Um Qasim* was within eight hundred yards and pressing on with a bow wave spreading wide.

At that moment, Nolan put a line around his waist, cinched it tight, and dove over the rail. He went under, turned like a gannet, and banked toward the surface in a stream of bubbles. In three powerful strokes he was over to Nordhoff and Vanhall and bundled them both into his arms.

"Haul away!" Nolan shouted up at the deck. "Haul away! I have them."

Kanoa and Guild led a dozen hands in heaving on the line.

The Marine called down from the foremast, "On deck! They are training weapons."

Nolan, Nordhoff, and Vanhall were still a dozen yards from the ship. Curran could not wait. "Sheet home. Sheet home! Padeen get under way, steer fair and by."

The sails were cleated and *Yunis* began to gather speed. On deck, a dozen hands joined Kanoa and Guild pulling in the line. Nolan lifted his face from the water and his teeth clapped down on a mouthful of air.

Rolling over on his back, Nolan held tightly to Vanhall and Nordhoff. Spray parted around them as *Yunis* gathered way and Padeen steered downwind, doing his best to pendulum the three men toward the side of the ship.

The water about them seemed to twitch, and the air in the sails cracked like a whip. "She has fired," the lookout cried. There was a deep boom and the howl of a shot screaming overhead. A column of water went up off the starboard bow. The water returned to the sea with a protracted snarl.

"Heave!" Guild yelled. "*Heave!*"

The combined weight of the men in the water was too much; the gathering speed of the ship worked them closer to the side, but it was impossible for even a dozen men to lift them from the water and over the gunwale.

"Make the line fast," Kanoa shouted. "Fast with a round turn. Now, out with some nippers! Get a purchase on this. Turn to!"

Someone found a set of tackles and Guild knotted them to the line. This process took half a minute, and in that time Nolan was again towed under. The three faces disappeared for an agonizing span of seconds; the line went taut as a harp string and then suddenly slack.

"Goddamn me!" Kanoa spat. The line angled sharply against the counter and then veered back out. There was a kick and splash on the near side of a swell, and Nolan's head popped out, his face streaming. His right fist clung to the rope, and his left hand pulled Nordhoff along by the collar. Vanhall was nowhere to be seen.

Nordhoff coughed out, "He's gone under!" But there was nothing to be done. Curran saw the sailor pass by the mizzen chains three feet underwater. Vanhall's striped jersey showed red and black through the blood-streaked water. Waving his arm, Vanhall went over a swell and then disappeared from sight.

The blocks were now fixed to the line, and Guild clamped onto it. "Lay hold!" he grunted, "Heave! Heave!"

Another pair of lines was sent down; a bowline and a figure eight. Nolan shoved his foot into the bowline, stepped up on it, and put a turn under the shoulders of the exhausted boy. Grabbing him by the waist of his pants, Nolan shoved Nordhoff up into Fante's outstretched hands.

Kanoa leaned out over the main chains and his hands clamped onto the midshipman's shoulders. Kanoa got him up as far as his chest and then the hands of a dozen shipmates closed over Nordhoff's shirt, shoulders, arms, and hair. As they struggled, Fante reached down and with one powerful heave brought Nolan onto the deck.

"Let her run, Padeen!" Curran said, and the ship began to make way.

Dripping, exhausted, Nolan slapped Fante on his back.

Um Qasim was within six hundred yards, almost rifle shot, and she was coming up fast. The corsair's after carronade went off like a thunderclap. The corsair trembled, and the space between the ships was rent by a white nimbus shot through with fire. Curran could see the ball flying at them, a deadly blur, and he turned and yelled, "Lay down!"

The crew fell to the deck, but Curran remained on his feet, too fascinated to move. He watched the ball come on, first a speck surrounded by a smudged rainbow, and then a screaming, wobbling blur. He felt its breath as the round went howling over the starboard side. The ball struck the water just off the bow, atomizing the sea before the prow and then sending a fountain skyward. Running into the empty space, *Yunis* pitched violently forward and down. A tower of green water went up as high as the foremast and then poured down onto the forecastle like a torrent. The foredeck was filled ankle deep with water and the flood ran aft, tangling together the cut gun tackles and stripping clean the shot racks. *Yunis* shuddered and found her stride, but as she came from under the flood she seemed tremulous under her helm.

Nolan trotted down the companionway and sloshed aft to his guns. Through the sternlights *Um Qasim* loomed like a cloudbank. Nolan shouted to the gun crews "Together now, hit them on the rise!"

Nolan worked a pry bar under the carriage of the larboard chaser. "Three inches," he said, wiping the seawater from his eyes. "And the quinion up too, an inch. Easy now, another, heave! That's it. That's it."

Through the skylight, Curran heard Nolan's command: "Smartly now, lads. As they bear, on the roll . . . fire!" The starboard chaser went off with a deck-rattling bang. A jet of smoke stabbed astern and then returned, swirling over the quarterdeck.

Curran went to the rail to observe the fall of the shot. Nolan's round went home, hitting the corsair square. The ball tore straight through *Um Qasim's* jibs and cracked off her foremast in a shower of splinters.

"Stand clear, now," Nolan said. The portside chaser was trained and aimed precisely, and at the top of the swell he thumbed a match into the touchhole. The gun went off, filling the cabin with a stupefying crash and bucking the cannon straight back against its breeching. The smoke went out and came back, and Nolan saw a pair of blurs streak toward *Um Qasim*. He had aimed for the bow, where the upper cheek met the fore end, intending to sweep the deck. His shot, loaded double, struck exactly where he had aimed.

With a terrific crash the cannonballs tore through *Um Qasim's* bow, ripping off an entire plank and plowing straight through the forward carriage. They did further mischief aft, striking either the helmsman or the ship's wheel itself, with the immediate result that *Um Qasim* bucked suddenly and fell off the wind. Her spanker banged over in an uncontrolled jibe, and the ship yawed off to starboard.

A cheer went up along the decks of *Yunis*. They had struck the enemy, but Curran knew that to survive they had to stay lucky; the enemy had only to get lucky once.

Corporal Hackman came on deck cradling his freshly made incendiaries. "Stinkpots, sir."

"Hand them out, Corporal, if you would be so kind. And in the meantime detail your riflemen into each of the tops—reliable fellows with Kentucks'. They may fire at will."

It is an axiom of naval warfare that if the enemy is in range, so are you. As soon as *Yunis'* Marines began to snipe at the enemy's deck, they were answered shot for shot. The corsairs may not have had weapons as accurate as Kentucky rifles, but they made up for any deficiency with enthusiasm and diligence. Their tops, also being taller, gave the corsair's miquelet men a decided advantage. Bullets snapped through the sails and soon cracked through the transom.

"All hands not returning fire may repair below," Curran said. "Those below, load your weapons, fill powder horns, and distribute grenadoes and stinkpots to each mess. Corporal Hackman, see to it that every three men share a match."

The order to go below was obeyed reluctantly. Nolan's head again popped out of the skylight; his battle grin gave him the appearance of a fiendish jack-in-the-box. "I am reloading with chain," he said. "Have you any objection?"

"I do not," Curran answered, checking his watch. "And I think this issue will soon come to a head. Can you fire and have another salvo ready in five minutes?"

"I can. Shall I reload with ball?"

"Grape or canister might answer—if you can find them."

"We have musket balls in plenty. I'll make canister out of a tin lantern."

"The faster the better." The decks were clear and Curran stood close to Padeen. Behind them, *Um Qasim* had sorted herself out and was again running before the wind. Without his glass Curran could see the loaders swarming over her great guns, sponging and swabbing and carrying up the huge rounds on four-handled stretchers.

"Keep us off her bow, Padeen. She cannot fire directly ahead."

"And what if she yaws, sir?"

Curran held his watch in his hand. "I expect she will, in two minutes. Until then, Padeen, you may tease her."

The deck shivered beneath them as Nolan fired the chasers, first larboard then starboard. A whirling mass of chain ripped through *Um Qasim*'s forecastle, shredding her spritsail and parting her dolphin striker. Nolan's second round, aimed higher, went hissing through the main courses, ripping holes that the wind immediately made larger. Curran watched as the corsair's starboard staysails were let go and brailed up.

Both guns were trained at them, and Curran watched as the loaders jumped clear. He could hear the shouted syllable "*Nar!*" float over the sea as *Um Qasim* fired her aftermost 50-pounder.

The concussion snapped *Yunis'* mizzen sail, and Curran could feel the blast on his face. The ball went overhead as high as the gunwale, and as it passed, the lateen mainsail was shaken from cap to foot. The deadly missile went by the main shrouds, missing them by a whisper. Fifty yards ahead, an astounding column of water pitched up.

Curran said to Padeen, "Now jink her, Padeen! Port your helm."

Padeen yanked the tiller, and *Yunis* surged to leeward just as the corsair fired. Again the thunder and smoke, but this time there was an ear-splitting crackle like the noise of a close-burning fuse. A cloud of grapeshot skittered through the air, a deadly blur that lashed the water fifty feet back into the wake. The splash thrown up was not as tall but was twice as wide as the one made by the round shot. Two hundred fist-sized balls had been fired at them—a deadly puff that would have killed every living thing aboard.

The corsair had fired both her guns, and now her crew scrambled to reload. "All hands!" Curran shouted. "All hands! Starbolines to make sail, larbolines to arms!" Armed with muskets and grenadoes, the crew scrambled out of the holds. Curran observed a few expressions of awe as sailors looked up—*Um Qasim* was towering over the stern no more than a cable's length behind them.

"About ship!" Curran barked. "Clap on the braces!"

Comprehension spread across the decks, and the looks of fear were replaced with something like malignant joy. *Um Qasim* had shot her load, both guns had fired, and it would be a full six minutes until she could load them: an eternity.

It was *Yunis'* turn to dish. "Ready about!" Curran yelled. "Hard alee!"

Padeen shoved the tiller over, the yards went across onto a full tack, and the xebec nimbly reversed course. *Yunis* had turned on her pursuer, the fox lunging at the hound.

"Pass her, port to port. As close as you dare," Curran said.

Not twenty yards before the enemy's bow, Padeen put the helm over, sheering across the whaler's cutwater, then swinging into her long shadow.

As *Yunis* passed to larboard, her sails ate the larger ship's wind. The corsair's torn canvas started to luff, and *Yunis'*, brisk and taut, scratched past what was left of the whale ship's jib boom. As soon as a view opened to the deck, Curran pulled both of his pistols from the bandoleer across his chest. "On deck, by messes, fire!"

The starboard Marines were the first to pull their triggers, and did so just as the corsairs revealed themselves over the rails. *Um Qasim's* bulwarks were ripped by a dozen musketballs, and splinters chirruped away to windward. The corsairs presented themselves to return fire, but Corporal Hackman's cunning had reserved the fire of nearly all of the larboard watch. A second volley swept through the corsair's miquelet men, tearing them to pieces.

Musket smoke rolled back and forth, and as *Yunis* passed under *Um Qasim's* towering port side, Curran could see the corsair's two gigantic guns, empty and pointed blankly overhead: *Yunis* was now too close to hit.

A handful of bearded, turbaned riflemen were scrambling on top of the guns to fire down at the xebec. A final volley from the Kentucks' in the maintop swept them down.

"Now grenadoes!" Curran shouted.

Five went over, trailing wisps of smoke. One skipped off the rail and fell into the sea, but four of them clanked onto the corsair's deck and went off with orange-black bangs. Under *Yunis'* mainmast, Hackman lit the fuse of the first stinkpot and Fante heaved it with two hands up and over the rail of the whale ship. It bounced through the fore shrouds and spilled onto the deck, instantly bursting into smoke and fire.

The ships were passing five or six feet apart, and the swell splashed up between them. From the tops, Arab marksmen fired down onto the deck, and Hackman and Guild fell. The corsair put her helm over and bashed into the side of *Yunis*. The main chains briefly locked together, and the xebec shook and slowed. A pair of grapnels sailed over, and Curran looked up to see a large party preparing to jump down onto the deck. Two grenadoes were tossed into the mass of corsairs, flattening them and sending the bloody, burnt survivors reeling aft.

Running onto the midship deck, Curran slashed at the grapnel lines with his cutlass. "Fend off aft! Fend us away!"

A dozen corsairs jumped from the whale ship's gangway and made it to the edge of the forward hatch. They had landed in a close knot, and Fante and Kanoa waded into them, Kanoa swinging his *pahoa* and Fante applying a six-foot iron pry bar. The Marines, freshly reloaded, turned and fired across the deck—the boarders fell in the smoke.

A bullet snapped past Curran's head and he flinched. "Get us away, Padeen. They've had their chance!"

Padeen put the helm over and *Yunis* went away to windward. Crouching, Curran moved aft on his own deck as the whale ship slid past. Looking up, he could see a tall, thin man with a black turban and a hennaed red beard. There was a musket in his hand and Curran watched him lift it and aim. Curran ducked as a bullet struck the rail next to him.

In that instant there was a staggering explosion. The whale ship lurched up, and a roiling mass of smoke burst from the forward gun. Shot through with sparks, another whooshing gust swept along her decks—a cartridge box had ignited. Fueled by a series of gunpowder explosions, the corsair began to burn, and a swath of fire seethed up into the rigging.

As *Yunis* turned away, Nolan aimed a chaser, pointed as high as he could fire, double-shotted with grape. A deadly swarm tore into the transom of the corsair, obliterating her stern windows and shattering her taffrail. Aimed slightly higher, Nolan's second gun pumped a cloud of grapeshot along the corsair's deck.

Padeen looked to see the red-bearded man fall and another hissing tongue of flame burst up from *Um Qasim*'s deck. They were clear. Padeen felt the tiller strengthen under his hand as the sails filled and *Yunis* gathered speed. Smoke now curled away to leeward as the fire aboard the corsair became general. The Marines in the tops fired a few parting shots, plucking off those of the corsairs who showed themselves outside of the smoke.

The xebec was galloping again, the wind nearly on her beam. The deck was slanting and water rushed along her sides; there would be no catching her now.

Nolan climbed up out of the skylight, his face smeared with soot and powder. His eyes were bright. "We did it, sir!" Padeen shouted. "We have whooped them sons of bitches!"

Nolan stood next to Padeen, delighting in the sight of their burning antagonist.

Yunis heeled as she worked to windward, her wake streamed out straight behind her. *Um Qasim* was blazing three hundred yards astern, and they had the heels of her. As the distance opened, Nolan could see more of the corsair, her guns turned uselessly to larboard, her rigging and sails now aflame, and her yards cock-eyed and smoldering. Those of her crew who were not wounded were fighting fires forward and amidships.

"Parse that, ya boogers," Padeen shouted. "Come back if ya want more!"

Kanoa staggered onto the quarterdeck, panting and spattered with blood. Nolan saw at once that his face was streaked with tears.

"Come forward, sir. Please come at once," Kanoa cried out. "Mister Curran has been shot."

TURNED ASHORE

I T IS RARE FOR AN AMERICAN SAILOR TO BE BURIED IN A FOREIGN LAND. Interment at sea was more common for that class of man—the traditions and custom of the service demanded it—and so a naval burial in a Spanish churchyard was, for that reason, a doubly mournful event. *Yunis* had suffered three dead and six wounded in her encounter with *Um Qasim*. Mulherrin, Moody, and Finch had been buried at sea off Cabo de Gata, Nolan saying over them what words he could, and the wounded were transferred to *Enterprise*'s sickbay at Cartagena. Of these, three succumbed despite Doctor Darby's valiant efforts. Guild and Hackman were Catholics and O'Mara was thought to be, and the following day they were rendered full military honors behind the small Franciscan chapel next to the American consulate.

In dress uniforms with swords reversed, Pelles and his officers escorted three simple wooden caskets up from the harbor. Behind them, the ship's company marched, mustered by divisions, their hats under their arms and black bands of crepe around the right arms of their best shore-going rigs. The familiar, heartfelt words were spoken, prayers were whispered, the Marines fired their volleys, and it was over.

After the service Pelles walked alone down the Calle Real. A rainy morning had somehow turned into a beautiful day, the wind plain out of the north and the sky as blue as a Dresden cup. A little before noon, *Enterprise* had been joined in Cartagena roads by the flagship of the Mediterranean squadron, USS *Constitution*. Anchored inboard of *Enterprise*, *Constitution* wore her jack and ensign at half-staff, and after a decent interval she ran up a signal: captain repair aboard flag.

On the quay, Pelles signaled for his barge. "Flagship, Mister Wolfe," he said to a tall, lanky, and brand-new midshipman.

"Give way," the boy said firmly. "Smart and dry."

As the barge pulled across the harbor, Pelles had a moment to compare the two frigates. *Enterprise* and *Constitution* had been laid down by the same hand, Joshua Humphries, and they looked very much like sisters. Each ship had her own superlatives and foibles, but it would be very hard for a landsman, or even many sailors, to tell them apart from the bows. *Enterprise* had a more gimcrack stern; it was rounded in the modern style and had a pair of galleries and the glory of a poop deck. *Enterprise* was longer by seven feet six inches, and though stoutly made was as lean as a thoroughbred. To Pelles' not impartial eye, it was *Enterprise* who was the beauty, and Easy E was renowned for sailing plain and true—a dry, weatherly ship, snug as a duck.

At twenty-three, her sister *Constitution* was starting to show her age. Old Ironsides was still a formidable ship, and without doubt the most glorious frigate in the United States Navy. It was a compliment to the ship as well as the senior-ity of her captain that *Constitution* wore the pennant, a burgee with twenty-four stars encircling a single large, five-pointed star. But even this distinction did not go unanswered by *Enterprise*. Since the sinking of *Ar R'ad*, Easy E had sported a broom fixed to her mainmast, a time-honored signal meaning that she had swept the seas.

The sailors of the flagship were spurred to something like envy when they came to moor and saw not only *Enterprise*, the victor over *Ar R'ad*, but two corsair ships taken in that same action. At anchor, the snow *Courier* and the xebec *Yunis* both wore the Stars and Stripes over the three green crescents of Bou Regreg. They were taken ships—lawful prizes; this meant, for the crew of *Enterprise*, honor, a certain moral superiority ashore, and the delight of all: prize money. Scuttlebutt had it that both ships would be "bought in"; that is, purchased directly by the Navy. This meant cash on the barrelhead for every man jack aboard *Enterprise*, paid in shares calculated down to the last glorious golden quarter eagle, silver half dime, and copper cent.

As Pelles approached the flagship, he could see that *Courier* and *Yunis* were being swarmed over by carpenters, sailmakers, gunners, and bo'suns; to judge by the multilingual curses wafting from both decks, there were some differences of opinion between the American and Spanish shipwrights. More somber, and per-haps less fussed over, *Yunis* was tied up to the ordnance dock taking aboard guns, powder, and shot—arms and ammunition to replace those thrown overboard in her costly escape from *Um Qasim*. Unlike *Courier*, that happy ship, *Yunis* wore her lateens crossed in a token of mourning. Work aboard her had been suspended for the funerals and would resume tomorrow after the hands had time to eat, drink, and mourn their shipmates.

Enterprise's barge pulled within hail, and a sentry called from the flagship, "Ahoy the boat!" Midshipman Wolfe answered, "*Enterprise*," indicating that the commanding officer of that ship was approaching. This exchange set in motion ceremonies appropriate for the arrival of a frigate captain, and as the barge came gently against *Constitution*, Pelles went up the side to the sound of bells, pipes, and the measured stamp of a squad of Marines.

With a look of calculated severity, Pelles saluted the colors and the quarterdeck in turn. The commodore, Jacob Jones, was a friend of thirty years. Both knew it was a matter of seniority rather than strictly merit that had granted Jones his office. Jacob Jones and Arthur Pelles had been mids together, and Jones was senior by three weeks.

The commodore returned Pelles' salute with due gravity but could not hide the frank and familiar pleasure of his smile. "Welcome aboard, Captain Pelles. Congratulations on your cruise." Jones took his friend by the hand and added, "I am sorry to hear of your losses."

Pelles nodded, and the commodore introduced his officers. They were memorably young. Jones' flag captain, Ezra Mullins, was not quite so young, but a spry man of forty. Pelles clasped his hand with a grin. Mullins had once been Pelles' exec in *John Adams*.

"Good to see you, Skipper," Mullins said, or rather mumbled, for since *John Adams* Commander Mullins had somehow lost all of his teeth.

"Howdy, Ezra. Good to see you."

A young officer, scrubbed pink, stepped forward and waved a white-gloved hand. "This way, sirs, if you please." Pelles had to look at the young man twice to believe that he wore an epaulette. No, *two* epaulettes.

Jones smiled. "I thought you might take some lunch, Captain."

In the great cabin the two august personages could be more like themselves, and not the living, breathing representatives of Yahweh. Jones took off his coat at once. "Sit, Art, sit. How are you? You look trim."

Pelles tossed his hat on the chart table, found a chair, and stretched out his legs. Commodore Jones' cabin was the mirror of his own, though perhaps polished more ferociously.

"Will you have some monongahela?" Jacob asked. He poured himself half a tumbler.

"Just beer."

Jacob touched a bell, and the steward nipped in with a brown ceramic bottle. He opened it, poured the contents into a glass, and disappeared like a phantom. Jacob slipped on a pair of spectacles and sat at his desk.

"By God, you look like a schoolmaster," Pelles said, sipping his beer.

Jacob poked through a pile of papers. "I am a mere scribbler. And a seagoing nanny. I've fifteen mids about, four of them squeakers."

"I might have vacancies for your oldsters. Can you spare me a few?"

"I am amazed at how you go through lieutenants. How many did you lose in the last go?"

"Three against *Ar R'ad*. And the rest pretty well banged up. Only two of them can count all the arms and legs God gave them."

Jacob sipped his drink. He remembered getting wounded himself. "I have a pair of master's mates that I can make into lieutenants, they're ready," he said. "But it will be up to you to make them sea officers."

"I should be able to do that."

"I am sure you will. Who is the officer you mentioned in the dispatch? The one who fought the captured whale ship?" Jones lifted one of the pages and looked at it approvingly. "Fought with grenadoes and stinkpots, by God. What was his name?"

"Curran."

"Just so. A Marylander?"

"Virginian. His father was a diplomat."

"Mnnn," Jones hummed. "Is he the one you buried today?"

"No. He was wounded while in command. Probably the last man shot in the engagement. A rifle bullet struck him, went under his shoulder, and traveled right round his rib cage. Do you believe it?"

"Will he live?"

"It seems so. The surgeon has put him ashore."

"He's likely to become religious, that boy."

"I would, too. The fact that he's walking seems a miracle."

"As was his escape from that corsair." Jacob touched the report. "A close enough shave."

"He is the first to say that he was lucky," Pelles answered. "And it is better to be lucky than dead. He's been given three weeks' leave."

"I wish someone would give me leave." Jacob found a file. "I hate to talk about money, Art, especially when I am drinking, and especially when most of it is going to you and not me. Shall I get the matter of the prizes out of the way?"

"I would be obliged."

"The cargo condemned, head money for the slaves, gun money—altogether a pretty penny. Pretty indeed. All the particulars are under the red cover." Pelles squinted around. "The red one, you blind bastard, and the shares to be paid out on the top sheet."

Pelles borrowed Jacob's glasses and looked at the numbers.

"A fair afternoon's work, by God," Jacob said. *And a pretty one for the commodore, too.* As *Enterprise* was at least nominally under his orders, Jacob's own share of the prizes was definitely enough to pay for lunch.

"We earned it," Pelles said. "Seventeen killed aboard *Enterprise*, and three aboard *Yunis.* A score of wounded."

"Twenty lives for two enemies taken, one sunk, and one left burning. You've done shrewdly, Arthur. If you'd lost a hundred men, Crowninshield would strike you off a medal. The Secretary does love the blood of sailors."

Pelles tossed the file on the desk. He suddenly felt tired.

"I've bought *Courier* into the service," Jacob said. "I can always use gun brigs, and her French owners were happy to part with her. I intend to put her to sea at once. Would you like to give command to the young officer who brought her in?"

"Fentress? No, I would like to place Kim Erskine in her, my exec. He's lost an arm and is due his step. Fentress may be kept on as his number one."

"Done."

There was a rap on the door, and the commodore's chief of staff stepped in. He was the same man-child Pelles had seen on the quarterdeck. "Captain Mullins' duty, Commodore. The political gent has sent his apologies. He is unaccommodated today, pleading the flux, and hopes it will be convenient to wait upon you in the morning."

"That will be excellent, Mister Kidd. Thank you."

The officer ducked out.

"Tell me, how old is that child?"

"I will not oppress you with numbers. He was the youngest lieutenant in the fleet, and then a commander in two years."

"His father is a congressman?"

"A senator."

"It is a different sort of Navy, Jacob."

"No it's not. Another beer?" By some hidden signal the pantry was alerted, a new bottle of beer appeared, and a rattling of crockery announced the imminent arrival of dinner. The cabin door opened and in came a silver platter carried by two men. The dome was lifted on a mound of saffron-colored rice that would have fed a half a dozen commodores. It was studded with mussels, bits of chorizo, fish, chicken, and whole langoustines.

"Capital. The prawns alone are the glory of the world. They were milling about at a hundred fathoms just last night." Jacob made a gesture for the stewards to serve and he walked over to the mess table.

"You will give yourself the gout, Jacob."

"We can't all be lean sea wolves, Art. We can't all sleep on wool blankets in wet peacoats. And a certain amount of sizzle does impress the natives." Jacob tucked his napkin under his chin. "*In bocca al lupo.*"

Pelles drew at his beer. "*Cin cin.*"

When the stewards retired, Jacob said, "Eat while you can, Art. There will soon be enough gun smoke to go around."

"Tell me about the cannon," Pelles said. "Who gave the Dey of Bou Regreg such prodigious guns?"

"The 42s were Portuguese, as you discerned. Delivered by that slippery bastard you shot the rocket over. It was thought originally that the Portuguese gave the Dey of Bou Regreg four guns, but our Sicilian allies . . . "

"Allies? The shits."

"Our esteemed friends, and allies, Captain Pelles, have confirmed that the actual number is six. Six guns were delivered to the Dey of Bou Regreg."

"And pray, how would the Sicilians know this?"

"Those remarkable carriages you reported—"

Pelles frowned. "The armored pivots? Infernal bits of equipment."

"They did not spring from the genius of the Arab corsair. They were a gift from His Majesty Ferdinand, King of the Two Sicilys. He gave them, gratis and for nothing, to the dey."

"Jesus Christ."

"Peace be upon him," Jacob smiled.

"Is there not one upright man in the entire continent of Europe?"

"You should have been a philosopher, Art. This is about money, which makes it about politics, and politics will always find an outlet in war. Ferdinand of Sicily has a merchant fleet and no way to protect it. He can't even protect his fishing boats, for that matter. Last year the Sallees kidnapped two hundred of his fishermen during the run of tunny. Snatched them up in sight of shore—right in front of their families. They are presently slaves at Arzeou—that means he pays. Portugal has African slaves to ship to Brazil, a very lucrative industry, and the Portuguese have only the stub of a navy to uphold the trade. That means they pay. In guns."

Pelles tried not to look appalled.

Jacob continued with his mouth full, "It is not all the end of the world. Their six guns will not make them bring on the Apocalypse. You sank two of them when you sank *Ar R'ad*, and two were put aboard *McKendrie Evans*, which they now call *Um Qasim*. Your young prodigy blackened their eye, and likely those two guns will have to put in and refit before they can serve again." Jacob chewed thoughtfully, his jaw clicking. "The question is, where is the *other* pair of guns?"

"Now I have an interesting story," Pelles said. "They are in the Med."

Jacob blotted his mouth with his napkin and then looked at it. "I don't think so."

"They were delivered to Bou Regreg and hauled north toward Cape Spatal."

"How do you know that?"

"Not only is Mister Curran a dashing naval commander, he is fluent in Turkish and the Arabic. Since he has been at leisure due to his wound, he has had occasion to reexamine the papers captured when we took *Ar R'ad*. He found within them several coded documents that yielded to his cryptological skills. They revealed that two of the guns were the property of the Bashaw of Arzeou."

"Another damn pirate?"

"The bashaw is nominally a sovereign prince under the Ottoman sultan. The bashaw rules a voracious little city-state on the Baie des Andaluces on the Barbary Coast."

"Why have I not heard of this place?" asked Jones.

"It is a Shia emirate, like Bou Regreg. Until now they have been content to operate in obscurity. They have preyed mostly on the coastwise trade of their neighbors, and exacted tolls from the caravans and pilgrims that pass through the Wadi Misserghin."

"They prey on their own?"

"Not quite their own. As you know, the Shiites do occasionally find themselves at odds with their more orthodox Sunnite brothers."

"I scarcely care for my own religion, Art."

"But you care about war and money, so listen." Pelles cracked a tail off one of the langostines and continued, "The bashaw is entered into a secret agreement to condemn and sell the prizes taken by the Dey of Bou Regreg. They are after all both Shiites, and regardless of how other Muslims feel about heretics, their hatred for infidels is far more violent. Bou Regreg and Arzeou have made a secret treaty to cruise on us and a few other far-off, weak-willed countries. In return for that privilege, the Bashaw of Arzeou is to outfit his own ships and also raid our commerce."

"How very ambitious. But there is 1,500 miles of desert between Bou Regreg and Arzeou. The Spanish closely watch the port of Tangiers, and they have a well-developed network of spies. They would have not let the guns be exported."

"Who knows what the Spanish would allow? Any gate, the dey's gunners did not even reach Tangiers. They put the cannon across the beach at Diasra."

"How could they get 42-pound guns across a sandy beach? Flying carpets?"

"Palm mats, Jacob. Woven palm mats. The same way we get field guns ashore. Off Diasra, the guns were put into the hold of a Russian ship and covered with grain. The Spanish boarded her in the strait but did not find the cannon. The Russian put into Arzeou three days ago."

"You amaze me."

Pelles lifted his glass. "I should."

"Then I am no longer left to wonder why *Um Qasim* did not try for the open ocean. After your xebec set her afire, I thought they would run back through the strait."

"Didn't they?"

"No. *Um Qasim*, formerly *McKendrie Evans*, put into Arzeou. Her captain, we understand, was killed in the engagement, so the bashaw was left to express his displeasure to the officers and gun captains by decapitating one-third of their number."

"Good for the bashaw. May he kill all his sailors until he has none left."

"Frigate captains are a glut on the market—at least ones who used to work for Napoleon." Jacob poured beer for them both. "The bashaw has hired Gaston de Puys, a French renegado, and he is scheduled to take *Um Qasim* back out after they refit."

"How do you know all this?"

"Penniman aboard USS *Torch* has them penned up in the harbor."

"Not Bob Penniman?

"August Penniman, his son."

"Is he also a doorknob?

"He is much like his father. Young Mister Penniman has the personality and brains of a terrier, but that qualifies him to bottle up a harbor. I am sure he will continue to do so with great zeal. Please pass the catsup."

"And what will young Mister Penniman do, in a sloop, should *Um Qasim* put to sea?"

"His instructions are to run like hell. Any gate, that ship will not be a factor for several weeks, and if she does come out, Penniman has the sense to lay off her quarter, as you did with *Ar R'ad*." The commodore pushed his plate away with a thumb.

"If *Um Qasim* does come out, we will know it. I have no doubt that *Enterprise* and *Constitution* will put an end to the bashaw's capers."

"They secretly moved the guns once," Pelles said. "They might move them again."

"I am certain they will—and they will put them to sea as fast as ever they can. With Bonaparte out of business, French officers are not the only things on sale. Now *I* shall surprise *you*: there is an ex-imperial frigate that the Bashaw of Arzeou has purchased from the Cretans."

"What ship?"

"*Le Combattant*, 28 guns, what might be called a sixth-rate, but a handy little craft. She kept herself out of the way of the Royal Navy, and there was a squadron out looking for her in the Adriatic. They never caught a whiff. After the Hundred Days, she put into Crete and surrendered. The Cretans kept her in ordinary and have recently offered to sell her to the Greeks as a fireship. The bashaw had alert people about, and they snapped her up. She is anchored in Trachilos."

"Just so."

"I am going to take *Constitution* to Crete and find the frigate. If they have put to sea, I will sink them. If she is docked or careened or pierside, I will burn her in the stocks."

"And you would have me mother convoys in the meantime?"

"Not you. I will deploy *Ontario* and *Courier* to do that," Jacob said. "You are to stay at Cartagena, or near here. We can convoy to hell and back, but the root problem is that our ships are being attacked. I intend to deny the enemy his weapons. As long as *Um Qasim* remains in Arzeou I am happy. As soon as I can sink *Le Combattant*, the corsairs cannot put their guns into her."

"You are a strategical guy, Jacob."

"I am very highly thought of, even by myself."

Pelles sipped his beer. "I'm sure it has occurred to you that they might take the guns out of *Um Qasim* and put them in some other ship. No matter how industrious *Enterprise* is, I will not be able to search every likely ship off the coast of Arzeou."

Jacob rolled a crumb against the tablecloth. "And there is the rub. You may patrol, but we cannot impose anything that looks like a blockade, and some of the merchants are damn touchy, particularly the English. But with you positioned in the east we will have a deterrent force. At present the strait is the only point of vulnerability. With *Enterprise* perched here and *Um Qasim* repairing, I do not expect you will have much to do until I get back."

"Brilliant."

"Thank you."

Pelles finished his beer. "You have covered almost everything, Jacob—all that is interesting and tactical. May I ask you about an administrative issue?" Jacob cocked his head. "You read the letter I sent to the Navy Department?"

"What of it?" Jacob asked.

"Nolan."

The commodore narrowed his eyes. "The old Iron Mask. How is he?"

"Older. He is forty, but he looks sixty."

"Hmm."

"He fought a division of guns when we took *Ar R'ad*."

"That is commendable," Jacob said flatly.

"It was more than commendable, Jacob. It was brave and resolute. It was above and beyond the call. And now he has brought in *Yunis* after Curran fell wounded. He navigated her himself—made as pretty a landfall as you'd care to see."

"I am happy for him."

"He owes the United States no obligations, Jacob. He could have taken the ship and sailed it into Algiers. He would have made himself rich."

"Do you want me to congratulate him for not turning Turk?"

Pelles fixed his eyes on his friend. "Did you forward my letter?"

"I did."

"Did you add an endorsement?"

Jacob leaned back in his chair. "I forwarded it, Art."

"You are not as brave as I remember you."

"I am not. Nolan's confinement is a political matter, not a naval one. I have enough to do."

"Nolan does not deserve to be held any longer."

Jacob folded his hands behind his plate. "How do you know?"

"I saw what he did on the deck of *Enterprise*."

"And how do we know what he did with Burr? How do we know what else he did with Wilkinson, or any of those other traitors?"

"It is ancient history." Pelles said flatly.

"Were they traitors?" Jacob asked.

"Jacob . . ."

"Yes or no?" Jacob insisted. "Were they traitors?"

"Burr certainly was," Pelles admitted.

"And Nolan was a conspirator."

"How grand you make him sound. He was a lieutenant then."

"So were you, Art. So was I. But we had nothing to do with Aaron Burr."

Pelles was not used to contradiction. "Wilkinson, Jackson, and Dayton, just to name a few. They knew Burr, they certainly knew what he was up to, and they walked free. Hell, that rascal Jackson may even run for president."

"Soldiers," Jacob sniffed. "Though I will grant you Wilkinson was truly a shit."

"What about Commodore Truxton?" Pelles retorted. "He corresponded with Burr, did he not?"

"Truxton did not leave his post," Jacob said.

In their thirty-year friendship, Arthur Pelles and Jacob Jones had never had an angry word. Silence strained them both.

"I don't think Nolan should be held any longer," Pelles said. "If the decision is that he should be imprisoned forever, then I no longer want to be his keeper."

"Art, this is a political matter. Nolan's crimes were political. We are in the Navy. We're not politicians."

Pelles stood. "Perhaps you have become one, Jacob."

"Maybe I have."

Pelles went to the chart table and picked up his hat. "Tell me something, Jacob. What if they decided to do this to you? Make you disappear? What if they didn't like your politics?"

Jones considered his friend for a moment and then said quietly, "Let this go, Arthur. If you ever want to hoist your own pennant, do not write another letter."

"I will never hoist a pennant, Jacob. And I am happy to command a frigate." Pelles put on his hat and looked at himself in the quarter galley's small mirror. "Thank you for luncheon, Commodore Jones," Pelles said. "And thank you for sharing your plans." He walked to the cabin door, paused for a moment, and then passed through it.

Jacob sat alone in the cabin. The silence was just permeable enough to admit the sounds of his friend's departure—the trill of the pipe and the tramp of Marines presenting arms. Then the ship's bell tolled out two double strokes and through the skylight came the bo'sun's strong, clear voice from the quarterdeck: "*Enterprise* departing."

———

After a few tense days Curran was declared out of immediate danger. Pneumonia following a chest wound was to be feared, though, and when Curran was well enough to be moved he was taken from *Enterprise*'s sickbay and put up at the villa of the Conde Desagoado, a rambling stone-and-stucco affair overlooking the Puerto de Escombreras. The *hidalgo* was not wealthy, and Darby had rented the sunny, windswept place for *Yunis*' wounded to convalesce. The clean, pleasant air and of course liberal amounts of beechwood-aged lager soon did their work, and after two weeks Curran and the others were coming along as well as any physician could hope.

As he mended, Curran read through a pile of the *hidalgo*'s newspapers: French, Spanish, and Italian mostly, with a few issues of *The Times* of London. On the Hellenic peninsula, Greek nationalists, encouraged by romantic Englishmen, had risen against the Ottoman Empire. Spain's overseas colonies were slipping away, and Peru and Chile were battling one another. Napoleon, long dead and buried at St. Helena, was reported by the *Gazzata di Parma* to be alive and at the head of an army in Brazil. There were wars and rumors of war and calamities in diverse places. A comet was seen twisting over the polar sea, and a whale ship in the southern ocean reported hearing a blast like the trumpets of Armageddon.

From *Constitution*, Darby brought up American papers, the packet press, and among them were a few of the weekly magazines from Washington and New York. Curran read that Secretary of State Henry Clay had challenged Senator John Randolph to fight a duel in Arlington, Virginia. Both of the political gentlemen managed to miss each other after firing four shots: one wide, one low, and two into the air. In the *Pilot and Ledger*, Curran scanned a dozen less stirring pieces. Thomas Jefferson, greatly encumbered by debt, had asked for permission to raffle off some of his property; this was followed by an informative article claiming to prove, once and for certain, that the tomato was a nonpoisonous fruit. These stories were punctuated with fascinating splashes of advertising, an annoyance to ordinary readers but a treat for sailors halfway around the globe. Between advertisements for Daffy's Elixir and Doctor Morse's Beet Root Bolus was a small, black-bordered column that struck Curran like a blow.

> *The Loss of the U.S. Brig* Epevier
> *No Survivors*
> *Last Seen at Cádiz*

Curran felt a sickening pang. In his mind, a voice instantly said, *No, it is not possible.* Had he not just left that ship six months ago? Had he not shaken hands all around the quarterdeck as he took his leave? The words seemed to expand on the paper, and he felt his stomach turn: "The melancholy news is received that the sloop-of-war *Epevier*, 18 guns, under the command of Captain John T. Gormly, is confirmed lost by the Department of the Navy at Washington. *Epevier* carried seven officers and a crew of 123 sailors as well as a detachment of United States Marines."

Every man aboard was known to Curran, all had been shipmates and many his friends. The words "no survivors" flickered up again at him from the page. It must be hyperbole, vile sensationalist exaltation, and it made Curran dizzy with woe and anger. *Epevier* had put him ashore at Cádiz, he had watched the men sail away, and it was sickening for him to think that he might have been the last man to see any of them alive.

Epevier had detached from the Atlantic Squadron and was expected at Newport in the last week of March. Confirming the loss was the testimony of the master of the trading brig *L'Aimable Louise* of Collioure. That ship, sailing in proximity to *Epevier*, encountered a heavy gale off the Grand Banks. The brig's master witnessed the foundering of *Epevier* in a blizzard on the evening of February 27. Dismasted in that same storm, *L'Aimable Louise* managed with great difficulty to make Halifax to report the calamity.

Horror-struck, Curran tried repeatedly to dismiss the story, but he had been aboard *Epevier* in a gale. She had been a spirited ship, a runner, but inclined to gripe in a heavy sea—she might easily have succumbed in a North Atlantic gale. Curran remembered a passage aboard *President* when he was a youngster, the first time he had stood in terror of the sea. On a lashing night, *President*, every inch as big as *Enterprise*, had plunged into a valley between two monstrous waves; her stern had been lifted and her bow pressed down as she took a wicked lurch. Green water had surged aft, a wall of it that quickly filled the ship to the waist, stopping her dead and snap-rolling all of her two hundred feet on her beam ends. Curran had been forward, alone, and remembered the terror he'd felt when he had been snatched off his feet and had tumbled upside down. By a flat miracle his fist had clamped onto a stray line, and as he had held on he had been turned over and over, never knowing if he had stayed with the ship or had been cast over the bulwark.

Epevier had faced a similar storm; but she was a sloop, not a frigate. In such a gale, Curran could easily imagine a port lid coming loose or a hatchway caving in. Aboard *Epevier*, the chain pumps were directly across from the midshipmen's berth. The main pipe, number one, had transected his own bunk.

The ship was gone, but for a long time Curran could not believe anything could possibly have killed Mister Morell, the gunner. That bear of a man who had taught him not only gunnery but how to reef, steer, and splice. Curran had seen Morell swim after men gone overboard, an indefatigable marine animal if there ever was one, and Curran's patient mentor. But no man could ever survive overboard in a Grand Banks gale. They were gone—Captain Gormly and the exec, Mister Club. Tommy, Murph, and Vince: his friends and messmates. Curran knew it was only mere a quiddity that had saved him. Had Captain Gormly not endorsed his orders, transferring him directly to *Enterprise*, Curran, too, would have perished. He had been spared from eternity by the jot of a pen.

Darby announced at the end of June that Curran might rejoin *Enterprise*. Curran returned to the harbor, surprised to find the frigate no longer anchored in the roads but tied up to the principal pier at the Tarcanal. Instead of a boat ride he had only to debark from the coach at the foot of the pier. He was even more pleased to find Fancher standing duty on the quarterdeck, resplendent in the uniform not of a midshipman but of a newly made lieutenant. Curran saluted the colors as he came up the gangway. "Permission to come aboard?"

"Permission granted." Fancher smiled. "Welcome aboard, shipmate." As if Fancher's smile weren't enough, Curran was soon surrounded by men welcoming him with winks and claps on the back. "Tell 'im, sir," Padeen said to Fancher. Kanoa nodded. "He oughta know."

"Know what?" Curran looked about. There were a score of sailors and Marines smiling at him from all over the deck. They were joined by a dozen more peering out of hatches and companionways. "What's going on?"

"You are the new exec, Mister Curran," Fancher smiled.

Curran shook his head. How could that be possible? When he went to hospital ashore he had been the ship's most junior lieutenant.

"You've been kicked upstairs, Mister C," Padeen said. "Congratulations."

It was true. Commodore Jones had made a series of transfers, some made necessary by *Enterprise*'s losses, others made possible by her captures. Aside from Fancher, Doctor Darby was presently the only other officer aboard; the rest of *Enterprise*'s wardroom was now scattered about the harbor on other duties and new assignments. In sickbay, between personal questions, pokes, taps, and the examination of Curran's tongue, Darby explained as best he could.

"The captain is ashore, of course, as there is an opera to be seen. Though he is aboard most nights—well, at least for supper. He has generally been in a merry, even jovial mood. Please turn your head and cough."

Curran complied. "Where is everyone else?"

"If by 'else' you mean our former messmates, they are scattered. Before he left, Commodore Jones made several transfers. Our good friend Mister Erskine has been given command of *Courier*, bought into the Navy and newly christened USS *Seafox*."

"Excellent, he will be a capital commander," Curran said. The transfer meant also that Erskine had been promoted to master commandant, the next waypoint to the rank of captain and a lifelong sinecure. "How was *Seafox* armed?" Curran asked. *Courier* had been practically without guns when she was taken.

"*Constitution*, that commodious vessel, carried nearly twenty carronades in her hold. Guns as ballast! Sixteen of these were put aboard *Seafox*. She has become a very warlike ship."

And maybe a bit overarmed, Curran thought. With sixteen guns, she would be a ship to be reckoned with.

"The carronades are her bite," Darby said, "Fentress went with Mister Erskine as his exec. He is the bark, I believe you'd say." Darby chuckled to himself, "*Seafox*, bark and bite. I *am* a wit, I am."

"Fentress as exec," Curran smiled. "He is fit for it."

"We are almost the only ones left. Mister Pybus, of course, continues as master."

"I am delighted to hear it." The master was one of the ship's standing officers, like the gunner and purser, and their appointments were usually for the life of the vessel. Pybus knew the frigate better than anyone else aboard. He was a plank owner, had helped put Easy E into commission, and it was impossible for Curran to imagine the ship even floating without the redoubtable Pybus to conn and sail her.

"Your wound is doing admirably, but I must recommend a glass of lager." Darby took down a pair of green jars from his cupboard and drew two pints from the tank and spigot on the bulkhead. "As you see, I have that noble antiscorbutic near at hand. I believe I have the only sickbay in the Navy that can serve out a salubrious draught."

Curran took a sip and said, "What of Mister Ward? And I did not see Captain MacQuarrie when I came aboard."

Darby looked at his beer. "Perhaps my own failures. Neither has thrived under my care, and I have invalided them both home."

Curran drank the rest of his beer. It amazed and puzzled him that he had somehow become the most senior lieutenant aboard.

"Oh," Darby said, "I forgot to mention, your hammock and kit have been moved into the exec's cabin." Darby clinked his mason jar against Curran's. "We are now neighbors!"

After his agreeable beer Curran went down to the orlop. Aft of the cockpit, Curran knocked at Nolan's cabin. There was no sentry on duty in the passageway, a change in condition ordered by Pelles when they had come back aboard from their cruise. Curran knocked again and pushed open the door. Nolan's things were gone, the mattress was rolled up, and carpenters' tools were piled on the deck. One of the frames overhead was being replaced.

Curran saw a lantern shine behind him. When he turned, he saw Padeen and Stephen Bannon edge-rolling a keg from the after hold. "Hullo, Mister C. Better gang way."

"Padeen, where is Mister Nolan?"

"Why, transferred, sir."

"Transferred? Where?"

"Just temporary like. Chips says he's got to get at the knees here in this frame. Mister Nolan has repaired aboard *Yunis*, sir, moored outboard; got himself set up in the great cabin. Happy as a clam."

From the cockpit, forward, came a stifled series of snorts punctuated occasionally by Nordhoff's whooping laughter. Curran walked down the passageway and pulled back the curtain screening the midshipmen's berth. When his face appeared, the occupants came to their feet, dodging the lantern over their mess table and stooping under the low ceiling. "Good evening, sir," they said, pretty much at once. Their dirks, buttons, and side arms covered the table, as did a handful of rags and pots of polish. Curran was instantly suspicious. It was not often that the devil's children did the Lord's work.

"Carry on, gentlemen," Curran said. They dropped back into their cramped seats. The smell of shiny brass wafted through the stagnant air. "What are you about?"

"Why, we are shining our brass, sir," said Hall.

Curran saw that in addition to a pair of brushed coats, clean linen and collars had been piled atop their cruise boxes. "You are shining buttons of your own initiative?"

"Why yes, sir," Nordhoff said. "We'll be on display come Friday. Inspection, in course, and then the ball, sir. The dancing."

"What dancing, Mister Nordhoff?"

"Why, it's the Fourth of July, sir. And there is to be an open house of the ship. Dignitaries and Spanish *dons*."

"Ladies too, sir," Hall enthused. "Spanish ladies, like in the song."

"I see." Curran had almost forgotten. That explained the paint stages over the side and the work aloft, as well as the industrious scrubbing by both watches. As he came aboard he had noticed that the painting and swabbing were being undertaken with a degree of enthusiasm rare for a ship in port.

"All right, gentlemen. I must say your zeal impresses me." Curran started away, but Hall called after him.

"And give us joy, sir!"

"Of what, Mister Hall?"

"Why sir," the boy said, almost blushing, "Nordhoff and me, we were both made master's mates by the Old Mo—"

"Captain Pelles, sir," Nordhoff said quickly. "Skipper's orders, sir. We are both rated master's mates."

"Oh, my God," Curran said.

———————

CAPTAIN PELLES RETURNED ABOARD FOR DINNER RATHER THAN SUPPER, catching the working parties hard at it. As *Enterprise* was pierside they did not have the usual warning of the approach of the captain's gig, and it took several minutes, much to Fancher's mortification, for the Marines to form, the bo'sun of the watch to be found, and for the captain to be piped aboard. Pelles took no notice; a French company was playing *Valentine de Milan* at the opera house, the contralto was of long acquaintance, and he had spent a marvelous night ashore. Fancher made a furious gesture as the bo'sun pattered up. While he waited for the ceremony of his own arrival, Pelles looked about. The yards had been reblackened, and the topmen were aloft painting the trestletrees with rapid strokes. Finally the Marines presented arms and the pipe warbled. Absorbed by the work aloft, the captain was almost surprised when the bell rang and Fancher said formally: "*Enterprise* arriving."

Pelles, pretending he had just magically appeared, returned the officer's salute. "Is Mister Curran returned to duty?"

"I am here, sir," Curran said, coming up the ladder.

"Ah, the lion of the sea returneth. Are you recovered, sir?"

"Yes, sir. I am feeling prime." It was mostly true.

"Excellent," Pelles said. "Outstanding. You will please join me in my cabin in five minutes."

"Yes, sir." Curran saluted.

"And Mister Fancher?"

"Yes, Captain?"

"A gull has shit on your hat."

The captain's cabin had been spared the shambles of the general over-haul, as it was usually kept in a pristine condition. "Mister Curran, please come in."

Pelles was in the quarter galley, stepping backward to allow Grimble to pour a pitcher of hot water into his shaving basin. Curran watched as the captain slipped out of his coat and pulled his shirt off over his head. He noticed that in addition to the loss of his arm, Pelles had a small, circular scar in his right shoulder: a bullet wound.

"I can come back, sir," Curran said, "when you've finished shaving."

"When I finish shaving I am going ashore. Come in. Sit down." Pelles splashed water on his face, and his shaving brush clinked into a mug of soap. Using the fingers of his right hand, Pelles scraped the razor over his cheek, dipped it into the basin, then flicked his wrist so that a facecloth flipped over the blade, blotting it dry. This was the sleight-of-hand necessary for a one-armed man to shave his own face. Curran stared in genuine amazement, then remembered himself.

"Sir, I want to thank you for my—"

Pelles rapped the razor against the basin. "Don't thank me. You earned the opportunity. Now you must keep the job." Pelles' tone was not gruff, but rather the opposite. He seemed to have descended from the Olympian heights. As he watched the captain ply his razor, it occurred to Curran that he had only been in the captain's cabin on two occasions. He would now become a frequent guest.

Pelles scraped away. "I think you are acquainted with the manner in which I expect the ship to be run."

"I believe so, sir."

Pelles made a face into the mirror. "I will be sleeping out of the ship for the next two or three nights. I have taken a room at the Rialto. You will notify me immediately, night or day, of any incident, accident, explosion, fire, grounding, or material casualty to the ship." Pelles flipped his wrist; the towel went round, he rinsed the blade and started on the other side of his jaw. "I am to be informed if there is a message, dispatch, or order, coded or plain, from the fleet, squadron, embassy, or the Department of the Navy. You may consult the ship's standing orders if you are compelled to act in my absence."

"Yes, sir."

The razor dropped into the bowl with a clang. Pelles felt behind the door, located a towel, and dabbed at his face. This was the signal for Grimble to advance with a clean shirt. "We have received aboard three new officers. Mister Easton will relieve you as navigator, but you will remain responsible for the custody of Mister Nolan."

"May I ask, sir, are the new officers aware of the circumstances of Nolan's sentence?"

"They are not. You will tell them."

Pelles tucked in his shirt and was handed his stock. Curran watched in admiration as he wound it around his throat and then tied it with one hand. "Mister Ruggles and Mister Easton are hatched from the commodore's own followers. I do not know them, but I know Jacob Jones, and I think you will find them right seamen. It will be your job to inform them how I like things done." Pelles checked his reflection in the mirror and bared his teeth for inspection. "I have promoted Nordhoff and Hall to master's mates."

"They told me, sir. They were overjoyed."

"I hope that their enthusiasm may not recoil on us."

Curran remembered the boy standing alone at *Yunis'* helm when the corsairs tried to take her back, and his steady, firm conduct when cast overboard with Vanhall. "Nordhoff is game, sir," Curran said. "I was most satisfied with his conduct aboard *Yunis*."

"And that has counterbalanced the fact that he is a menace to navigation. A few months sweating over the celestial tables will bring them both to their duty. See that they do not tax Mister Pybus overmuch. He is a genial soul, but I know not how far he might be pushed should they spill catsup on his charts."

"Yes, sir. May I ask where the rest of the squadron has gone?"

"You may not. I will say only that the commodore has ordered us to remain here showing the flag, and that accords us an opportunity to put on the dog for the Fourth of July. The ambassador and his retinue will come down from Madrid to help us celebrate. I understand our envoy is bringing with him some sort of duke or prince, or someone whose birth entitles him to a job. Our orders are to impress the natives. That will include a twenty-one-gun salute and an open house for the ship. I want everything two-blocked, Mister Curran, everything squared away. This is on my head, which means I will have yours if anything goes awry."

"Squared away, sir."

"Two-blocked," the captain said with a trace of smile. Pelles gave some other orders relevant to the celebrations—times for meetings and specific evolutions he wanted performed. "If you have a question, you need only ask yourself, how would Erskine have handled this? You will not go far wrong if you act accordingly."

DUTY KEPT CURRAN IN THE TRACES UNTIL SIX BELLS IN THE EVENING WATCH. He found that his work expanded to fill the available time, and that the arrangements for the celebration were proving every bit as complex as planning for a fleet engagement. The precise cleaning of the ship was nothing new, even carried to the ridiculous extremes taken by sailors when they are to show their ship to landsmen. More complex by far was the coordination of the firing of the salutes (nineteen for the duke and his entourage, fifteen guns for the envoy, and five for the vice consul);

this in addition to the exhibition of flares and rockets (in lieu of fireworks) that would compose the grand finale, which included another twenty-one guns to mark the day. The firing of naval ordnance was always an occasion for potential mishap, and though it was frequently undertaken in the face of the enemy, the practice was not often conducted with a deck full of gaping civilians. At the end of the day Curran staggered to his new cabin forward on the starboard side, only to find that it had been partially dismantled. Parked in the space he would have slung his hammock was the bulk of a 24-pound gun and the several wrought iron racks that would be used to fire the rockets. Curran was not too tired to remember that *Yunis* was still alongside and that his former cabin was grander even than *Enterprise*'s first starboard.

Taking a clean shirt, he went forward to the quarterdeck. Outboard of *Enterprise*, *Yunis* was moored head and stern. Her lateens had been struck on deck for a coat of pitch, and her decks were, by that necessity, covered with lines, spars, lumber, and sawhorses. Piled aboard her as well was everything not being immediately used to titivate *Enterprise*: ladders, stages, heaps of drying hammocks, strings of laundry, and parts of gun carriages. Being a humble native craft, *Yunis* would have always come off badly in comparison with the frigate, but now, pressed into service as a paint punt, she looked very shabby indeed.

Curran went down the ladder onto *Yunis*' main deck. Here, his former command showed to even less flattering advantage. The sides, masts, and yards of the frigate towered above, pristine and exact geometry. There was a Marine posted at *Yunis*' gangway, a dark blur in the glow of a lantern. "Good evening, sir," the sentry said automatically, presenting arms.

Curran touched his hat. "Good Evening, Gerrity. I will be sleeping aboard if I should be wanted."

"Very good, sir." The sentry was the only sign that marked the xebec as a naval concern. When *Yunis* came into the harbor she had worn the Stars and Stripes over the three crescents. She showed nothing aloft now, not even the partique, and to Curran's eye she seemed to droop for shame. *Courier* had been bought in and rechristened as a United States ship, but *Yunis*, too exotic or too humble, had not been deemed worthy of the honor.

As Curran started toward the hatch the sentry called out, "You'd better take along a glim, sir. It's black as hell down there."

Black it was, and perplexing as well; the ladders and passages were strewn with sawhorses and chunks of lumber, many of them diabolically placed at the perfect height to bark a shin. It took resolve as well as memory for Curran to feel his way down and aft toward the great cabin. The ship that had been so crammed with people, so alive with sounds and sights and smells, was now a dark blank to ear and eye. Carrying his light, he found his way through the peculiar maze of cuddies and compartments that fronted the great cabin. In the solemn darkness Curran could not help but be reminded of *Epevier*, now sunk and dead at the bottom of the sea.

Ahead he could see a light, and a door was open; in the great cabin, Nolan was crouched over the small desk. He had a trio of lanterns before him, putting down a concentrated pool of brightness. As Curran approached he could hear the soft crinkle of paper as Nolan's hand lifted into and out of the light; he was sewing.

"Shipmate," Curran said, stepping over the threshold.

Nolan squinted up from the lantern, blinking from it. "Hello, friend," he said, coming to his feet. "Mind your step. I have made a mess of the cabin."

There were bits of cloth and paper patterns scattered about, and Nolan gathered them up, smiling happily. "Let me make a place. Here. How are you?" Nolan hung one of the lanterns from a crossbeam and peered into Curran's face—he seemed drawn and pale. "Did they not feed you in that place? You look like a sparrow!"

"I am much better."

"Have you eaten? There is some manchego, that noble commodity, and even some soft tommy here somewhere."

"Thank you. I had supper," Curran said quietly.

"Ginger beer?"

"Yes," Curran said. "I reckon I will." Nolan poured it out and sat in the lamplight smiling, obviously glad for the company. Curran thought that Nolan looked careworn and older—he could not know that Nolan thought the same of him.

"I am paid out," Curran said, falling into the chair behind the desk. "Tired as a saw."

"It's the crushing burden of command," Nolan smiled. "Give you joy, sir, of your promotion."

"Thank you, Philip. Thank you. I am pretty sure I didn't deserve it." Curran pried off his boots and let them fall to the deck. He fell into his hammock at once.

"Something is the matter," Nolan said. "You've had bad news?"

Curran was too tired and heartsore to spin a story. He heard himself say, "*Epevier* was lost."

"Your old ship? I am grieved to hear it." Nolan was sitting at the table, his face turned toward the lantern. Almost a minute passed before he spoke. "How did it happen?"

"A gale, on the Grand Banks. A French brig saw her founder in a blizzard. There was no chance of lending assistance. The merchant was herself dismasted and made it only by the hardest effort into Halifax."

"Were there survivors?"

"Not one." Curran shook his head. After a moment he said bitterly, "What sort of God would smite a homebound ship?" Curran heard Nolan draw a breath and felt suddenly ashamed. "I am sorry. That was a selfish thing to say."

"Not at all, friend," Nolan answered. He had lost in his lifetime not a hundred friends or a thousand, not merely his ship but his country.

After a moment, Curran asked, "How do you stand it, Philip?"

Nolan was quiet for a long moment and then said, "If you were to ask me how to overcome grief, I would tell you that all of the business and all of the work done to distract oneself are perfectly useless. So are postures and attitudes; pretending not to care, which is obscene, or to profess not to hurt, which is simply false.

Nolan let a long moment pass, then said slowly, "Grief is an odd commodity. It is the only thing I know that is at once both dull and implacable. You can fight sorrow for a decade. You can stand up to it and think you have overcome it, face the hardest hours, and then some small thing will happen. You'll see a cloud or hear a voice behind you—you'll see a sunrise, and everything breaks down."

Curran wondered at how long Nolan had been at sea with only grief as a shipmate. What a small, simple comfort it was to have a home—and what a cruel, wicked thing it was to have had it taken away.

Nolan put the lanterns out but left the glim flickering in a holder by the cabin door. Curran watched Nolan's shadow move across the cabin floor and saw it stop by the stern lights. "I am very sorry about your friends. But I can tell you that the ache in your heart will pass. One can make an accommodation with grief. A truce. The more we have loved the more we grieve, and that is right. But it is wrong to surrender to regret."

Curran had no answer. For a while he stared at Cádiz: a row of amber dots, and they seemed as far away as stars.

Nolan stood looking out across the harbor and the glittering band of water. "Sleep and dream," said Nolan at last. "Tomorrow always comes for the brave."

DRESSED WITH BUNTING AND SIGNAL FLAGS, THE WARDROOM HAD BEEN transformed into the very den of patriotism. Dinner had been served early, as reveille had been early—the morning watch had passed in a state of vigorous industry, all hands scrubbing and polishing and putting things right enough for an admiral's inspection. Second meal on the mess deck and in the wardroom was light—fried chicken, biscuits, and yellow potato salad. Supper was to be barbeque served out pierside. Overseen by Old Chick and Gustavo Gubbins, three whole hogs had been turning over a hickory fire since the end of the mid-watch.

In various stages of military splendor, the officers lounged around the wardroom. Those who knew about the Spanish sun were waiting until the last minute to venture on deck in their fine blue broadcloth coats.

"We can't just pretend he doesn't know what day it is," Pybus said.

"No, we cannot," Fancher agreed, looking a little overwhelmed. Fancher's chair had been covered with the Don't Tread on Me flag, garishly red, white, and rattlesnake. The decoration of the wardroom had been the final step in the complete dressing of the ship for the Glorious Fourth. "What are we to do? Keep him below hatches?"

Pybus considered that a fair enough idea, but the others thought it a barbarous way to treat a shipmate.

"What is normally done with Nolan on the Fourth of July?"

No one knew. Nolan had come aboard *Enterprise* in January, before the Fourth of July was even considered a remote possibility.

"Isn't he supposed to be kept in the brig or something?" asked Easton, just aboard from *Constitution*. The old Enterprises stared at him. "I only asked," he spluttered.

"He's not supposed to hear or read anything about the United States," Ruggles corrected him. Slouching in his chair, Darby folded a newspaper in front of his face: it was cut through, censored in a dozen places. "Well," he said, "it would be a shame if Nolan were to hear of the United States now—seeing how Mister Curran has prevented him reading about it."

Curran sat at the head of the table, opening a letter that had arrived on embassy letterhead. He read the note, smiling, oblivious to the swirling debate.

"He isn't a prisoner, really," said Fancher. "Well, I reckon he is, technically."

"He can read a calendar," Ruggles said.

Darby put the paper down. "A dilemma. Our prisoner now imprisons us."

"He fought with us, gentlemen," Curran said. "It would be a dishonor not to have him enjoy the afternoon with us."

"But how can that be done?"

"I have an idea," Ruggles smiled.

"Not again," sneered Easton.

Ruggles gave his messmate a wintry glare and continued, "We put him into the longboat and row him around the harbor until the patriotic speeches are over."

The suggestion was met with guffaws.

"What? Anyone have a better plan?" he huffed.

"Mister Ruggles, you have a fine idea," Curran said.

"One of many," Ruggles said, and he narrowed his eyes at Easton.

"We will have our Fourth of July, and so will Nolan," Curran said. "He will be chaperoned."

"How do you mean?" asked Darby.

"The captain will escort the ambassador and the Duke of Murcia from the hotel to the ship." Curran looked at his watch. "They will arrive precisely at one forty-five."

"The red carpet is laid," Easton said. He was in charge of the side boys.

Curran went on. "The captain, the chargé, the duke, and the ambassador will travel in the first carriage. Nordhoff, Hall, and I will escort the ladies of the delegation."

"Did you say ladies, sir?" Ruggles asked.

"I did, sir. In prodigious numbers." Curran passed around the letter. "That grateful intelligence is confirmed on embassy letterhead. Ambassador Forsyth has six lovely daughters." The entire wardroom, all of them unmarried, now listened closely.

"I suggest the following: before any overt display of patriotism, Mister Nolan will accompany me to the hotel. We will gather the fair ones, embark them in the carriages, and Nordhoff and Hall will deliver them to the ship."

"You hope," Darby sniffed. To the doctor, the thought of the two scamps actually completing an assignment seemed a remote possibility.

Curran answered, "Should duty fail to animate them, there is always the threat of flogging. To continue: Nordhoff and Hall will deliver the ladies in time for the opening ceremonies. I will gather two of the loveliest, and Nolan and I, accompanying them, will arrive conveniently late—say, just after the orators have left the quarterdeck."

Glances were passed. It seemed an eminently plausible idea. "Once the barbeque and dancing are under way, one of us will stand with Nolan by turns to make sure he is not spoken to inappropriately by our guests. We all get the Fourth, we all get to convene with Bacchus, and Nolan is not excluded from the fun."

Mister Easton lifted his glass. "To our exec! You are a hero, sir! By land and sea!"

NOLAN COULD VERY WELL READ A CALENDAR. DURING ALL THE YEARS OF HIS sentence it was usual for him to spend the Fourth of July under some sort of close custody, segregated from the crew. *Hornet* put him in irons; most ships treated him better (they could have hardly treated him worse), but during the celebration he was always, at the very least, confined to quarters, and very often put in the brig.

While his cabin was being repaired, Nolan had stayed aboard *Yunis*. This was in itself no punishment. He had the ship virtually to himself, and the great cabin on the xebec was a far more spacious and airy place than his cubby aboard *Enterprise*. No one specifically ordered that Nolan was to be confined aboard *Yunis*; Pelles gave no positive order to that effect, and no one else besides Curran ever communicated with him in matters regarding his custody. A sentry was put on *Yunis'* gangway, and another stood on the pier; this was not without some mutual embarrassment. After the fights with *Ar R'ad* and *Um Qasim*, the vast majority of *Enterprise*'s crew felt Nolan was a shipmate, and was as entitled as anyone to celebrate the Republic's birthday.

Though almost no one aboard knew exactly *why* Nolan was being punished, all hands understood what his custody entailed. There were still a few who thought a traitor deserved worse; one can always find patriots of the punishing stripe. Piggen remained adamant that Nolan was as evil as Burr, but there were few aboard anymore who would listen to his rants. During the engagement with *Ar R'ad*, Piggen had remained firm at a station far below the waterline. The men knew this, as they knew that the purser had quailed when Curran had bid him join Varney in the duel.

Nolan was esteemed by his shipmates; he had sweat and bled with them, and even the dullest hand realized that the political creatures who had persecuted Philip Nolan were not much inclined to do either—sweat or bleed. It did not sit well with the men before the mast that they not only defended these clever men in Washington, but now had to dish their punishment too. But sailors, perhaps better than any other men, know that life is not fair. Reluctantly, all hands aboard *Enterprise* upheld the conditions of his confinement, but it would be easier for them, and for Nolan, if they might not have to do it on the Fourth of July.

Nolan, as always, was keenly aware of the feelings of others. He knew it was uncomfortable for the men who were set to watch him, and he knew that his presence was especially a burden during the celebration of holidays. As the Glorious Fourth approached, he stayed almost exclusively aboard *Yunis*. As preparations went forward, and *Enterprise* was warped pierside, Nolan retired completely to the xebec's great cabin and put himself out of the way of the patriotic bustle. There would be no safe place for him on deck or even aloft, and he did not wish to make a sailor or Marine ask him to do what he had sense enough to do on his own.

There was a knock on the cabin door. Nolan turned in his chair as Padeen entered. "Afternoon, sir. And Mister Curran's compliments."

"Yes, Padeen?"

"Are you ready, sir?" Before Nolan could ask what for, Padeen stepped aside. Into the cabin came Shakin' George, the ship's barber. The lanky Tennessean had been diverted from the barbeque pit.

"Just a trim, sir," George said, "which is the exec's orders." In a gust of hickory smoke George wafted an apron over Nolan's shoulders and set to work lathering and scraping. In a matter of minutes Nolan was shaved, patted dry, and powdered fragrantly. His queue was retied with a black silk ribbon, and done proper, as Shakin' George, along with Captain Pelles, was one of the score of men aboard who still wore a tail. Padeen produced a clean, pressed shirt and a brilliantly starched collar. With tuts and clucks they got Nolan into the fresh shirt (his pants were passable) and handed him a long silk cravat.

"Is my leather stock not perfectly fine?" he asked.

"Sure it is, sir," said Padeen. "But it's a bit familiar after all these years." Nolan had for twenty years worn a leather stock identical to the sort the Marines wore; it had gone gray with salt. Padeen and George, taking little regard of Nolan, tossed away his old one and wrapped the new silk cravat around his neck. In a moment it was tied competently, and Padeen tweaked out the tips of the collar. He stood back to look as George dumped the basin out of the stern windows.

"That is splendid," Padeen said. "Now sir, if you'd be coming along, I'll take you to Mister Curran." Nolan started to say something, but George had his elbow. "This way 'yer honor," he twanged. "Better step lively." They led him onto *Yunis'* deck, across the gangplank, and onto the deck of the frigate.

Nolan found the ship transformed. There was a large, white awning put up between foremast and main, and another over the quarterdeck. Signal flags in profusion were hung from the stays, and as Nolan looked up he saw topmen a hundred feet above the deck acrobatically stringing more between the caps. It was the ritual of dressing ship, and in all his years at sea Nolan had never seen it.

"Mister Nolan," Curran said, "there you are." Dressed in his best uniform and number one hat, Curran bounced down the quarterdeck ladder. Sailors and Marines, also in their best, were giving a last-minute sweep and swab to the deck that would soon become a dance floor. The mood was holiday. "Are you ready, Philip?"

"For what?" Nolan answered blankly.

"We have an extra duty. I think you will find it agreeable."

Kanoa and his mates approached looking particularly dapper in red waistcoats with beribboned seams. "Here you are, sir," Kanoa said. He held out a Prussian blue cutaway jacket. It had a high collar with red facings and gold lace. The buttons were brass, but they had been polished like the flintlocks on the carronades, smooth and glimmering, nearly white in the sun.

"What is this?" Nolan asked.

"Why, they are your duds, sir. Me and old Otho Newsome here made them up. We used your old coatee as a pattern. It's to the letter, sir, as you can see."

It was a nearly perfect copy of an artillery officer's dress coat, less insignia. It was of the old design, the type worn before the last war, but neither Nolan nor the seamen had seen the new pattern uniforms. Some of them had never seen an American soldier in their lives. They had merely copied his old coat. Though Nolan always took pains with his appearance, the new garment made him aware at once how shabby he must have looked.

"Try it on, sir," said Kanoa. "Let's see ya."

Stunned, Nolan put on the coat. He was speechless. In almost two decades it was the first new, purpose-made piece of clothing he had even touched. And now it was his, and it fit perfectly.

"There. Now you are a credit to the ship, sir," Newsome said proudly. The jacket was a credit to his scissors, too.

"Handsome is as handsome does, Mister Nolan," said Kanoa. "You look like, a what do you call it? A paramour."

"Paragon," Curran suggested.

"'*Ono nō ka 'oi*, sir," Kanoa beamed.

"Like he said," grinned Newsome.

Nordhoff and Hall handed over a round hat, freshly lacquered. "Here, sir. We did a little overhaul on your scraper."

The hat was of the old Army pattern as well; it had a cockade but did not bear the eagle or crossed cannon. This was as close to martial glory as Philip Nolan was allowed to come. Not knowing what else to do, he put the hat on his head. Curran smiled, and a couple of the men started to clap. Soon the applause was general around the decks.

Nolan was touched and glad that he was not called upon to speak, for his throat had closed off. He made himself smile; it came easily once he started, and he gave the crew a stately bow. Nolan continued to grin, but his eyes were stinging. Curran guided him aft. The crew opened to let them pass, still clapping, some cheering and whooping. They went onto the quarterdeck and then past the sentry and into the great cabin.

Pelles was standing next to his desk, prepared to meet them. "Good afternoon, Mister Nolan."

"Sir," was all Nolan could say in return. Pelles and Curran both judged that he was very close to being overwhelmed, but the captain had yet another gift to bestow.

Pelles thought it best to make the presentation with as little bombast as possible. "I am not one for speeches, Mister Nolan," he said. "I am a man who judges the actions of persons rather than their words. As I told you after our brush with *Ar R'ad*, I have every reason to be pleased with your conduct—or should I say your example aboard my ship. I am extremely pleased with your alacrity in bringing *Yunis* into port after Mister Curran's wounding. It was an intrepid deed, and would have earned any other sailor in the Navy a medal, or another stripe. It is not in my power to grant you those tokens, and I am not yet able to give you what I wish for you most. But I do wish to show my personal gratitude to you, and to recognize your valor."

Old Chick came forward carrying an oblong velvet bag. Pelles balanced it on the desk and flicked open the drawstrings with one finger. He took out an officer's sword, of French manufacture, a beautiful object of silver, steel, and gilt.

"I captured this on the deck of *Hecate* during the Quasi-War off St. Barth. It was honorably won and is honorably given." Pelles held it out with the belt and scabbard. "I would be honored, the ship would be honored, if you would wear it today as we celebrate, and keep it as a memento of our gratitude for your service and bravery."

Nolan lowered his head and tears flowed down his face. Pelles stepped forward and with Curran's help buckled on the belt, frog, and knot. Nolan had not worn a sword since his was taken from him in Richmond, the day he lost every other emblem of rank and nation. He was staggered, affected to the soul, as they all were, but Nolan brought himself about quickly, wiped his eyes, and said, "Thank you, Captain, I am very grateful."

Pelles placed his hand in Nolan's and shook it firmly. "I can think of no officer who has done more to deserve this honor," Pelles said.

Nolan's face shone. "Thank you, sir. I will ever try to be worthy of it."

As the carriage went up the Calle Real, the two uniformed men in it were an object of curiosity. The Spanish driver, aware that this was some sort of American holy day, had dressed himself in his best carnival livery, purple, green, and gold. Some passersby thought Nolan and Curran to be Vatican officials and either knelt or crossed themselves as the carriage passed.

"They are certainly mistaken as to who we are," Nolan said.

"They are." Curran smiled. "Isn't it just the thing?"

At the Calosa Latour, a boy ran through the alley from the next block squeaking out that the Duke of Murcia was in a coach and four heading for the harbor. It was quickly put about that His Serene Highness Gonzalo was in the company of an American officer, a very grave, tall, one-armed man who (it was said) was some sort of republican high executioner. The boy spoke breathlessly to the driver, asking him if it were true that the Americans were going to hang a murderer aboard their ship.

The driver answered, "God knows what is in the hearts of heretics."

This was taken, per force, as a confirmation. Curran overhead this chatter, as did Nolan, but neither remarked on it. By the time they arrived at the Hotel Rialto, the pavement outside was filling with people, carts, horses, and mules, all heading generally toward the harbor, a crowd as happy and jovial as any off to witness a bullfight. The ladies of the ambassadorial party were in the ballroom of the hotel, happily chatting and sampling sorbet. Captain Pelles, the duke, and Ambassador Forsyth had already departed, and Mister Nordhoff and Mister Hall were trying to charm and cajole the women into the waiting carriages. This without much success, for though their immaculate uniforms were the very emblems of authority, their voices had only just broken, and it is not very often that women will pay attention to little boys.

Like all parties, this gathering was resistant to relocation. Curran surveyed the task at hand: about fifty persons remained. Clinging with the women in the ballroom were a few of the secretaries of the legation, as well as some of the ducal entourage. The Spanish and Americans were stylishly, if severely, dressed. The duke's men were beribboned, studded with stars, and were of a type. A few of each crowd seemed put out to have been left behind by the ducal departure. Those grandees and beaver hats who had their own transportation eventually heeded the midshipmen and started the journey for the ship. This left the dawdlers.

Where the midshipmen had failed, Curran succeeded by main force, announcing once and plainly that it was now time to depart, and that those not wishing to ride might find the ship by taking a right-hand turn, walking downhill, and looking for a tall black object with checks painted on its side. At Curran's command were three carriages: a landau, a phaeton, and a large four-in-hand: enough seats to accommodate the ladies and the most pompous and obese of the men. The threat of walking spurred the torpid of both sexes toward the carriages. Curran was no stranger to diplomatic receptions and now made a few tactical introductions, thus restraining the more eager embassy types from taking ladies' seats in the carriages. Curran presented Nolan to Mrs. Forsyth, who'd known Curran as a boy in the Levant. The ambassador's wife was very pleased to make Nolan's acquaintance. There were other necessary introductions. Curran presented Nolan to the *acalde* and his beautiful wife, several *dons* and *doñas*, and *hidalgos* both those who were rich and those who were merely proud.

Nolan began to find the experience overwhelming. He was still somewhat overcome by the ceremony aboard *Enterprise*, and for the first time in many years he was thrust into society. The flit of fans and the rustle of silk dresses distracted him. Curran presented Nolan to Ambassador Forsyth's six daughters—Emily, Anna, Lisa, Laura, Makalah, and Marigot—whose names he somehow retained for the requisite ninety seconds. Nolan bowed to each of the ladies, somewhat unsteadily.

Truth be told, he felt somewhat dizzy; it had been many, many years since he had spoken to a woman, and now he was surrounded by six of them. Nolan could not prevent himself from looking up at the ceiling, and this pose, as well as his swaying sailor's posture, made several persons stare at him.

Curran made sure Hall continued to offer his arm and maintain a steady flow toward the front door and the carriages. As the crowd thinned, the vice consul, Mister Slonecker, introduced himself. He was a thin, pale, shrew-faced person, between Curran and Nolan in age. Slonecker wore a lippy, condescending smile, and to Curran he looked like the sort of gentleman who might live in an apartment full of cats.

"An honor, sir," Curran said, shaking the diplomat's cold, sagging hand. "May I present my particular friend, Mister Philip Nolan."

The vice consul responded by holding two limp fingers an inch in front of his protruding belly, as ill-bred persons will do when an introduction does not interest them. Nolan looked briefly at the pudgy hand and returned a rigidly formal bow. "Good afternoon, sir," Nolan said coolly.

Slonecker began to walk away, but then an odd look came to his face. He turned to look at Nolan, trying to place him. "You, sir. Don't I know you?"

Nolan did not recognize the man's flabby, unfriendly face, but he knew his expression well enough.

"You are the man who dueled with Colonel Bell, are you not?" Slonecker sneered.

"I believe I was the last to have had that pleasure," Nolan said flatly. Nolan was out of sorts and found that he was suddenly vexed; but he was not without resource enough to give back every second of the secretary's queer gaze with a steady, blank expression of disregard.

Curran was certainly aware of this silent bout of wills; he quickly turned around, selected the ambassador's two prettiest daughters, and said to Slonecker, "Though it would be a pleasure to renew your acquaintance, sir, Mister Nolan and I have been ordered to convoy these ladies specially to the ship."

"Really?" one of the ladies giggled. Perhaps she was Emily. Nolan took his cue and offered his arm to another, perhaps Marigot, and said, "I am honored, mademoiselle." Nolan then bowed to Slonecker with a precisely dosed bit of insolence: "Good day to you, sir."

They left the vice consul muttering, and Curran led the party from the ballroom into the lobby. Hall and Nordhoff had by then completed their sweep and hovered under the awning by the curb.

"Got them rounded up, sir," Hall reported. "We are ready to get under way."

Curran noticed that Hall and Nordhoff had managed to cut the ambassador's two youngest daughters from the pack. By dint of careful stowage, the large coach had departed full, leaving the landau for the midshipmen and the phaeton for Curran, Nolan, and the sisters Emily and Marigot. It was a neat bit of maneuvering.

"We can go, sir?" asked Nordhoff.

"You may," Curran assented. Hall and Nordhoff bounded into the landau and pulled the girls in after them. "Mister Nordhoff," Curran said after them, "a direct course for the ship, if you please."

Nordhoff looked crestfallen. Hall wore the dazed expression of a person who has had a plan unraveled by a mind reader. "How's that, sir?"

"To the frigate, Mister Hall. Directly."

"Aye, aye sir, right away," Nordhoff said. The landau went off, the girls smiling and the midshipmen trying to look as though they always rode in coaches when on liberty.

Curran opened the carriage door. As he handed Emily up, Slonecker crossed the street and tried to wave down a hackney coach. The driver, an old and mellow Catholic, turned up his nose and hissed, "*Hereje sucia!*"

Slonecker was nearly made apoplectic. It did not help that at that moment Nordhoff chose to stand on the seat of the landau and flourish his handkerchief at the crowd.

Curran caught sight of both the boy and the seething diplomat. "Damn that little imp. I'll have him kiss the gunner's daughter."

Across the street, Slonecker stared crossly at Nordhoff and then again at Nolan, who scrupulously ignored him. Marigot found her seat and Curran nodded to the driver, "*Quisiéramos ir, señor.*"

The carriage pulled away from the curb and into the sunshine.

When they had gone some distance from the hotel Marigot said, "Mister Slonecker could use the walk."

"He is perfectly obnoxious," clucked Emily. "Rude and pompous as Nero."

"Perhaps he was indisposed," said Nolan.

"Would it be possible, do you think, to press-gang Mister Slonecker?" asked Marigot.

"We do not resort to the press," said Curran. "We are volunteers aboard *Enterprise.*"

"But could you not have some burly Marine merely knock him on the head to remind him of his manners?" asked Emily. She glanced at Nolan and thought to herself that he was not unattractive, and it occurred to Marigot that though the older gentleman seemed distracted she could not find fault with his manners.

"I so look forward to the firing of the cannon," Marigot said.

"I hope the frigate's guns will not disappoint," Nolan replied. "They are as loud as any I have heard."

"I am sure they will be thrilling, Mister Nolan," Marigot said complaisantly. "It's been a long time since I have enjoyed a really good bang!"

The midshipmen had been admonished to proceed directly to the ship, but their superiors were under no such constraints. Curran asked the coachman if they might pass by the Rambla de Benipita and then ascend to the battery at the Castillo de Galareas. The promontory there, more than three hundred feet above the harbor, would grant a splendid view of the bay. It was also a perfect way to get rid of the better part of two hours.

As the carriage passed out of the town and into the countryside, Nolan was able to compose himself. The sun was bright but not intolerably hot, and the road was shaded as it began a long series of hairpin turns up and toward the battery. Nolan was surprised at how anxious he now was. He had felt suffocated by the crowd, though he realized that there had been no real crush of people; Nolan had not really yet recovered from the gift of his jacket or the presentation of the sword. And now the presence of two pretty, sociable young women seemed to have made him stupid. To be so suddenly in an open carriage, so very much like a free man, so very much like a normal human being, was close to incomprehensible. Nolan was happy, but the greater part of his mind advised against it. He kept thinking, frighteningly, that all this might be a dream. Every now and then he placed his hand to the pommel of the sword and touched the buckle cinched about his waist.

The castle had a grand, sweeping view of much of Murcia. In the distance, sharp-ruled against the sky, could be seen the embarcadero, and beyond it Punta Caldiera and the bright blue sea. Below, palm trees fluttered on the hillside. When they arrived at the battery, Curran gave his compliments to the officer commanding, a Spanish ensign hardly older than Mister Hall. He was told, without even asking, that the Paloma battery would join the other guns of the harbor in returning *Enterprise*'s salute.

"*Cuántos cañones, señor?*" Curran asked. More than a hundred, came the answer—it would be a very grand sight. Nolan, who had been standing aside, came forward and exchanged compliments with the ensign and the grizzled sergeant major of the battery. They all seemed pleased to speak French, the language of artillery and fortification. Nolan remarked knowledgably on brattices and belvederes, chemins de ronde, chevaux de frise, and counterscarps until, from below in the harbor, came the low grumble of a signal gun. Aboard *Enterprise*, the Blue Peter went up at the main, a white rectangle within a blue one. The flag of recall was nearly lost in the profusion of the hundred others put out to dress the ship.

"That will be our signal, ladies," Curran said.

Nolan gave his best compliments to the men of the battery (the cannoneers had been assembled for his inspection) and then very self-consciously returned their salutes. It had been an age since he had been rendered the honor.

The phaeton went down the steep gravel road, then onto the cobbles of the streets near the *rambla*. By the time they came to the quayside Curran could see that the ship's complement was mustered on the spar deck. He checked his watch. They were on time almost to the minute.

As the carriage halted, the notes of a song came to them: a beautiful, bright operatic voice singing a capella. The tune was a slightly obscure one, "To Anacreon in Heaven"; it had gained popularity when the words were rewritten as "In Defense of Fort McHenry." Since the last British war it had become a popular, if extraordinarily difficult to sing patriotic song. They were close enough for Curran to see that Captain Pelles, together with the dignitaries, was standing at the quarterdeck rail. A golden-haired, petite woman was singing. Her voice carried remarkably, flawlessly in tune, but she had varied the lyrics slightly. She had obviously memorized the words phonetically, a skill not unusual for divas, and the lyrics drifted to them only slightly distorted:

José doth el star spaniel banter and bay—

Before any could form a reproof, the beautiful, singular voice went back to the true libretto, finishing the last bars with a soaring cadenza:

O'er the land of the free, and the home of the brave!

The ship erupted in applause, genuine and boisterous from the sailors and civilians before the masts, polite and admiring from those elevated on the quarterdeck. Pelles stepped forward, took the beautiful diva's hand, and bowed to her. There was another wave of applause. Apparently the performance had been one of extremely gratifying quality.

Curran was relieved that Nolan had caught wind of nothing that he should not have. Captain Pelles had asked his friend Mademoiselle de Chaplet to sing for that exact reason. There was, of course, the pleasure of teaching the song to her (Pelles did love a soprano), but it was to be recommended for several other reasons. "My Country, 'Tis of Thee" was America's unofficial anthem, but it was not always fitted to an occasion where the British might be encountered as its melody was cribbed shamelessly from "God Save the King." "The Star Spangled Banner" was perfect for *Enterprise*'s celebration, and not only because Mademoiselle de Chaplet's voice so well suited it. The song was unique in the patriotic line, for not once in its four sprawling verses did the lyrics contain the word "America," or even mention the United States.

In the carriage, Curran said, "I think this is the time we should debark."

As Nolan helped the ladies, Curran reminded the coachman to set his brakes. While a mid aboard *Epevier* he'd a previous experience with post horses and signal guns, and did not wish to repeat it in front of a frigate full of distinguished visitors. Perhaps the driver was tired, perhaps he was distracted by Miss Marigot's décolletage, or he was simply beyond taking advice, but the coachman did not depress the lever. The results were nearly instantaneous.

When *Enterprise* fired the first cannon of the five comprising the vice consul's salute, the old gelding in the traces seemed to levitate on four legs. Nolan had just handed Miss Emily down from the carriage when the second gun fired, and at that moment the horse put back its ears and bolted.

As a gust of cannon smoke jetted from the quarterdeck, the carriage jerked forward, the horse's iron shoes threw sparks from the cobbles, and the entire contraption thundered at an alarming rate diagonally down the pier and toward the warehouses. The driver's commands, curses, and eventually prayers were swallowed up by the continued thunder of the guns. As the carriage rattled off toward the town, powder smoke gushed across the harbor, brilliantly white and then pearl gray as it scattered. And in the space of a few seconds the coach was far, far out of sight.

"Well," Curran said, brushing his hat and fixing it securely on his head, "shall we go aboard?"

MISTER SLONECKER, THAT VEXED SOUL, WAS NOT AT PIERSIDE TO WITNESS THE salute fired in his honor; he was not at the gangway either, and as the echoes boomed back after many seconds from the walls of the city, they reached him on his sweaty, angry walk down the Calle Real. Slonecker plucked his watch from his pocket and listened as *Enterprise*'s gun crews went directly into the next salute, fifteen for the ambassador and his party, and then nineteen more for the Duke of Murcia. Miffed, he continued downhill toward the harbor.

Nolan and Curran watched as the important people continued to come aboard and *Enterprise*'s guns were bowsed and made fast. From the several batteries around the harbor the salute was returned gun for gun, a grand, rolling syncopation. There were all of the hundred guns the Spanish ensign had promised, those and others from emplacements that were not obvious from the sea. It was all of six minutes before the redoubling echoes faded. When the last of the smoke lifted, the air was still, as though the wind had been stunned.

The decks under the awning were full of people. The sailors were delighted and expansive, and the civilians congratulated them. Mister Bent (another of the new midshipmen) came over to Curran carrying a leather tankard and a cut glass goblet from the wardroom. "A taste, sir," he said. "You didn't get a chance to approve the refreshments." Bent handed the glass to Curran.

A sip: "It is delicious."

Bent smiled. "Raspberry shrub. For the ladies." Bent took a furtive look around and handed Curran the tankard. "Now, sir, try this," he whispered.

Curran touched his lips to the rim and his head flinched involuntarily. "Woah."

"Schwimmerhorn, the Dutchman, calls this one 'Green Goddamn.'"

"A drink not to be underestimated."

Curran handed the tankard to Nolan. He took a sip and grimaced. "Good God!"

Bent was delighted. "We're having a contest, to see who can come up with a better name. One more genteel like, so the ladies will try it."

"How about . . . 'Liquid Concussion'?" Nolan asked.

"That sounds scholarly, sir." Bent nodded, "Like it was medicinal. But we'll be serving this belowdecks." Bent took back the tankard and said confidentially, "And no open flames, just to be safe."

It would be an unusual ship, as well as an unhappy one, that did not have its share of musicians aboard. *Enterprise* had among her four hundred–odd souls a share of fiddlers and tin whistle players. There were also drums, fifes and bugles, gut bucket basses, and a violin cello or two. Added to a few very gifted players were dozens of others who made up with enthusiasm what they wanted for technique, and they added triangles, bells, washboards, tambourines, and even Jew's harps. *Enterprise* was able to put a creditable band on the forecastle, and though they were not up to Mozart, or even to accompanying Mademoiselle de Chaplet, they were to be counted on to deliver reels, jigs, and contra dances by the score. All hands were determined that *Enterprise*'s Fourth would be the finest that was ever known: no man o'war's ball is ever done by half measures. After the speeches and salutes, the frigate's musicians assembled with the alacrity of a boarding party.

Old Chick, a master of skillet and camboose, likewise the banjo box, bent forward and said, "Gen'elmans and ladies, 'Money Musk,' if you please!" The tune was followed by "The Virginny Reel," "The Old Thirteen," and "The Lakes of Pontchartrain." And merriment was contagious.

A Fourth of July abroad will unfailingly attract American expatriates, and besides the young women who were the relations of the embassy there were also the daughters of several Baltimore merchants and dozens of *señoras* and *señoritas* willing to dance. The hands were unabashed, and fell in to teaching the ladies the figures. Mostly they were contra dances, and soon the decks were full of swirling skirts and gliding sailors.

Every celebration, large or small, has currents in it; some are obvious, some unseen. Friends meet, people are introduced, and new acquaintances come together. There is a general flow of persons, dancers and spectators, as well as the gradual, almost random circulation of groups coming together or going apart.

As in the ocean, the obvious currents have evident and predictable effects; these are usually benign. It is the unseen currents, like rip tides, that do peril to the unwary.

There was already a trace of tension. Ambassador Forsyth could not be called a sensitive or particularly astute man. He owed his appointment to political contributions rather than any ability with language or the diplomatic arts. The ambassador was a Democrat of the stripe of Thomas Jefferson and James Madison, meaning he was a slaveholding plantation owner, and he had alienated every *Enterprise* sailor in hearing when he asked Captain Pelles how much he would accept in gold to purchase Fante.

With a look that might have enlightened a less opaque man, Pelles informed the ambassador that Fante was rated able, a free man, and not a piece of property. Thereafter, Pelles tried to remain out of the ambassador's way. This was noticed.

The captain was the host, and by and by the ambassador had occasion to remark that he found it rather vulgar that Captain Pelles was cavorting with an opera singer. This little tidbit also made its way around the party, ricocheting through the quarterdeck where the diplomats and the grandees congregated.

Eventually Mister Slonecker completed his perishing journey from the hotel and clomped sweating over the gangway. He was in a lather and quickly buttonholed Ambassador Forsyth. The ambassador was further ruffled by the news Slonecker brought from the consulate: a newspaper clipping from a filed copy of the *Richmond Virginia Gazette* dated September 8, 1807. In it was a short piece about Nolan's trial and a picturesque bit of prose about his "traitor's" march from the city gaol to the armed galley that rowed him down to Norfolk. Slonecker triumphantly thrust the paper under the ambassador's nose and pointed Nolan out on deck.

Nolan, of course, was unaware of any of these machinations. Self-conscious in his new uniform, he could not help but feel generally that he was a special object of attention. Congratulated by various crewmembers and introduced to an increasing number of strange faces, Nolan felt increasingly that he was a specimen on display. He did realize that he was being spelled by different officers; this he knew to be necessary, but it is awkward for a forty-year-old man to be chaperoned, no matter how well meaning are his guardians. Nolan did his best to be polite, but there was around him an unavoidable diminishment of levity. Though well regarded, even cherished by his shipmates, no one wanted to be the person who slipped up, and as the punch began to take hold Nolan found that his presence tended to induce a certain staring silence in the sailors who were around him.

The party continued until it reached its predictable culmination. There are several versions of what, exactly, transpired on the quarterdeck between Captain Pelles and the ambassador—all of them to the greater credit of *Enterprise* and her captain. Ambassador Forsyth had been a member of the Virginia bar and clerked for Justice Marshall during Aaron Burr's trial. Having failed to bring the traitor to justice, Forsyth had taken a sharp and malignant interest in the secondary cases. He had rejoiced at Nolan's conviction and had ever after smugly pronounced that the cruel sentence was just. When Slonecker presented the ambassador with the newspaper and informed him that the infamous person was here in attendance, Forsyth was incensed. That Philip Nolan was wearing a sword and was dressed in a semblance of a uniform—well, that was beyond the pale. Ambassador Forsyth spoke to Captain Pelles only after he had made known to several persons, including the duke, what he thought about Nolan, traitors in general, and the manner in which he inferred that *Enterprise* was commanded. When the ambassador confronted Captain Pelles, demanding that Nolan be "disarmed and stripped of his uniform," he received a very undiplomatic response.

Word of the contretemps eventually found Curran, and complicated his life immediately. In any other situation, the disagreeing parties could merely separate. The ambassador was escorting the Duke of Murcia, who was, with his several dozen valuable friends, waiting for the fireworks. The duke was an important person, not far removed from the Spanish throne; it was of the first importance to impress him. Ambassador Forsyth realized that regardless of Captain Pelles' temerity, he would have to wait until he could decently storm off the ship. The timing of his tantrum (and he was determined to pitch a fit) was complicated by the fact that the Duke of Murcia had once also commanded a frigate. The duke, too, had fought the British and French, and it was with redoubling frustration that the ambassador realized that His Serene Ducal Highness had taken a very personal and pronounced liking to both the insolent Captain Pelles and the singing trollop Mademoiselle de Chaplet. The ambassador watched with his jaws clamped shut as Pelles and the duke spoke and laughed and drank, growing ever more frank, friendly, and familiar.

The band played, Mister Slonecker's betrayal became well known, and every sailor aboard *Enterprise* took to staring long and narrowly at the ambassador and his busybody minion. The punch was strong, the day had been hot, and a brawl was certainly not out of the question. Curran spoke to Old Chick, who did his best to keep the dancers engaged. Quadrilles were being played, and as those dances go, one couple does the figures while the others watch and then join in turn. There were dancers arrayed in squares about the decks.

By this time, Nolan was standing alone by the carronades in Bastard's Alley, watching and smiling. The lanterns in the awnings put a golden light on the dancers, a glow that made even the present into a sort of living nostalgia. And out of this pleasantness, very suddenly, Philip Nolan was struck by a bolt of heartache.

He recognized Lorina Rutledge immediately. As Nolan watched from across the deck, Lorina turned to speak to a woman next to her, a pink, willowy creature with gray eyes and reddish hair. Both were dressed in the manner of La Belle Assemblée. The men standing around Lorina included a Spanish grandee and a French officer, profusely embroidered. Behind her lurked a civilian dressed in a black cutaway and tight pantaloons, a man who looked like a dancing master.

Lorina was talking to one of the duke's men, a sad-faced noble who wore the Order of the Knights of Malta. Nolan watched as Lorina flirted her ostrich plume fan and tittered at something the duke's man said. It was a contrived, fawning laugh, so artfully rendered that no one who had not known her well could ever think that she was not entirely sincere. This small falsity struck Nolan first among many other perplexing impressions. He had remembered and cherished Lorina's simple, graceful movements and her bright, interested smile. Now she was unsteady on her feet and seemed to lean upon the men and even the women who came close to her. When she spoke, her gestures seemed outré and exaggerated. Between bouts of laughter she wore a careless, distracted expression, a bemused and haughty smirk. This disaffection was so totally alien to the woman he had known that Nolan thought he must be mistaken; it could not be Lorina after all. But the delicate line of her shoulders was unmistakable. Her long, white gloves clapped along with the music. Her expression and her movements confirmed the charms Nolan had treasured so many years before.

On the improvised bandstand, Old Chick smiled brightly and tapped at his banjo. "Gen'elmens and ladies," he said happily, "now if you might form a quadrille for 'Biloxi Bay'!" Click, click, click went Chick's nails upon the box. Then the fiddles squeaked and the fifes played the happy tune. The band sawed into the music, Chick in front, rocking back and forth as he rumbled the banjo. Nolan wondered how so much happiness could surround his sudden and astonished misery. But a moment before he had been as happy as he had ever been in two decades—now he felt wretched and broken.

How did he dare to judge Lorina when he had so despised those who had judged him? Self-reproach was now added to his despair. Nolan turned, intending to go below, but Lorina saw him. She stopped talking and peered at him across the swirling dancers. Their eyes met. Nolan thought to bow, or at least to nod to her, but either his determination or his Stoicism failed him. Between them, the deck was full of moving, laughing, singing people—Nolan deliberately went into the crowd and headed aft. He made his way down the larboard side, and behind him the dancers moved together and apart, up and down. Nolan walked aft to the quarterdeck break with his fists clenched. He was almost to the gangway of *Yunis* and the safety of his cabin when he heard someone call behind him.

"Can that be you, Philip?"

The voice was precisely as he had remembered it, every note and tone exact. He turned to see Lorina standing just forward of the companionway, her head tipped slightly to one side. "I wonder if you have forgotten me?"

"I do remember, Miss Rutledge."

"Only I am Miss Rutledge no longer, but Mrs. Graff." She gestured with her fan. "That is my husband there with the *alcalde*."

A moment passed; for them both the music seemed suddenly to have stopped, and the dancers too. Nolan felt his mouth go dry; the silence between them seemed to strangle his thoughts.

"The most remarkable coincidence," Lorina said. "It is just the most extraordinary thing to see you. I heard the ambassador making some sort of fuss, I won't bore you with it, prisoners at large, traitors even, but I had the oddest thought that he could only have been talking about you. And here you are."

"May I ask to whom you were married?"

"Oh, it is no one you knew, Philip, a physician. He has a practice in Europe. A phrenologist. He is standing just there with the Marqués de Algaba."

Across the deck, Nolan at once picked out the eminent Doctor Graff: a cadaverous, stoop-shouldered man in a suit of dove gray silk. About Nolan's age, Graff looked older and debauched, a man wafted over by Morpheus.

"We live a gypsy life, and he treats famous heads. Isn't that droll?"

Her face, her figure, her movements, and her voice, all of these Nolan recognized; but Lorina's manner had changed so completely as to make her seem a different person. Her smiling kindness had quite vanished, and seemed to have been replaced by a meager and pitiless curiosity. She glanced at his coat, the plain buttons and the curious French sword. "Tell me, are you a soldier again?"

"I am not."

"You are a prisoner, still? I am surprised." She looked out at the party. "Your confinement seems very genteel. They don't treat you too badly, I declare. I don't suppose it would do to ask if you need money?"

His cheeks burning, Nolan shook his head. "My needs are met," he said. Nolan felt crushed and empty, riven by the insurmountable distance between past and present. "Why did I never hear from you?" he blurted out. "After the trial, why did you not write to me?"

Her eyes narrowed slightly. "Oh. Did you not receive letters? Really? I did send some—and heartsick ones they were too. Of course, when I never heard from you, I concluded that it was you who did not wish to correspond." She paused. "After all, I thought you never wanted to hear of home again."

A Marine, Corporal Tappert, had caught sight of them speaking together; though mindful of his duty, he had the decency to remain just out of earshot.

Later, Nolan was quite astonished at himself, but he asked quietly: "What of the paper I gave to you?"

Lorina looked blankly at him.

"The note. In the courtroom—before I was sentenced."

"The paper you put into my hand?" Her face darkened at the thought.

"Did you not read it?"

"I did not. It fell from my hand during the riot. We were set upon by Jacobins. It was all so dreadful. Had Wendell not been there we might certainly have come to . . . I was so shocked and I still am. I have tried very much to put it all out of mind." Her green eyes searched his face. She said, "What did it say?"

"It said that I *would* go away with you."

Nolan noticed a minute stiffening of her mouth. "I was foolish to have ever made the offer, Philip. It was all quite impossible. And childish. There is no place you could have run; and if you had, I would certainly come to hate you."

Around them, fiddles went on and there was laughter wrapped around the music. Nolan was silent, and after a long interval he heard Lorina say sharply: "Really, Philip, it is ungentlemanly to stand there and simply gape. Why don't you ask how I have been?"

Nolan took a breath and bowed. "Mrs. Graff, it was polite of you to notice me," he said. Lorina blinked at the Marine standing close by, at first uncomprehending. She then realized that Nolan was, in fact, under guard and made a slight shake of her head. "Now, I wonder if you would please excuse me, it is late, and I am required to retire," Nolan said. He bowed again and moved for the gangway.

Lorina called after him: "You needn't be so righteous, Philip."

Nolan stopped and turned.

"It's you that has hurt me. Not the other way around. Your pride and insolence have separated you from all decent society. You have never made any effort to make amends or to apologize, to your country or your friends, and it should not surprise you that you are still held in contempt by those who have not chosen to forget you. Pride led you to grief—and it was your friends that suffered too. Wendell and Alden were much maligned, and now he is dead, given up his life for the country you casually damned, and Alden a widow. My own reputation and prospects were so sullied that I had no choice but to consent to the proposal of a laudanum-addled quack. You have hurt many more people than yourself."

At that moment a veteran officer of le Grand Armée joined Lorina and asked her to dance. She curtseyed, declined, and said in measured Parisian that she had an amusing person for the colonel to meet, a singular gentleman, but when she turned around, Nolan was gone.

The first rocket roared up from *Enterprise*'s quarterdeck and burst into a red ball of light. It was followed by another star shell, a blue one, and then by the lurching white of a flare. The lights pitched shadows across *Yunis'* deck. It had been years since Nolan had been gripped by bitterness and resentment; their jaws closed around him now, and he felt tears stinging his eyes. He had vowed never again to give another person the power to hurt him; that resolution had melted away like a dusting of snow. He had commanded himself so long and with such masterful dignity that his failure made him almost physically sick. Harried, provoked, and as desolate as he had ever been in his life, Nolan stepped down the gangplank and onto the high, slanted afterdeck of *Yunis*.

The silence of the smaller ship was a relief; it was dark and low and shadowed. He did not head aft, for the cabin, but forward, down the ladder at the quarterdeck break and then along the outboard side in the splintered light below the masts and rigging. The decks had been cleared, more or less, the yards and booms rigged, and the hatch covers replaced, but it would have required a powerful eye, and a practiced one, to detect Nolan's dark shape moving across the forecastle and out onto the forepeak. More rockets went off above the ship, and the crowds on the frigate's deck and the other people around the town looked into the sky. No one saw Nolan move out onto *Yunis'* bowsprit, crawl out to the very end of it, and lower himself down onto the quay.

Nolan did not think about the next step, or the next, or what it meant, but he started to walk quickly, and then he started to run. Trotting down the darkened pier, Nolan felt himself to be more alone than he had ever felt in his life—what shuddered inside him was the distilled miasma of two decades in confinement, the desolated aguish of a man not only without a country but now, apparently, even without a history. There were dozens, hundreds of people about, but no one paid

him any mind. All of them were looking out over the harbor at the jets and cascade
of rockets. As the fireworks transformed the sky, few realized that a prisoner had
just turned himself into a fugitive.

Nolan jumped down onto one of the low docks. He lifted a line from a cleat
and pulled the bow of a fishing boat toward the pier until it thumped against the
piling. The little craft was a scabrous, desperate-looking thing; it was weathered
and its stretchers were cracked, but it seemed all that he needed. He had to flee.

Coiling the painter in his hand, Nolan's fist clamped onto the thwart and
pulled the boat beside the pier.

"Where away, Philip?"

Nolan turned. Curran stepped out into the moonlight, his hand wrapped
around a pistol, the lock drawn back.

"Would you stop me?"

Curran sat on a piling and balanced the weapon on his knee. "I'm not sure I
have to. It takes more than one man to row a longboat." Behind him, a rocket went
into the sky and came down, a shower of yellow sparks. "Which probably don't
signify, for I doubt one man would be able to sheet and steer, as the wind is straight
upon the harbor."

"I would do all right," Nolan choked. "I could not do worse than to stay here."

Curran considered the distance between them; less than a dozen feet. He
would not be likely to miss if he fired. "Where would you go?"

Nolan's voice was tight. "Anywhere."

"I doubt you would even make it to the Gut. The glass is falling. There is likely
to be a sirocco, and there would certainly be galleys about. It would be safer to head
west, across to Italy. But then, of course, the corsairs might take you, and make a
slave of you."

"You mock me, sir."

"You step into that boat, Philip and you will be jumping from the end of the
Earth."

Nolan stared out the mouth of the harbor to the moon-spilled sea beyond. He
seemed willing to chance it, to chance everything.

Curran continued: "You have no water, and in a day the sun would beat your
brains out. If the sun does not kill you the corsairs will. And even should you live,
Pelles would come after you. He would hunt you and never stop."

Easton ran onto the wharf. He saw Curran, saw the pistol, and saw Nolan
pulling the boat closer. He stopped instantly and drew his dress sword from its
scabbard.

"Don't throw your life away, Philip," Curran said.

"Life?" Nolan scoffed. "I have no life. It would be better to be eaten by rats
than to live as I do. What does it matter if I am dead?"

"You are still undefeated. Do not surrender to despair."

Nolan swallowed back frustration and rage. "I cannot stand it any more. I will not. If you must stop me, then . . . "

Nolan turned toward the boat, and Curran's hand lifted the pistol. "Don't," he said, and there was a noise behind them: shouts and hurried footsteps. With a thump and rattle a pair of Marines jumped onto the pier. "Sir!" one yelled. "Mister Curran! Look! Look out there in the harbor!"

The Marine's hand waved past Nolan, past the feluccas in the anchorage toward a pair of salt-yellowed sails. A squalid-looking craft came out of the darkness, rode over one of the mooring buoys, and came on toward the quay. It was heeled awkwardly in the wind; its sails were tied off, and it steered wildly. The boat was coming on much, much too fast. Kanoa thumped down onto the pier—in his hand was a rammer from one of the guns. All could see it was a cutter, blue over white, a ship's boat. They could see no one in it, but it was being jibed right and left, the boom cracking against the mast, and it was sure to collide head-on with the pier.

"Lend a hand!" Curran barked. Curran and Kanoa used the rammer to try to fend off the boat, but it slammed into the fishing boat, stoving in part of its bow. It banged off in a crackle of splinters and drove up onto the wharf between Curran and Nolan. The boat's foremast snapped by the boards, dumping a heavy chunk of the mast and the boom onto the pier.

Kanoa managed to jump into the boat, kick the tiller over, and unsheet the remaining sails. Into the fluttering noise he called out, "Here's a man! No, a body. And another!"

"Bring me light!" Curran called.

A lantern came down. More Marines and a few crewmen spilled onto the pier. Curran took the lantern and jumped aboard. He crawled over the fallen mast and the tangled rigging. He could see a body curled around the tiller. It was still.

Easton reached out and managed to pull the stern of the whaleboat alongside the pier. Nolan found a line and made it fast. There was another shadow crouched inside the boat, thin and ragged. Nolan could hear a wheezing noise, a rasping sound, and he could smell something putrid.

"Help me," someone mumbled. "In the name of God."

Curran lifted the lantern overhead. The light came down on a lurid, hideous face. A pair of hollow cheeks were powdered with sea salt, and the eyes above them ringed with crusted blood—a man's face, made into a monster. His eyelids had been cut off, as had the end of his nose. The corners of his mouth had been sliced back almost as far as his back teeth, a festering, twitching wound.

The tongue rasped again, "Help me."

Someone behind Nolan said quietly, "Christ almighty."

The death's head spoke: "I am a United States naval officer. From the brig sloop *Torch.*"

Curran took the man into his arms. "Get Doctor Darby, at once!"

Nolan came over the thwart and joined Curran in the stern of the boat. He helped pull the man out and lay him on the pier. Bundled in rags, the man's skin was covered with ulcerous wounds.

"The plague," a Marine gasped, staggering backward.

Nolan held up the lantern as Curran looked into the man's maimed, blackened, lopsided face. "No. Not the plague. Pirates did this," Curran said. "Pirates."

CAPTAIN'S MAST

DOCTOR DARBY SAT BY HIS PATIENT IN THE DIM LIGHT OF THE SICKBAY. The man in the cot was bandaged like a pharaoh, his face and hands wrapped in strips of linen that concealed a number of deliberate and horrific mutilations. His name was Joseph Fuller, first lieutenant of *Torch*. When he was brought below, Darby could hardly tell him apart from the pair of corpses he had been found with. Even now Darby did not care for the victim's thin, rapid pulse or the wheezing grumble in his chest.

Captain Pelles leaned over the cot. He had his head turned, bent close to the place where the bandages moved. Pelles held the scrap of parchment Lieutenant Fuller had put into his hand, and looked at it now and again as he listened. What came from the bandaged face were hardly more than grunts. The words were mumbled and occasionally disjointed, but they made known a tale of shipwreck, a battle lost, captivity, and torture. Fuller's voice was a rattle, an increasingly incoherent one, and Darby feared that his patient might talk himself to death.

"He must rest now, sir," Darby said.

The captain stood, touched the man on his shoulder, and walked from the sickbay. As he climbed the ladders up from the orlop, the eyes beneath the bandages haunted him. Fuller and the men with him had gone five days without water. All of them had been maimed and emasculated by the cruel scimitars of the bashaw's Janissaries.

A SINGLE CANDLE GUTTERED IN THE LANTERN ON NOLAN'S FOLD-DOWN DESK. A dull light was projected onto the ceiling, casting shadows onto the cabin walls, accenting the gloom rather than illuminating space. The cabin was thick with the smell of fresh paint and cut wood. One of the diagonal knees above Nolan's cot had been replaced, and he had leisure now, lying on his back, to study it closely. Nothing else, materially, had changed. His clothing and possessions had been gathered up on *Yunis* and returned to him. They were placed back on their shelves and hung from dowel hooks: his ditty bag, sketchbooks, colored pencils, and his pins, threads, patterns, and needles all stowed. Nolan's hands were folded behind his head and his feet were crossed on the foot of the cot. It was in just this position that he had waited on his first evening aboard *Enterprise*, expecting to be rousted out by the ship's corporal. He closed his eyes and made himself still. As silent hours passed, it was easy to believe that he had never stirred from this place and that all of the events of the last months had been a dream.

Nolan had been returned to the ship under ambiguous circumstances. He had helped carry the wounded man from the boat. In the tumult that followed, the celebration aboard *Enterprise* had been instantly terminated. As the disfigured survivor from *Torch*'s whaleboat was carried aboard, some looked away in horror while others stared in mute fascination. The frigate had been cleared of visitors, the guests hurried over the brow and back to their carriages. Curran ordered Nolan to be put under guard and confined to his cabin.

At four bells, Nolan had heard the pipe and the call of the bo'suns to unmoor ship. It was followed by the stamp and go of the men at the capstan as the frigate warped away from the pier and recovered her boats. The increasingly deep, easy roll told him that *Enterprise* had left port and then cleared the bay. The frigate was under way—but bound where? The crew was mute. Gone were the half-facetious comments, jokes, and semi-insults that passed between the watches. Even the midshipmen's berth, a place of almost constant laughter, was as quiet as the moon. Nolan heard the sentry relieved outside his cabin door; that he had again been placed under guard did not surprise him. His attempted escape had been both ill conceived and badly executed. Thrust from one extreme to the other, from future's impossibly bright promise to the past's regrets, Nolan had once again forsworn optimism.

In his cabin he closed his eyes but could not block out the sight of Lorina. Her movements had been languid, her complexion pale and sallow, and he thought now that her breath had the sweet, deadly smell of opium. She had spoken slowly, but the words she gathered struck Nolan like stones. He was gripped again by the same searing pain he'd felt when he went over the bow of *Yunis*.

When he ran down the quay, he'd had no idea where he would go. It was an instinct to flee—which is simply and always an impulse for self-preservation. He did not care much now that he'd failed to get away from the ship; confinement was his fate, ironbound and forever. Nolan cursed himself for having thought that anything could have changed: hope was the cruelest blade a man could ever turn upon himself.

In the passageway the sentry came to attention and Nolan heard the rattle of keys. The lock in the louvered door was opened and a light shined into the compartment. "You're wanted, Mister Nolan," said a voice behind a battle lantern. "Right directly, if you please."

Up the ladders and aft, led by a Marine and followed by another, Nolan went across the spar deck. Above, the masts whispered. The wind was abaft the beam, and the frigate was under all plain sail. Land was a low, red smudge far away to starboard, and the sea around was the sapphire blue of deep soundings. Nolan, so long a nautical creature, could tell that the frigate was headed south-southwest. He did not trouble to ask why.

Nolan was led into the wardroom. Pelles was there at a small podium. Papers covered the desks on either side, letters and orders and files; black tape, green, and red. As he entered, Nolan stole a glance at Curran, seated at Pelles' right hand. Some of the other officers looked up as he came in, but most did not. Nolan scarcely knew the recently appointed officers. It was obvious they were gathered to dispense some sort of justice. All wore their dress uniforms and sat rigidly. Nolan could glean nothing from their expressions, and even Curran's face seemed to be veiled with grave, silent authority.

Pelles asked that Nolan be given a chair. Newsome, the captain's clerk, held a board in the crook of his left arm; clipped to it was a short stack of papers. His pen scratched as Pelles spoke.

"Mister Nolan, do you know what a captain's mast is?"

"I do, sir."

It was the ritual of shipboard justice. A person charged with an offense was brought before the captain, *masted*, as they said, and charges were read out. It was the captain who sat as judge and jury, and his power to chastise, even to flog, was immense. Nolan had known Captains Bainbridge, Lawrence, and even Decatur to routinely sentence malefactors to floggings or confinement on bread and water.

"I am convening a captain's mast," Pelles continued, "as charges have been laid against you, Mister Nolan."

Nolan glanced across the table. Curran sat with his knees together, looking at the painted black and white squares on the deck cloth.

"Mister Nolan, you are aware that you continue to be under the custody of the United States Navy and are bound by the conditions of the sentence you received at general court-martial on September 2, 1807?"

"I never thought anything had changed sir," Nolan said.

Pelles let a moment pass. He went on in a cold, official baritone. "Mister Piggen has placed you on report. He has made several serious allegations: quitting the ship without permission, disobedience of a direct order, evasion, and attempted desertion."

Nolan looked at Piggen, gray-faced and pinched. The room was so still that Newsome's scratching pen could plainly be heard.

"I am compelled," Pelles said, "on hearing Mister Piggen's charges, to inquire into the circumstances. Several of these are serious allegations. One is a capital offense." Pelles put down the paper. "You are aware that as a result of this mast, the material conditions of your custody may be affected?"

"Yes, sir."

The pen went on and then hissed to a stop. Pelles said, "I will question you and the other officers and come to a judgment regarding this matter. My decision is final and binding. You will be accorded an opportunity to speak after I have heard the evidence against you. You may call any witnesses you think may help your case. In the case that a capital offense is judged to have occurred, your sentence will automatically be appealed and referred to the commodore of the Mediterranean Squadron."

Nolan lowered his eyes. He thought of the execution he had witnessed once in Gibraltar. Three deserters were hanged from the yardarm of the frigate HMS *Bellerphon*. Captain Bainbridge had thought the spectacle would enlighten Nolan and had him rowed over in one of *Constitution*'s boats so he could witness the horror close at hand. Nolan had not forgotten what a hanged man looked like.

"Am I to plead guilty or innocent?" Nolan asked.

"You are not," Pelles said.

Nolan looked at Darby. The doctor seemed extraordinarily sad.

"Do you wish to name any persons of the crew to speak on your behalf?" Pelles asked.

"No, sir."

"Will you call any witnesses?"

Witnesses to what? Nolan thought. Easton had seen Curran and Nolan on the wharf. He saw plainly that Curran had pointed his pistol at Nolan. Nolan could not know how much the young officer had heard, but what he'd seen was certainly enough.

Nolan said clearly: "I will not call any witnesses."

"Mister Piggen, please repeat what you told me."

"I will, Captain. Last night, I saw Nolan going over the side of *Yunis*. He went over the bow and lowered himself to the pier by the spirit yard. And then he went running down the pier, toward town. I called out to him and remembered him of his duty, but he went along pretending not to hear. I told him twice."

Nolan watched Piggen closely. He might have seen him go over the bow, but no one had hailed him. Nolan wondered why Piggen would choose to embellish this point.

"Who else saw Nolan quit the ship?" Pelles asked. No one answered. "Did anyone hear Mister Piggen order Nolan to return?" Again, silence. "Mister Piggen," Pelles continued, "what did you do after seeing Nolan leave the ship?"

"I told him to return, like I said," Piggen jerked his chin toward Curran, "then I told the exec."

Pelles turned to Curran. "Did you see Nolan leave *Yunis*?"

"No, sir," he answered. "I did not see him leave the ship."

"Go on, Mister Piggen."

"That was it, sir," Piggen nodded. "I saw him try to escape. I ordered him to halt, twice, and then I told Mister Curran and Mister Easton, him being officer of the day."

"Did you make any attempt to go after Mister Nolan?" asked Pelles.

Piggen blinked. "Me? No, sir. He was wearing a sword."

"But you are sure it was Mister Nolan," Pelles asked, "and not someone else going ashore from *Yunis*?"

"I saw him, sir," Piggen said. He pointed at Nolan's face. "He knows I did, too."

Nolan shook his head. "Captain, I was—"

Pelles lifted his hand from the table; the gesture cut Nolan short. "You'll be given an opportunity to make a statement, Mister Nolan."

Piggen seemed delighted. Around the wardroom, the other officers were sullen and mute. Darby ran his fingernail up and down the edge of the table. Pelles cleared his throat and put on his glasses.

"Mister Nolan, yesterday afternoon you were ashore with permission and in the custody of the executive officer. Is that correct?"

"Yes, sir," Nolan said.

"At any time did Mister Curran ask you for a formal parole or elicit a promise that you would not try to escape?"

"No, sir."

"Did you ask Mister Curran to clarify the conditions under which you had been allowed liberty ashore?"

"No, sir. I did not."

"In June of this year, you assumed command of the prize vessel *Yunis*, navigating her to the port of Cartagena, after Mister Curran had been wounded, is that correct?"

"It is."

"Mister Curran, during the time at the Lofa River, or later in Sierra Leone, did you ever fear that Mister Nolan would attempt to leave the ship?"

"No, sir, I did not."

"Did you think at any time ashore during liberty yesterday afternoon that Mister Nolan might attempt to flee?"

"No, sir."

Pelles looked down at one of the files. "The ambassador seems to have been particularly animated against you, Mister Nolan. And I am informed that a certain Mister Slingeker . . . "

"Slonecker, sir," Piggen corrected him.

"The ambassador's vice consul has alleged that you were disrespectful to him while you were ashore."

Nolan looked down and shook his head.

The captain asked Piggen: "Did you speak to Mister Slonecker about this?"

"I did, sir. He mentioned that the prisoner had been disrespectful of his person while ashore."

Pelles frowned. "Disrespectful how?"

"Well I don't know exactly what he said. He asked me about Nolan, so I told him about his confinement."

Pelles put his hand to the side of his face, cradling his chin. "Were you not informed, Mister Piggen, that the conditions of Nolan's sentence and confinement are a confidential matter?"

Piggen was flustered. "Well, he already knew, sir. I mean about Nolan being a traitor. The ambassador, too. I told 'em how Nolan was supposed to be kept."

Pelles said, "Did you discuss any other confidential matters with Mister Slonecker?"

Piggen was taken aback but managed to press on. "Well, no, sir. We both saw Nolan go over the side. I saw him first, then I pointed it out to Mister Slonecker."

"Were you watching Mister Nolan particularly?" asked Pelles.

"I was, sir. I saw Nolan on deck talking to a woman. I thought there might be some possibility of him asking inappropriate questions."

"Who was this person?" Pelles asked.

"She looked like an American, sir. I would say she was a lady of quality."

"Did Mister Nolan seem acquainted with her?"

"He did, sir."

"Why do you say that?" Pelles asked. Nolan felt his stomach churn.

"They was talking close. They was talking, and then all of a sudden Nolan walks off. Angry like. He went right over to the gangway and down onto *Yunis*. I was watching, sir, from the larboard rail. I saw him go forward and then I saw him go over the bow."

Pelles turned his gaze on Easton. "You were officer of the day yesterday, Mister Easton?"

"Yes, sir."

"You were aware that Mister Nolan was out of the ship?"

Easton took a second to think. "In the morning, sir."

"How many times, Mister Easton, did Mister Nolan leave the ship yesterday?" Pelles asked.

Easton exhaled. "I am not aware that Mister Nolan ever left the ship without permission, sir."

"That isn't what I asked, Mister Easton. How many times did Nolan leave the ship?"

Several seconds passed. Nolan did not expect Easton to lie for him. "I left the ship twice, Captain," Nolan said firmly.

"To whom did you speak while you were on deck?" Pelles asked.

"I had occasion, sir, to meet an acquaintance," Nolan said. "An old friend. The result of that meeting put me into a state of something, I regret to say, that was very much like melancholy. I went aboard *Yunis*."

"Did you tell anyone you were quitting *Enterprise*?"

"He told me, sir," Fancher said.

Nolan looked at Fancher. This was a lie, a perfect, blatant lie. Nolan remembered that Fancher was near the larboard gangway, but he did not ask his permission to leave the ship.

"He went aboard *Yunis* just after eleven o'clock," Fancher said, utterly straight-faced.

"Do you own a watch, Mister Fancher?"

"No, sir. Mister Nolan spoke to me just as the fireworks was going. Per schedule that was eleven o'clock."

Nolan looked at Fancher. *He is risking his career and honor for me—why?*

Pelles made a note and turned to Nolan. "Mister Curran tells me that when *Torch*'s whaleboat collided with the wharf, you were with him. Is that correct?"

Nolan hesitated.

"Yes or no, please, Mister Nolan."

"Yes, sir, I was there."

"And Mister Easton has stated that you helped fend off the boat when it looked like it would strike the pier."

Nolan looked at Easton. It was Easton who had fended off the boat, and he certainly knew that Curran had been holding him at pistol point. Now Easton was protecting him too.

Pelles said, "Is it correct that you all went together when you saw the whaleboat coming through the anchorage?"

"I saw him go over the side," Piggen croaked. "Nolan was scooting out."

"Thank you, Piggen. I heard you the first time," Pelles said. "Mister Fancher, when you saw Nolan go aboard *Yunis*, was it before or after *Torch*'s boat came into the harbor?"

Fancher automatically said the thing that would favor Nolan: "After, sir, right after it came across the bar."

Pelles was not likely fooled; but he did not want to see Nolan hang. "Mister Piggen, did you speak to Mister Nolan last night?"

"Why no, sir."

"Do you have any idea why he might choose to go ashore from *Yunis* by the bow? By dropping off the bowsprit?"

"I reckon he was running, sir. It was the fastest way to the pier. I still think that."

"You said it looked like he was in a hurry, did you not?"

"He was sneaking, like," Piggen minced.

"Was this during the fireworks?"

"Around that time, sir."

Pelles leaned back in his chair and smoothed the empty sleeve pinned to the front of his coat. "Seeing that the entire harbor was illuminated by star shells, could it have been that Nolan had seen the whaleboat enter the harbor?"

"*I* didn't see anything, sir," Piggen said.

"You stated previously that you were on the larboard side. Were you looking out into the harbor, Mister Piggen?"

"I was looking over the side, sir. I saw Nolan go forward on *Yunis*. Outboard. Staying in the shadows, like. It was right dark, sir. A black night."

"It was, Mister Piggen," Pelles said. "It very often is dark when the sun is down and there is no moon; I am heartily glad you noticed. Now, Doctor Darby, when the call came for stretchers, you went down to the pier?"

"I did, sir."

Pelles removed his glasses. "Was Mister Nolan on the wharf when you arrived with surgeon's mates?"

"He was."

"Did Nolan assist in carrying the wounded man aboard the frigate?"

"He did, sir."

"Did he come freely or was he forced?"

"Forced, sir?" Darby blinked.

"Did anyone compel Mister Nolan to carry the stretcher? Was he compelled by force, or threat of force, to assist in bringing the wounded man aboard?"

"No, sir. He did it of his own."

There was a long, strained silence. Pelles went though some of the papers in front of him. Nolan had an instant to look into Curran's eyes—he looked tired and bereft.

"I must conclude that you did leave the ship, Mister Nolan," Pelles said. The room was still. "But I can draw no conclusion as to your motives." Pelles flipped closed the file in front of him. "But given that you were previously at liberty, both when in command of *Yunis* and ashore yesterday afternoon, I am not willing to pronounce that you were attempting to desert the ship. Especially as *Torch*'s boat, obviously in distress, was visible from the deck. I have been given proofs of your courage, and I believe that you are an honorable man. I choose to think that you were more disposed to help than to run."

Nolan felt shame rather than relief. He barely heard Pelles say, "This matter is closed."

Nolan stood, ready to depart. Pelles moved away from the podium and toward the wardroom table. He said, "Sit down, Mister Nolan. There are other matters before me that I would like to discuss with you."

Pelles turned to Piggen and said coldly, "These will be tactical matters, Mister Purser. I do not think you need trouble yourself with them."

Piggen surveyed the faces. Every eye was on him, and in every one there was nothing but loathing. Piggen went out of the wardroom, his shoes squeaking.

As the door closed, the captain handed a piece of parchment to Curran. It was written in extravagant, flourishing Turkish—wafered and sealed and beribboned.

"This was found in *Torch*'s boat. I suppose that it is some sort of ransom demand. Can you confirm it?"

Beyond the opening remarks, in the name of the most merciful, etc., the message was very far from mercy or peace. "It is a demand for compensation," Curran said. "It announces that the Bashaw of Arzeou has captured the gun sloop USS *Torch* and her crew."

"Captured? How is that possible?" Ruggles stammered.

"From the survivor we know this much," Pelles said. He nodded, and Pybus unrolled a chart of the Barbary Coast. "*Torch* was on patrol off Arzeou, here." Pelles put his finger down between Algiers and Tangiers. "Her orders were to observe the harbor and fortress at Arzeou. After Mister Curran gave *Um Qasim* a shiner, she took refuge there in the harbor at Arzeou. *Torch*'s orders were to observe, but their commander, Mister Penniman, showed a bit too much zeal. A week ago, in a calm, a dozen galleys came from the harbor and made for *Torch*. Penniman was not surprised and managed to sink three and maul the rest. But while *Torch* was withdrawing she struck a reef to the west of the fortress."

"It ain't on the large-scale charts, sir," said Pybus.

"Which doesn't mean it isn't there," Pelles said. "*Torch* went hard aground and came under constant attack by the batteries at the mouth of the harbor. It was not long before they had her range. *Torch* did what they could to get off, starting their water, guns, and supplies. When it was clear that they could not make her swim, Commander Penniman sent the unfortunate Mister Fuller and three men in the cutter to get help. Their boat was overtaken by one of the bashaw's row galleys. You saw what was done to the men."

"Don't we have a treaty with the Bashaw of Arzeou?" asked Pybus.

"We did," Curran answered. "The bashaw's public treaties are worth less than his private ones. The bashaw has entered into an agreement to sell prizes taken by the Dey of Bou Regreg, whose normal remit is on the Atlantic."

"That is why he allowed *Um Qasim* to refit in Arzeou's harbor," Pelles said. "It is also believed that the bashaw is holding the crew of *McKendrie Evans*—what remains of them." The captain smoothed the chart and continued, "Now the Arabs have refloated *Torch* and taken her under protection of their guns at Arzeou. The crews of the whale ship and USS *Torch* are being held as captives."

Pybus frowned, "If they were to repair *Torch* and *Um Qasim*, sir, and arm them with the Portuguese guns . . . "

Easton piped up, "And I have seen Arab divers recover guns from the seabed . . . diving to more than five fathoms. They're likely to recover *Torch*'s guns as well."

"Suffice it to say that our task to protect American shipping would become burdensome."

Ruggles asked, "What do they want?"

Curran scanned the document. "An apology. That was put in rather strenuous language. They demand a payment, as an indemnity for *Torch*'s violation of their territorial waters. They also want the recommencement of tribute. They are asking for the same payment made by President Jefferson to the previous Dey of Algiers."

"What is the sum?"

"Five hundred thousand Spanish dollars, sir. In gold."

"Who is it that makes this demand?"

"It is signed by the vizier, sir, the bashaw's chief of staff."

"Not the sovereign himself?"

"No, sir. That is not unusual; should the demand be refused, it will not reflect upon the bashaw's authority."

"I *shall* refuse, Mister Curran," Pelles said pleasantly. "And the bashaw's authority shall look rather funny hanging out of his arse."

At the bottom of the letter was a notation, added in a compact, flowing hand. It was written in English and read, "Witnessed, and attested: Taken with the frigate under my command are one hundred fifty-six men; seventeen sergeants and petty officers. During the engagement, one hundred and twenty men were killed and sixty-three wounded. Signed, Lieutenant August L. Penniman, USN."

Torch's unfortunate commander had been prevailed upon to certify that the demand was genuine. Though his pen was steady, you might see distress plain in the neatly ruled and smallish letters. The S in USN was written backward.

"What do you make of it, Mister Curran?"

Curran studied the paper. "It was obviously written under duress. There are of course no sergeants in the navy, and Commander Penniman commands a brig sloop, sir, not a frigate, and he did not carry any Marines."

"Might this letter say anything else?"

Curran looked closely at the addendum, and then at the spaces between the lines. He looked briefly at the back of the document. "Can you tell me something about the officer, sir?" Curran asked.

"Penniman? Not very much. He is unlucky."

"*Torch* was his first command sir?"

"It was."

"May I ask, Captain, where he served previously?"

"*Brister, Vesuvius*, and I believe he was attached to the mission in Paris."

Curran looked again at the postscript. The man had taken his time to write this. It was closely, neatly written and as lined up as though he had used a straight rule.

"If he had been with the Paris mission, sir, he probably knows of secret writing."

"I am not sure I can put Commander Penniman among intelligence agents," Pelles said blandly.

"The technique is very commonplace in embassies, sir. When I was a boy I sometimes helped my father with his correspondence." Curran peered at the back of the paper, angling it in the lantern light.

"Would he not have required secret ink?" asked Fancher.

"He would not, but he *would* require privacy—just a few moments without the guards hovering around." Curran held the parchment up to the top of the lantern's globe. "There is another message on the parchment, sir, written on the back."

To the naked eye, the paper showed nothing. Curran let the flame climb out of the shade, toward the paper with a series of rhythmic stabs. The parchment was brought nearly to the point of combustion and a series of lines appeared. Slanted large across the back were a scrawl of letters and numbers: ME62T124EBBAGNO.

"I'll be damned," said Fancher.

"Commander Penniman was apparently left alone to add his postscript." Curran tapped the paper. "He used a pen and ink to write the confirmation but used an old trick to write the other. It is visible now, sir, as you see."

Pelles took his glasses and threaded them behind his ears. "Pray, what was it written in?"

"Urine, sir," Curran said. "Daubed on with a matchstick."

"Piss on a stick?" frowned Pybus.

"Now," Pelles mused, "what does it mean?"

Five silent faces starred down at the parchment. Finally Nolan spoke, "*McKendrie Evans*, 62. *Torch*, 124 . . . "

"And EB?"

"East Battery," said Nolan.

"And a bagnio is a prison, sir," said Curran.

"Now we must question whether Commander Penniman's gaolers might have discovered his secret message or written it themselves. Mister Pybus, the chart of Arzeou, please."

"It's here, sir. Only one we got is a French one, imperial, that I bought off'n a French merchant when we was off New Providence, the bashaw being a former pal of Napoleon, as you might say. As 'yer can see, the emperor's navy gents surveyed his harbor nice and regular."

"Commander Penniman might have appreciated your chart, Mister Pybus. It clearly shows the reef straddling the offshore approach."

The chart showed a harbor open to the north and enclosed by two fortified causeways. The wall on the eastern side was a short, slightly squat affair, the first part perpendicular and the second angled to the west and ending in a two-story Martello tower.

"I ain't never been there, sir, but old Franklin in *Constitution*, he was captured with Bainbridge in ought three. They sold him as a slave over to Arzeou. Used him cruelly. He told me that Arzeou and Tripoli is of a type, sir. Very similar with walls and batteries, but with Arzeou having less people, it's of a smaller scale."

The longer, eastern causeway went nearly straight out to a rocky islet, most of a mile from the shore. Like the other causeway, this one was studded with gun emplacements and had a steep wall facing seaward. It led to the island, which was itself walled and towered. The islet, tear shaped, looked to be a little over four acres, and nearly all of it was filled with a warren of buildings. The narrowest part was a battery facing over the harbor mouth, positioned to support its neighbor half a mile across the channel. The town was layered up in terraces overlooking the anchorage. The city had been fortified from time out of mind, first by the Romans and Vandals, and before them the Greeks and probably the Carthaginians. The walls had been expanded several times to enclose a greater urban area, and these expansions had been made by knowing engineers.

"Mister Nolan, I wonder if you might share your lights? We need your opinion as an artillerist."

"I am at your service, sir," Nolan said quietly.

"I thought you'd feel that way . . . the wounded Mister Fuller has plainly sketched us an idea of the bashaw's guns at Arzeou." Pelles handed Nolan the paper Fuller had given him in sickbay.

Nolan studied it—the merest scratches of lead, numbers that looked like fractions, which he finally determined were weight of shot and the height of guns. "These are very plausible emplacements, sir," Nolan said. "At these heights, with the calibers mentioned, nearly the entire harbor and most of the approaches are well covered."

The imperial chart was marked with two anchorages: a military anchorage to the west and merchant piers to the east. The chart showed that it was deep right up to the longer causeway, and there was a beach and yard at the foot of it. It was a perfect naval base and port, valuable commercially and militarily, which explained why the French had troubled to make such a painstaking chart.

Nolan opened a pair of dividers, touched them to the scale, and then swung them in an arc pivoted from several places on the chart. "The strongest point, or rather the best-covered point, is here." Nolan touched the chart off the inside of the longer causeway. "The guns from the island and those in the main fortress cover this location and the approaches. And it is close to the causeway and this, which I take to be a beach. An easy place to haul out or load a derrick."

"Very well, I understand their strengths," Pelles said. "Now what, tell me, are their weaknesses?"

"There appear to be none, sir." Nolan said. "The arrangements are most complete."

Pelles let his eyes roam over the chart. There had to be a way into the harbor. "These two batteries at the head of the channel. Am I right to suppose that if they are suppressed, the harbor could be entered?"

"Yes, sir, certainly. I believe it might be done, especially if the eastern battery were to be attacked, say, from the north and close offshore. If the approaches could be commanded long enough to put a party ashore, I believe the battery might be taken from the land side, by assaulting down the causeway."

"And the world would hear that," grunted Pybus. "Nothing would stop the Prophet's own army from marching down the causeway to take back the battery."

Pelles frowned. "Mister Pybus, could *Enterprise* cross into the harbor?"

"Past the batteries? I reckon if we fired both sides we could. But I'd not like to try to put about in the harbor, sir. Oh, no. It is damned close, and that would be presuming it was empty."

"Which it is not," Curran said. "*Um Qasim* and *Torch* are there, at least."

"It has been my experience with the Barbary corsairs that they are not to be underestimated," said Pelles. "As they have two important ships, it has surely come to mind to moor a couple of gunboats about to augment what Mister Nolan calls this interlocking fire."

"This all presumes that we would have to fight our way in," Curran said. Nolan looked over at him. Curran's eyes narrowed: "What if we didn't fight the batteries but just sailed past them?"

"In *Enterprise*?"

"In *Yunis*. She doesn't draw much, so we could surely cross the bar. It doesn't matter if the batteries are taken or not taken—if they don't fire at us." Curran looked at Pelles. "*Yunis*, sir. Disguised as a coastal trader—what disguise—she is a coastal trader. We could enter the harbor and cut *Torch* out."

"I am not an enthusiast for desperate missions, Mister Curran."

"They would delay fire, surely, until they were certain of trouble. The key to our operation would be stealth. We could transfer the prisoners, sir, to *Yunis*, and get them from harm's way. We would then try to get *Torch* under sail."

"What if she is anchored with chain? What if the Arabs have taken her sails to make tents?" Pybus grunted.

"Then we burn her." Curran answered.

Pelles looked again at the chart, considering every angle. "Mister Nolan, if I had a flood tide, and entered the harbor with *Enterprise*, would I have enough time to free the prisoners and sink *Torch*?"

"You might, sir. But one thing is certain, the fort might sink you . . . but you will never sink the fort."

A moment passed: Pelles lost in thought. "I do not think much of councils of war, gentlemen—as they are talking shops in case of defeat. I do not plan on being defeated. There is a chance that Mister Curran's plan might work. In any event, should it fail, it would be less bloody than for *Enterprise* to wallow into the harbor and present a target for Arab guns. The xebec will be fitted out to carry seventy sailors and Marines. Command will devolve to you, Mister Curran, as I think this expedition will call for a two-armed commander." Pelles again tapped the chart, "Mister Curran will take *Yunis* into the harbor, rescue the hostages, and attempt to cut *Torch* out. Failing that—you will burn the sloop to deny her use to the Arabs."

"Captain Pelles, I'd like to accompany Mister Curran."

"I had anticipated that request, Mister Nolan. But I must decline. I cannot place a prisoner in my charge in such obvious jeopardy. I will also need you aboard *Enterprise* to help direct suppressive fire against the harbor batteries. We will have to be close offshore to cover their exit."

"Sir—"

"We do not question orders in the naval service, Mister Nolan. Make ready the plan we have discussed. There is not a moment to be lost."

TWENTY MILES OFF CABO DE GATA *ENTERPRISE* WAS HEAVED TO, HER TOPSAILS aback. As befitted a tender, *Yunis* was under her lee, lolling under sad, backwinded lateens. Pelles said the familiar words, hats were lifted, the hatch cover was tilted up, and the canvas-shrouded body of Lieutenant Fuller splashed into the waves. That he had survived five days in his mutilated state was something of a cruel miracle, and it was considered a mercy that he had passed away. His wounds had been diabolical and were intended to appall and dishearten all who saw them. They had shocked every soul aboard *Enterprise*, both for their ingenious cruelty and for the malice they evinced. But where the corsairs attempted to sow fear they would reap only cold, determined anger.

The grindstone was in constant use putting a razor's edge on cutlasses and tomahawks, boarding axes, Bowie knives, and steel bayonets. Fresh flints were passed out for musketoons, pistols, carbines, and shotguns; powder horns were filled; and leather cartridge boxes were lined with freshly waxed linen. The men with Kentucky rifles fussed over their flints and prepared paper cartridges filled with fine-corned powder and freshly cast bullets.

Under an opalescent sky, the barge and cutters shuttled between *Enterprise* and *Yunis* transporting arms chests and several of the stubby brass howitzers the Marines served in the frigate's tops. These guns were mounted on swivels and concealed by canvas on *Yunis*' waist and forecastle. They were double-shotted with canister—a rude, lethal surprise for any ship curious enough to look closely.

Curran had a thousand details to attend to, tactical and administrative. There were, in addition to the weapons, a variety of incendiaries, grenadoes, and stink bombs, as well as twenty deadly barrels filled with tow, tar, sulfur, and gunpowder, short-fused to burn *Torch* if she could not be cut out. Not the least among Curran's chores was the selection of the sailors and Marines who would go with him. In one way, this was the easiest of the jobs he faced. There was not a man aboard *Enterprise* who did not want to go, even though *Yunis* would carry only a pitiful few cannon and was bound for one of the most heavily armed fortresses in all of the Maghreb.

Curran sat in his cabin writing out a plan of signals when there was a knock. "Come," he said.

Piggen entered, eyes narrowed, and his thick, wet frown set as usual. "Curran, I have come to offer my services on your expedition." Before Curran could speak Piggen continued, "Please, sir, hear me out. I have a very good idea what you think of me. And I believe you have formed an incorrect opinion of my firmness as an officer. I can command as well as anyone, and I am not shy."

"I am surprised you have chosen to volunteer, Mister Piggen."

"I have taken the liberty, sir. I am sure you would not have selected me."

"That's correct. I would not have. And I will not now." Piggen tried to interrupt. "Hear me, sir," Curran said. "I listened to you. You are surely aware of the disrepute in which you are held aboard this ship. I will not venture whether your character is deserved or not. You are one who *calculates*, Piggen, and I am sure you realized that volunteering could only elevate your standing aboard. You must have known I would refuse to take you, so you faced little physical danger, only the upside of ameliorating your reputation as a poltroon."

"I would fight," Piggen huffed.

"If you were put in a box and prodded. A rat would do that. I am sure your performance in combat would be satisfactory—only that—satisfactory. I am declining to take you because I am certain that if our expedition should fail and we should become captives, your conduct would be exactly what it has been aboard this frigate."

"How do you mean?"

"I mean, sir, that should we fall into the enemy's hands, I would expect you to be a gossip, a hoarder, a creature of faction—an informer and even a collaborator. You might declare yourself willing to fight, Piggen, I hardly know a man in the Navy who is a truly born coward, but you are certainly not a person who has the character to lead in adversity."

"I will ask the captain, then," Piggen said.

"You might, sir. Though if I were you I would not press him for a recommendation. I will decline to take you regardless."

Later in the afternoon Doctor Darby also applied to join *Yunis*, and it was with genuine regret that Curran had to refuse. He agreed with Darby that his services would be needed at the point of attack, but he did not want to risk the only surgeon aboard. If the mission were successful, there would be wounded in plenty and the liberated prisoners also to care for. If the expedition failed, Curran did not want to see the frigate's only medical officer captured or killed. Darby, a man of reason as well as philosophy, could not disagree. Unlike Piggen, Darby knew his own reputation in the ship and did not doubt his own courage. Neither did Curran.

The ships carried on slowly toward Arzeou. The blue cutter was sent far to windward as a lookout, and an early supper was served aboard *Enterprise*: Chick's own New Orleans concoction of chili beef and beans, soft bread, cheddar, and fresh green beans. Great wooden mess kits were rowed over to the hands working aboard *Yunis*, and the smell of rich chili wafted though the salt air.

Curran would have normally eaten his share, chili beef being one of his favorites, but his appetite was gone. While mirth came up from the mess decks, he stood at the taffrail looking into the last, fading light of sunset. The wake stretched away, straight and luminous as the night came on. As Curran's eyes became increasingly accustomed to the dark, he could see the cutter far to windward. It showed no lights, but would shine a blue lantern should a stranger be sighted. By full dark the transfer of volunteers and ordinance was nearly complete—Curran might yet enter the harbor with an element of surprise.

Since retreat, no bells had been struck aboard, no pipes were sounded, and what remained of the work was carried out in measured voices, though they were still a hundred odd miles from the coast. The ship took on the tense, expectant air of battle, made more concentrated by the darkness and the instinctive need for quiet.

The raiders were assembled on the spar deck. The orders to make themselves look like natives rather than United States Navy sailors had been obeyed enthusiastically. Most of the hands had seen corsairs close up and made *thawbs* and *djellabas* closely resembling the real articles (there were some remarkable tailors among the hands). Others, more avid still, made up the garb of pirates of another century. But none had outdone the Bannon brothers for ornateness or style. Stephen Bannon sported a mountainous black turban with a foot-long feather. Christopher wore petticoats and a veil, both probably the trophies of a July Fourth conquest. Their disguises were topped off with pistols and boarding axes, and both had blackened their faces with soot from the camboose.

"Which Bannon are you?" asked Curran, peering under the turban.

"Which it's Stephen, sir. I am dressed as the sultan himself."

It wasn't likely that the sultan owned a bigger turban. It was certain that the sultan did not have Bannon's bright green eyes, which were set off starkly by the soot he had painted across his cheeks. Curran looked next at the veiled figure standing next to him.

"Which it's Christopher, your honor," said the other Bannon. "And I am the sultan's harem."

"Admirable," Curran said. "You have the devil's own cunning." The brothers winked at each other. Curran went on thoughtfully, "But it might not be fair to confuse the enemy so completely. Indeed, Stephen Bannon, you look so much like a bashaw, I am sure the enemy would be too concerned with their salaams to even raise a finger." Curran reached up and took the turban off Steven's head. He was surprised to find a loaded horse pistol tucked in it.

"My backup, sir." Bannon winked.

"Excellent," Curran said. "But perhaps it would ride easier in a hanger or perhaps even a leather holster." Then, with the greatest delicacy, Curran said to Christopher, "And I might have you take off one or two of the petticoats, Christopher

Bannon. Though I am not completely versed in the couture of the *harim*, I do not seem to recall so much lace or flattering calico."

"Really, sir?" asked Christopher sadly.

"I am afraid so. You might wish to consult your own safety as well. Should you be captured, it would not do to have the enemy overcome with precipitate lust."

Curran walked down the line addressing each man in the raiding party, asking how they did and approving of their preparations. Kanoa had made a short *thobe* out of his mattress ticking. His garment was not very far off from what a real Algerian slave might wear. "No other weapon, Petty Officer Kanoa? Just your ax?"

Kanoa shouldered his fearsome, shark tooth–studded *pahoa*. "You only get one shot with a pistol, sir," he smiled. "A'sides, there's always plenty of weapons to pick up after a boarding."

Curran smiled. Behind the first rank of volunteers Fante was sitting on a hatch combing. He was unarmed and he was wearing Nolan's old duck trousers and a blue jacket made out of brushed blankets. "Fante," Curran said, "I am surprised you are not among the storming party."

"I'm surprised too. Me having been to Arzeou. And me speaking like a corsair," Fante said.

Curran was surprised. "You speak Arabic, sir?"

Fante delivered a blistering Arab curse. It used half a dozen nouns and three verbs that were among the most obscene Curran knew. Together, they defied translation. "You certainly command the language," Curran said. "Why will you not be joining us?"

Fante stood, arms crossed. "In the first place, no one asked me."

There were smiles about the deck. "Ask him, sir," someone said.

"And in the second place," Fante continued, "I don't see why you are going to so much trouble."

"How do you mean?" Curran asked.

"There are more slaves than masters in Tripoli and Arzeou. Every time there is a battle in Africa, slaves are taken. Why is it so important to get these?"

"They are our countrymen."

Fante shrugged. "They could free themselves instantly by becoming Muslims," he said. "Everyone knows it is forbidden for a good musselman to own a Muslim slave. Why do you not send ashore a letter to tell them to turn Turk—then they would not have to be slaves and you would not have to be knocked on the head."

"I'm not sure it is so simple. Nor do I think that the bashaw or even the sultan would scruple from keeping a fellow Muslim as a slave. Any gate, they are Christians, and you would not ask a man to give up his religion."

"Bah," Fante said. "I have given up mine. The religions of other people are just superstitions." Fante's smile showed no trace of sarcasm. "The slaves in your country," he asked, "are they Muslims?"

"They are Christians."

"Then it is a victim's religion. I think you should simply tell the captured men to become Muslims. Then they can be free."

"We must fight, Fante," Curran said. "We cannot submit."

Fante narrowed his eyes. "Are there white slaves in America?"

"No."

Fante towered over Curran, his crooked shark's teeth set in a wry smile. "So it is not slavery that you object to, but when *white* people are made into slaves?"

"I can see how you might think that."

Fante gestured to the men gathered in the waist of the ship. "And here you are, every one of you a slave too."

"We are not slaves," Curran answered.

"Psssh." Fante leered. "Do you not bow down to the captain? There is not one here who dares contradict him. He is like a sultan," Fante said. "Tell me, if you are not slaves, why do what he tells you?"

"Because we took an oath to obey."

Fante looked astonished. "Were you forced to take this oath?"

"No."

Fante shook his great, solid, wooly head. "Then why would you do it? Why did you give up your own freedom?"

"When the Portuguese came to your village, did you fight?"

"Of course."

"When they took away your people, did you fight to get them back?" Curran asked.

"I did, but I was a prince," Fante said. "They were my own people. These men who were taken, what are they to you?"

"Countrymen."

"Ha! What does that mean? A king is a countryman, but he would not die for a farmer. You are a free man, yet you bind yourself unto death? You don't seem to have thought very deeply about this."

"You make some good points, Fante. And I cannot refute them. I am a naval officer, not a philosopher. I am going to Arzeou because it is my duty."

Fante grunted. "Why don't you just order me to fight?" Fante asked. "Am I not a slave?"

"Certainly not. You are member of the ship's company. There are no slaves aboard *Enterprise*."

"None of these men are ordered to go?"

"They are all volunteers."

"The other Africans, Old Chick and Gubbins, the others who are not white men, they are not slaves?"

"They are free. And as you see, Young Dave and Tommy and others have volunteered," Curran said.

"But they are Africans. They were slaves in your country?"

"Yes. They were slaves, but they are free men now."

Curran looked around. A dozen sailors had gathered to listen to the debate. All were smiling. Curran said calmly, "Fante, I would be honored if you would join us in storming the sultan's fortress and freeing the American hostages."

Fante considered the offer with the expression of a banker calculating a loan.

Curran said, "Please?"

A grudging smile came over the big man's face. "Well, I might enjoy it." Fante ran the tip of his tongue along the pointed row of his teeth. "I have changed my mind. Now I say yes. Let's go kill some pirate bastards."

THE FORTRESS AT ARZEOU

YUNIS TOOK ON THE LAST OF HER VOLUNTEERS AND TURNED AWAY south-southwest for Cap Falcon. The wind was steady, a mild Levanter, just enough to tease up whitecaps from the tourmaline-colored water. Under courses, *Enterprise* recovered the blue cutter and set off to the east, pitching in a moderate swell. Aboard *Yunis* Curran paced the quarterdeck, walking with measured steps from binnacle to taffrail. As the moon coasted into the western sky he could see the frigate's gun ports lit in a display of self-conscious innocence. Curran knew that by the end of the first watch, Pelles would douse his lights and steer the darkened ship downwind into the Baie des Andaluces west of Arzeou.

As their courses opened, Curran would occasionally fix his glass on the frigate, scanning her closely. He wondered whether was he looking for a signal of recall, or even hoping for one. Along the larboard side, Orion wheeled up from the sea, his arching bow aimed into the blackness at the top of the sky. South-southwest, directly marking his course, Curran could see Venus and Jupiter together in the sky just above the horizon. It was less than thirty leagues to the mouth of the harbor, an easy, even languid day and night's sail for a vessel as handy as *Yunis*. Curran would time his arrival with the setting of the moon, a few minutes before midnight, tomorrow. It would be too much to hope for a rain squall, but a hazy night was likely, and after the setting of the moon the sea-darkness would be nearly opaque. If all went to plan, *Enterprise* would complete a slow, semicircular approach and appear within gunshot of the fortress three hours after *Yunis'* arrival. By then, one way or another, Curran's mission would be decided. The frigate would be offshore to either welcome the victors or gather up survivors.

Curran settled with his arm wrapped through the mizzen shrouds, looking back into the long, luminous wake. He listened as the sounds of supper came up from below. He'd ordered a whole bullock to be served out, having learned long ago that a full belly was as important as dry powder for men going into combat. As dinner was consumed (and with it, a twenty-two-pound jelly roll) the noise below changed to the rattle of mess cranks gathering and scrubbing wooden kids, leather mugs, pewter spoons, and copper kettles. The watch changed, the sentries intoned "All's well," and Curran saw to it that the lookouts took night glasses up with them. As the last Dog Watch was being piped down, Curran had Padeen order divisions.

Seventy-five men had come from *Enterprise*; every man aboard the frigate had volunteered, and Curran had the pick of the best hands. Soon they were on deck, thoroughly counted and roughly toeing the seams inboard of the hidden guns. Mister Nordhoff and Mister Hall climbed to the quarterdeck and lifted their hats, "All present and accounted for, sir."

Curran looked out at the faces. Even in the pale moonlight they looked eager. "Padeen, will you go into the forepeak?" Curran asked quietly. "There is a coil of line and a bolt of painted canvas. Look under it and ask Mister Nolan to join us."

Padeen gave back a knowing smile, and Hall gagged like a boy discovered with a pocket full of stolen candy. "In the forepeak, sir?" Hall spluttered.

"What makes you think he's in there?" blinked Nordhoff.

"Because it's the only place I haven't looked," Curran said. "Run along and bring him to divisions."

Hall went forward and returned with Nolan in tow. As they passed through the assembled crew there were murmurs of welcome and approval, but none really of surprise. Nolan walked up the ladder to the poop and joined Curran by the rail.

"Good evening, Mister Nolan," Curran said. "Thank you for joining us."

"I hope you will forgive me for taking the liberty," Nolan said.

"I would be disappointed, sir, if you had not."

Nordhoff and Hall stood like wooden posts—both had helped Nolan stow away. The midshipmen stepped back as Curran put his hands on the quarterdeck railing. His voice carried easily to the assembled crew: "Tomorrow night we will fetch the Barbary Coast. Until then it is imperative that you stay hidden. For the crowding belowdecks I apologize, but your discomfort now will become the enemy's nightmare. You all know what needs to be done. The bashaw has made slaves of more than a hundred of our brothers, whalermen from *McKendrie Evans* and men o'war from USS *Torch*. We will restore them to their liberty and take back *Torch* to bring them home. If we cannot take back the sloop, then we will burn her to the waterline. I do not intend to leave Arzeou without the captives or the ship. We will have to be quick about our work, for I am sure the bashaw will see things differently."

"So what?" Kanoa grunted. He swung his *pāhoa* overhead and there was a ripple of laughter.

Curran went on: "When we have made the harbor, boarders—get onto *Torch* quick as you can. Topmen, do not wait to be told, get aloft and let loose her sails. Those noted to go below, quickly see to the safety of the prisoners and cut the anchor cables. You all know your duty. We are depending on surprise and audacity. We may not count on the laziness of the enemy. I do not have to remind you that the Arab sails and fights as well as any man. With luck, we will sneak into their harbor, but it is sure we shall have to fight our way out."

A moment passed.

"Does anyone want to speak?"

Nolan said, "I would like to say something." He stepped to the rail and took off his hat. "When we go in, I can promise you that the fortress will appear to be as big as a mountain. More than a score of the batteries are dug into the cliffs above and behind the citadel. I can also tell you that it is the habit of elevated gunners to overshoot their targets for the first several salvos. You may be sure that they will improve their aim and fight until the last ounce of powder. But they are fighting for their bashaw and are compelled to battle in fear of their lives. We are fighting as volunteers and for the freedom of our own people. That will tell the evening's business."

Nolan paused for a moment. Behind him the mizzen sail rumbled in a short gust, and he said, "I am proud . . . I am honored to sail with you."

"Hear him!" someone said. Applause swept the decks and then cheers. "Huzzah, Mister Nolan! Huzzah!" The crew's affection was plain, and Curran joined in the applause.

"All right, all hands back into the hold," Curran said. "Turn in and get what sleep you can. We will be about this business soon enough."

As the hands went below, Fante touched Nolan on the shoulder. His filed teeth flashed in the moonlight. "You speak well," Fante said. "One day you will be a prince. Like me."

Nolan smiled. "I'd be happy to be half of you, Fante."

DAWN CAME AS A HALFHEARTED SMUDGE OF GRAY. A DULL GLOW CLUNG TO the eastern horizon, spreading toward the south and gradually ascending in hazy shades of maroon. During the first watch the wind had veered and sputtered out. Now the sea was flat save for a long, uneven swell from the east. *Yunis* slowed and rolled, sails flapping, until she would barely answer the helm. Throughout the night watches Curran had three or four good sights, and had worked out their position as fifty miles north and a dozen miles east of Arzeou. Despite the tranquil dawn it would be a hard-won fifty miles to the coast. The perverse combination of a rapidly falling glass and a building swell presaged a savage blow. Over the larboard rail, the eastern sky was furrowed in the color of blood.

To the south could be seen a solid, rust-colored band of cloud: a sirocco. It is one of the characteristics of this fierce Mediterranean wind that it is preceded by a clock calm, almost as though the wind has been gathered and held like a giant breath. Curran knew that the deadliest of the gale would be felt out to sea. After the tomb-stillness of the dawn, the first gusts of hot air were already whispering over the bow.

"Padeen, pipe all hands. We will delay breakfast until we have recovered the boat." Curran said this as calmly and cheerfully as he could, but both men expected the day to get ugly. He had not wished to recover the cutter towing astern—he would need it to board *Torch*—but now he felt that it must be taken aboard or lost. The old Mediterranean hands knew what was up; by now the sky had taken on a copper color and spray was peeling aft from the cutwater. They were in for a beating.

Kanoa touched his hat and came forward. "Beggin' your pardon sir," he said, "I'm not so sure these old booms will handle some bad tacks. Specially like they been groaning."

The xebec gave a skip, and a sheet of spray came hissing back as far as the waist. The horizon was wavering under an ochre-colored band. The wind was already coming at them. "How long would it take to strike the yards and rig courses?"

"About as long as we got," Kanoa said.

"Then get about it."

By the time the cutter was made to the stern davits and the yards were lashed down, the wind had risen to a half gale; stronger winds were to come. Curran placed three men at the tiller, all of them holding fast as the ship rushed forward on a larboard tack. Roiling, the dark band on the horizon hurried toward them.

The sky turned pewter and then impenetrably thick as the dust came, and soon even the coppery sunlight was snuffed out. In abrupt darkness the sea changed from blue to black and the air was filled with stinging, then slashing gusts of sand. The wind in the rigging rose a tone and gradually transformed into a howling shriek. As the dust came the visibility went to half a mile, then four hundred yards, then finally to less than a hundred feet. The men at the tiller wrapped bandanas around their faces, their fanciful Arab costumes now put into real service.

The binnacle was lit and the helmsmen steered by compass, southwest by south, as they would on a moonless night. Curran had Hall toss the log—they were making better than ten knots under a scrap of trysail and a double-reefed main course. Sand hissed off the sails, and the water that came over the deck was mixed with blowing grit; it made a red slurry that stuck to everything.

"How long will this last?" Nolan shouted over the wind.

"Three hours or three days," Curran answered. "If it lasts beyond sundown it will likely go on for seventy-two hours."

Nolan lurched forward as the ship staggered. A cross swell came over the larboard bow and sent a knee-deep torrent as far aft as the quarterdeck break. The forecastle was buried almost to the heads and then came up, scuppers streaming mud-colored water.

"A slapper," Curran grunted. "This is not even the worst of it."

Nolan held his scarf up over his nose and peered around in the artificial darkness. "By God, it's unbelievable that we are at sea and not in the middle of some vile desert."

"The desert has come to us."

So it went, tack upon tack, watch after watch. Sometimes a rift would open in the blowing sand, but never was the sun revealed, and only once could they see as far as a mile. Curran spent most of his time on the quarterdeck, now and again ducking into the cabin to update and check Nordhoff's plotting. It was merely dead reckoning, course and speed, glorified guesswork, and at the start of the second dogwatch Curran tacked again and reduced sail. The reckoning put them within two leagues of the fortress, a distance well within the error of so rough an estimation, and Curran was painfully aware of the several rock ledges scattered to the east of Cap Falcon. It was on one of these that *Torch* had come to grief.

There was so much sand in the air that sundown came on in an instant. The night was stubbornly dark, but the wind began to lift and veer, several times gusting round sharp enough to backwind the trysail and send the jib club banging wildly against the mast. Curran gave orders to run preventer stays to the main and mizzen, and to bring the kedge aft to the quarterdeck and bend a cable to it.

Nolan stood for most of this time on the leeward side of quarterdeck, respecting the custom that granted the skipper the windward rail as a holy sanctuary. Nolan had a long while to watch his friend and observe the isolation of command. Curran was part of the ship, a vital part of it, but as captain he was separated completely from the crew. No one spoke to him unless spoken to, and no one approached him as he paced the windward rail, peering at the sails, testing the tension of lines and sheets, and staring into the sky at the slightest break in the blowing sand. Sometimes as he passed he would nod to Nolan, sometimes he would order the log to be thrown, and when he was told the speed he would stand with his arms crossed and his eyes narrowed, calculating time and distance, which could be estimated, and the leeway of the ship, which had to be foretold by a divine sort of sailor's magic.

The mess fires had been put out at dawn, and supper was cold: ship's biscuit, a sharp Roncal cheese, and cold leftover beef slathered with Old Chick's chili catsup. After supper the swell diminished, though the wind remained strong and the sandstorm continued without respite. Curran tacked ship and cocked his ear into the wind, listening for the dreaded roar of breaking surf. He heard nothing but the high howl of the wind.

The leadsman in the bow heaved and took in his line, whispering back to his mates who relayed, "No bottom with this line." Nolan watched as Curran took the tiller, feeling the living pressure strong against his hand. Eyes fixed on the binnacle Curran put the helm up. The lubber's line turned over the compass card: southwest, west by south, and finally dead west.

Curran stepped back and returned the tiller to Padeen and his mates. "Steady on," he said. "Steady as you go." Curran walked to the larboard rail and squinted into the musty blackness.

After a few moments he said to Nolan, "I believe we are past Pointe de l'Aiguille. Oran should be to the south, maybe five miles."

"Is it not a major port?"

"It is, but we are not likely to meet anyone coming out of it, not on a night like this." Curran looked away into the inky, swirling darkness. "And it would be foolishness for anyone to approach the coast blinded." Curran did not mention that they, too, were blinded, and that they not only had approached the coast but were now turned parallel to it, groping west and hoping to sight Cap Falcon before they ran upon an uncharted reef. If it was foolishness to try to make the harbor of Oran on a night like this, it was lunacy to try to make Arzeou. Oran was a city, a seat of commerce, and its approaches were straightforward and well known; Arzeou was a smaller place, its approaches strewn with reefs, ledges, and rocks, and both the town and the harbor were enclosed by high walls and batteries. Of all the city-states of the Barbary Coast, Arzeou had the least enviable situation. Behind its well-manned bastions, five thousand people and twice that many slaves existed in what was really not much more than a fortified sheikdom. The city and its surrounds were ruled by a particularly uncompromising form of Sharia law, administered by stern-hearted mullahs. The fact that Arzeou's rulers and people were Shia isolated it, as did a long history of violence, piracy, and slave trading dating back to the blood-drenched epoch of Genseric and the Vandals.

Curran leaned into the binnacle light and opened his watch. Curran knew the moon must have set by now or would be concealed against the tops of the Jebel Murdadjo. Nolan had detected a slight drop in the wind (more southwest than south now), though perhaps he had only imagined it, as they were on a larboard tack. His impression seem confirmed when a messenger came scurrying back from the forecastle hissing, "Where is the skipper?"

"Here," Curran said. A shadow came up the quarterdeck ladder: one of the Bannons. "Sir, bow lookout thinks he sees land, off the larboard bow."

"Where away?" Curran asked, already starting forward.

"Maybe a mile, sir. He says the sand stopped for a moment. He's pretty sure."

Curran made his way to the forecastle and climbed up into the fore chains. It was Kanoa who had glimpsed the land, and he was still adamant, though the sand had closed back over the night. Kanoa lifted his hand and said quietly, "One point to starboard, Mister Curran. Maybe about a mile off. A point, steep to, with a kind of low beach in front of it."

Curran put his telescope to his eye. "How high? How much did you see?"

"Only about a cable's length," Kanoa said, "and the mountain behind it goin' mostly straight up."

"How tall was it? A hundred feet? Five hundred?"

"More like a thousand, sir. It went into the sky."

Curran handed the glass to Nolan. He pointed it into the blackness; whatever Kanoa had seen was not there now. The Hawaiian was one of the best seamen aboard and Curran did not doubt what he said, but a moonless night and sheets of blowing sand could play deadly tricks.

"Did you see breakers, Kanoa?"

"None, sir."

Nolan handed Curran back the glass. They stood quietly, listening to the bow wave splash in front of the cutwater. Then there was a glimmer of light off to the right.

"Could that be a village?" Nolan asked.

Curran and Kanoa stared off to starboard. Again the sand parted, revealing four or five lights; stationary. Might they be fishermen? But who would be out on a night like this? Curran looked back to larboard—there was nothing to be seen there, not a scrap of anything, just a black void.

Kanoa seemed to be reading his commander's mind. "I saw a mountain, sir. Damn sure. With a flat cape in front of it."

The ship was heading west. If Oran was to the south, and if these lights were not fishermen, this little village could only be Ain et Turk, three miles below Cap Falcon. They would have to tack to clear the headland, and they would have to do so quickly, before they were embayed. Cap Falcon must be to starboard; that is, if Kanoa had sighted Mers el-Kebir and not some other nameless cape.

Curran turned these deductions over in his mind. All navigation, even celestial navigation, is mere theory. Any position plotted on a chart is a guess, informed more or less by things that can be seen. Curran could see nothing except half a dozen small, hazy, winking lights. He had to assume they had penetrated the Gulf of Oran, that they had made their way to the western part of it. If he believed that, he should immediately turn north, keep an eye to larboard, and round Cap Falcon and then south into Arzeou. That *is* what he believed. They might have indeed seen the lights of Ain et Turk, or they might have seen boats. When there are consequences attached to a belief, opinion is transformed into a higher concept called faith. For Curran, having faith now meant believing in himself and trusting his dead reckoning. He had checked and rechecked Nordhoff's plotting. Now in the balance rode not only his ship and all of the men aboard her, but also his mission and the 150 captives kept at Arzeou.

Nolan watched as Curran pushed the telescope closed against his chest and put his jaw forward. A splash came up over the bow, pattering them all with big, salty drops, and Curran said, "Prepare to wear ship." As Curran walked back to the quarterdeck, the hands went to the sheets. Nolan was amazed that the men fell in and found their positions without a word.

They went up the quarterdeck ladder and Curran nodded to Padeen at the tiller. "Tack ship." Padeen pushed the helm over. Quickly *Yunis* turned away from the wind, and Curran said in a conversational tone, "Brace about." Sheets were hauled and made fast, and the xebec settled on a course downwind.

With the wind aft, the ship suddenly became silent, and the wind across the deck seemed stilled. The crew completed making fast the sheets and faking down the lines. As silently as they had worked, the shadow men scuttled below and back out of sight. Curran stood at the larboard rail looking at the lights scattered to the west. A mile away now, perhaps a bit more, it was easier now to see the lights as houses. To the north and south there was nothing, not a glimmer; but now there seemed to be less, much less, sand in the air. Still not a star could be seen, and the darkness above was total. *Yunis* surged though the blackness, throwing a snowy wake to either side and now pitching slowly rather than rolling as she had done for the last ten hours.

For the first time Curran thought he could make out a cliff looming to larboard, a firmer sort of darkness sloping up and into the murk. It was impossible to determine how far offshore they were. As they sailed north, he watched as the lights of the houses were occulted one by one. Nolan thought the village might have disappeared behind a promontory, and as he turned toward Curran, he saw only a silhouette against a less firm darkness. Now that the ship was on a stern reach, Curran could sense the swell change; the lift was no longer grand and gradual but steeper and more abrupt. A cross swell had also developed—this variation became bigger and more pronounced.

"Finch," Curran said, "take up the twenty-fathom line and man the chains for sounding." As the lead and line were readied, Curran considered the vagaries of steering a dead-reckoning course in conditions of reduced visibility; never a star, not even Orion, and the effect of current and tide this close to an unknown shore could only be guessed at. And though it was improbable, there was a nagging thought that *Yunis* had made more progress to the west than had been chalked onto the log board.

There was a splash forward and then the cry, "No bottom with this line."

"Carry on, Finch. Arm your lead."

The line was recovered and a piece of tallow put into the recess of the plummet to catch particles off the bottom. Again a splash, and then a call, "By the deep, twelve."

Twelve fathoms; that was the reason the swell had steepened. For much of the last watch the wind had been out of the east, dead astern, and combined with *Yunis'* slight tendency to steer wide, their south-by-southwest heading may have placed them closer to Cap Falcon than was either prudent or desirable.

Curran called to Finch, "What is your bottom?"

Finch took up the lead and examined it. "Shell, sir, and gravel."

The swirling littoral current had put *Yunis* very much closer to Cap Falcon's deadly reefs than any of them knew; very much closer. Again the splash of the lead, and again the call, "No bottom with this line."

Deep water. Had they passed over a reef, or were they still approaching an invisible coast? Now through the sandy darkness Curran watched as a wave broke over the starboard rail, throwing white spray as high as the tops.

Curran said to himself, *We shall put about.* And then aloud: "All hands, clap on. Prepare to about ship."

From Kanoa: "Ready, sir."

"Bear up," cried Curran. "Ready about." Before he could order "helm alee" the ship seemed to skip, checked for an instant by an unexpected blow, and Curran's posture changed instantly. Nolan stood back as Curran took a single bounding step across the quarterdeck toward Padeen and clapped his hands on the tiller. Curran detected a pulse in it, a pressure more forceful than he expected.

"Did you feel it?" Curran said to the astounded helmsman. "Padeen, did you feel it?"

Another jolt went through the ship. The darkness in front of the ship became suddenly more opaque, and *Yunis* lifted up and then struck through the trough of a wave that made the entire ship ring like a wooden bell.

"Jesus," Padeen gasped. "We have touched!"

Cap Falcon, thought to be a league to the west, now loomed up before them, terrifying and black. To larboard Nolan watched as Curran and Padeen shoved over the helm, running it all the way to the larboard rail. Nolan was bowled over as the xebec turned forcefully to starboard, her deck inclined like a steeply pitched roof. As the sails flogged, Nolan saw what Curran and Padeen had comprehended just a second before: a solid, vertical wall of rock looming a hundred yards in front of the ship. At its base was a booming line of whitewater surging and retreating.

"Let go the sheets!" Curran shouted. "Foresail sheets and aft! Let go!"

There were a handful of seconds and an even smaller number of yards in which to save the ship. As the forecastle heaved upward, *Yunis* was struck on the bow by a monstrous swell, a wave reflected back by the rock wall. Green water broke over the prow, surging back along the decks, sweeping men from their feet.

A second reflected wave struck them, passing under the bow and lifting the forecastle high into the darkness. She fell quickly and for a desperate moment *Yunis* pearled under, her stern nearly vertical, her rudder exposed, biting air. The ship wrenched to starboard, the masts groaning. The trysail blew out of its boltrope with the sound of a whip crack, and the sails flogged wildly, filling the night with the sound of a thousand galloping horses.

Curran and Padeen wrestled with the tiller to try to get the wind onto *Yunis'* beam. "We have to get the stern anchor down," Curran shouted. There was another staggering lurch and the sound of a deep, resonating thud belowdecks. The ship was still beam-on to the gale, rolling dangerously and drifting toward the cliff.

By now the entire crew was on deck, grave but not panicked. Above them in the murk they could make out the sheer face of the cliff, and others farther forward on the bow could see that there was a huge, pyramidal rock to leeward, a rock the size of a frigate. Beyond the great, jagged islet was another void, one less solidly dark and flicked through with whitecaps: open water.

Curran saw the pyramidal rock and realized instantly that it was Ras al-Qaria, the islet directly east of Arzeou. Incredibly, they had not been merely to windward of Cap Falcon but south of it as well. There was a narrow channel between the headland and Ras al-Qaria, a surging reach of water called al-Humazah, "the

Slanderer." The name was apt. What Curran could see in the darkness was a treacherous, doglegged channel between Ras al-Qaria and the cliff that formed the east side of the cape. They had only one chance: to sail into the chasm and the headland.

Curran shouted to Nolan, "Get the kedge over! We'll try to warp into the channel!"

The kedge anchor was stored under the taffrail knee, aft of the sternpost—the most exposed part of the ship. Crawling on hands and knees, Nolan and Kanoa made it to the stern. Kanoa threw himself on top of the anchor and had Nolan cut away the gripes that held it fast. Another wave crashed across the deck, burying them in dark water and then in swirling foam. Clawing to his feet Kanoa pulled an ax from the stern locker and smashed it down on the taffrail; the wood was mere fancywork and shattered at the first blow. Together they crawled back to the kedge and dragged it across the lurching deck.

"Get back!" Kanoa bellowed. He put his feet against the shank and kicked. The anchor plunged off the stern, and the stock clanged against the broken rail. Curran looked back from the tiller in time to see the anchor drop free. The hawser screamed after it, spiraling up from the Flemish coil on the deck.

"Brace!" he shouted.

Five fathoms deep the anchor took to the bottom and the line went tight against the stern bits. Nolan could see it rip through the surface in a straight line behind the sternpost. The ship was checked, momentarily, and the cable wound toward the starboard side, chewing off the remaining bits of taffrail as it went. The line was stretched iron tight, but held. The kedge had bought the ship maybe twenty-five seconds of life.

Held like a dog on a leash, *Yunis* struggled into a starboard turn, the swells bashing her quarter and throwing whitewater over the stern. A hundred yards off the bow, the foot of the cliff exploded in luminous foam. Scattered around the base of Ras al-Qaria the tops of a dozen rocks showed like teeth. The sails strained against the sheets, the spars bowing. The anchor line slackened and then jerked tight. As long as the kedge held, they had a chance to get her head around to starboard, away from the cliff and toward the slender hope of the al-Humazah channel. Curran and Padeen put the helm on the larboard rail, and the ship continued a laborious, wallowing turn to starboard.

"Grab hold!" Curran shouted to Nolan. "Lay hold!"

Nolan rushed to the tiller and applied all his weight. The ship continued to pitch and roll, and the sails thundered as the stern came again through the eye of the wind. Pushing at the tiller with all his strength, Padeen cursed, damning the wind and goddamning all of Africa too. The anchor line crunched over to larboard, sheering through the stern locker at the base. Fifty yards remained until the knifelike tower of Ras al-Qaria. Turning, turning, the xebec was within sixty yards of the base of the cliff, and then the blackness opened at the ship's waist: the channel.

"Hoist the main!" Curran bellowed. "Haul away!"

On deck, the men stood transfixed, gaping up at the thunderous tumult of the whitewater against the rocks—as spellbound as the crew of Odysseus. Finally Nordhoff waded into them pushing and shouting. "Lay hold! Lay hold!" The midshipman's orders could barely be heard over the deafening crash of the flogging sails. "Backwind the jib," he screamed. "Heave it round!" Hall uncleated the jib sheet and was quickly joined on it by Fante. "Pull!" he shrilled. "Pull for your lives!"

The huge triangular main went up, filling as it went, rumbling and billowing. At the tiller, Nolan could feel the ship surge under his feet. The deck flinched, and the anchor line parted with a searing bang. The bits were jerked up from the deck and whizzed through the air. *Yunis* lurched forward, gathering way obliquely toward the maw of Ras al-Qaria.

"Now back!" Curran boomed.

Padeen ducked under the helm and popped up on the other side, pushing hard. The sails rumbled again, the sound of the world shaking apart, and the broken jib club banged against the beakhead, but the ship gathered speed. They were now heading diagonally toward the western face of the rock. Curran and Padeen dipped the tiller back and forth, putting the ship into a series of shallow upwind turns, shivering the sails and letting her fall off and fill, nursing every inch out of her.

There was a staggering crash; the deck jerked up and then went sharply down. *Yunis* had struck again. On deck, men went down like tenpins, but not one went over the side. Time seemed suspended, all hands holding their breath, but then the ship settled and surged forward. The impact had jerked the bow sharply to starboard, and she entered the channel, her main filling and pulling her forward.

Padeen mutely pulled on the tiller; the ship jinked in response—they had water under them. "She steers, sir." It was a miracle the rudder had not been shorn off.

Between the headland and the rock, the wind was again firmly out of the south. Nolan pulled himself up onto the mizzen shrouds to look ahead. They would pass through the channel—but to where?

Finch came up onto the quarterdeck. "Been below, sir; can't even believe it."

"What is the damage?"

"Can't hope for better, sir. There's a hole forward, big as man—got a rock jammed in it like a plug. Chips is getting it shored, and just two feet of water in the well."

"Nothing else?"

Finch shrugged. "Not yet, sir."

Nolan would not have been surprised if her back had been broken. He walked to the rail and looked up into the swirling black. The cliff directly to the east rose in a steep curve. Below them, to larboard, was a short stretch of beach ringed by nearly vertical stone. As they moved northeast up the channel the rock face became increasingly smooth, and it was only after a moment that Curran could see that the impressive height was composed of blocks of stone. They were sailing now not under a cliff but a rampart.

In the swirling, opaque sandstorm they had blundered under Arzeou itself. Nolan cupped his hands around his eyes. There were lights high above, and against their dim glow could be seen the right angles of towers and turrets. The channel opened as they went north, and on the larboard side what had been a wild rock face became more ordered and lower. There was a flicker of yellow light, then it became steady, swinging, swinging and descending a stairway cut into the rock. Just off the larboard beam, looming above them in the sand-blown darkness were the walls of the bashaw's palace.

"There are sentries on the breakwater," Nolan whispered.

"A merchant ship would pay them no heed." Curran tried to believe his own words. "Keep us two hundred yards off, Padeen," he said quietly.

Without a word the men went down into the hatchways. Padeen, Curran, Nolan, and Fante remained on the quarterdeck. First the deadly cliffs and then Ras al-Qaria had appeared out of darkness, and now the same fateful hand had conjured a fortress out of nothing.

For the first time in twelve hours Curran had the consolation of knowing his position exactly. It was cold comfort. He could see that they were outside the eastern breakwater of the Arzeou harbor, closer than musket shot. Near aboard he made out the stone causeway, half a mile long and topped with crenellated embrasures. Curran knew that at the end of it there would be a Martello tower—and a dozen cannon.

"Fante, go below and tell the boarders to be ready. Keep them silent and have Kanoa report to me."

Kanoa's head poked through the skylight. "Here, sir," he whispered.

"Kanoa, light the pilot lights and take a white lantern into the maintop," Curran said quietly.

"Light the pilots and a white light into the tops, aye, aye."

By their shabby appearance and by the audacity of their course they would certainly be taken for a local vessel. Now everything depended on it. *Yunis* would do what any merchant would do on entering the fortress at night—she would light her masts and pilots. The breakwater slid past to larboard. As they rounded, Nolan could see a watch fire flickering through a brazier in a stone sentry box.

Now under the lee of the fortress, *Yunis* sailed in peace and silence. Nolan pulled his scarf around his neck and unconsciously hunched his shoulders. He had a second to wonder if the bellowed commands that put them through the channel had been heard in the fortress. Kanoa appeared from the main hatchway and lit the starboard and then the larboard pilot lights in the waist. He put a pair of tapers into a brass lantern, clamped the handle in his teeth, and then went up the shrouds into the mainmast.

The mainsail rattled and luffed. "Don't trim her, Padeen," Curran whispered. "Make us look like a slug."

Nolan looked ahead. The battery was close to larboard, and he could just see across the mouth of the harbor to the tower on the other side. A burst of laughter floated down from the ramparts to the deck of the ship. The mirth seemed pointed, derisive. "*Ohe o barco!*"

Curran cocked his head. The words were not Arabic or Turkic. "*Ohe!*" came the voice again. They were being hailed in Portuguese. Curran put his hand on Nolan's shoulder.

"They ask if we are bringing cannon," Nolan muttered.

"Tell them we are carrying the sultan's dispatches."

"*Viemos de Tunis,*" Nolan shouted. "*Nós transportar escravos do sultão.*"

A lantern swept a feeble light at their shattered stern. Another voice called out an insult followed by laughter.

Yunis went past the hulking eastern tower, came about, and ghosted across the harbor. The wind was unsteady below the headland, and wide breaks began to open in the blowing sand. A mile southeast, a series of dark terraces and then a high-walled citadel soared over the central and inner parts of the harbor: the bashaw's palace. A quartet of minarets crowned the center of the complex.

All hands waited in silence, jaws clenched, expecting any second for the night to rip open and the hundred guns of the citadel to fire and smother them with shot. But nothing happened. Arzeou's defenders were not interested in a battered tub like *Yunis*. The anchorage behind the eastern battery was full of galleys and French-built calliope cannoniéres, the latter proof of the late Emperor Napoleon's affection (or perhaps respect) for the bashaw. Fast and maneuverable, each of these gun sloops carried a 32-pound carronade. A single round from one of them would cripple *Yunis*; mercifully, their decks were dark and their sails furled.

Yunis ghosted on, groping toward the western tower. Off the starboard bow they could see the mile-long causeway that linked the Bastille Nord and the mainland. There were a dozen more feluccas moored in a basin under the lee of the west battery, as well as a trio of canted masts, each crowned by a crooked crow's nest, sticking up from the water. They were the masts of a whale ship; they marked the place where *McKendrie Evans*, the would-be corsair ship *Um Qasim*, had settled and sunk at pierside.

"That is the corsair we tangled with," Nolan whispered.

"We sunk their nasty ass," Kanoa clucked in surly triumph.

The looming shape of the Bastille Nord soared over the starboard rail. *Yunis* passed within a hundred feet of the western tower, but there was no hail. Nolan could see sentries outlined on the parapets and heard the sound of music, a tingling *maqamat* playing from one of the dark structures beyond the demi-bastion. Standing by the broken taffrail, Curran could see one of the sentries shielding his eyes with the palm of his hand. He lifted his lantern and touched his hand to his heart; the sentry on the parapet merely turned away. There was no challenge from the east tower, or from the two Janissary riflemen sitting on the short pier behind the Bastille Nord.

"South-southeast," Curran whispered to Padeen. "Steady on."

Where the causeway joined the Bastille Nord was a forest of masts, mostly lateens, moored close together and filling the two basins under the island's south side. Still there was no sign of *Torch*. The gray dark walls and the perfect blackness of the sky gave the impression of sailing into a vast box.

Nolan went down from the quarterdeck and stood by the starboard main chains. He was looking forward when he finally saw the American sloop. *Torch* was moored head and stern to the causeway, her bow made to a finger jetty at right angles to the long quay. She had been hard to spot because her topgallant masts had been struck and her yards were scandalized, tilted at a forty-five-degree angle to the deck. This simple ploy had made the American sloop (normally a square-rigged vessel) nearly impossible to pick out among the hundreds of like rigs, poleacres, feluccas, and *barca longas*. A wide, heavy gangway had been put over her starboard side to the causeway.

Two vessels were moored under *Torch*'s stern, forming a sort of floating barricade—a narrow galliot of 70 feet and an ornate, gilded row galley—tied up perpendicular to the quay. The larger galley was moored outboard, toward the citadel. To judge from the carving, it was likely the bashaw's own. The galleys had their long ramming bows resting in steps cut into the causeway, and their sterns were tied to buoys in the channel basin. Guns and trucks were lined up neatly on the causeway in front of the inboard galley, as were piles of cordage, lumber, sails, and cooperage; *Torch* was obviously being refitted.

The larger galley was bigger than any Curran had ever seen, more than sixty oars; a tapering, oblong canopy was laid fore-and-aft over her decks—perhaps living quarters. It gave the craft the appearance of a hump-backed, reptilian creature. Smoke wafted from a stovepipe forward of the mainmast, and the long lateen yards made the ship seem even more like a dragon in repose. Curran could see a pair of wide-mouthed stern chasers mounted on the galley's aft deck. The gilded dragon was not merely a pet.

Holding his robe about his throat, Nolan walked back to the quarterdeck. Even in the darkness he could see Curran's thin, tight frown. Although *Torch* was moored away from the guns of the citadel, she was hemmed in by a pair of very awkwardly placed consorts. And without her topmasts *Torch* would be difficult to maneuver; assuming, that is, that they managed to get close enough to board, and were then lucky enough to cut her out.

Curran knelt by the skylight and looked down into a ring of darkened faces, the boarders assembled in the great cabin. "We are within a biscuit toss," he said. "I am going to lay us alongside. When you feel us touch, get quickly over the starboard rail. Then it's up and take her."

"Damn me if we don't," someone whispered.

"Your armbands now. Starboard side, above the elbow. The word is 'Halloween.'"

Curran could see smiles as he lowered the skylight. Nolan handed him a pistol wrapped in a strip of white cloth. Curran put the pistol into his waist, and Nolan helped him tie the cloth around his left arm. The water in the harbor seemed flat, embraced by the causeways and loomed over by the Bastille Nord on one side and the citadel on the other. It was easy to imagine that the fortress had swallowed them alive.

"Down helm, Padeen," Curran whispered. "Loose the sheets."

Yunis' head came into the wind and her sails luffed. They were a hundred yards away, and after a tense, silent span of three minutes, fifty yards.

A voice barked at them from the bashaw's galley. This was Arabic, harshly intoned: "What are you doing, you wetness? Stay off my buoy!"

Padeen's hands gripped the tiller and Curran said quietly, "Lay me for his quarter." Curran went to the rail and put his hands to his face. "*Masaa al-khair!* We are from Damur with dispatches from Beyrut!"

"I don't give a turd!" the sentry in the galley barked. "Sheer off!"

"We lost our anchors in the storm," Curran called out. "Allow us moor to your buoy."

Another figure joined him—a tall, white-turbaned man who wore a scimitar at his hip. "What are you doing, piss stain?"

"I am carrying tobacco," Curran called, "and will pay for mooring."

Nolan stood by the starboard rail, willing the ships closer. Under his cloak his hand was tight around the butt of a pistol. The turbaned man called back, "Then take the buoy and send over the tobacco, but do not come alongside."

Padeen slyly eased the tiller. "They will soon run out of patience or disbelief," Curran said softly to Nolan. "When you see that they intend to raise an alarm, give them a grenado."

"I will, too."

Nolan bent down by the lantern and lit a piece of slow match. Cupping the burning end, he wrapped the fuse around his left hand. *Yunis'* bow was coming around. From the helm, Curran looked forward to see a dozen hostile faces lining *Torch's* stern. A light came across *Torch's* deck, there was a sudden shout, the blast of a trumpet, and then from the quarterdeck of the sloop a rifleman fired at them.

"Now!" Curran barked. Nolan stood and windmilled the grenado at the galley. The fuse crackled orange and yellow, and as it arced through the air, a second sentry on *Torch* fired down at *Yunis*. The bullet ripped a long spark off the binnacle in front of Padeen.

"Boarders away!" Curran yelled.

Padeen shoved the helm over and *Yunis'* head thumped against *Torch's* quarter. Nolan's second grenade exploded on the sloop's stern; a dirty puff of smoke and fire scythed through the densely packed men. Kanoa lit a pair of fuses and hurled both at the galley, the first bounding off the canopy and into the stern, the second tumbling into the thwart, where they both exploded with a pair of muffled thumps.

Yunis' hatches came up and the crew burst from their hiding places. Nolan ripped the canvas off the larboard swivel gun and thumbed a powder quill into the touchhole. He trained the muzzle forward and shoved his match at the vent. The gun went off with a blinding crash, spattering the galliot and the bashaw's galley with a cloud of canister. The smoke blew away to reveal a pair of floating shambles. On the quarterdeck, Curran took up a cutlass and handed the tiller to Hall.

"You have the ship, sir. When the boarders are over, throw us a line and tow her stern out." Hall took the tiller and clung to it. "Can you do it?" Curran asked.

A bullet hissed between them. The boy did not flinch. "I will do my best, sir."

"I know you will, Mister Hall. Watch for our signal."

Curran swung his foot onto the mizzen chains. "Second division," he yelled, "follow me!" Twenty men surged over the rail and up the sides.

Nolan tossed a grenado through *Torch*'s quarter galley. The glass shattered and a second later a flash ripped through the aft cabin, lifting the skylight and blowing the deadlights off the windows. Nolan waved his pistol and jumped across through *Torch*'s shattered stern; a dozen men followed shouting, "Halloween! Halloween!"

Curran pulled himself up the sloop's starboard side next to the gangway. Incredibly, the manropes were shipped, as if *Torch* had been expecting visitors. Half a dozen men were already above him, climbing the shrouds and straight into the tops. To Curran's left there was a flash and a soul-shattering boom. *Torch* had fired one of her outboard guns at *Yunis*. The muzzle was within three feet of his head, and as it went off the explosion seemed to suck the life out of him. Blind and deaf, Curran nearly missed his handhold as he tumbled across the hammock netting onto *Torch*'s deck. Kanoa went past, his blanket headdress askew and his *pahoa* hissing through the air. The shark's teeth ripped through a lunging figure, and a pistol went off close behind. Curran was aware of a blur going by his head and a pike was shoved at his face. He parried and then from the darkness a huge hand grabbed him by the hair. Curran turned and slashed; the hand was gone.

The clang of steel and shouts of "Halloween" rang fore and aft, and within a minute the defenders were being driven back to the quarterdeck break.

"Topmen! Cut clues and gaskets!" Curran shouted. Already there was rustling overhead and the foretopsail was dropping like a curtain. *Torch*'s deck was a violent darkness shot through with muzzle flashes and bayonets. A musket went off, and Nolan saw Gerrity stumble in a cloud of smoke. Another cannon went off on *Torch*'s deck—the gun had been depressed, aimed down at *Yunis*, but the carronade had been set off before it could be properly secured. As the weapon recoiled, the carriage spun around its train tackle and turned over like a market cart, scattering the gun crew.

The aft hatch came up, and the first of *Torch*'s prisoners surged out on deck. A dozen more followed, ragged and filthy, and a score after that. Curran saw an officer's coat among the mob. Curran called out, "Commander Penniman!"

A small, ragged lieutenant shoved toward Curran. Despite the Enterprisers' costumes, the Torches saw at once what was up. "Penniman is dead," the officer said. "I am Amick, third lieutenant."

A mortar shell burst overhead, a red-orange blast and a tearing sound like close thunder. "Mister Amick, we are from *Enterprise* and mean to cut you out," Curran shouted.

"I am for it, sir." Amick grinned and picked up a Mameluk sword from the deck. A 50-pound ball whistled overhead, fluttering the sails and rattling the stays. It landed with a resounding clang at the foot of the Bastille Nord.

"Have your men cut the moorings," Curran said. "I'd like not to linger."

A hundred ragged prisoners surged across the deck, hallooing and shouting. There was not much more to be done. The corsairs were beaten into a pocket on the forecastle and a diminishing heap in front of the gangway. Two more cannonballs passed close, growling over the sloop and smashing into the causeway, shattering paving stones and sending splinters skittering through the sails. As Nolan had predicted, the first shots were going long. Several smashed into the wall on the far side of the causeway, shooting sparks and dust into the darkness.

"Torches! Torches! Hear me!" Curran bawled. "Over the side and into the boat! Get under way and pull our stern out!" Directed by Amick, *Torch*'s crew dropped off onto the stern and into the xebec. Nordhoff coolly ordered them into the tops, and *Yunis* made sail.

Torch was taken: well enough. Curran climbed the quarterdeck ladder. There were a dozen white armbands around the ship's wheel, pulling at the chain that had wrapped around the wheel, fouling the barrel and spindles. The blow of an ax and a link was shattered. As the wheel was freed, Curran saw Nolan emerge from the companionway dragging a red-bearded *sayyid* by the arm. As the ship was being taken, the Moor had fired a blunderbuss through the door of his cabin, killing half a dozen of the boarders as they came down the passageway. When Nolan and his prisoner reached the deck, Fante plucked up red beard, broke him over his knee like a stick, and tossed the corpse over the rail.

Padeen appeared from the bow. "The cable's slipped sir! We're ready to get under way."

"Topmen!" Curran shouted. "Let fall!"

Ashore, drums were beating and trumpets sounded from half a dozen points. Nolan could see troops of cavalry galloping down the causeway from the citadel. The big galley's lines had burned through, and she was drifting into the harbor, fully engulfed in flames. Thick, choking smoke swept across *Torch*'s deck. Above, the topsails came down from the yards. A flare tore into the sky from the citadel. In its lurching fire Curran could see *Yunis*' sails filling, and as she began to make way the cable lifted from the water, tightening and squirting water. Hall was at the tiller, and a dozen Torches were on deck setting main and mizzen. The xebec's big lateen sails fluttered and shook, the towline wrung itself dry and *Torch*'s stern came away.

A Mameluk horseman jumped his mount up from the causeway just as the gangplank jerked free. Fante lifted a long sweep from the deck and thrust it like a pike: mount and rider fell screaming and splashed between the quay and the ship. Other Mameluks clambered onto the bulwarks and were stuck by a volley fired from the forecastle.

The cannon in the citadel put down a steady and increasingly accurate fire. At the end of long, stuttering whistles, columns of water exploded up and came spinning down onto *Torch*'s deck. Curran was amazed to see Nolan climb into the hammock netting and pull an American flag from beneath his cloak. Stitched together from ribbons, linen, and bits of blanket, Nolan's creation looked like a quilt.

"Where did you get that?"

"I made it," Nolan said, fixing it to the halyard.

"Made it?" Curran sputtered. "When?"

Nolan pulled the halyard and the flag went rippling into the mizzen tuck. "It's not as if I lacked the time."

Another flare floated down out of the dusty gloom, lighting the harbor in a red, cloying glare. When the men aboard *Yunis* saw the Stars and Stripes rise over *Torch* they broke into cheers. At the end of the tow rope, the xebec tacked onto a beam reach. At the tiller, Hall steered expertly; the cable connecting the ships groaned, and *Torch*'s prow swung inboard and ground across the jetty. When it reached the end, the sloop gave a jolt, the bow lifted up and over the rocks, and she went forward.

"She swims, sir," Kanoa said. "We're out of the berth."

"Part the tow!" Curran said, and Finch brought down an ax on the hawser. In three chops it parted. *Yunis* went quickly away, and *Torch*, much larger and slower to start, drifted north toward the outer harbor.

The wind gusted again, filling the sails of both ships and thickening the air with sand. The immense darkness of the harbor was now ringed with brilliant flashes. The guns of the bastilles and even the palace itself were now brought into action. Most of them, ranged to protect the port from threats offshore, continued to fire long; but several gun crews had been made wise, and two crashing blows struck *Torch*. The first shattered the main rail under the bowsprit, and the second, fired obliquely across the harbor, smashed the capstan, sending a cloud of deadly brass and oaken splinters across the waist.

Muskets and miquelets fired randomly from the bastille, a few shots popped off from windows, but as they passed the first basin Curran could see a body of men marching down one of the alleys toward the harbor. Another flare tore into the sky, adding a pitching set of shadows to the red light of the burning galleys. *Torch* was nearly at the end of the sandbar that divided the basins from the main harbor. A hundred riflemen surged out of the sally port and onto the causeway; they were quickly formed by company, the front rank knelt, and a crashing volley was fired into *Torch*'s side. The bullets came in a swarm, striking the oaken gunwales, entering the gun ports, and ripping sparks from the guns. Five men went down as the rifle smoke gushed across *Torch*'s deck.

Another volley of musketry, fired high, ripped through the hammock netting. Climbing down from the mainmast, Nordhoff yelped and whirled around, shot through the foot.

"One through seven!" Nolan called. "Out quinions, depress them as far as they will go!" *Torch* was now abreast of the sally port. "Fire!" Nolan barked.

The larboard guns went off in a rippling peal of smoke. The salvo was fired point-blank, and its effect on the massed riflemen was horrific. The galleys in the basin were plowed from the water and blown into shreds. The balls struck the edge of the breakwater and caromed up into the packed ranks; the men on the quay were mowed down in rows. The wind blew the smoke back down on *Torch*'s decks, and when it lifted not a rifleman was left standing. In the flare light Nolan saw a pair of wounded Janissaries stagger back toward the sally port as the ironbound doors pulled closed.

Torch rounded the bagnio, and just as the west tower became visible, six rounds struck her in the span of as many seconds. The bowsprit exploded in a cyclone of wood, line, and block fragments. A second ball struck number two, picked the 1,500-pound carronade from the deck, and sent it spinning end over end down the starboard side. Atop the bagnio tower, Curran saw a rifleman stalking across the parapet; as he watched, the man framed himself between two of the crenels, lifted his weapon, and fired down onto the quarterdeck. The bullet thumped harmlessly into the deck; a second later, Curran felt a pressure against his back and comprehended a searing, blinding light. That brightness enveloped him in silence. A 50-pound shot had struck *Torch* square on her quarter, there was nothing for an eye-blink—a numb, unpleasant blank—and then Curran felt himself turned upside down, his feet gone over his head, and he landed on the deck in a miasma of smoke and pain.

When he opened his eyes, he saw the shattered wheel and then Kanoa's empty shirt fluttering across the mizzen jeer bits. In the jerky light he could see the tattooed Hawaiian sprawled on the shattered deck, naked to the waist, unmoving, his arms wrapped around his face. Curran's head swam, he could not hear or see; the battle and all its crashings lurched round him in a vertiginous spiral. Then, before his eyes, Nolan appeared outlined in flames. Curran saw that he was carrying Pelles' sword—the tip of it had been sheered off by a bullet. Curran crawled to his hands and knees and then lurched to his feet.

"There you are," Nolan said in a calm, conversational voice. He placed his hand under Curran's arm and lifted him. "May I suggest that we transfer to the xebec?"

Nolan's tone was so nonchalant that Curran had the awful feeling that he was in a nightmare, in a sort of spark-torn hell, and not on earth. Concussed and bleeding, Curran's head ached, his limbs were numb, and he could scarcely form a thought in his head. For the past seventy-two hours his every nerve had strained in an effort to take back USS *Torch*: so firm was that intention that even now as it was being shot to pieces under him, it had not occurred to Curran to abandon ship. Nolan knew, as did Padeen, that *Torch*'s back had been broken and it was time to go.

Another ball slammed into the bow, and splinters went caterwauling into the darkness. Nolan said something Curran could not understand; Curran turned to look forward. The foremast was gone—simply gone—and when his eyes could focus he saw that the main was by the boards, slowly falling over the starboard side. *Torch* had only a single mast standing.

Nolan put his arm around Curran's waist and caught him as he passed out. "We shall abandon ship, Padeen," Nolan said. "Please see to it that Mister Curran and the other wounded are put aboard *Yunis*."

Hall had seen the salvo rip into *Torch* and knew that the wound to the ship was mortal. He quickly clapped the helm over and steered into the sloop's starboard bow, coming alongside as daintily as though he were picking up a commodore.

Nolan called down to the boy. "You're a smart sort of lad, Mister Hall. Now, keep her alongside as we take off the wounded." Two men took Curran by the shoulders and heels. "Handsome does it," Nolan said. And then to the crew, "Who are the firing party?"

Finch answered, "Here, yer honor! Stinkpots and pitch bombs, which we have set."

"Excellent, Finch." Nolan said. "Below, then, and start her at once. Make sure you have a full muster when you come back on deck. Go now and set her up."

The boarders crowded onto *Torch*'s starboard bow. The first few jumped down to *Yunis*' deck and lowered down the wounded. Now that *Torch* was clear of the bastille, fire opened again from all sides of the harbor. As balls hissed past, Nolan paced the quarterdeck. From the inner roads, the low shapes of three galleys were rowing toward them. A swivel gun spat from one of their bows, and a 4-pound ball bounced off the sternpost and rolled across the deck. Nolan trapped the rolling ball under this boot and flicked it toward the scupper. After the barrage of the citadel's guns, a 4-pound shot seemed like an insult.

"They will likely try boarding," Nolan said to Fante.

"I doubt it," the big man said. As the first boat came under the counter, Fante heaved up a 30-pound cannonball. He leaned over the rail and dropped it squarely into the galley. It struck the bow oarsman in his lap and drove him through the bottom of the boat. The galley pitched up at the stern and started to swamp; its oarsmen cast away their sweeps and weapons and dove into the water—not a single one of them tried to come up the side.

Fire was now burning in the waist of the sloop, and thick black bellows of smoke were sweeping high as the maintop. Nolan could see Finch at the bow, waving. "Mister Nolan, she's afire below!" Already flames could be seen licking through the screens of the forward hatch.

Fante said, "Come now, Nolan."

"Just one moment, and I am your man," Nolan answered. He tossed away the stump of his sword, went to the mizzen halyard, and calmly hauled down his flag. Another round struck the larboard side, passed though a gun port, and plowed through the burning hold. There was a small explosion, and then a mounting wall of sparks and fire swept aft. Nolan and Fante crouched behind the wreckage of the helm until the tongues of flame lifted. Fante touched Nolan's shoulder and found it covered in blood. He lifted him by the collar of his coat. "You are bleeding!"

"So I am. Think little of it," Nolan rasped. "This is not the first time I have been shot by a bastard."

"Then maybe you shouldn't give him another chance. Now, Nolan, if you please, we must go." Fante dragged Nolan toward the waist of the ship.

The xebec was now making all the sail she could, heeling over on a starboard tack and crunching along the side of the burning ship.

Across the harbor, the bashaw's galley, all ablaze, drifted wide of the causeway, the flames leaping from her deck putting about a hot, red light. The galley's magazine took light, there was a towering flash, and then a deep, rumbling detonation shook the harbor. The detonation echoed back from the ramparts, silencing all the guns, stunning attackers and defenders alike into awed silence. Perched on *Torch*'s bow, Nolan and Fante watched the fire mushroom over the harbor.

On the deck of *Yunis*, Hall had the Torches ship sweeps; the long oars bristled down the ship's sides like the legs of an insect, flailing and then falling into rhythm. The starboard side was backing water, and the oars were pulling round to keep the bow in contact. It was a seven-foot drop from the sloop; Fante stepped into the air without a thought and landed like a cat on *Yunis*' bow. Cradling his wounded arm in the flag, Nolan swung his legs over the rail and surveyed the deck. He felt the heat at his back; it was almost impossible to judge the distance in the flickering light. He hesitated, considering the distances, and a 32-pound ball whizzed overhead, sucking flames up in its wake. Among the faces on *Yunis*' deck Nolan saw Curran's, freshly bandaged, looking up at him. "Cut along, Philip!"

Around the two vessels, the cannon of the fortress boomed like a concert of drums. Nolan stepped onto the bulwark, stood, and threw himself off the cathead. There was a thunderclap and a crackling hiss, a noise like the flight of a million bees, and a round of canister ripped through *Torch*'s bow. Nolan was caught by it in midair, lofted skyward, and then cast down at the foot of *Yunis*' foremast.

Curran and Fante ran to the place Nolan had fallen. His robe had been blown off, his shirt and waistcoat torn open, and his face pierced twice. As he landed, his right arm had been twisted at the shoulder and broken hideously. As Curran and Fante tried to lift Nolan, riflemen in the bastion let go a volley. As ricochets twittered around them Curran managed to turn Nolan over and Fante dragged him to cover behind one of the carronades.

Nolan wore an expression of unalarmed bafflement. He tried to lift his right hand; two of his fingers were gone, and his broken wrist stuck through a hole torn in the flag. "Damn me," he grunted.

All aboard saw that Nolan had been hideously wounded. The thundering of guns, the slap of shot hitting the two ships, the crackle of musketry, all seemed to stop. All hands stood frozen in their places, paralyzed and mute.

Finally, at the helm, Hall bawled out, "Turn to, you lubbers! Shove off and man the sweeps! Pull and pull or we'll die here!"

A mortar shell burst over them, red-orange for a second and then a fleeting gray cloud. The boy's words galvanized the crew, and the hands turned to with a will. *Yunis* was soon under way, her sweeps churning.

Curran looked aft as *Yunis* made her last tack through the jaws of the harbor and into open sea; in the flicker of the battle light he could see that the soot on Hall's cheeks was streaking with tears. When the boy caught sight of Curran, he wiped his face, shamed by his grief.

Padeen knelt beside Nolan, tore a strip from his own shirt, and started to bind the gaping wound now pumping blood from Nolan's shoulder. As Curran and Fante elevated Nolan's shoulders they could see that blood was also dripping from his nose and the corners of his eyes.

Hands trembling, Curran drew back Nolan's jacket and was distraught to find that he'd been hit by a bullet in the center of his chest. He pressed his hand against Nolan's wound, the bleeding slowed, but the blood that had spilled around him continued to expand in a malignant black pool.

Sprawled on the deck, Nolan twitched his limbs and tried to sit up—he fell back with a grunt. "I can't see," he said calmly. His right eye fluttered closed, and his breathing became shallow.

"Oh, Jaysus, Mister Nolan." Padeen's voice broke and he touched Nolan's forehead, his finger tracing the sign of the cross.

"Hold fast, Philip," Curran said, the words strangled in his throat. Nolan's arm moved and his broken and bloody hand closed over Curran's. Fante knelt beside them and Curran bundled Nolan close. "Hold hard. We will return to the frigate, all of us together."

"*Enterprise*," Nolan whispered. From his chest came a deep, ugly gurgling, and he began to tremble. Curran watched as Nolan drew another breath and his lips moved silently.

"Stay with us, Philip," Curran choked. "Stay with us." Curran felt Nolan's grip tighten, and he pulled him closer.

The xebec was moving out of the harbor now, the wind on her quarter; the guns of the bagnio and the harbor batteries all firing in impotent fury. The sky was lowering, red with the glare of fires and smoke. Curran and Fante cradled Nolan between them and clamped on fiercely—trying, with all their might, to keep his soul from flying free.

THE MAN WITHOUT A COUNTRY

THOSE WHO HAD SURVIVED AND THOSE WHO HAD BEEN RESCUED CLIMBED up onto the frigate. Nolan was put onto a litter and made fast with strips of linen around his legs and a turn of line around his chest. The flag he stitched together was put into his hands, and the stretcher was lifted from *Yunis* to the spar deck of *Enterprise*. The men on both ships were silent, and the sky was bone white and still from horizon to horizon.

Curran was the last man to come off *Yunis*, jumping from the main shrouds to the mizzen chains of *Enterprise*. Nolan was lowered to the deck, and Darby knelt beside the stretcher. He put his fingers to Nolan's throat, felt the cool, damp skin, and lifted up the flag to see the dime-sized hole bored into his friend's heart. Darby lowered the eyelids down with his thumb and forefinger, took out his lancet, and cut away the linen and the shot line that bound Nolan to the litter. When he called for bearers his voice sounded like it was coming across a hundred miles.

At first, no one stirred. No one wanted to hear. Curran stood by Pelles, unable to move and incapable of speech, hardly able to believe. Darby asked again, stood, and Lieutenant Amick and four of the Torches came forward. Curran watched as they took up the litter, and a shadow rose behind them. Fante brushed the men away. The big man went to Darby's side, leaned over, and scooped Nolan's body up into his arms, bundling him up as though he were a sleeping child. Fante looked up at Curran and Pelles, and tears streaked his black, powder-scorched face. The crew parted before him as he carried Nolan toward the companionway with slow, measured steps.

Until this instant Curran had felt almost no pain; now it seemed to consume him. His skull ached as though it had been punched through with a handspike. He staggered toward the rail and gripped it with both his hands. To starboard, in the place where *Yunis* had been, there was only a debris-strewn slick. Shot through a dozen times between wind and water, she had sunk alongside, going down by the bow with only a whisper. Far to the south, near the line of the horizon, a thin trickle of smoke wound up from Arzeou, a distant blank marked by a curious smudge. Curran looked across the deck; in Fante's arms there was another empty place, a thing that had once been a man, a friend, a shipmate; now it was a burned and broken thing, dripping dead blood from dirty rags.

Curran saw faces turning toward him. Pelles, Padeen, Nordhoff, and Hall. His head swirled, and he saw others who were not there: Hackman, Kanoa, and Finch and Guild, a dozen other fallen shipmates. In his mind's eye, Curran saw Nolan on the pier at Cádiz; he saw one of Nolan's papers picked up by the wind and blowing off the quay, the wind lifting it, turning it end over end and out into the bay. Grief; desolation; an agony of want and sorrow, all these things welled up in the place behind his heart. Curran felt his joints crumbling; he felt his pulse pound and his mind flying to atoms—as he fell, Pelles caught him up with his good arm and lowered him to the deck.

CURRAN'S EYES OPENED. SLOWLY HE MADE OUT A LIGHT, A WHALE OIL LANTERN turned low, spilling thin light across the foot of his bedstead and the curving space of his stateroom. He turned his head painfully. His boots, sword belt, and pistol were on the deck. He only vaguely remembered the ministrations of Doctor Darby and speaking to Pelles, telling him of the sandstorm and the passage through the al-Humazah channel, of the burning galleys and the harbor lit by flare and cannon, and of Nolan twisting in the air.

For a while, Curran lay staring at the beams of the overhead. He had been washed and his wounds dressed, but still the smell of gunpowder clung to him. His hand reached and fumbled across his desk; there was blood under his fingernails. He found his watch and opened it. Curran could see blue moonlight through the scuttle in the bulkhead; he had slept for the better part of fifteen hours. It was nearly midnight when he walked into the empty wardroom. He drank a cup of ginger beer. Old Chick came in silently and put down a sandwich of cheddar, ham, and mustard. Curran ate it slowly.

Two bells in the middle watch; Curran walked through the ship, down ladders to the gun deck, then aft and down again to the berth deck. Through the swinging hammocks he could see the lighted place where Nolan was laid out on a hatch cover, a sailor and a Marine standing armed over the body. Curran stood at the end of the deck, unable or unwilling to come any closer. A dozen hands passed by him, the men of his division and the crews of *Yunis* and *Torch* touching their hats in salute, and his older shipmates patting him with rough, open hands. No one spoke a word, though some were streaked with tears, and it seemed that the entire ship was mute and still.

Curran watched as the guard over the body changed, Marine for Marine, sailor for sailor, then went down into the orlop to Nolan's cabin. He stood in front of the door for a long moment, then took a lantern off the bulkhead and opened the door.

His light revealed the small, tidy place: Nolan's bunk, a sea chest, some books and papers. Curran hung the lamp in the ringbolt over the desk. He looked at the bookshelf and Nolan's modest library: Epictetus, Seneca, Linnaeus' *Systema Naturae*, and three untitled leather volumes. Curran took them down and put them on the desk.

The first was a chapbook devoted to insects, beautifully illustrated in Nolan's own hand. The exotic mantises of the tropical Pacific, moths and butterflies from three continents, and even the humblest of shipboard roaches were faithfully and exactly rendered in watercolors and ink. The second was a book of pencil sketches. Spanning the pages were line drawings of various ships, frigates, gun sloops, and schooners neatly drafted from bobstay to counter: *Constitution, Holyoke, Hornet, Vixen, Warren, Brister.* There were watercolors of sailors around their mess tables, a cartoon of a midshipman exiled aloft, and a fine likeness of Curran, laughing. There was a haunting ink sketch of a man standing alone at a ship's rail, his back turned, a tremendous thundercloud looming on an ink-washed horizon. The figure was tall and wore a neatly ribboned queue. Perhaps it was Captain Pelles; perhaps it was someone else.

Curran opened the third book, its pages stuck through with needles and cards wound with multicolored thread. Stuck in the book's leaves were patterns traced on tissue paper: arrowheads and clouds and olive branches.

Curran sat and listened to the sound of the water against the hull. A seabag swayed on its dowel and the lamp rolled in its handle. Nolan's bloody clothing had been bundled into a white sheet and placed onto the foot of the berth by Doctor Darby. Nolan's flag was folded into a triangle and placed atop it. After a long time Curran leaned across and pulled it open. He had only glimpsed it during the battle, and now, looking closely at it, he was astounded by its intricacy.

Nolan's blood was spattered over the fly; in places the flag was burned through by powder and shot. No part of the whole was larger than a hand's breadth. Nolan had sewn it together from hundreds of small pieces of fabric, like a quilt. The stripes were pieced together from bits of red ribbon and bunting. Other parts were cut from bits of cloth or bandanas in shades from crimson to copper red, united into rectangular strips with careful, even stiches. Some parts were linen, white as snow, fabric cut from the simple shirts Nolan wore in hot weather. Other parts were a sun-bleached shade of tan sewn onto butternut-colored cotton.

The blue of the flag's canton was composed of a hundred patches and as many shades of that color; sapphire bits of silk, navy blue bits of pea jackets, rectangles of denim, strips from Nolan's old coat sleeves dyed with India ink in shades of azure, cornflower, and deepest indigo. On very close examination parts of the blue rectangle not blue at all, but ebony-black as Fante's brow. Over the canton Nolan had sewn stars for all the states, those that he knew. Twenty-three stars were ordered in a wavering set of rows: five, and six, and six again twice. Some were applied as embroidered patches, layered with stiches, some were cut and sewn with five- and even six-sided stars, each star cut from a unique piece of fabric, a constellation in shades of white duck, rough homespun, and yellow flax almost the color of sunflowers.

Up close, the miscellany of patches made the flag seem almost abstract, the smallest parts quite distinct; but taken together, the whole became not only unified but interdependent, its rectangular and lopsided pieces melding into harmony and order, as sublime and beautiful as an ideal.

Curran looked at Nolan's seabag, still hanging from a dowel on the door. He took it down and opened it. It contained shirts and a pair of duck trousers, some darned socks, and what looked like a pillowcase made of two pieces of satin. He pulled it out and noticed that dozens of threaded needles were stuck into its corners. Curran turned the case inside out and found it to be embroidered from end to end: a map of the United States, drawn from memory.

Needlepoint piled up, stitch upon stitch; the original Thirteen were there, and Delaware; Louisiana, of course, and Kentucky and Ohio: all the states extant on the day of his conviction. In the years of his sentence Nolan had somehow divined most of the ten states that were added to the Union.

In the south Nolan had stitched in the boundaries of Alabama and Mississippi quite exactly, and above them Tennessee. The peninsula of Florida was there, but not demarked as a state, Nolan probably mistaking that the lack of a war with Spain had resulted in continued Spanish possession of that place. In the northwest where he had served, Nolan had correctly sewn in Illinois and Indiana but seemed not to know about the Minnesota and Missouri Territories. The Arkansas Territory was unknown to him, though he had stitched in the Sabine and Red Rivers with a fair degree of accuracy. Curran was surprised that Nolan had embroidered most of Texas, bordered in the south by the Rio Grande, and unbounded to the west. He had sewn a star at a place Curran did not know: Arroyo Nogal. Rivers and mountains, plains and lakes were all in their places. It was a beautiful, ornate, and detailed piece of work.

"It must have taken years."

Curran stood and turned to find Captain Pelles standing in the doorway. He placed the silk map back on top of the flag.

"I often saw him staring up at the ensign," Pelles said. They stood in silence for a moment. "In my memory he never missed a reveille in any of the ships he was on. On *Holyoke* and *Constitution* he was always there, at dawn, in fair weather or foul." Pelles traced his fingers around the stars.

"I don't know why I didn't notice," Curran said softly. "But he was on deck at the end of the middle watch, the day we sailed for Arzeou. He saw the sunrise." Curran touched the map. "He must have counted the stars. When another was added, he was sure another state had come into the Union."

Pelles sat down at Nolan's desk and adjusted the lantern on its ringbolt. Among the other books, the captain's eyes fell on the copy of Epictetus. He opened the cover to the dedication he had written years earlier.

"I remember when he first came aboard *Vixen*," Pelles said. "I met him in the West Indies, before the second British war. I was third under Captain Scholley. I'd just made lieutenant, not more than a year. It was 1809, I reckon, early in his sentence. *Wasp* rendezvoused with us off St. Barth's. Her patrol was over and all hands knew there would be a run up the Gulf Stream, then Christmas and snow in Boston.

"The morning *Wasp* was to part company, Nolan was put into a boat and sent aboard us. He looked very blank when he was told he was being exchanged into the outbound ship. There would be no going home for him, not even to a prison. Until then, I'm sure he thought he was going home. I remember he had stitched together a boat cloak out of a wool blanket—that one there, on the hook—he made it when he thought he would be returned to Boston. Instead he was turned over to us. I was the officer of the deck; I am ashamed to say that I signed for him as though he were a bag of nails.

"When he came aboard in that old coat of his I thought he must be some sort of lay chaplain. I was so green I thought every ship must have one. It was only when Captain Scholley called us together to explain Nolan's sentence that I had any idea he was a prisoner. In the first six months he was on *Vixen* almost no one talked to him. No one dared."

Pelles looked older, grayer, and sadder than Curran had ever seen him.

"I met him again when he came aboard *Holyoke* off the Marquesas; by then he was an old salt—he'd sailed with Porter to Tahiti. I know for a fact that Porter thought to leave him there to command the garrison with Gamble . . . exile in paradise." The captain paused for a long moment. "But Porter did not put him ashore." Pelles' green eyes fixed on Curran. "The commodore didn't want to exceed his orders. So Nolan was sent on. No ship wanted to carry him. And no officer wanted to be complicit in Washington's vengeance—but we went along. We all did."

Pelles looked down at his hands. "Truxton and Gamble complained to the Navy Department. I did too. But none of us had the guts to alter his orders. Nolan was braver than any of us." Pelles looked around at the cabin, scarcely eight feet by seven. Everything Nolan had owned would not even fill half a seabag.

"Did he ever speak to you of family, sir?" Curran asked.

"He did not."

Curran said softly, "I am embarrassed to say that I never asked."

After a pause the captain said, "Now he is punished and we are guilty." Pelles opened Nolan's Bible. There was a slip of paper marking Isaiah 2:4. He turned over the bookmark and unfolded it. Nolan's firm hand had written:

> Bury me in the sea; it has been my home and I love it. But will
> not someone set up a stone for my memory at Fort Adams in
> Newport, that my disgrace not be more than I ought to bear.

Say on it: In memory of Philip Nolan, Lieutenant in the Army
of the United States. He loved his country as no other man had
loved her; but no man deserved less at her hands.

Pelles handed the paper to Curran. "I will leave it to you to gather his personal
effects."

"Yes, sir." Pelles had never seemed small to Curran, but now, in the shadow of
the lantern, he seemed shrunken, grave, and wounded.

"I have lost a shipmate and it pains me," Pelles said.

"You were his friend, sir."

"I cannot call myself one. A friend would have done more."

For the rest of the evening Nolan's body lay on the gun deck, guarded
in turns until each division, each squad of Marines, and each mess had paid him
the honor. He was washed and his hair combed, and his head was placed on the
pillowcase he had made. He was covered in plain sailcloth until his uniform was
made ready. His best blue coat was brushed up, and the old brass buttons were
taken off. The plain ones were replaced with officer's buttons bearing the eagle and
anchor: they were sewn onto his waistcoat. For the cuffs of his coatee, the sailors of
each division gave blue-dyed, anchor-carved buttons from their peacoats, thirteen
of them, one from each department and division of the ship.

A shroud was stitched from the ticking of Nolan's own mattress, and a black
hat ribbon embroidered with the words U.S. FRIGATE ENTERPRISE. Three
marble cannonballs from *Ar R'ad* were placed at Nolan's feet and the ticking was
pulled gently up over him. As the canvas was being sewn, Curran stepped forward
and removed his own sword. He placed the pommel in Nolan's hands and the scabbard by his side. Men wept openly as Padeen sewed shut the canvas.

Philip Clinton Nolan was buried at sea at 36° 44' North and 0° 58' East. The
Mediterranean was at her most beautiful to receive him; the sky was pure and
infinite and the sea blue-dark and calm. As his remains were put over the side and
the volley was fired, Curran walked to the quarterdeck.

The bo'sun's pipes shrilled a long, plaintive wail. The crew held its salute, every
officer, sailor, and midshipman. As Curran went up the ladder to the quarterdeck
Fante readied a halyard. At the taffrail, the Marines were called to attention and
presented arms with a firm clash, their gloved hands slapping the stocks of their
rifles, their bayonets moving as one machine, up from port arms in a gleaming blur,
then perpendicular and white in the sun.

Together, Curran and Fante hoisted Nolan's battered flag into the mizzen.
Rippling in the wind, the powder-stained ribbons and patches were a perfect
emblem of his shipmates' esteem, grief, and proud resolve.

The United States frigate *Enterprise* flew Philip Nolan's flag until the day she was stricken from the list.

———————

For many years it was rumored in the fleet that Nolan was not killed at Arzeou. It was put about that he was allowed to go ashore at Cádiz and that he came home to the United States. Others said that he went to New York and saw Aaron Burr, and that on that day Burr died of shame and grief. Some think that the ghost of Nolan still rides over the sea, that he became a Flying Dutchman, a phantom, moving from ship to ship. But in the end, Philip Nolan proved to be a mortal man—merely flesh and blood.

Arthur Pelles wrote a special letter to the Secretary of the Navy demanding that Nolan be pardoned. The letter was returned, and Pelles went to Fort Adams, at Newport, and had a marker placed in the graveyard there. When the garrison commander removed it, Pelles challenged the man to a duel. The interview was declined; the officer preferred charges (assault and insubordination), and Pelles was briefly arrested. Exonerated at court-martial, Pelles was ordered to duty in a dingy garret in the Capitol. There he found his friends few on the ground and his prospects greatly diminished. Told he would never again command a ship, Pelles resigned his commission and took a wagon south and west as far as he could conveniently travel. He settled on the Bay of Biloxi in Mississippi, where he lived as a semirecluse for the rest of his life.

Curran, himself later a captain and then a commodore, also wrote to secure a pardon and to restore to Philip Nolan the privileges of a citizen. The authorities in Washington ignored the whole business. You may be sure that the people of that city will always serve their own interests first, and there are few among them, then or now, who might do anything to set right a cleverly hidden wrong. Curran, too, eventually resigned his commission. After serving as captain of a China ship in the merchant service, Curran retired to the town of Staunton, in his native Virginia. He married, had two daughters, and never laid eyes on the sea again.

No stone or marker exists to honor Philip Nolan, and no records mark his part in the actions at Arzeou or the cutting out of USS *Torch*. The country that Nolan loved did everything in its power to erase him from history.

They will tell you still in Washington that there was no Philip Nolan—that he never lived, and that this story never happened. Believe what you will. But as long as there is a United States Navy it will have a ship named *Enterprise*. And as long as there is a ship that bears the name, it will carry Philip Nolan's flag.

Acknowledgments

No book can come to press without the hard work and dedication of dozens of people, and I have many to thank for their kind assistance in bringing Philip Nolan to life. I first heard the story of "The Man Without a Country" from my father, who had loved the book when he was a young man and read it aloud to me when I was a boy. It was a story I never forgot, and a fascination with tall ships, sailing, and the sea has remained with me all my life. The world of imagination that is opened and the love of reading and literature that results are gifts that truly last a lifetime. Thanks, Pop.

Thank you also to my friend and agent, Julia Lord, who patiently navigated the changing currents of the literary world and found Nolan a berth—not an easy task in a day when Twitter and Facebook are much more in vogue than topsails and frigate battles. At the Naval Institute Press, special thanks to Susan Todd Brook, who was an early fan and brought Nolan "into the service." Thanks also to Taylor Skord and Richard Russell.

Thanks to novelist, screenwriter, and war correspondent David Freed, who read early drafts and provided encouragement. He is a friend of many years and a constant example of how to write well. Many thanks to Anna and Emily Iannucci, their brother, Matt, and his wife, Yoam Yoreh, for constant interest and encouragement. To Minsky, who always believed, and to Paddy, who reminds me that life is to be fun. Special thanks to Tripp Newsome and Matt Wolfe, companions these many years and stalwart friends through the ups and downs of the writing life.

Most of all, I want to thank my wife and my love, Louise: she is my muse, my editor writing coach; I count on her discerningly critical eye. Through the long process of researching and writing this book, she patiently endured—and hoped. I love you KKC.

About the Author

Chuck Pfarrer is a former Navy SEAL turned screenwriter and author. He has written seven Hollywood blockbusters, including *The Jackal, Red Planet, Darkman, Hard Target, Navy SEALs,* and *Virus.* He is also the *New York Times* best-selling author of *SEAL Target Geronimo*: *Inside the Mission to Kill Osama bin Laden, Warrior Soul: The Memoir of a Navy SEAL*, and the critically acclaimed novel *Killing Che.*